TRAIN

TRAINERS

LOUISE BRODERICK

This book is entirely a work of fiction. The names, characters and incidents in it are the work of the author's imagination. Any resemblance to actual persons, living or dead, events or localities is entirely coincidental and have no relation to anyone bearing the same name or names. All incidents are pure invention and not even distantly inspired by any individual known or unknown to the author.

Published 2018
By Lavender and White Publishing,
Cornwall,
England.
Email info@lavenderandwhite.co.uk

LOUISE BRODERICK 2018

The moral right of the author has been asserted.
Typesetting, layout and design Lavender and White Publishing.

A huge vote of thanks to superb artist Tony O'Connor of White Tree Studio for allowing me to use some of his amazing paintings for my book covers. More of Tony's equestrian and animal paintings can be found on his website www.whitetreestudio.ie

All rights reserved. No part of the text of this publication may be reproduced or transmitted in any form or by any means, electronically or mechanical, including photocopying, recording, or any information storage or retrieval system without the written permission of the publisher.

The book is sold subject to the condition that it shall not, by way of trade or otherwise, be lent, resold, or otherwise circulated without the publisher's prior consent in any form of binding or cover other than that in which it is published without a similar condition, including this condition being imposed on the subsequent purchaser.

www.lavenderandwhite.co.uk

CONTENTS

CHAPTER ONE	1
CHAPTER TWO	8
CHAPTER THREE	14
CHAPTER FOUR	20
CHAPTER FIVE	27
CHAPTER SIX	34
CHAPTER SEVEN	40
CHAPTER EIGHT	46
CHAPTER NINE	52
CHAPTER TEN	59
CHAPTER ELEVEN	65
CHAPTER TWELVE	72
CHAPTER THIRTEEN	78
CHAPTER FOURTEEN	85
CHAPTER FIFTEEN	91
CHAPTER SIXTEEN	97
CHAPTER SEVENTEEN	104
CHAPTER EIGHTEEN	111
CHAPTER NINETEEN	117
CHAPTER TWENTY	123
CHAPTER TWENTY ONE	129
CHAPTER TWENTY TWO	135
CHAPTER TWENTY THREE	141
CHAPTER TWENTY FOUR	148
CHAPTER TWENTY FIVE	155
CHAPTER TWENTY SIX	162
CHAPTER TWENTY SEVEN	168
CHAPTER TWENTY EIGHT	175
CHAPTER TWENTY NINE	182
CHAPTER THIRTY	190
CHAPTER THIRTY ONE	197
CHAPTER THIRTY TWO	204
CHAPTER THIRTY THREE	211
CHAPTER THIRTY FOUR	218

CHAPTER THIRTY FIVE	225
CHAPTER THIRTY SIX	232
CHAPTER THIRTY SEVEN	238
CHAPTER THIRTY EIGHT	245
CHAPTER THIRTY NINE	252
CHAPTER FORTY	259
CHAPTER FORTY ONE	265
CHAPTER FORTY TWO	272
CHAPTER FORTY THREE	279
CHAPTER FORTY FOUR	285
CHAPTER FORTY FIVE	292
CHAPTER FORTY SIX	298
CHAPTER FORTY SEVEN	304
CHAPTER FORTY EIGHT	311
CHAPTER FORTY NINE	318
CHAPTER FIFTY	325
ABOUT LOUISE BRODERICK	332

TRAINERS

CHAPTER ONE

Coming home to Westwood Park was like waking from a nightmare. But as the taxi circled in the wide gravelled forecourt outside the house Tara Blake felt a sense of disappointment seep over her. No car stood at the foot of the steps. Derry was not there. The house was in darkness. She waited, oblivious of the bitter cold, watching the tail-lights of the taxi growing smaller as it went down the drive. Then it turned a bend and was lost from view. Finally, as the last notes of the engine faded away Tara turned to look properly at the house.

It slumbered in the darkness, square against the inky-black starlit sky, the windows gazing blankly out at the parkland that lay beyond the gardens. Home. She felt a huge sigh rush past her lips as the tension slid out of her. Slowly, feeling stiff from the long journey and tired beyond exhaustion, she pulled her suitcase and bags up the wide curved flight of steps that led to the tall front door. She dug deep in her travel-bag for the front-door key that had remained there since she left so full of love and hope two years previously.

Hank Maxwell had proved to be like all the rest of the men she had ever got involved with: a lying, two-timing cheat. Derry, her older brother, had been the first person she thought of when she found Hank in bed with a girl who was supposed to be her friend. Derry was the only man she could trust never to let her down. She had been on a plane back to Ireland a few hours later.

As she inserted the key in the lock the door swung open, creaking inwards on its hinges. Scowling, she pushed it open fully and walked into the hall, fumbling for and then finding the light-switch.

She blinked as the light flooded the hall and then, opening her eyes, shut them again in disbelief. "Derry!" she hissed in temper. The house was filthy. Piles of unopened mail and unread newspapers littered every surface in the vast expanse of the hall. They cluttered the tables and chairs and in places had spilled untended onto the floor. Empty coffee cups and glasses lay upended amongst the debris. Tara slammed the door shut behind herself in fury. It was evident that no one was looking after the house.

There was a cook, Mrs McDonagh — she had been the housekeeper when Tara was growing up. Then as she and Derry had become older Mrs McDonagh had slipped into semi-retirement, coming to the house just to cook, something which had never been her forte. The cleaning and looking after the house had then been the duty of au pairs, many of whom had come and gone, usually not before they had fallen for and then fallen out with Derry.

Growing more and more angry by the second, Tara prowled around the downstairs. The house was filthy. Straw and what looked suspiciously like horse-dung littered the carpets and thick dust coated every surface. Only the kitchens, Mrs McDonagh's province, looked relatively clean although the sink was full of dirty plates and takeaway cartons. Miserable tears of exhaustion pricked the back of Tara's eyes. Dashing them angrily away, she collected her suitcase and bags and trudged upstairs.

Her room was at the back of the house, a peaceful room that overlooked the once carefully tended garden that had been her mother's pride and joy. It was a light airy room with a small bathroom and a tiny sitting-room that had been her bolthole when Derry used to come home from school for the holidays with hordes of loud friends. That room also, she was horrified to find, was filthy with dust and neglect. The bed was crumpled, the sheets heaped at the bottom. Half-full glasses of wine growing mould lay on the bedside table along with a used condom. She shoved her case over to the bed.

"Welcome home, Tara," she whispered wryly.

The icy air amplified the noise. In the distance a powerful car was hurtling down the narrow Tipperary road towards the racehorses making their way to the gallops for their morning exercise. A hard frost had dusted the long strands of grass at the side of the road with fine white powder. Cobwebs spun into the bare hawthorn hedges hung heavy with thousands of tiny droplets of ice. The riders guided their horses gingerly along roads slick with treacherous black ice that shimmered maliciously in the intense winter sunlight. Morgan Flynn swore under his breath at the stupidity of the driver of the as yet unseen car, who was on a collision course with thousands of pounds' worth of horse-flesh. He felt his stomach knot with fear and a cold sweat of panic drenched his body as he imagined the car ploughing into the horses. The sickening, slow-motion moment as the driver tried to bring the car to a stop. The screech of tyres on tarmac, then the appalling thud of metal hitting delicate limbs. Carnage. In his mind's eye he could picture the broken bodies of the animals who were his pride and joy. The imagery was as clear as it was horrific. Broken limbs, screaming horses, a slick of blood oozing along the tarmac, thick as treacle — and a car, crushed beyond recognition, wisps of smoke escaping from the engine. He tightened his grip on the rubber-covered reins, willing the fit racehorse, Brackley Gate, to behave. Long months of hard, backbreaking, mind-numbing work had gone into turning the tall chestnut horse from a bony unbroken four-year-old with a mind of his own, into an impressive racing-machine with rippling muscles, breathtaking speed and awesome staying power. And, Morgan was certain, one of the hottest prospects for the Ladbroke Hurdle at Leopardstown tomorrow. The only thing that he had not been able to change was Brackley Gate's unpredictable temperament. The sudden appearance of a speeding car coming towards him over the brow of the hill could scare the volatile horse. As Morgan knew only too well a frightened horse was a dangerous one. An accident could wipe out the hopes and ambitions of everyone at Radford Lodge, Morgan's training stables.

Beside him, Morgan heard Kate, his groom, say in a frightened voice: "Jeez, that car's going too fast." As always she was mistress of the understatement. "Whoever the eejit is that's driving it, he's going to really scare the horses when it comes over the hill."

Morgan bit his lip, hard, to prevent himself from yelling at the young girl to shut her up. He could not trust himself to speak without his voice betraying the fear that he felt. He tasted the salty tang of blood as the sharp edge of a chipped front tooth, the result of a fall over an open ditch while in the lead in a race, pierced the delicate skin on the inside of his lip. He glanced quickly at Kate, suddenly afraid for her. Would she be able to hold the powerful horse she was riding if it decided to bolt, buck or rear? Her face was white beneath the brightly coloured crash-hat. Eyes the colour of a warm tropical sea gazed fearfully from beneath the peak of the hat in the direction of the noise and her mouth was pressed into a tight tense line.

The car was close now, but still unseen. The engine noise changed as the driver slowed for a corner, changed gear and then powered rapidly on the accelerator. The horses pricked their ears and held their necks high, tense at the unfamiliar noise. The moments oozed by painfully towards the inevitable split-second confrontation of horsepower and horseflesh. An accident was inevitable.

Behind him, Morgan could sense the other riders tightening their reins and gripping their knees into the exercise-saddles, ready to stop the horses spinning into the road if the sudden appearance of the car startled them.

Suddenly, in an explosion of noise and colour, a bright red sports car hurtled over the brow of the hill. Rust-coloured bracken and the bare branches of the hedges lining the road rattled in a Mexican wave as it shot past. The terrified horses scattered in all directions. Morgan heard hooves clattering on the tarmac and branches breaking as one of the horses tried to escape through the thorny barbs of the hedge. There was a scream of protest from the tyres as the white-faced driver slammed on the brakes. In slow motion the car slid along the road, by some miracle missing the horses.

Morgan saw its bonnet glide by Brackley Gate's belly. Then, with a dull thud, the car slammed into the grass bank and came to an abrupt halt.

After the cacophony of noise and movement, all was very silent and still. Then the driver's door opened and a tall, well-dressed young man exploded from the car, expletives streaming from him in a raging torrent of abuse as he marched towards the quivering horses and their trembling riders.

"You fucking bunch of cowboys!" he yelled, his handsome face contorted in anger. "Why the hell don't you keep your ponies in the corral until you can ride them!" His dark eyes flashed with fury and his wide mouth twisted in rage over a line of very perfect white teeth.

"You bastard," Kate hissed, riding towards him, "you nearly killed us!"

Her horse, still snorting in fear, pranced sideways forcing him to jump out of the way in order to avoid being trampled by the dancing hooves.

"These are valuable racehorses," she continued, breathless in her anger, "and you were driving far too fast."

Morgan recognised the young man as Derry Blake, owner of Westwood Park training stables, Ireland's champion jockey five times over and now high up on the list of top trainers.

"Racehorses?" sneered Derry, running a hand through his dark hair to slick back a lock that had fallen over his forehead. "Well, I'm glad that you pointed that out to me, darling, otherwise I wouldn't have known! What are you going to enter them in? The Donkey Derby?" He thrust his hands into the pockets of his well-cut and obviously very expensive sports jacket, and looked Kate up and down slowly, straight dark eyebrows raised sardonically.

"Leave it, Kate," Morgan said, tonelessly, finding his voice at last.

"Ah," Derry gloated, a smirk twisting the corners of his lips, "these are your horses are they, Flynn?" He ran his eyes over the quivering horses, scathingly appraising them.

Morgan had been a jockey when Derry was racing — he had been his only serious competition. For a while they had goaded each other over which of them could win the most races and attain the accolade of being champion jockey. And then Morgan had been horrifically injured in an accident, when the horse that he was riding had bolted on the road and been hit by a car. That had ended his career and killed the best horse from the stables that belonged to Ralph Hardwicke, the trainer he was working for. Dismissed and in disgrace, he had disappeared from the racing scene, helping his father run his chain of hardware shops instead. But being away from racing and horses had proved to be an unendurable torture.

A few years ago he had resurfaced, persuading his father to lend him money to buy the run-down Radford Lodge and train a few point-to-point horses, then graduating to training racehorses for a few minor races. He and Derry had moved in different spheres of the same world. Derry training the best horses for hugely rich owners entering the biggest races, Morgan entering his for races at small country racecourses. It suited Derry that their paths never crossed. He had never forgiven Morgan for challenging him to the crown of champion jockey, a position that Derry had always assumed was his by divine right.

"I thought that you killed horses, not trained them!" said Derry, disdain clearly etched on his handsome face. "Well," he said haughtily, "I knew you had some runners in point-to-points, but I really don't think that your nags are in the same class as the ones I train."

"Their paths will be crossing sooner than you think," Morgan enunciated quietly, meeting Derry's incredulous gaze with his own icy stare. "If you look in the race entries you will see that my horse is entered in the Ladbroke, with your Sloe Gin."

Derry exploded with forced laughter. "See you at the races," he then drawled sarcastically as he spun on his heel and stalked back to the car.

"Prick!" Kate screamed after him. "We'll bloody beat your horse!"

Derry turned and surveyed the group of horses with amusement. "You haven't a hope, darling!"

"Leave it, Kate," said Morgan.

Derry fired the powerful car back into life and with an aggressive roar of the engine reversed back onto the road and shot off at high speed down the narrow lane.

"Bloody amateurs," he snarled, scowling at the rapidly diminishing figures of the racehorses and their riders in the rear-view mirror.

A few miles further Derry reached Westwood Park. He slowed the car, his anger gone as quickly as it had erupted. A high wall, built of grey limestone, marked the boundary of the estate where he had grown up. Derry let out an enormous sigh of pleasure. As always, when he looked at the house from the end of the long straight driveway with the avenue of beech trees with their silver trunks, he felt a surge of love for his home.

Westwood Park had been built at the end of the 19th century. It was a tall imposing house, built in red brick that had now mellowed to the rusty shade of a damp fox. Although, like many who had grown up amongst great wealth, Derry took much of his life for granted, the beauty of the house never failed to take his breath away. The house was covered with a mass of dark ivy, wisteria and jasmine that fought to take over the brickwork, draping themselves languidly against the sloping structures of the roof.

Even with a pounding headache from a hard night spent drinking and the confrontation on the road, Derry could not help but feel that familiar surge of love and pride, tinged with the now less painful sense of regret that his father was no longer there to share the house and the training stables with him. Captain Blake and Derry's mother, Celia, had been killed two years previously when the car in which they were travelling crashed. They had been on the way to England to watch Captain Blake's favourite horse run in a big race on a wet Tuesday at Haydock. The horse had won, but the Captain and Celia had never seen it run. The car had crashed on the motorway a few miles from the racecourse, killing them both instantly.

Derry's sports car swept through a second set of pillars, the smooth tarmac of the drive ending as the gravel forecourt of the main house began. Derry manoeuvred the car around to the front of the house and switched off the engine. The house towered above the car, the dark windows looking out. Derry pushed open the car door and the familiar scent of home wafted into the interior: the heavy scent of the yew trees mingling with the overlying odour of the stables — hot horses and horse muck. He let out a long sigh of pleasure, savouring the silence.

He unfolded his long legs and swung them out onto the gravel, getting out of the car with the grace of a cat. He ran lightly up the stone steps and into the house.

"Derry!" called a voice from above him.

In a split second he recognised the voice and pounded up the stairs, his long legs taking the stairs two at a time. "Tara!" he yelled in delight. "My darling little sister!" He reached the first landing, where the stairs bent before climbing upwards again, and paused.

Tara leant against the banisters at the top, looking down at him, a broad grin of delight lighting up her face. The Blake good looks that made Derry so stunning sat strangely on Tara, making her seem striking rather than beautiful. The Florida tan didn't suit her features and fine hair at all, thought Derry.

"Welcome home!" he grinned, bounding up the remaining stairs to sweep her into his arms, making her squeal in protest as he squashed the breath out of her. "Thank goodness you're back," he said, releasing her. "This house needs a woman's touch!"

CHAPTER TWO

The powerful chestnut horse began to buck, arching his back and plunging furiously as soon as his feet touched the springy old turf of the twenty-acre field. Morgan dug his knees into the hard leather of the tiny exercise-saddle and dragged at the reins, every muscle straining with the effort, trying to force Brackley Gate's head up from between his knees to end the ferocious cavorting.

Then Brackley Gate gave with a titanic, twisting leap that would have done justice to a rodeo horse, and Morgan felt himself being launched skywards high above the saddle. He landed with a thud that rattled his teeth, on the horse's neck in front of the saddle, without reins or stirrups. Clinging on with his legs and hands he grappled for the reins which were swinging wildly beneath the horse's neck while he wriggled back into the saddle and searched furiously for his stirrups, the ground flashing at an alarming rate of knots beneath him. He wrestled the horse back under control, slowing his headlong gallop into a more sedate canter.

Kate, thanking her lucky stars that she was not riding the terrifying Brackley Gate, caught up with Morgan. "Fresh, isn't he?" she laughed, tossing a stray strand of hair from her eyes as she rode.

Morgan had gone deathly white and his teeth were chattering despite the sweat that darkened his hair beneath his crash-hat. He snorted in reply, not trusting his voice to conceal the panic that he had felt. If he had fallen off, there could have been thousands of pounds' worth of horseflesh loose on the road at this very moment.

The lads who were riding the other horses from the yard cantered slowly up the slope to join Morgan and Kate. They had watched Brackley Gate's antics, open-mouthed in horror.

They all cantered the horses alongside each other around the long field. Then on the last circuit Morgan eased the reins, letting Brackley Gate gallop ahead, stretching his legs, revelling in the super fitness and stamina that had been so carefully nurtured and worked on over the last few months. Everything over that period had been leading up to tomorrow's race.

Finally they slowed the horses back to a canter, then to a trot and then to a walk before they made their way back to the stable yard. Morgan rode ahead of the others, whistling tunelessly. He was thrilled with how the horse had worked, and was convinced that he could win the race.

Radford Lodge was the rather glamorous name for the ramshackle set of buildings that housed Morgan and the horses. The cottage that he lived in had once been the groom's accommodation. It stood to one side of the extremely beautiful but rundown stables which had been built around a square yard of dark cobbles. The stable doors, although sagging on age-old hinges and patched with planks of wood where time had made its mark, were smartly painted giving the old yard the faded dignity of an ancient duchess. All the buildings stood in the shadow of the enormous ruin of Radford House, a once glorious mansion that now stood derelict and forlorn, raising its roofless stonework to the sky as if imploring to be repaired.

They rode the tired horses into the stable yard and Morgan slid from Brackley Gate, tossed the reins to Kate and grabbed the copy of the Racing Post that the newsagent had shoved in the bars of the gate. As he unfolded the newspaper the headlines seemed to leap off the page to taunt him: Derry Blake's Horse Sloe Gin Certain Winner at Leopardstown, screamed the headline. The earlier argument had left a sour taste in Morgan's mouth. He hated confrontation, but Derry Blake's arrogance had stung.

Derry had always been the golden boy of racing; he had even shone on the pony-racing circuit as a child. Once he had gone into racing proper, he had gone straight to the top — his father's contacts had made sure of that. Now he was one of the top trainers in Ireland. Morgan hated him, with a bitter vengeance. Derry had always had it so easy: good horses, training facilities, owners with bottomless purses to fund it all. Morgan wondered bitterly how Derry would manage to train horses with the facilities, or lack of them, he himself had. His growling stomach reminded him that he hadn't eaten. Still grumbling to himself, he stalked off to the house.

A large dark-brown mouse ran swiftly along the draining-board and took refuge in the cupboard as Morgan opened the kitchen door. The tiny kitchen was always dark, the one small window only letting in a narrow shaft of light. Morgan surveyed the room numbly. A gale was blowing under the door, rattling the heap of bills that were piled on the table. He scowled; he did not need to be reminded about the unpaid bills — they seemed to glare at him maliciously enough already. He had no chance of paying them, so what was the point of even opening them? He switched on the kettle and took a chipped mug out of the cupboard. While the kettle boiled he threw a tea bag into the mug and pulled the fridge door open. A single carton of milk held pride of place in the empty fridge. He sniffed the milk gingerly - it didn't smell great. He poured the boiling water into the mug and put it onto the table, pushing aside a clutter of dishes. He always seemed to be too tired to wash up, even when there was hot water. Delving into the bread-bin, he selected two slices of bread that weren't too dried out and threw them under the grill.

As the bread toasted he went into the tiny lounge and raked out the ashes from the fire. The chimney desperately needed sweeping. Smoke and ash were blown backwards into the room, covering his racehorse portraits and the point-to-point trophies he had accumulated and which lined every available surface. The smell of burning toast made him dash back to the kitchen. Thick smoke poured from the grill. He grabbed the handle and wrenched it out, spilling the toast onto the floor in the process. Sighing, he retrieved the toast, dusted the horse - and dog - hairs and the worst of the charcoal off it and scraped butter onto the surface.

Most of the horses in the yard belonged to his two owners: Eddie Gallagher, a rough and bullying building-contractor, and Lynn Moore, a very merry widow. Lynn's best horse, the small, wiry, bay mare Frottage was as highly strung and difficult as her owner. If she had been a person, Kate had once said, Frottage would have been a drug-addict or an alcoholic. Because he was only a small-time trainer, Morgan could not charge the large training fees that could be demanded by the larger, more prestigious establishments. The result of this was a hand-to-mouth existence. The horses were better looked after than he was.

Toast eaten, he threw his dirty plate into the sink and picked up the telephone. Eddie Gallagher answered his mobile phone on the first ring.

"Morgan," he said brusquely, seeing the telephone number come up on the display. Morgan knew that he wanted only the basic facts about his horse, no small talk, of which he was glad. His phone bills were horrific and calls to mobile phones were expensive.

"I've just worked the horse," Morgan said. "He's spot on for tomorrow."

"Worth a bet then," said Eddie, over the roar of noise from the building site. It was a statement rather than a question.

Morgan paused, trying to frame his words to tell Eddie that while he had every hope for the horse, anything could go wrong while the race was being run. The horse could fall or be brought down or could just not perform on the day. However, before he had time to put his thoughts into a sentence, Eddie said, "See you at Leopardstown" and the telephone went dead.

Morgan was suddenly gripped with fear. What if Eddie thought that the horse was a dead cert and put loads of money on him? What if he didn't win? What if Eddie put no money on him and the horse romped home? What if, what if — the endless possibilities of disaster ran through his head making it spin. There was nothing that he could do now. He just had to get Brackley Gate to Leopardstown and the rest was up to the horse.

Kate stomped into the kitchen. With an enormous sigh she pulled out a chair and sank down in it as if the cares of the world were being carried on her young shoulders. She watched from behind the mane of red hair that she had let fall across her face as Morgan made her a cup of tea and put the steaming mug onto the pine table in front of her.

"Mum's still nagging at me to get a better job," she sighed, dreamily stirring sugar into the mug and reaching for one of the biscuits that Morgan had unearthed in a cupboard and put on the table. "How am I ever going to tell her that I don't want to be someone's personal assistant," she complained, looking at Morgan earnestly through enormous blue eyes, "that all I want to do is to ride horses and shovel horse-shit?"

"Have you tried just telling her that you're happy doing what you do?" he said wearily. The conversation was one that was repeated over and over again.

"I never get the opportunity," she complained, her wide mouth framing a grimace.

Kate's mother was one of life's super-achievers, always on the go, desperately trying to better her social standing and way of life and pushing

Kate to do the same. But all that Kate ever wanted to do was to be near horses and Morgan.

She pushed aside the mane of hair and looked at him coyly, but something out of the window had caught his attention. Kate spun around and, following his gaze, groaned as she saw Lynn Moore's jeep careering into the yard. Kate noticed the look of dislike that clouded over Morgan's eyes.

The jeep slewed to a stop in the middle of the drive and Lynn got out. For a woman in her mid-forties she had a great figure, tall and toned, dressed in jeans that clung to the contours of her firm thighs and a pale shirt with the outline of a lacy bra visible beneath the fabric. She slammed the car door and strolled towards the cottage with a model's sashay and wriggling hips.

Kate felt Morgan freeze. He stared out of the tiny window with the watchful gaze of a hunted fox. "I'll go and groom the horses," Kate mumbled bleakly, painfully aware that Morgan was not listening to her. She stood up so hurriedly that the chair fell backwards and crashed loudly onto the tiled floor. Suddenly boiling with jealous rage, Kate righted the chair and turned to go, only to find the doorway blocked by Lynn.

Close to, her age was more obvious. Orange make-up was smeared liberally over her wide cheekbones and her collagen-pumped-up mouth was covered by a broad slash of bright colour. Heavy mascara and dark shadow accentuated her eyes and collected in the fine lines at the edges. Her dark hair, dyed presumably to hide any telltale grey strands that ran through it, was teased into enormous curls that drooped around her face.

Lynn had risen from very humble beginnings, but was very ambitious. She had caught the eye of Liam Moore, her boss at the factory where she worked. He did not know what hit him when they began an extremely torrid affair. The affair eventually became public when his suspicious wife caught the two of them together in a very compromising position in a hotel bedroom while he was supposedly away on a business trip to Dublin. Liam left his wife and set up home with Lynn. She never forgot her gratitude for the sudden change in her circumstances and never tired of showing it to the man who was some thirty-five years her senior. After enjoying the best few years of his life he finally expired during an exceptionally energetic sex session one lunch-time. The episode left Lynn with a substantial income and a desire to find herself another rich husband. Her husband had often entertained his clients in plush hospitality boxes at race meetings and, fascinated by the super-wealthy and glamorous people that she had met at the races, she soon began to think about having a horse in training. Regular trips to the races would afford her an excellent opportunity to suss out new prospects for husband number two.

A friend recommended Morgan. He was, at the time, having a lot of success with the point-to-pointers, was good at training horses and certainly needed the business. Lynn set off to see him, reluctantly. She had a far more glamorous trainer in mind.

She almost turned back when she saw the ramshackle yard, but when Morgan emerged from one of the stables she was immediately hooked by his brooding good looks and decided to stick around. She had quickly made him aware that it was more than her horses that needed looking after and that if he wanted her business, he had to do the business.

"Have you got time for coffee?" she said in a voice that demanded rather than asked, glancing over her shoulder in amusement at the angry set of Kate's back as she hurried away from the cottage.

Morgan glanced pointedly at his watch, trying desperately to think of an excuse to get out of the house, but before he could think of one she was breast to chest with him, saying huskily: "We must discuss my horse."

A knot of distaste wrapped itself around his stomach. The last thing she wanted was to talk about horses. Then he thought of the pile of unpaid bills and the cheque that she would leave him. "Coffee would be lovely," he said, forcing a smile onto his face as she reached out a hand and began to undo the buttons on his shirt.

"Feel how hot I am," she whispered huskily, catching his hand and pulling him towards her.

He felt himself go rigid with tension and repulsion. He wanted to shove her away from him and run, but he knew that he needed her money and if this was part of what he had to do to get it then so be it. As her body brushed against his, she parted her lips and touched them gently to his. Then, despite himself, he closed his eyes and felt his body betray him as he responded to her demanding touch.

CHAPTER THREE

Sarah Connors gasped in pain as Sloe Gin trod on her foot for the second time that morning. The horse was in a frenzy of excitement. His small ears were flattened against his elegant black neck and he glared at the girl who was plaiting his mane, showing the whites of his mean, piggy eyes. Sloe Gin knew that he was going racing and barged backwards and forwards, fighting against the restraint of the lead-rope that anchored him to the wall. He waved a long and delicate hind foot, ready to lash out whenever Sarah got within his range. His front end was just as deadly — he snapped viciously at her with his long yellow front teeth whenever he got the chance — her arm was already dotted with bruises in an assortment of vivid colours.

As she neared his ears to put in the final plaits, he flung his head violently sideways in temper, giving her a hard bang on the side of her face. Only by sheer discipline did she prevent herself from thrashing the horse that had hurt her, a discipline instilled in her through the years that she had worked with horses. Instead, once the stars had stopped dancing in front of her eyes, she began to work again and finished the last plait. Sloe Gin stood still long enough for her to complete the intricate twisting of the wiry hair.

Relieved that she had completed her work before Derry appeared, in his usual frenzy of temper and arrogance, she walked across the silent yard to the tack room. A short while earlier the yard had buzzed with the chatter of the stable staff as they worked, mucking out the horses and riding them off to the gallops. Now, at nine in the morning, they had all gone off to their lodgings in the village for breakfast.

The tack room was silent apart from the faint snoring of an ancient terrier snoozing in one of the sagging armchairs that occupied the corners of the room, amongst the clutter of rugs and grooming kits. The large room was lined with dark mahogany which dated back to when the house was built. Bridles and saddles festooned every available inch of three walls, filling the air with the smell of leather and horse-sweat. On the other wall hung the jockey silks, brightly coloured nylon jackets in a myriad of loud colours and clashing patterns, like giant tropical butterflies pinned to the wall.

Sarah poured herself a cup of tea from the flask that she had brought with her from the garden cottage where she lived. She evicted the sleeping terrier who limped stiffly away, growling with temper, and sank down gladly onto the hair-and-mud-encrusted armchair. Sighing with tiredness she sipped the scalding liquid, feeling it revive her flagging energy. Her day had started long before it was light, the buzzing of the alarm-clock dragging her from a restless sleep to begin another day supervising the staff that cared for the forty horses at Westwood Park.

The previous evening the sound of Derry's powerful car roaring up the drive as he returned from the pub had woken her from an exhausted slumber in front of the television. But he hadn't come to visit her. Derry would often turn up at her door in the middle of the night, randy as hell, when he had nothing better to do. Or no one better to do, she sometimes thought bitterly, acutely aware of her lowly place in Derry's life. She could never quite believe her luck when he came to visit her. He was so gorgeous and she was, she had realised long ago, so very ordinary.

There were no men like Derry on the rough Dublin estate where she came from, just rough, tough men with no manners or money. Sarah loved her job and she loved Derry. She had worked for him for over a year and had been his lover for most of that time. She knew that he used her when he had nothing better on offer, but she felt that any crumbs of affection that he gave her were better than starving. She had tried to find other boyfriends, but quickly discovered that although Derry did not practise monogamy she was very definitely expected to be his exclusive property. She discovered too, that after having Derry as a lover no one else really compared. Anyone else was rather like having to eat fish fingers after being used to dining on smoked salmon. So she often spent long evenings, night after night, watching for his car returning from whatever jaunt he had been on and hoping to hear his footsteps approaching.

Sarah loved Westwood Park almost as much as she loved Derry. A tiny cottage went with the job, set into the wall of the enclosed garden, a short walk from the stable yard. After the noisy chaos of her parents' home, the peace of the cottage was wonderful. Derry had redecorated it for her when she had taken the job. She had chosen Laura Ashley wallpaper to cover the stains where the last groom had thrown hoof-oil against the walls in a fit of temper when Derry had become bored with her.

The stable yard was her pride and joy and she supervised it with great care. It was built in a rectangular shape in the same mellowed red brick as the house. Spacious loose boxes with green painted wooden doors looked out onto an oval of carefully manicured grass.

Sarah heard the click as the gate-latch was sprung back. She glanced out of the cobweb-encrusted window to watch Derry, unobserved. A tall archway, crowned with a rearing-horse weather vane separated the stable yard from the gravel drive that led up to the house. She watched as Derry pushed the gate open and glanced around the yard. Even though they were lovers, Sarah knew that he would not tolerate any slackness in her work. But the yard was immaculate. Sarah smiled as Derry nodded to himself in satisfaction. She swallowed the biscuit that she had been eating. The diet that she had begun two days ago had already been abandoned. She ran dirt-engrained fingers ineffectually through the wind-tangled thick strands of her dark hair. She jumped as he came into the tack room, spilling half a cup of tea down the front of her jeans which were already filthy with horse-muck and straw.

"Ready?" he said shortly, tense as always on a racing morning.

"As always," she quipped, but the joke was lost on him.

"How's the horse?" he demanded, his eyes taking in the tack room, checking to see if she had the racing colours ready and the tack that they would need for the race.

"He's fine." As always his tremendous animal magnetism left her trembling inwardly and unable to do anything for the paralysis he wrought on her.

He left the tack room as abruptly as he had entered it. Sarah followed him, trotting to keep up as he marched rapidly across the yard to the stable that housed Sloe Gin. Sloe Gin belonged to JT Healy, and was the best of the large string of horses that the professional gambler owned on the yard.

Derry flung open the stable door and stood to one side as Sarah unfastened the horse's rug and slid it back over his muscular quarters. The black horse looked magnificent. He stood almost seventeen hands high, with strong, finely chiselled legs supporting a huge barrel-like chest. He lifted a delicate back leg in a threatening gesture and laid his ears flat against his head, annoyed at the intrusion. Derry ran a hand down each of his legs, checking for the telltale signs of heat that would foretell any approaching lameness. Satisfied at last, he stood up and peered into the horse's feed bowl to check that he had eaten all of his oats.

"How has he been working?" he demanded.

"Very well," she said and began to relate the work that the horse had done, but Derry was sliding his hand around the back of her neck and pushing her slowly backwards to trap her against the rough wall of the stable.

Afterwards he left the stable abruptly and a few moments later she heard the engine roar as the lorry was started. Sloe Gin pricked his intelligent ears to listen to the noise. Sarah slipped a head-collar over his finely chiselled head. Then, as she rolled a bandage over the silken hair of his tail, to protect it in the lorry, Derry barged back into the stable.

"Time to load the horse," he snapped. "Where's Paul?"

Sarah swallowed; inwardly preparing herself for the wave of temper she knew would erupt. "He's late, he rang me to say he had to change a tyre on his wife's car, it had a puncture while she was taking their little boy to school."

"That's not my problem," Derry raged. "He should be here to drive the lorry. I can't wait for him. I'll have to do it myself. Make sure his wages get docked."

Without answering, Sarah led Sloe Gin from the stable. She knew from bitter experience that it was best not to talk to Derry when he was wound up on a race morning. For him the sex had been a quick and mindless release of his tension, but now he was back in work mode, efficient and deadly if crossed. Any wrong word from her and he would give her a verbal lashing from his sharp tongue that would leave her stinging for the day, even though he would forget it instantly and then wonder why she was quiet with him. He had reversed the lorry onto the tarmac of the stable yard and now it stood with the ramp down and the engine running.

Sloe Gin, the week before, had gone into the lorry only to be cooped up for hours as it made a long journey to a racecourse in England. He had been trapped in the narrow stall as the lorry swayed with the rocking movement of the boat. He had been terrified and he was unwilling to repeat the experience. At the bottom of the ramp he stopped and swung his rounded muscular quarters away from the lorry as Sarah prepared to lead him into the dark interior.

"Come on, Ginny," she coaxed. She tugged at the lead-rope but Sloe Gin, sensing his greater strength, pulled back, dragging her away from the lorry.

"Get in there, you bloody animal," snarled Derry. They were running late and he could not afford to waste any time messing around with a badly behaved horse. About to explode in temper, he stamped to the cab to fetch a long whip.

Sarah had led the horse back to the lorry and had succeeded in getting him halfway up the ramp when Derry suddenly appeared at the side, surprising both of them. Sloe Gin pulled back violently, rearing up and wrenching the lead-rope from her hand, leaving a burning red wheal across the palm where the nylon had chafed against the skin. Derry let out an angry roar as Sloe Gin spun around and galloped across the immaculate turf in the centre of the yard, leaving huge holes in the damp grass. As he spotted another horse looking out of his stable, watching to see what all of the commotion was about, Sloe Gin slid back onto the tarmac, sparks from his hooves showering high into the air.

"Catch that damn horse!" roared Derry slamming his toe into the rubber of the lorry tyre in temper.

Sarah, trembling all over and feeling a red-hot flush spreading over her pale cheeks, ran across the defiled turf in pursuit of Sloe Gin. The holes in the grass seemed to mock her. Sloe Gin, excited, with his head high and his tail kinked over his back, was now thoroughly enjoying himself. He watched her approach until one hand almost grasped the dangling lead-rope and then he cantered away, snorting in delight as his hooves danced with jaunty amusement. "Please," she muttered through clenched teeth, desperately hoping that the horse would let her catch him before he damaged himself or more of the yard, "Derry will go mad."

Sloe Gin cantered to the far end of the yard and skidded to a halt at the gate that led into the hay-barns and the gardens. For a horrible stomach-churning moment she thought that he was going to attempt to jump the gate from a standstill. But then something caught his eye, the sight of other horses in the paddocks, and for a second he forgot his red-faced and tearful pursuer who finally managed to seize the end of the lead-rope.

As she reached the lorry Derry snatched the lead-rope from her and pulled the horse towards the ramp. He thrust the long whip into her hand.

"Use this," he snapped, his eyes flashing in temper.

Gingerly she hit Sloe Gin's back-quarters with the long whip, dodging quickly out of the way as one long hind leg lashed out resentfully at her. Finally the horse gave into their combined force and bounded up the lorry-ramp. Derry tied the lead-rope and landed a hefty kick in the horse's belly with such a force that the horse grunted in surprise, "I'll teach you to mess me around," he hissed. Sarah stood by the side of the lorry, quivering in anticipation of the wrath which she knew was about to be unleashed on her. However, the assault on the horse had eased his temper and he emerged from the lorry in a better mood. He flung the lorry-ramp up and with a curt "Come on then!" pinched her rounded bottom to show that she was forgiven, climbed into the cab and started the engine.

She climbed into the passenger side, relieved that the episode was over and that his vile mood had evaporated. She was used to these violent shows of temper when the excitement and tension of a race day erupted suddenly.

"Tara's come home," he told her.

Sarah pulled an interested face. Derry had told her a little about his younger sister and she was curious to meet her.

His anger had vanished as quickly as it appeared. As he turned the lorry out of the stable yard he turned on the radio and was soon singing to a banal pop song in a loud and tuneless voice. As the lorry, which was custom-painted in the dark blue and red of the Blake racing colours, sped through the lanes, Sarah wedged her feet on the dashboard and lit a cigarette for Derry. He accepted it wordlessly and dragged on it with obvious delight, drawing the smoke deep into his lungs pleasurably and exhaling in a long sigh, the earlier violence completely forgotten.

CHAPTER FOUR

Tara shivered miserably and pulled the collar of her thick overcoat tighter around her neck. Two years in the Florida sunshine had ill-equipped her for the bitter cold of a wet and windy racecourse on a horrible January afternoon. How on earth, she wondered bleakly, had she let Derry persuade her to come to the races?

They were standing in the centre of the parade-ring, watching as the horses were led around before the race. Beside them was the bulky, red-faced form of JT Healy. The two men were studying the horses intently Tara felt a surge of annoyance - she hated JT, who she felt was a dreadful old lecher.

"Which horse is going to win this race?" demanded JT, making Tara jump back in alarm as he thrust his race card under Derry's nose, almost knocking Tara out of the way as he did so. He exhaled a cloud of noxious cigar and brandy fumes into the air. Tara blinked as the smoke from the Havana cigar, which was as long and thick as a jockey's arm, stung her eyes.

Derry took the race card, which was already crumpled and battered from being folded and stuffed into JT's pocket half a dozen times. "Badminton Boy won last time out," he mused, narrowing his eyes in concentration.

Tara could feel the bulky form of JT prickle with impatience beside her, as he waited for Derry to make his decision.

A successful day's betting was crucial to JT who had spent most of his life making a substantial income from the proceeds of gambling. The money that he had won over the last thirty years had been put to good use, funding a succession of property deals which had made him one of the wealthiest men in Ireland.

"Blaze-a-trail — he fell, yet again," Derry read from the form guide at the side of the horse's names m the catalogue.

Tara let her eyes roam over the horses — thousands and thousands of pounds' worth of rain soaked horses all being led around while their drenched owners and the spectators crowded around the ring watching them. What a bloody pointless activity this was! She wished that she had stayed at home to lick her wounds and get over Hank.

Derry's voice droned on as he expertly appraised the horses. "Carnmore Cross is the horse," he decided at last, tapping his finger against the horse's name on the race card.

"He ran well last ..." he continued, but his words trailed off as JT snatched the race card from him and hurried away, head down against the rain, his mobile phone firmly clamped to his ear as he rang the multitude of men that he had lined up to place bets for him in bookies around the country.

"Watch this," Derry said, a thin smile of amusement playing around his wide mouth as JT approached the on-course bookies that lined the area around the main stand. Whenever he went onto a racecourse JT attracted a huge crowd of followers, eager to share his success and place their own hard-earned money on the same horses as he did. The bookmakers, however, were not so thrilled to see him — many had lost a lot of money on bets that he had placed.

Tara screwed up her eyes against the rain and wind as JT waved a wad of money at the first bookie, who shook his head, refusing to take his bet. As JT disappeared into the crowds that surrounded the bookies, Derry raised his hands in front of Tara's face to show her his crossed fingers, hoping the horse he had selected won.

The bell that signalled it was time for the jockeys to mount their horses rang out loudly across the parade-ring. The jockeys, who had been standing in clusters with the owners and trainers of the horses that they were to ride, their brightly coloured silks gaudy against the tweeds and waxed jackets, walked towards their horses, shivering against the cold and the nerves that wracked their painfully thin bodies. With final claps on the back and whispered words of instruction and reassurance ringing in their ears, they were legged up onto horses that spun with excitement. The horses were led for another circuit of the parade-ring. Eager spectators crowded against the rail to watch and pick out last-minute bets. "I'm going to bet on that one," rang out a shrill female voice. "He has a nice face!" There was a collective titter of amusement from the more authoritative gamblers.

The steward pulled back the guard-rail to allow the horses onto the course. "The going is officially soft," JT muttered, seeing Derry scowling at the state of the turf on the course. The first race had churned the grass up so that it resembled a ploughed field, huge chunks of the prized turf littering the track. Deep soft mud that would cling to the horses' legs, tiring them and straining delicate tendons, oozed like a quagmire. The white-faced jockeys clung to the reins and tried to look nonchalant as they were led past a group of eager-faced teenage girls.

"We can get a good view from the owners' and trainers' stand," Derry said, already following the spectators who were hurrying to get in place before the race began. Tara followed him, scowling. She longed to be at home, in a deep bath of hot water, letting the warmth soak into her frozen bones.

The horses lined up at the start and moments later the starter's flag fluttered down and the race was underway. Derry clamped his binoculars to his eyes, concentrating on the distant blur of movement. Tara gazed uninterestedly across the desolate acres of the racecourse. The rain had eased off and far away on the other side of the track she could see the group of horses, moving fast, a flash of colour against the dull spring landscape. Tension gripped the spectators as everyone gazed, white knuckles clutching race tickets, whispering silent prayers for success.

Suddenly Tara forgot the aching cold that bit into her bones and froze her toes. Despite herself, she began to will Carnmore Cross forward, every sense concentrated on the race. He was running in third place. With two fences left to jump the pace began to quicken. The horses turned towards the stands and a collective roar of excitement rang through the course. A gasp of horror slipped through Tara's lips when Carnmore Cross stumbled as he landed over the final jump, losing precious ground. Then the horse surged forward to win by a short nose on the finishing line. Tara was dismayed to find herself leaping up and down and shrieking with excitement with the rest of the spectators. Below them JT shoved his way through the crowds, his red moon-face beaming with delight at the thought of the money that he had won.

The cold forgotten, Tara felt excitement begin to build within her: it was time for their race. The Ladbroke was one of the biggest races in the Irish calendar. It was a day when everyone flocked to the racecourse, from the experts to those who merely wanted to come and be seen.

Derry strode ahead of her towards the parade-ring. The crowd parted almost of one accord as he walked through. Tara trotted in his wake, jostled by the crowd who stopped to stare and nudge one another and say "Is that Derry Blake?" She wriggled her way under the guard-rail that separated the horses from the crowds and shot across the tarmac walkway, narrowly avoiding the dancing hooves of a sweating grey horse that was being led around the ring. In the centre of the ring the owners and trainers of the horses for the big race stood in silent contemplation of their animals. The tension hung heavily in the air as each one weighed up the competition.

"That's my horse," Derry announced, unable to disguise the pride in his voice. Sarah was leading a majestic-looking Sloe Gin around the ring, his hooves echoing dully on the rubberised tarmac walkway. Noticing Derry, Sarah's face, pinched with the cold, split into a grin of delight.

"Would you bloody look at that!" exploded Derry suddenly. Tara looked in the direction of his incredulous stare and saw a tall chestnut horse being led around the ring. "It's the horse that belongs to that idiot who nearly made me crash the car."

A tall good-looking man was glaring aggressively back at them. Tara instinctively moved away. Whatever fight Derry had with the other trainer, she wanted no part of it. She distanced herself from the men as the stranger stalked over to Derry.

"Your horse doesn't look his best," she heard the stranger say in mocking tones.

"He'll still beat your old nag," Derry sniped back. The man laughed — a deep, mocking laugh of amusement. "We'll see," he snorted.

Still tense with anger Derry waved his hand at Sarah, commanding her wordlessly to take the horse to the saddling area. Tara followed them to the small saddling stalls. Tempers were short as horses stood on toes and snapped their long yellow teeth at the grooms as their girths were pulled up tight.

Sarah stood in front of Sloe Gin, clutching his bridle and trying to avoid his restless feet and snapping teeth.

"Well, look who it is," drawled Derry.

The man he had been rowing with was leading his horse into the adjoining stall. "Giving him a head start for next week's race, are you?" snorted Derry, giving his horse a hefty slap on the neck.

"Fuck off," snapped the man, turning his attention to his horse.

Tara lolled against the partition, watching surreptitiously. Sloe Gin quivered with excitement, his hard muscular body racked with tremors. A dark film of sweat had broken out on his neck.

Sarah stroked his shoulder. "Easy, old lad," she whispered gently, her voice calm.

"Horse looks well," boomed a voice, making them all jump. JT shoved his way into the saddling stall, booting a rug out of the way in order to lean against the wooden partition. "I hope that he's going to win," he snapped. "Costing me a bloody fortune, he is!"

Tara saw Derry close his eyes in horror. He had enough to worry about without JT giving him grief just at this moment in time.

"I'm off to get my bets on," boomed JT, his loud voice echoing around the saddling-area as he shoved his way out of the stall and strode away.

"I didn't see much money going on your horse," mocked Derry, shoving his head over the partition to survey his opponent's horse critically.

Tara heard the snarled reply: "This horse is going to win!"

Derry gave a loud snort of amusement. "Well, we are about to find out," he said, as he slapped Sloe Gin on his broad black quarters.

Sarah led Sloe Gin out of the saddling stall, glaring coldly at the red-haired girl with the tall chestnut horse. Sloe Gin danced beside her, snorting in mock terror at unseen dangers in the shadows. Tara watched the horse dancing away down the pathway towards the parade-ring, feeling a quiver of terror for them all. The horse was so precious and the racing game so dangerous — the horse could so easily be cavorting his way merrily to his death.

The entrants in the race marched around the parade-ring. Tara stood on the damp turf of the paddock, huddling into her heavy coat, shivering with the cold and excitement. Beside her Derry was making inane small talk with JT, reassuring him about the horse's chances in the race and how useless all of the others were.

There were ten horses in the race, all there to prove which one of them was the best over the tough Leopardstown course.

Morgan felt desperately sick. What was he doing here? All of the horses were far superior to Brackley Gate. This was the big-time — and he was going to make such a fool of himself. He watched as the favourite, Ashford Supreme, walked majestically around the paddock with his nonchalant jockey coolly waving at someone in the crowd. He looked bound to win. Then there was Rowan Rock who had come all the way from England with his trainer and a French jockey. Horse after horse swept past on long proud strides. Seemingly confident jockeys sat astride them with cocky stable lads and girls leading them. Then he saw the pink, excited face of Kate clutching the reins of Brackley Gate as if her life depended on it and the green face of Josh Drake, his jockey, who looked as if he was going to throw up at any second. Brackley Gate snatched at the reins unhappily.

Kate slipped the lead-rein from Brackley Gate's bit and stepped quickly out of the way as his flying hooves rushed past her. Morgan's sick feeling and fear vanished as he concentrated on the horse. With his long powerful stride and sharply pricked ears, he looked every bit as good as any of the others in the race.

The horses cantered to the start. Everyone involved with them was gripped with a fresh bout of terror. Tara stood with the others, her eyes glued intently to the television screen that relayed pictures of the race. She thought Sloe Gin walked majestically, looking like a king amongst the others. Then the horses lined up at the start and in a moment the race was underway.

The pace was fast and furious. Sloe Gin galloped in the middle of the horses, his shining black coat making him stand out from the others.

"Come on, lad," Tara heard Derry mutter, lost to the world as he stared intently at the screen.

The horses turned towards home and then with horror she saw the tall chestnut, Bracklev Gate, powering through the horses. With two fences left to jump he took the lead, his long stride eating up the ground as he pounded towards the finish line. Sloe Gin was completely outpaced. The crowd began to roar with excitement, encouraging the horse, delighted that the underdog was going to win.

Then seconds later Brackley Gate flashed over the finish line to a cheer that rang around the course.

Tara stole a glance at Derry whose face was dark as thunder. She saw the trainer of Brackley Gate running down the steps towards the winner's enclosure, his feet light with joy. She watched as he punched the air in triumph. Then she turned and saw JT making his way slowly up the high steps, his ruddy face purple with rage.

CHAPTER FIVE

Although it had seemed like a good idea at the time, Tara was now not so convinced of the wisdom of taking one of Derry's young point-to-point racehorses hunting.

She followed Derry across the yard dressed in her hunting clothes. Her jodhpurs felt too tight and the stock that she had tied around her neck seemed to be cutting off the circulation to her head. He flung open the stable door and stepped inside. Tara followed. Her heart sank when she saw the young grey thoroughbred already saddled and bridled, his mane neatly plaited by Sarah. The horse was wild-eyed, careering around the stable in his excitement, knowing that something was happening.

"Quiet as a lamb when he's out," announced Derry firmly, making a grab for the horse's reins and bringing him skidding to a halt.

Tara eyed the horse who was looking at her through wild, suspicious eyes, his nostrils flared red with his exertions and his grey neck damp with sweat. Patches of foam, like whipped cream, had appeared where the leather straps had chafed against the sweat.

"He looks a bit wild," she volunteered, not wanting to go anywhere near him. There was a world of difference between her capabilities and those of Derry. He had always had nerves of steel, honed by the series of frisky but brilliant ponies that their father had bought for him, and then when he had gone on to be a jockey getting on wild, excited horses was all part of the day's work. Tara, however, had inherited none of his steely nerve. She had preferred the ancient ponies that plodded quietly around the paddock, or stood gently to eat the grass while she sat on board enjoying the feeling of their soft hair and delighting in breathing in the glorious equine smell.

"He'll settle when he gets there," Derry told her, leading the quivering horse out of the stable. Tara jumped out of the way in order to avoid being crushed by the fearsome animal. She stepped back into the comforting bulk of Sarah who had appeared from one of the stables.

"Wouldn't Tara be better taking Mr Clever?" Sarah said. "He could do with the exercise and perhaps Diary Date might be a bit strong for her?"

Derry stopped abruptly and wheeled to face Sarah, fixing her with an icy glare that made even Tara quail. She felt Sarah perceptibly shrink beside her.

"I think that 1 can manage to find a horse for my sister, thank you, and it I need the groom's opinion I will ask for it."

Sarah wheeled on the heel of her Wellington boot and shot back into the stable she had been cleaning out.

Diary Date, as if sensing Derry's temper, behaved impeccably and walked across the yard and into the lorry like an old horse. Derry helped Tara into the cab.

"Have a good day," he said, winking cheerily at her as he slammed the door shut.

Tara fumbled with the key and finally got the huge lorry started and moving out of the yard. As she crawled slowly down the drive she began to feel a sense of excitement washing over her. It was a glorious day. The sun shone, brightening the rain-washed fields and lightening the bare bark on the beech trees that lined the drive.

She was glad to find that she had arrived early at the hunt meet and that she had plenty of time to manoeuvre the large lorry into place before the car park filled with the assortment of lorries and trailers that were bound to come later.

It was years since Tara had been to a hunt meet, yet, as the trailers and lorries began to arrive, she was greeted as if it had been only yesterday.

Paddy Moran, the Hunt Master, recognised her instantly. "Tara!" he boomed, his voice carrying the length of the pub, and everyone turned to stare at her. She smilingly made her way to the far end of the pub where Paddy was untangling himself from a heap of young blonde jodhpur-clad girls. He stood up, shaking off the last of the girls. He was tall, clad in tight-fitting jodhpurs, a brightly coloured waistcoat and a bright red tailcoat. He wore a top hat at a rakish angle and the buttonhole of his coat sported a tightly closed rosebud, which he proceeded to pull out and present to her.

"Welcome back to Ireland!" He gave her the full benefit of his megawatt smile, sweeping the top hat low off his head with a dramatic bow. Tara noticed with a strange feeling of satisfaction that the dandy's hair was streaked with grey and the famous ponytail that women had once swooned over was no longer in existence, the result she had heard, of falling asleep at a dinner party once too often. The furious hostess had taken a kitchen-shears to his pride and joy, severed it as he slept face down in a plate of chocolate cheesecake and stuffed the severed remnant into his jacket buttonhole instead of his famous rosebud. Someone had commented wryly that with the lifestyle he led he was lucky his ponytail was the only thing that ever had got severed.

Tara ordered a large port and moved away from the crowd at the bar to drink it, feeling the comfort of Dutch courage seeping into the knot in her stomach as she drank. The glass was halfway to her lips when a tall man pushing into the pub jolted her elbow and the contents of the glass showered over her face. She gasped in shock as the cold liquid hit her skin.

"Well, I've never seen anyone get blooded before a hunt!" brayed the Hunt Secretary of a neighbouring pack, laughing uproariously.

Tara tried to wipe her face with as much dignity as she could, with the whole pub giggling at her predicament.

"Sorry," said the man who had jolted her elbow. "Let me get you another one."

"No, thanks," she snapped, scowling at him through port-soaked eyelashes.

"Suit yourself," he shrugged, before joining the crowd at the bar.

The Huntsman suddenly banged his empty glass down on the table and lurched to his feet. It was time to begin.

Tara went outside, put on her crash-hat and lowered the lorry-ramp. The grey horse regarded her from the dark depths of the lorry. He was quivering all over and sweat dripped slowly off his belly into a growing pool on the rubber floor. She wanted to go home, but it was too late to back out now. She led him outside.

A helpful farmer seized the bridle and her leg and heaved her up into the saddle, all in one swift movement. Suddenly she was on the horse, her fingers clutching onto his sweat-lathered reins, her feet thrust into stirrups that felt far too long. The horse cavorted sideways beneath her, his tail kinked over his back, his neck arched, making noises like a dragon, barely aware that there was someone on his back.

The hounds spilled out into the car park, barking excitedly, a swirling mass of black and tan and white with waving tails. Diary Date found the whole thing too much — he reared up, pawing at the air with his front legs, and then, coming down to earth, he leapt up again on all four legs. Tara, clutching his mane, was surprised to find herself still in the saddle as they were swept along with the rest of the horses and riders.

A vaguely familiar man trotted up beside her on a beautiful chestnut horse.

"Are you OK?" he asked.

Tara, struggling to keep the capering Diary Date under control, hissed between gritted teeth: "I think so." She recognised the man who had showered her with port and felt a surge of dislike for him. He trotted on past, leaving her to glare at the straight line of his back as best she could from beneath a riding-hat that was slipping down over her eyes.

The hunt clattered along the road, sweeping Tara in its wake. Diary Date pulled against her ineffective hands, his feet sliding uncontrollably on the slippery surface. She was relieved when at last they turned off the road into a field gateway. The Huntsman led the hounds towards a large thicket to look for a fox. The rest of the riders settled down for a long wait, pulling out hip-flasks and lighting cigarettes. Paddy, the Hunt Master, took advantage of the situation to slide his hand onto the thigh of the chubby redhead who was constantly beside him. There was a sudden crash of baying as the hounds swept out of the wood m the wake of a fox. The Huntsman spurred his ugly black cob after them. Paddy abandoned his surreptitious examination of the redhead's cellulite and spurred his horse in pursuit.

Diary Date, wildly excited by the horses and ponies who were cavorting beside him began to canter sideways, jerking his head down to snatch the reins from Tara's hands. He leapt the first wall, so excited that he barely seemed to notice the solid obstacle, his flailing legs reducing the stone to rubble. Tara, hauled on his reins with all of her might, trying to exert some control over the headstrong horse. Ahead, Tara could see that the riders had stopped, queuing to jump a fence into some woodland. Diary Date had no intention of stopping. He plunged through the riders, scattering them in all directions, and flew over the fence. Then, mindless with excitement, instead of turning right down the forest track after the other horses Diary Date bolted straight on into the woodland, swerving past the trees. His head dropped lower and lower as his pace increased, hooves thundering along the track. Tara ducked low to avoid being hit by the branches, desperately clinging to his mane in terror, knowing she could not stop him. At the far side of the forest was a wire fence. Diary Date hurtled straight towards it and leapt, but failed to clear it. His headlong gallop was brought to an abrupt end and Tara was sent sprawling headlong over his ears to land some way into the field.

For a moment she lay still, glad to be alive. Then, as she got up, she was aware of Diary Date trying to struggle to his feet. The wire was wound tightly around his delicate legs. He lay stretched out on the grass, his grey sides heaving like bellows, his eyes rolling in panic as he fought against the constraining strands. She knelt beside him. If she could just reach across him then she might just be able to pull the wire off his leg.

"Stop!" A sudden yell made her jump.

She looked up to see the man who had flung port in her face riding fast towards them through the woodland. In a fluid motion he flung himself off his horse and tossed her its reins.

"He'll kick seven bells out of you once he's free from that wire," he said, pulling her roughly out of the way.

"Well, he's got to be freed!" she snapped, nerves and fear making her short-tempered.

Ignoring her, the man carefully unwound the wire from Diary Date's leg and stood back. "OK," he said, holding out his hand to pull her to her feet.

Reluctantly she took the offered hand and he pulled her upwards. However, she did not have long to contemplate her new companion. Diary Date suddenly heaved himself to his feet and stood dejectedly, his head hanging, grey flanks quivering. Blood streamed from a nasty-looking gash on his shoulder.

"He needs a vet, that's a nasty cut," said the man. "Look, you lead him to the road - I'll go and get my lorry and bring you down to John Burke's to get that wound stitched up." He swung himself into the saddle. Before she had time to reply he was gone, cantering off across the turf before casually jumping the horse over a formidable-looking stone wall and disappearing.

Slowly Tara led the trembling, dejected Diary Date towards a gate, following the direction he had taken.

At a snail's pace she led Diary Date onto the road. A short while later a horse-lorry pulled up beside her. The man took the reins off her and led the horse into the lorry. Then with a swift movement he slammed up the ramp and turned to face her. "For the second time of asking today, are you OK?" he said gently.

For the first time she looked at him properly, nodding her head. He was tall, wiry in a hard, fit sort of way - the body of a man who makes his living outside, manually and he was extremely attractive. He had blue eyes that were soft with concern, set beneath straight brows. His hair was dark with sweat and stuck to his forehead in damp curls where he had taken off his riding-hat, and his mouth, though set in a hard and determined line, was decidedly kissable. She was startled at her last thought and, to her annoyance, felt herself blushing faintly.

"Well, then, let's go," he said, with a smile that meant he had seen her blush.

Later, back in the lorry. Diary Date's wound tended, Tara felt embarrassed that the visit to the vet's had taken so much time and that she had put her rescuer to such trouble.

"I've spoilt your day - I'm sorry," she said, stealing a look at him from under her eyelashes.

"No problem," he shrugged. "I'm always available to help damsels in distress, especially beautiful ones." Then, as if the words had escaped from his mouth unawares, he clammed up and they completed their journey in silence.

She was disappointed when the lorry drew up at the now empty pub car park. A damp soft drizzle had started to fall and the light of the day had now gone. Sitting in the warm protection of the cab with him she wanted the drive to go on forever. Instead, they took down his ramp and moved a very stiff-looking and miserable Diary Date into Derry's lorry. Then he threw up the ramp behind the horse and paused, obviously about to take his leave.

Desperately wanting him to stay, Tara fought to find something to say. "I . . ." was all that she could blurt out.

He gazed at her. His face was in shadow, but she knew that his expression was gentle. Suddenly, she longed to go to him, to throw herself into his arms and kiss the taut line of his mouth. But she couldn't — he would think that she was mad. Long seconds trickled past as they stood, face to face, longing and mistrust heavy between them.

"See you again, then," he said suddenly, by way of farewell. Then he was gone.

Shivering now and scared of the wrath of Derry for bringing his horse home maimed, she drove slowly home. As she turned into the stable yard to give the horse to a furious Sarah, she noticed that every light in the house was blazing away into the night and the sound of music was thumping across towards the stable yard. Derry was having a party. He had not even given her a second thought.

CHAPTER SIX

Tara pressed her face deep into the pillow, willing sleep to return. She had been lost in the pleasurable half-world between waking and sleep, thinking about her rescuer. Any thought or regret that she might have had about Hank had now been replaced by a delicious fantasy about the stranger where he had drawn her into his arms after he had thrown up the lorry-ramp. She rolled over and lay gazing at the patterns made by the bare branches in the shadows that reflected on the bedroom ceiling, idly pondering on how she could get to meet him again. Hunting was out of the question; she really could not face that ordeal again. How extraordinary that they had parted without ever exchanging names! How could she have been so stupid? But perhaps he already knew who she was — after all, many of the people at the hunt knew her and, besides, he must have heard her give her name at the vet's. She wondered whether she dared telephone the vet's surgery to find out who he was.

Then with a jolt that made her sit abruptly upright in bed she remembered the horse. She had not seen Derry to report the dreadful accident to him. He would be furious when he saw what she had done to his horse. Derry had been so drunk the night before that it had been impossible to tell him and so she had just gone straight to her room after making herself a sandwich, while the party had raged on downstairs. Now she had to face him and tell him what had happened.

There was only one place that Derry would be at this time of the morning and Tara made straight for the stables. The yard was a hive of activity, the grooms busily sweeping it. Soon it would be so clean that not a piece of straw or manure would mar its pristine condition. Diary Date's loose-box door was open. Tara crossed the yard and peered into the box.

Derry was not there, but Sarah was bathing the horse's wounds while a girl groom held him.

"How is he?" ventured Tara, sidling into the stable.

Sarah regarded her balefully, dabbing dramatically at the wound with a piece of cotton wool. "He's bound to have a nasty scar," she said coldly, looking at Tara as if she regarded her as one of the worst mass murderers since Harold Shipman. "It's doubtful if he will be sound on the leg for a long time."

"Where's Derry?" Tara asked impatiently. She felt bad enough about the horse without Sarah carrying on as if she had deliberately maimed him.

"He's on the gallops," Sarah said curtly, flinging the cotton wool into a bucket.

Derry's Jeep was parked high on the hillside above Westwood Park where it had the best view of the horses as they were ridden on the all-weather gallop. Tara toiled up the hill towards it. She stood to watch the horses being exercised — three bay horses wearing striped rugs that billowed beneath their saddles as they powered up the hillside, each stride eating up the ground as they galloped. Each was a mass of muscle and sinew, carefully honed to the peak of physical performance. Astride the horses, the lads perched high above their backs in the ridiculously small saddles, balancing over the horses' shoulders as they pounded around the track.

Derry was in the front seat of the Jeep, large field glasses glued to his eyes.

"Afternoon, Tara," he said sarcastically as she climbed into the back seat of the Jeep.

"Derry, I'm so sorry about Diary Date . . ." She touched his shoulder to get his attention, but Derry was miles away, his attention focused on the two horses galloping towards them. All that she received in reply was a distant "Hmm?" Then the horses shot past the Jeep and carried on down the gallops.

"Brilliant!" Derry exclaimed. He laid down the field glasses. "He'll win a race soon."

He leant forward to press his face towards the car windscreen in order to peer at the long blue horse-lorry that was weaving its way slowly down the lanes below them.

"But this horse is going to be a champion." He inclined his head at the approaching lorry.

Then he started the engine and shoved the gear-stick forwards. The Jeep bounced over the rough turf at an alarming speed, Tara clinging to the back of Derry's seat as she was bumped and bounced all over the place. They shot out of the gate just behind the horse-lorry, which swayed and jolted up the lane in front of them.

As the lorry turned into the driveway, Derry pulled onto the grass and with a spurt of speed overtook it. He sped into the yard and parked the Jeep. His excitement was palpable. He shifted from one foot to another like a small, excited boy.

The driver hobbled to the rear of the lorry clutching his back. "One of yer lads will have to take him," he whined pitifully. "My back's too bad these days to be leading horses about, especially ones like him!" He gestured at the lorry with a twisted thumb.

The ramp crashed to the gravel yard with a thud and they all peered into the gloom. A tall grey horse glared back at them from the near-darkness. He lifted his head suddenly and whinnied, a loud, shrill challenge. One of the lads, sent by Sarah, dashed up the ramp and pulled the partition to one side. The horse lifted a hind leg menacingly as the lad shot nimbly past him to tug the lead-rope free at his head. The horse snatched his head forward, twisting it like a snake, to seize a mouthful of the lad's sweatshirt.

"Well, he certainly has spirit," commented Tara, stepping abruptly behind Derry as the lad began to lead the horse down the ramp.

"I bought this horse cheap," Derry said smugly. "His owner bred some of the greatest horses in racing, then went bust after which his wife fucked off with the stud groom."

He stepped back abruptly as the horse stood on his back legs, raking the air with his front legs in temper. "He's bred to be a champion — I'm convinced he'll win me some good races if he performs as well as his pedigree suggests."

Derry ordered the nervous lad to saddle the horse and take him into the paddock. The lad walked off across the yard towing the tall grey horse unwillingly behind him.

"Come and see what this horse can do," Derry said, steering Tara across the expanse of lawn to the post-and-rail fence of the schooling paddock, where the horses were jumped for the first time and ridden when they had just been broken in. They leant on the fence waiting for the horse to come back. "Now you are going to see something," Derry told her. Around the edge of the paddock the faint breeze gently stirred the bare branches of the beech trees.

A short time later the lad appeared leading the horse, now saddled and bridled. Sarah accompanied him, her face dark with concern. The horse's long, black tipped ears were laid back against the long black mane that swept almost down to his shoulders. He rolled a disdainful eye at the assembled gathering.

"I don't think Tommy knows enough to manage this horse," said Sarah, catching Derry's eye. "He's only just started on the yard."

"Rubbish!" snapped Derry. "If he can't ride then I'm not prepared to pay him. You shouldn't employ fools that can't ride – it's wasting my time and money!" His eyes were flashing in temper.

Sarah coloured in embarrassment and looked away. Before she had the chance to say another word Derry had seized the horse's bridle and Tommy's leg and heaved the lad skywards into the saddle where he landed with a thump that made the horse skit sideways.

Derry flung open the paddock gate. "Walk him around in here," he said gesturing with a nod of his head to the white-faced Tommy who was clutching the reins as if his life depended upon it. The grey horse marched majestically into the paddock.

"Look at his long stride," Derry said proudly as the horse walked around the outside of the paddock. "A horse like that would have the power to win at Cheltenham. Maybe even the Gold Cup," he added wistfully.

"He's magnificent, Derry" Tara whispered in a voice filled with awe, leaning her arms on the wooden fence that surrounded the paddock. Even plump without the muscle tone of the race fit horses Tara saw in Derry's stables the grey horse seemed to exude power and arrogance, from the high set of his head to his powerful hind quarters.

"Trot him on," commanded Derry.

Tommy booted the horse into a trot. His nervous fingers clutched the reins, making the horse feel restrained and throw his head up in the air to free himself. Tommy, more nervous, gripped tighter. The horse began to throw his head up and down, snatching on the reins, which began to slide through Tommy's fingers while the horse began to trot faster and then to canter.

Tara clutched the fence, her fingers tightening around the knotted surface of the wood. She could feel Tommy's fear as the horse went faster and faster. The boy leant back in the saddle in an effort to stop him, but the horse still went faster. Round and round the small paddock he went galloping, banking sharply at the corners, his long legs slipping and sliding to gain grip on the slippery grass surface as he shot around each bend.

"Stop him, you fool!" hissed Derry.

Finally Tommy remembered what Sarah had taught him and stopped pulling on the reins. Without anyone to fight against, the horse calmed down and slowed his pace until finally he began to walk. Sweat darkened his neck and his sides heaved with his exertions.

"That's enough. Bring him here!" bellowed Derry. As he spoke, his dog shot out of the woodland at the far side of the paddock just beside the horse which shied violently, leaping quickly away. Tommy, relaxed for the first time since he had got on the horse, slid sideways. The horse, feeling him unbalanced in the saddle, began to buck, leaping skywards and unseating Tommy who landed on the grass with a thud that was audible at the other side of the paddock.

At once the grey horse set off in a flat-out gallop. Too shocked to do anything other than watch, they all gasped in unison as the horse approached the fence, skidded as if he was going to stop, then jumped it and set off at a gallop across the fields. Derry, rigid with temper, stalked off to the house. Sarah, relieved to be away from Derry and the outburst of temper that could have accompanied the incident, set off across the fields in pursuit of the horse with a limping Tommy beside her.

Tara made her way back into the house. She realised that it was past lunch-time and that she had not yet eaten.

She took some coffee, went back to the kitchen to make herself a sandwich and took it to sit in the sunlit conservatory. This was her favourite room of the house. The tall windows looked out over acres of garden. There was a long, squashy comfortable wicker sofa in the conservatory and she stretched out on this, reaching occasionally for the sandwich, which she had placed on the green marble-topped table beside her. She closed her eyes and munched slowly, letting the warmth of the sun and the sunlight flicker on her eyes through the branches of the vines and the tall wisteria plants.

She let her mind wander back to "the man". She drifted over a fantasy of him riding up the drive to look for her. Finally she decided that she would find out where he lived from the Hunt Secretary and go around, looking her best, on the pretext of thanking him for helping her. He would be bowled over by her charms, and the strong sense of attraction that she had felt when she was beside him would have a chance to take its own course.

She was just imagining him taking her in his strong arms, enfolding her in a passionate embrace, and his lips reaching out to touch hers while his hands entwined in her hair when Derry burst into the room and threw himself down on one of the chairs.

"I'm going to kill that horse, if I ever see it again," he raged.

"Oh, Derry," Tara sighed, pulling herself upright with difficulty. Once the horse was back and under control, his anger at the animal would vanish as quickly as a summer mist.

Derry leant back, letting the sunlight play on his face. He unfolded the newspaper and began to read the racing pages. Suddenly he slammed the newspaper down with force on the chair. "New Golden Boy Wins Big Race!" he spat in temper. "I'll fucking show him who can win races!" With that, he jumped up and stamped out of the room.

Tara reached across and took the newspaper from where he had thrown it down, curious as to what had made him so angry. Her heart skipped a beat. There, beneath the headline, was a grainy but definite likeness of the man who had rescued her the previous day. Suddenly, she realised. It was the man Derry had argued with at the races. How could she not have remembered that! Hungrily she read about the big win at Leopardstown and how his small yard was now considered to be the best in the country. Then she read all about him: the yard that was only a few miles from Westwood Park, his horses, his training methods. And now she knew his name — Morgan Flynn.

CHAPTER SEVEN

Wriggling her hand into the pocket of her jeans Tara pulled out a scrap of newspaper, carefully folded into quarters. She spread out the newspaper cutting. Morgan Flynn, captured by the camera at his most gorgeous. He was smiling with delight at the photographer, clutching the cup that his horse had just won. His blue eyes danced with joy beneath a wild cap of dark curly hair and he was grinning broadly, mouth open wide, one front tooth chipped. What had happened between them? Had she imagined the way that he had looked at her? She had wanted him like no one ever before. That night, in the lorry cab, she had felt so close to him — she had longed to touch him, to kiss him, to go home with him. It would have all seemed so right, somehow, but she, or was it they, had let the moment go. Now the opportunity was gone. Now she knew who he was. Morgan Flynn, her brother's enemy. Did he know who she was? Was that why he had backed off?

If only, she thought, she could have the moment back again. If only there was another chance she would do things differently. She would take a chance. She would make the first move if that was what it took. She would have to find him again, see him at the races, go to his stables. She had to find out whether she had imagined it all. What if he was married? She frowned — the thought had never occurred to her. He couldn't be. He would never have looked at her like that if he loved someone else. Besides, the newspaper article had never mentioned a wife, never mentioned anyone. She folded up the cutting and shoved it back into the depths of her pocket.

"Tara! Where the hell are you?" shouted Derry.

Tara scrambled guiltily off the bed at the sound of Derry's footsteps thundering up the stairs. She was off the bed and out of the room like a shot, shutting the door behind her just as Derry reached the top of the stairs.

"There you are!" he exclaimed. "'What on earth were you doing in there?" And then, without bothering to wait for her reply, he continued, "some farmer from seven miles away has just rung to say that he has found my bloody horse in with his young ponies."

"That's great news," she smiled at him, still half in the dream world that she had just been inhabiting with Morgan Flynn.

"Well, come on then," he snapped impatiently. "We've got to go and catch the fucking creature!"

'We' turned out to be Tara, Derry and Sarah who was already waiting in the Jeep which was parked outside with the engine running.

Tara slid into the passenger seat beside Derry. She smiled at Sarah. "Hi."

Sarah said "Hi," in reply without, Tara noticed, taking her eyes off the back of Derry's head. Good grief, she did have it bad.

"Since this horse has been on the run for over a week now I don't see the need for this bloody urgency," complained Tara.

"That horse has made a big enough fool out of me already," snapped Derry, swinging the Jeep out onto the main road, narrowly missing one of the tall pillars and causing the driver of an approaching lorry to stand on his brakes to avoid hitting them.

"I want him back here under control. Now!" He shoved his foot down on the accelerator, as if it was his sports car, making the engine scream in protest.

Tara clung to the edge of the seat, thrown about with the vicious movement of the vehicle.

"Sounds like we are in for some fun," she said, turning to look at Sarah.

"Yes," Sarah smiled, her eyes fluttering briefly away from the back of Derry's head and meeting Tara's. Her eyes were grey, kind and gentle, with a wary look in them.

"Why does Derry want us all to go and catch the horse?" Tara asked, raising her voice over the roar of the engine.

Sarah smiled dreamily at the mention of Derry, making Tara feel sorry for her. She was going to be hurt and badly if she stayed worshipping him like that.

Sarah shrugged and made a little gesture of confusion with her hands. "We stand more chance of rounding up the horse with a few of us. Derry won't take a chance on the horse escaping again. He thinks that it has made a fool out of him once already."

Tara shook her head wryly. She had better things to do than rounding up wild horses.

A few minutes later they slid to a halt in a muddy farmyard. Tara heaved a sigh of relief that they had made it so far. Derry flung open the door and heaved himself out.

"What a dump!" he commented to no one in particular, rummaging in the depths of his cord trouser-pockets for a packet of cigarettes. "Sarah," he commanded, pulling out a cigarette, "go and find someone."

Obedient as a soppy spaniel, Sarah scrambled out of the jeep and went towards the house. Tara gazed out at the ramshackle buildings. Straw and manure were piled at every doorway with scraggy chickens scratching feverishly at the steaming heaps. Rusted farm machinery cluttered the muddy square of concrete between the sagging buildings. The slate roof of one shed had collapsed completely leaving a gaping hole open to the elements, the bare beams exposed like the ribs of a skeleton.

"That horse will be glad to get out of here," mused Tara.

Derry snorted in reply, glancing around the yard in disdain. "Aaah," he hissed softly, his voice loaded with sarcastic amusement, "here come the landed gentry." He drummed his fingers on the roof of the jeep, every pore oozing with impatience.

Tara peered out at the man that was shambling, beside Sarah, towards the car. He was tiny and his dark, beady eyes gave him the look of a small, inquisitive bird. He walked with a pronounced limp, raising one hip high in order to swing his leg forward, which pushed the whole upper part of his body to the side. As he walked the loose trousers that he wore fluttered around his legs above the bunched folds where he had shoved them into filthy Wellington boots.

"Howye," he nodded, rocking to a halt at the jeep and peering at them all from beneath a dark mane of curls.

"This is Paddy Corcoran," Sarah introduced the man.

Tara looked at him more closely. At first glance he had looked like a very old man, he was so bent and covered with grime, but closer to he was hardly over thirty.

"Oss is this way," he grinned, looking at them all with great amusement and seeming to find Derry's obvious scorn of him a big joke. He then shoved roughly past Sarah and scrambled into the front seat of the Jeep with surprising speed and nimbleness. Derry flung himself back into the driver's seat and gunned the engine into life.

"There!" gestured Paddy pointing with a grimy finger down the rutted farm drive. Derry set off again at breakneck pace. In the warmth of the Jeep, the strong odour of farm animals, unwashed bodies and clothes began to be emitted from Paddy. Tara caught Sarah's eye and they exchanged grimaces of distaste.

Paddy directed them to a field a few miles away from the farm. Derry drove the Jeep onto the grass verge and turned off the engine.

For a moment there was silence, and then Derry turned to Paddy and snapped, "well, where is he then?"

Paddy grinned inanely and shoved open the door. Tara took a gulp of clean air with relief. Still grinning with unconcealed amusement, Paddy heaved open a rickety gate and led the way over a wooden bridge made of old railway sleepers that spanned the wide ditch separating the field from the hedge that bordered it. Terrified of the obviously rotten timbers of the bridge, Tara picked her way in the wake of a sullen Derry.

"There!" gestured Paddy, waving his arm at a dark blur on the horizon. For a moment they were all silent, contemplating the field in front of them. The pasture Paddy's animals grazed was a strip of land that spanned into the distance without a fence in sight. The young ponies that the rogue grey horse had joined were so far away they were barely visible.

"Fuck!" muttered Derry in annoyance, looking at the vast distance they had to walk before they even got near to the animals.

Tara was aware of Sarah shaking her head in disbelief.

"How the hell are we supposed to catch the bloody creature in here?" moaned Derry.

"Best to drive them into the pen," Paddy told them, nodding towards a broken-down clutter of poles in one corner of the field. Then, obviously not going to be any more help, he shambled off towards the pen.

Sarah shrugged. "Come on then."

They set off in her wake, Derry stalking sullenly along. Sighing, Tara trudged behind. What a way to spend an afternoon! They were barely close enough for the animals to be seen properly when one of the ponies suddenly flung up its head and gave a loud snort of terror. In one mass movement the ponies wheeled away, already galloping in an instant, mud flying up from their heels. The grey horse galloped in the middle of them, tall and incongruous amongst the shaggy creatures.

"You bastard!" hissed Derry, glaring at the rapidly retreating figures. There was no choice but to trudge onwards to the end of the field.

The ponies stopped at the far end of the pasture, standing in one bunch, their ears sharply pricked, eyes wide with terror at the approach of the humans.

"Well handled obviously," commented Sarah wryly, looking at the animals.

"Hardly," Derry said. "From the look of this lot I doubt that they've even seen a human being for a long time." He glared at the tall grey horse who stared back from within the safety of his shaggy companions. "You wait until I get my hands on you!" Then, businesslike, he said, "our best bet is to drive the lot of them towards the pen. It's our only chance of catching him."

"I'll drive them back," Sarah told him. Tara stood to one side as Sarah ran at the ponies, yelling like a banshee, until terrified they scattered and then galloped towards the opposite corner of the field, towards Paddy and the pen.

After a walk that seemed to take forever over the rutted, boggy field they finally reached the far end. The ponies milled around, close to the pen, their eyes watchful, ears flickering in fear. The runaway grey grazed amongst them, amusement oozing from the arrogant lines of his body.

"Now, if we spread out —" commanded Derry. "Don't let them get away — we must guide them into the pen — otherwise they'll just be galloping up and down here all day, taking the piss out of us." They spread out, making a line across the field, pushing the ponies slowly towards the pen.

Tara moved her feet over the boggy patches and the clumps of rushes. Please don't let the horses run towards me, she prayed. She would never be able to stop them. At either side of her Derry and Sarah stalked the horses, like gamekeepers stalking wild animals in the jungle, watching their every move. Slowly the animals moved towards the pen and capture.

But suddenly, as if he knew their plan, the grey horse threw up his head and let out a loud whinny, a challenge that rang out loud over the pasture.

The ponies began to mill around, moving away from the pen again, their ears pricked.

Then, as if he could sense her fear, as if he knew that she was the weakest link in the human wall, the grey horse began to gallop straight at Tara.

"Shout at him!" she heard Derry yell. She was aware of Derry running towards her, but the horse was faster. He came straight at her, his eyes locking onto hers as he bore down at her. She threw up her arms and yelled, but the noise that came out sounded like a strangled squeak. The horse was so big, so powerful. He was going to gallop straight over her. At the last moment she flung herself out of the way, falling to the ground. He passed by so close that she could feel the heat from his body, smell the sweat and feel the earth shake as his hooves pounded close to her head. If she had not jumped out of the way he would have killed her.

Shaken, she scrambled to her knees. The ponies were already a blur on the distant horizon. She got up, shaking. Derry was stalking away, fury evident in every movement. Paddy was doubled up with laughter, leaning on the side of the pen.

"I thought he was going to run straight through you," said Sarah, laying a gentle hand on Tara's back.

They walked slowly back to the Jeep. Derry was already in the driver's seat, revving the engine. "Why the hell didn't you stop the horse?" he snarled, his lips curling with temper. "A bloody child could have stopped him!"

CHAPTER EIGHT

Sarah peered into the darkness through the sheets of rain that scythed across the stable yard. None of the forty horses' heads poked out to stare at the lorry headlights that were slowly crawling up the drive towards them. She was awaiting the arrival of the grey horse who had finally been caught. Paddy Corcoran had managed to herd all of the ponies into a pen with his farm workers and the horse had admitted defeat and allowed them to catch him. In the floodlights that lit up the yard the rain could be seen, heavy sheets that moved across it forming enormous puddles and falling in sheets down the guttering. She stepped back inside the relative warmth of the tack room, huddling close to the gas fire that she had lit more for comfort than warmth, until the lorry drew up into the yard.

Paul, the driver slid down out of his cab, pulling a thin waterproof coat on as he landed, splashing in the puddles that were threatening to become a lake. "Derry's bloody new horse home safe and sound!" he yelled at Sarah, over the noise of the wind and rain.

As she led the horse down the ramp, his ears flattened against the rain, he tried to turn sideways, wanting instinctively to turn his bottom to the rain to get protection from the cruel sheets of water that stung his eyes and battered his sensitive ears. Sarah hurried ahead of him, trying to avoid being trodden on by the large dancing hooves.

She heaved back the stable door, struggling against the rain and wind that threatened to pull it off its hinges. Finally she managed and the horse shot inside, casting her disparaging looks. He sank thankfully to his knees and rolled once in the deep bed of straw once she unclipped his lead-rope, and then began to tuck into the net of hay that hung in one corner.

His rounded grey quarters quivered with the cold, so Sarah darted across the yard, head bent against the wind and rain and fetched him another rug from the tack room. Then she spent a few minutes gently massaging his ice-cold ears. Once his ears were warm the horse was more comfortable and began to relax. Sarah fetched him his feed, which he tucked into with a huge sigh of relief. She stood in the corner of the stable watching him eat. She was in no rush to get home. She was happier out here, even though it was cold and wet.

"Derry will be furious with you, boy," she told the horse, rubbing the hard muscle of his neck. Derry's wonder horse had been a complete disaster and Derry did not take kindly to being made a fool of.

Finally tiredness swept over her. She gave him a final pat and straightening a corner of his rug she left the stable, bolting it securely. She dashed through the yard to her cottage, shivering with the cold, which seemed to have penetrated her body right through to the bones. A hot bath, she decided, was the only way to get warm before bedtime.

Soon she was relaxing in the deep fragrant water. Even now, a year after leaving home it was still a pleasure to have the luxury of plenty of hot water after the tiny tepid amount that the boiler at home could ever manage to pump out.

On the downside, even the deep hot water could not disguise her chunky body. It lapped against the cellulite on her thighs and made the mound of the pale flesh of her stomach seem like an island in the foam and, as for her breasts, they lolled like life-jackets against the sides of her arms. None of the diets she tried ever seemed to shift her excess weight. Even though she was working outside all day and lifting bales of hay and straw and feed and handling huge horses, she still could not lose weight. She knew though at the back of her mind that the reason she found it impossible was that she simply ate too much. Once the day's work was over she came back to the cottage and lazed on the settee and ate, more out of boredom and loneliness than hunger.

She soaped the mountains of her pale flesh and focused on the pinprick of worry that had been gnawing at her for the afternoon, ever since the disastrous horse had been found. Derry would be furious. Derry was intolerant of most things, but being made a fool of was the thing that he disliked the most. She could recall various horrendous incidents when someone had tried to make a fool of Derry: grooms who thought he would not see when they could not be bothered to clean out the horses or groom them properly, feed merchants who tried to leave fewer bags than ordered — nothing escaped his eagle eyes and nothing and no one ever made a fool of him and escaped lightly. His was a controlled rage, which was far more frightening than the 'throw your fists about and yell a lot' sort of temper that she had witnessed with ever-growing regularity from her father before she had left home.

This situation was a bad one. This was a horse that Derry had said was a champion in the making. He had repaid Derry's confidence and faith in him in the worst possible way. She was still thinking about it when she went to bed, finally warmed through, and she lay awake, worrying.

She woke with a start some time later. Footsteps were crunching on the gravel path outside the cottage. Footsteps that she recognised instantly. She sat up in bed, hazily pushing the dark bird's-nest of hair from her face. She reached over and snapped on the bedside lamp, flooding the room with pale light. Grimacing, she took in the piles of dirty clothes that she had not yet put into the washer and the untidy squalor of make-up and toiletries that littered her dressing-table. That paled in comparison when she caught sight of her own face with its shell-shocked expression in the mirror, miraculously, since going to bed, another huge spot had appeared on her chin, which seemed to glow maliciously at her in the half-light. She slid her legs out of the bed, the satin pyjama bottoms with their gaudy pink rose-pattern sliding silently across the rumpled cotton sheets.

She pushed her feet into her battered slippers and stood up, feeling a sense of triumph wash over her. Finally, after weeks of deliberating, she had come to the harsh truth about the relationship she had with Derry. And the fact was, there was no relationship except that of being a convenient fuck when Derry felt horny. But no more. She was sick of being used. Talk about kicking a man when he's down, she thought, gazing at herself in the mirror. Tonight, she was going to refuse him. Finally she knew she had the strength to tell him that he was no longer welcome in her bed.

She felt that she had suffered enough at Derry's hands. Since she had come to work at Westwood Park and he had first come to her bed, she had been made miserable by him. He would come to her when he felt like it. He would make her feel loved, he would talk to her as if she was important, as if he was interested, and then he would begin slowly to kiss her and caress her — and time after time she would melt. He kissed like no man she had ever kissed - slowly, luxuriously, his tongue exploring her mouth, her teeth, twining with her own tongue in a way she had never experienced before. She could be kissed like that forever and never want to stop. And his hands on her body were like no others that she had ever felt; experienced and caring, they covered her body, worshipping it, made her revel in his touch, and when he finally was inside her that too was like never before. He was the one man that she had ever had sex with who had made it feel like he was making love. He wanted to please her, he was skilful, waiting until she was satisfied before he finally gave in to his own pleasure — and he could do it over and over again.

But no more; she had suffered enough from him. He would come, love her for the evening and then he would be gone, leaving her wanting him, longing for him from afar. And unless he came to her she could not go to him. Her one tentative advance in public had met with very serious disapproval from him and she had never dared to try again. She never knew whether he cared about her or whether she was just a convenience. Every time he went away from her and then ignored her for days, weeks sometimes, she broke inside. Until he came again and then for a few days she was ecstatically happy. Now she had cured herself. She could not live with the suffering any longer; she would refuse to have any relationship with him other than that of a dedicated employee. It was not as if Derry did not have other women. He had strings of them, all flaunted under her nose, all leggy as colts, blonde hair down their backs and the sort of expressions and haughty demeanour that made her feel as if she was something that they had scraped off their well-heeled shoes.

So that was it. She would never again submit to his very dubious charms. She would get over him and get on with her life. She carried this thought downstairs with her.

Derry was silhouetted in the light outside the glass of the door, lounging against the doorframe. He was so sure - she could see it in his posture - that she would let him in and fall thankfully into his arms although he had not been near her for a fortnight.

She threw open the door. She glared at him. He stood up straight, one arm on either side of the doorframe - he was so tall that he seemed to fill it. The light outside the door meant that his face was in shadow as he stood in the tiny honeysuckle-covered porch, but she knew that he was smiling. She felt her heart lurch and then felt her legs carry her as if of their own volition straight towards him.

He came into the tiny lounge. He always made the room seem somehow smaller than it was, he was so tall, his long legs and arms sprawling over her small settee.

"Be a darling, will you, and make me a cup of coffee," he said, smiling gently at her.

She felt her reserve melt. Soon he would take her upstairs and she would have his flesh pressed against hers — she would have that gorgeous mouth to kiss. She pattered obediently off to the kitchen, switched on the kettle and busied herself with the coffee mugs and milk.

"God, I've had an awful day," he moaned from the lounge.

The kettle boiled and she took the full mug back to him.

"That bloody horse!" he complained bitterly, taking the mug from her hands and cupping his own around it as if to suck up the warmth from the pottery. "He's made a bloody fool out of me!"

"He will probably settle down," she said quietly, wrapping a loose thread around one of the buttons on her pyjama top.

Derry, however, did not seem to hear her, he was so involved in feeling sorry for himself. "He made a bloody fool of me," he repeated, running a distracted hand through a strand of hair that had fallen across his forehead.

Sarah wondered frantically what to say to him. One misplaced word and he would fly off the handle completely. Fortunately he did not seem to need or expect a reply so she kept silent. He drained the last of the coffee and held out the mug. She got up to take it from him and, as she moved forwards, he reached out and grabbed hold of her wrist. He pulled her down onto the sofa beside him. She lay sprawled over him, feeling desperately conscious of her plump body against his, her cheap satin fabric against the expensive cut of his tailored tweed jacket and moleskin trousers.

"Take me upstairs," he whispered into her ear.

She woke, sometime later, in his arms. She studied his handsome profile, his face relaxed now, in sleep, with none of the tension that was usually present. She loved these moments — it seemed a shame to waste them by being asleep. Now he belonged totally to her — she could touch the planes of his face, run her fingers through his thick straight hair, touch the flesh that lay beneath the bedclothes. She propped herself on one elbow and watched him. She ignored the nagging feeling at the back of her mind that told her she was being a fool.

He shifted in the bed, half waking, and reached out to pull her face towards him and cover her mouth with his. She slid thankfully into his grip, feeling the urgent need for him growing somewhere deep inside her.

The alarm-clock went off while it was still dark and raining. Derry sat up abruptly, instantly awake. Rain lashed against the windowpane in heavy squally sheets. He looked at her as if he was not sure how he had arrived in her bed and then smiled that beautiful and disarming smile. "I need coffee, darling." he said, reaching out to the side of the bed to grab his trousers.

By the time she returned with the coffee he was fully dressed. She felt very self-conscious in her pyjamas. He sat on the edge of the bed, watching as she dressed.

As she pulled a shapeless fleece top over her head he said, "I've decided I'm wasting my time with that horse."

Sarah turned towards him, the hairbrush halfway to her hair.

"So he can go to the next sales."

"Great, good idea," she replied, her mind already racing ahead. She would put the horse on a different feed that would fatten him up and calm him down. She could have him looking a picture in no time at all.

"Turn him out," Derry said, his voice breaking into her train of thought.

She stared at him, thinking she had misheard.

"Turn him out," he repeated.

"What!" she exclaimed. No one in their right mind would turn a horse out in this weather. The horse was used to being in a stable and had no thick winter coat to keep him warm.

"Today," he continued. "Now, in fact. First thing." He drained the last of his coffee and left without another word.

She arrived in the yard a short time later to see one of the lads leading the rugless horse across the yard and into one of the bare, shelterless paddocks.

"You bastard, Derry," she hissed under her breath as the horse was let loose into the field.

CHAPTER NINE

Tara felt a shiver of excitement run through her as she reached the racecourse. Morgan Flynn had a horse running. She was going to get a chance to see him again. All night her mind had replayed the most enticing fantasy of them getting together. She got out of the car and rushed across the car park, keen to get into the racecourse, her eyes darting from side to side, scanning the faces, hunting for the one person that she longed to see — Morgan.

She bought a race card from the kiosk and hurried towards the parade-ring. She shoved her way through the crowds that circled it gazing at the horses, trying to select a winner. The horses for the next race were being led around, marching disdainfully around the strip of tarmac on long, slender legs. In the centre was a large oval of immaculately manicured grass, where the owners and trainers congregated, perusing their horses and eyeing up the competition. At last she saw Derry. He was staring fixedly at another man who was approaching him and, from his stance and the hard set of his shoulders, she could see it wouldn't be a friendly encounter. Tara felt her heart give an enormous lurch in her chest as if it was trying to burst out through her jumper. The other man was Morgan Flynn. She got closer. Morgan's eyes were narrow with dislike as he squared up to Derry. He was gorgeous.

"Well, playing with the big boys today, are we?" Derry drawled, meeting Morgan's gaze with grey eyes that danced with amusement.

"It's a free country!" spat Morgan in reply, his fingers clenching as if they were itching to knock the supercilious grin off Derry's handsome face.

Tara saw Morgan give a start of recognition as she paused on the fringes of their argument.

"Hardly free," grinned Derry, baiting Morgan, "but then you have a good owner to pay your way into this league, don't you?"

The other trainers had stopped their conversations and were listening unashamedly to the exchange between the two men.

Suddenly Derry leant forward so that his face was inches from Morgan's. "I hear that you have to look after her in order to keep her horses," he said in a very loud stage whisper. Adding sardonically, "service with a smile, I hope!"

A collective titter of laughter swept around the paddock.

Prickling with annoyance, Tara slipped away from Derry and stood by the guard-rail, watching as the horses walked out onto the racecourse. Consulting the race card, she spotted Derry's horse, the evil-tempered Connemara King. Then Morgan's horse, Stone Cold, owned by someone called Lynn Moore, walked proudly onto the racecourse. His ears were pricked sharply as he jogged along beside his girl groom, dancing as some of the more unruly horses barged past, bucking and cavorting on their way to the start. One of the jockeys was bucked off on the start-line and the horse shot off up the course, its tail kinked over its back in delight. It was quickly cornered by the stewards and brought back to where the bruised jockey was hoisted straight back up into the saddle again.

The horses circled in the distance. Then Tara saw the starter's flag go up and then flutter down. The race was off. As she studied it, she became aware that she was being watched and turned suddenly. Leaning on the guard-rail a short way along from her was Morgan Flynn, staring unashamedly at her. She caught his eye and smiled. He met her eyes coolly, his gaze flickering over her face. She opened her mouth to say something to him, but he then turned abruptly to look at the race and the chance was gone.

The blur of brown topped with a bright flash of colour was coming closer, sweeping around the turn which would bring the horses to the finish line after the next circuit of the course. Tara jumped back as horses galloped beside the stands, the beat of their hooves loud on the hard ground, even above the roar of encouragement from the crowd. Stone Cold was galloping alongside Derry's horse Connemara King, far ahead of the others. The dark bay of Derry's horse gleamed maliciously in the pale sunlight. His jockey belted the horse hard down his shoulder, forcing him to gallop faster. Away from the stands they went. Tara watched them, her heart in her mouth. She turned to look at Morgan again. His face was set, concentrating hard on the horses, oblivious to everything else going on around him. She took in his handsome profile and ached to touch him, to be close to him.

The horses swept around the course, disappearing from view as they went into the countryside. When they came back into view there were only three fences to be jumped and still Connemara King and Stone Cold were neck and neck. They took the next jump together and landed in one movement. Tara saw Morgan clutch at his form guide, his long fingers clenched around the curled paper, willing the horse onwards. At the second fence from home Stone Cold put in a magnificent jump and landed slightly ahead of Connemara King. He was going to win. The crowd went crazy, jumping up and down and yelling roars of encouragement.

Then, at the final fence, there was a shower of brushwood as one of the horses hit it.

There was a collective gasp of horror as the horse went down amidst a flurry of hooves. The runners galloped on and the crowd began to scream Connemara King's name. Tara saw the dark bay horse sweep over the line, his jockey standing in the short stirrups waving his whip into the air in victory, a broad grin slicing across his mud-splattered face.

Tara felt herself let out a whoop of joy. Derry would be thrilled. Then in one awful moment she realised that Stone Cold had not come over the line. She turned, her heart in her mouth, to look at Morgan. He stood silently, his back to her, gazing down the course, grief etched into the slumped line of his shoulders, his eyes trained on the final fence. Stone Cold lay at the foot of the fence, his legs outstretched, the rounded hump of his belly still against the dark brushwood. Tara clutched at the rail, feeling her knees sag with shock. The horse was obviously dead.

As the crowds surged forward to welcome home Connemara King as the winner, Tara saw Derry hurry past the crowds onto the track. Beaming with delight, he clapped the horse on the neck and grabbed the triumphant jockey's outstretched hand. Tara turned away, unable to stomach such delight in the face of Morgan's grief. He was running up the course to where Stone Cold lay outstretched on the churned turf. Tara ducked under the guard-rail and walked slowly up the rutted turf towards the final fence.

A horseshoe lost in the race glittered in the late evening sunlight. A small crowd had assembled around the body of Stone Cold. Morgan stood there, looking down, his face a mask of sorrow. The jockey was pulling the saddle from the prone horse. He was white-faced and could barely speak, his gaudy silks horribly out of place in the desolation. "He just never took off — he went straight through the fence," he stammered.

Morgan was looking down at the body of the horse. His neck was broken. He must have died instantly. Behind them Tara heard the tractor approaching with the trailer that would cart off the horse's body. She watched Morgan unbuckle the bridle. The horse's teeth were clenched shut and Morgan had to lever the bit from his mouth. The jockey, not knowing what to say, walked away, a sorrowful hunched figure carrying the still-warm saddle. The tractor drew to a halt. The assembled crowd drew back as the stewards clipped a chain around Stone Cold's hind legs and revved up the engine to drag him into the trailer. Morgan, obviously unable to watch, walked away.

Tara watched him trailing miserably up the racecourse. On impulse she dashed after him.

"Morgan . . ." she said quietly, slowing to a walk beside him.

Morgan looked up scowling, as if the last thing that he wanted to do now was to have to talk to anyone.

"I'm so sorry," she said, laying a comforting hand on his arm. "He was going to win, wasn't he?"

He spun around to look at her, his face grey, all life swept brutally away from it.

"Shouldn't you be with your boyfriend?" he snarled bitterly, shaking off her hand.

"Boyfriend?" she said quizzically, looking at him with concerned eyes.

"The winning trainer, Derry Blake," he said sarcastically, his eyes filled with hate and grief.

"He's not my boyfriend!" she exclaimed. "He's my brother."

"Well, go to him," he said wearily. "You're not wanted here."

He shrugged off her arm and marched away through the racecourse buildings towards the stables. As he approached, a joyous crowd surged towards him. The winning horse, Connemara King, led by Derry, was being brought back to the stables. Derry saw Morgan and stopped, pulling hard on the lead-rein of the horse. For a long moment the two men glared at each other, bitter hatred exuding from every pore. Then, slowly, Morgan stretched out his hand.

"Congratulations," he murmured.

Derry's eyes glittered maliciously behind the dark sunglasses that he wore. He looked slowly down at the outstretched hand and very pointedly ignored it. "Connemara King would have won anyway," he said loudly.

Tara saw Morgan visibly reel at her brother's words.

"Stone Cold was finished," Derry continued maliciously. "And wasn't he well named? He'll be very stone cold in about an hour!" Laughing at his own humour, he pushed past Morgan with Tara trailing miserably behind. She wanted to comfort Morgan, to ease his pain and grief, but what was the point? He hated her as much as he hated Derry.

She was furious at Derry. There was no need for him to have been so awful. She was in no mood for celebrations when she knew that Morgan was so upset. She just wanted to be with him.

She hesitated, then slipped quietly away and made her way to Stone Cold's stable where she knew Morgan would be gathering up his things. He glanced up and saw her approaching. He looked at her coldly and then disappeared into the recesses of the stable.

Tara stood in the doorway. He was kneeling, bundling the bridle and rugs into his trainer's bag. "What do you want?" he snapped, raw emotion making his voice harsh.

"I wanted to say sorry for what Derry said to you," she said, wringing her hands nervously together.

He got slowly to his feet. "Sorry! Your sort doesn't know the meaning of the word!" He pushed roughly past her and stalked away towards the lorry park. Tara jogged after him. "Go away," he snarled.

"I'm not letting you go home like this on your own," she snarled back, desperately wanting to put her arms around him.

As they reached his lorry she was aware that tears were rolling down his face.

"Give me the keys," she demanded. "I'm taking you home." Obedient as a child, he handed her the keys and scrambled into the cab. She darted around to the driver's side and climbed into the cab, amazed at how forceful she was being. She pushed the keys into the ignition and started the engine. "Where exactly do you live?" she asked with a small laugh at the irony of the situation. Morgan told her. "Jeez," she whistled. "We're nearly neighbours!"

Morgan, sitting morosely as she drove, suddenly exploded into violent fury, making her start in horrified surprise. "That was my fucking best horse!" he raged, thumping his fist on the dashboard.

By the time Tara drove the lorry into the yard at Radford Lodge Morgan had regained a degree of control over himself. They slid out of the lorry.

"What needs to be done? I'll help you," Tara said, grimly surveying the ramshackle yard.

Morgan watched surreptitiously as she helped him feed the horses. He noticed the fear in her eyes as she shot into the stables, taking in the buckets of food that he had prepared. She was terrified of the horses.

Once the horses were fed she followed him into the house. He seemed no longer to care whether she was there or not. She looked around the untidy room and at his bent head and longed to touch his dark hair.

"You need to eat," she told him gently, looking warily around the dark kitchen. God only knew what lurked in those dirty cupboards.

He shrugged. She searched gingerly through the cupboards, unearthing eggs and some potatoes that looked as if they should be drawing a pension. A piece of mouldy cheese was the sole occupant of the fridge. Quickly she concocted a cheese omelette and chips.

"He was the best horse I had. How am I going to tell his owner?" Morgan mused bleakly when he had pushed the half-eaten meal away "She wasn't even there."

She was at a loss as to what to say.

"Your brother is an out-and-out bastard," he said suddenly, looking at her through glittering blue eyes, the lashes matted with tears.

"Tell me about it," she said wryly. "I've known him for years."

He laughed harshly at her small joke.

Intensely aware of the aching desire that she had for him, she got up abruptly and began to clear the table to distract herself. She began to wash up, plunging her hands into the tepid water and vigorously scrubbing the plates. She heard him get up from the table and was aware of him standing close behind her. She could feel the warmth of his body against her back. She put the last plate onto the draining-board and turned around slowly. He was very close. She slowly met his eyes.

"Thanks for staying with me," he whispered harshly. He raised a hand to her face and slowly touched her cheek, then slid his hand, achingly slowly, around the back of her neck and drew her towards him. He kissed her slowly. She let her arms slide around his neck, her whole being enthused with longing for him.

"I've wanted you since I first spilled drink across your face!" He smiled for the first time since the horse was killed. Then taking her hand he led her slowly up the stairs.

When he woke in the morning she was curled into his arms, her hair spilling across the pillow and over his outstretched arm. He kissed her forehead tenderly and then froze. A car was coming down the drive. It drew to a halt outside. A door slammed and footsteps sounded on the path towards the house. High heels tip-tapping on the concrete slabs. Lynn Moore.

CHAPTER TEN

The footsteps tapped closer down the path. Lynn, he knew, would be furious at finding Tara with him. She must know about the death of her horse by now and was probably furious that he had not telephoned to tell her the bad news. He groaned in anguish, frantically trying to disentangle his arm from Tara's body

She stirred in her sleep, trying to stay with the warmth of his body. For a moment, despite his anxiety, he was lost, filled with love and longing for her. Even in sleep, with all of her make-up kissed away, she was still incredibly beautiful. She looked like a little girl, innocent and trusting, and entirely unaware of the onslaught in the offing.

He heard the door slam and the steel-tipped high heels move slowly across the bare tiled floor downstairs. He hastily levered himself out of bed, pulling on the clothes he had worn the previous day. He shot downstairs, fear gripping his stomach like a vice.

Lynn stood at the bottom of the stairs. Her face was etched with a fury that hardened the lines around her mouth and eyes. She glared at him with eyes full of hatred and vengeance.

"What the fuck are you doing?" she spat viciously.

He was lost for words. She had every right to be angry — he should have spoken to her last night, should have telephoned and explained about the horse. He felt his mouth open and close but nothing came out.

"You were supposed to take me out to dinner last night," she raged. "I spent all night waiting for you. I've never been so insulted in all of my life — to be stood up by some two-bit horse-trainer like you. You little shit!"

Horrifying scenarios crashed into his brain. She did not know about the horse. It was even worse than he had expected. Not only had he stood her up, he had failed to tell her about the horse dying and had gone to bed with another woman who at this very moment was sleeping upstairs. "Oh God," was all he could manage to say. He went slowly towards her. He felt filthy — there was a sharp fuzz of stubble on his chin and he must reek of sex.

She turned abruptly and marched into the lounge where she sat down heavily in one of the battered armchairs. She wore a very short skirt that rode up as she sat down to reveal a tantalising glimpse of tanned and shapely thighs. He felt a huge pang of guilt that he had been so uncaring. Last night he had been so distraught about losing Stone Cold that he had not been aware of what he was doing. Normally, he would never have been so careless as to forget Lynn, his most important client. He needed her money, that was for sure, and if fucking her and taking her out to dinner was the way to keep her then that was what he would do. He swallowed hard. This was a tricky situation. He threw himself into the chair opposite her and ran both of his hands through his ruffled hair.

"Yesterday, something terrible happened," he said.

"Dead right it did," she growled, lighting a cigarette. "You stood me up and I don't like being stood up!"

"Stone Cold was killed yesterday. That was why I didn't come. I was so upset that I forgot all about our dinner date."

"Killed?" she mouthed, drawing hard on her cigarette and blowing out a plume of smoke towards the ceiling. "Killed?" she said again her voice becoming higher and more incredulous. "How the fuck did he get killed?"

Morgan clenched his fists together as he recalled the dreadful sight of the horse tailing, the tangle of legs and the prone body lying at the foot of the fence as he ran up the track towards him. Slowly he explained what had happened. Lynn picked at an imaginary spot of fluff on her black skirt. Then finally she raised her head. "But how the fuck could that make you forget our date?" she hissed. "It was only a horse, for Christ's sake!"

Morgan gazed at her, open-mouthed. Stone Cold had not been just a horse. He had been one of the best. He stared at her, seeing how the thick make-up had run into the hard lines around her mouth, how her eyes were heavy beneath the thick coat of mascara she wore.

He felt a heavy feeling of loathing for her, along with the fear that he could say something that he would regret. At the end of the day, her money was important to him.

"I was very upset," he muttered. "Stone Cold meant a lot to me, even if he was just a horse to you. I put a lot of time and work into him and he should have won that race — he should have been one of the great horses on the racing circuit." He was suddenly beyond caring whether she liked what he was saying or not.

Lynn softened, her tone becoming wheedling. "I was very hurt," she said, laying her head to one side and looking at him through lowered lashes. "I had been looking forward to going out with you for dinner."

Morgan leant forward and took hold of her hand. Her long red nails dug painfully into his palm. "Lynn, we can do it some other night — let's just forget that last night ever happened," he said softly.

"I don't want you to ever forget me again, Morgan Flynn," she threatened.

He smiled, meeting her hard ice-chip eyes with an innocent gaze. "How could I ever forget you?"

She leant forward to offer her thickly smeared red lips for him to kiss.

He leant forward and in that instant both of them heard an unmistakable creak of the bed upstairs.

"What's that?" Lynn snarled, suddenly as alert as a Rottweiler. "Who's upstairs?"

Before he had time to reply she stormed out of the room, marching upstairs with him trailing fearfully in her wake.

As they burst into the room Tara was lying with her back to the door. "I woke up and you had gone," she murmured sleepily.

"Well, now I'm back!" said Lynn through gritted teeth.

Tara sat up as if she had been electrocuted. "What the . .." She pulled the bedclothes up to her chin and brushed her tangled hair away from her face. She looked, thought Morgan even in his distress, utterly gorgeous and totally sexy with her tangled hair and dark frightened eyes.

"It's no use being coy now," fumed Lynn, glaring at Tara. Then she spun around to Morgan and slapped him hard across the face, the blow making his head reel.

"That's it, buster!" she spat viciously, spittle flying from her mouth as it twisted in hatred. "You're finished as my trainer!"

Morgan shot backwards out of her way as she barged roughly past him.

Tara and Morgan waited in silence as Lynn's high heels tapped rapidly down the path and then the engine of her Jeep roared into life and the wheels spun as she gunned the accelerator. He waited in the doorway, not knowing what to say, wanting to erase the terrible scene from his mind, wanting to erase the horrible hurt he could see reflected in Tara's eyes.

"Tara," he said, gently, pleadingly, stepping into the room again. He sat on the bed, but she leapt out of it and began to dress, self-conscious at her nakedness.

"Don't!" she said harshly, her voice coming out as a strangled sob. "Don't! I've just got away from one two-timing lying bastard and I don't want to get involved with another one!" She turned to face him, her face closed. "Take me home, please," she said quietly.

"Tara," he said, reaching for her hand. He touched her fingertips and she jerked her hand away. "Let me explain to you how things have been between Lynn and me." He was desperate for her not to reject him. "She means nothing to me. Last night was something special. You are special — don't walk out on this —"

"There isn't a 'this' — we just had sex," she snapped, reaching in her handbag and pulling out a comb which she attempted to drag through her hair.

"It wasn't just sex and you know it," he said, surprised at how calm his voice now sounded. He wanted to pin her to the bed, to shake her shoulders until she understood.

"Please take me home," she said again, abandoning all attempts to do anything with her hair.

Wearily he got off the bed and slowly went downstairs. He made coffee and sat trying to sip it. Eventually she came downstairs, her footsteps slow on the steps. She wrenched open the front door and went into the yard.

Outside Kate was cleaning out the horses. She had seen the whole scene unfold and had guessed at what had happened. "Talk about killing two birds with one Stone Cold," she muttered bleakly to herself.

Tara got into Morgan's Jeep. "Take me to Westwood Park," Tara said mechanically, as if talking to a taxi driver. They drove in silence. Then, as he turned the Jeep into the drive of her home, she snapped, "drop me here. I want to walk."

He jerked the Jeep to a standstill. "Tara, I really, truly did not mean to hurt you."

She stifled a sob and fumbled with the door-catch, trying desperately to get out. As the door swung open she turned and met his devastated gaze with eyes that were filled with tears. "Goodbye," she said bleakly. She walked away up the drive without glancing backwards, a slight, hunched figure.

As she walked she wondered how she could have been such a fool. How could she have fallen for yet another cheating bastard? Each footstep seemed an immense effort, each breath harder than the one before it. Splitting up with Hank had not hurt her at all — she was past caring when she had found him in bed with the blonde, one of many — but somehow, even though she hardly knew Morgan, his betrayal hurt immensely. She had felt that he was different, that he was special; something had happened the previous night. She shook away the thought. It was ridiculous. He was just like all of the others. An out-and-out bastard. She had been a complete fool.

Derry glanced through the window of his study as she approached the house. "That will be fine. Thank you very much, Lynn," he said, replacing the telephone receiver. He pushed his leather chair away from the enormous desk that dominated his office, and moved slowly to the tall French windows. Tara looked devastated as she walked up the drive. Derry put two and two together, guessing what may have happened. It was well known in the tight circles of the racing world that Lynn and Morgan were lovers, that he was a kept man. Kept by a tarty hag old enough to be his mother. He had been a thorn in Derry's side for a while, but now Derry was going to get his revenge in the nicest way possible, especially if Morgan had hurt Tara. How strange if she had been instrumental in Morgan's downfall! Now Derry was going to finish the bastard's training career once and for all. He would never rise again; he would sink back into the muckheap where he belonged.

Lynn Moore was true to her word. Derry's groom Sarah arrived at Radford Lodge in the middle of the afternoon. "I've come to collect Lynn's horses — she's sending them to Derry's yard," she said, her eyes not quite meeting Morgan's.

"What a bitch she is!" said Kate.

"Shut up," Morgan told her. "Let's get this done."

It took only moments to rug the four remaining horses in the purple and gold colours of the Westwood Park yard. Sarah slipped the battered nylon head-collars off and replaced them with the shiny leather ones that belonged to Derry. Then they led the horses out of the stables and loaded them into the expensive lorry.

Sarah, kindly as ever, touched Morgan's arm. "I'm really sorry about this. I think she's a cow, but I'm just doing my job. I will look after them, I promise."

She clambered into the lorry and shot out of the yard, barely missing the leaning wall as she drove hurriedly away.

Morgan went miserably to the tack room to put the discarded rugs away. Five empty boxes stared bleakly at him from across the yard. Without those horses he would have to let the lads go. They worked long and hard and were fiercely loyal to him — he hated having to let them go, but without the horses there was no way that he could keep them.

He lay on the sofa listening to music, hardly hearing it, yet unable to move, to do anything. Tomorrow he would face the world, but today he needed to sit quietly, to lick his wounds and let the problems churn around in his mind. Eventually he could bear it no longer. He had to try to see Tara, to try to explain about his relationship with Lynn. It meant nothing to him, she had meant nothing. He drove the few miles to Westwood Park in a daze. He pulled up outside the imposing front door and rang the doorbell. After a few moments the door was swung open and Derry stood before him, a tall glass of champagne in his hand.

"Ah," he said waving the glass, "I wondered how long it would be before you showed up!"

"I want to see Tara," demanded Morgan.

"Well," snorted Derry, "you can be assured that she doesn't want to see you. Not now. Not ever." And he swung the door slowly shut in Morgan's face.

CHAPTER ELEVEN

Morgan drove into the muddy field that served as a car park at the horse sales, stopped the lorry and got out. He glanced at the dark bay horse being exercised in the paddock a short distance away. Sighing he dragged his coat and hat from the passenger side of the vehicle and pulled them on, shivering in the biting wind and miserable drizzle, this, he mused could be a total waste of time, finding a horse good enough to sell on and make money out of was not an easy task. In order to supplement the meagre wage he was earning from training racehorses Morgan periodically bought a young half bred horse to break in and sell on as a hunter or show horse. As he watched, the dark bay horse began to buck on ground churned by the efforts of countless others being shown to potential customers that was one he wouldn't be looking at. Pulling his battered cowboy hat firmly over his ears, Morgan began to follow the line of people making their way to the sales yard.

A rusting sign by the gate bade visitors welcome to the spring sales. The sales yard was an ancient tight quadrangle of dilapidated stables, green paint peeling from the doors, many of which had spades propped against them to keep them shut. The serious business of the sales was conducted in a small ring covered with a high tin roof that kept the worst of the rain off but little more, with hard wooden benches circling it and a rickety podium where the red-faced bull-like auctioneer conducted the sales, bouncing bids off the wall, gabbling in unintelligible sales talk until no one knew who was bidding, even the bidders themselves. The yard was already crowded with serious-looking buyers who looked critically at the horses and made crosses against their numbers on windblown catalogues.

Morgan bought a catalogue from a shivering girl who had taken a day off school to do the job and was now regretting her rashness. He wandered towards the stables with his head buried in the catalogue. There were a few horses that he was interested in and he marked them with a stub of a pencil. He walked around the stables identifying the ones he had marked.

He looked at an elegant chestnut mare but dismissed the pretty horse as unsuitable because of a splint on one of her slender legs. He felt the tiny lump and stood up, sighing; it was hard enough to sell a good horse let alone one which already had problems. In the next box was the horse that was being exercised when he was parking the lorry. Morgan ran an expert hand over his chunky legs and body. The horse submitted to his touch, looking at Morgan out of the corner of his eye. He stood proudly, knowing that he was handsome. This one might make a nice hunter.

As Morgan came out of the stable and pushed the door shut, a horse being led across the yard caught his attention. The magnificent bay was rugged up in a warm wool blanket bound in red. He wore a leather head-collar and was being led by a tall, extremely attractive blond groom who looked as arrogant as the horse. Morgan leant against the door and watched the horse walk. He covered the ground in long proud strides, taking in his surroundings with intelligent kind eyes. Then Morgan realised that he was not the only one admiring the horse.

A man was lolling arrogantly against a stable door. Morgan scowled with distaste — Derry Blake.

As the horse was led past Derry noticed Morgan glaring at him.

"Morning," said Derry, nodding curtly. Morgan nodded briefly.

The very presence of Derry made the hairs on the back of his neck stand up in dislike.

"I imagine that horse is out of your league," drawled Derry, nodding in the direction of the tall bay horse.

Morgan shrugged, feeling bitter bile rising at the back of his throat. He clenched his fists tightly by his sides in order to prevent himself from punching the man.

"Maybe," he said shortly.

"Well, I think he will do me very nicely," said Derry, marking his catalogue with an expensive-looking pen, "I'm looking for a nice trainer's hack for myself."

Quivering in temper Morgan stalked away and tried to concentrate on the sale. He gradually got his frayed nerves under control. Once he had studied all of the horses he had marked, hunger drove him in the direction of the sales-yard cafe. He turned the corner towards the second yard and an obviously Thoroughbred grey head caught his eye. What was a Thoroughbred doing at these sales, Morgan wondered glancing down the catalogue he read: Property of a gentleman. Absently Morgan stroked the face of the horse, then, out of habit went into the box. He recoiled in horror: the horse was nothing but skin and bone. The hair was missing in huge raw patches from his back and legs from being out in the rain and mud. "Jesus," he whispered, his eyes taking in the horse's injuries and condition. "Poor lad," he said, touching the painfully thin neck of the horse. It would be kinder to put the horse down rather than sell it. Whoever had let the horse get into this state wanted shooting. No wonder the owner preferred to remain unnamed! He shook his head in disbelief. He left the stable feeling sick at heart.

A disjointed voice crackled over the loudspeaker, announcing that the sale was about to begin. The stable yard began to empty as the buyers made then: way to the auction ring. Morgan followed the exodus and squashed into one of the wooden seats which were slowly filling with buyers. He glanced quickly around the ring, recognising and nodding at a few familiar faces.

The loudspeaker crackled into life again and the auctioneer began to speak. "Good-morning-ladies-and-gentlemen-welcome-to-the-spring-sales," he said almost unintelligibly into the microphone. He surveyed the assembled audience with his piggy eyes. An expectant hush fell as he drew his glasses out of his coat pocket. He put them very deliberately onto the end of his nose and then, pausing for dramatic effect, picked up the sales catalogue from the rostrum. A short man led in the first horse, a leggy-looking gelding "Here-we-have-the-property-of . . ."

A tall bespectacled man and a hard-faced lady dealer from the north began a ferocious battle to buy the horse. The auctioneer beamed with delight at the bidding battle and rose spectacularly to the occasion. Eventually the horse was knocked down to the hard-faced lady. The bespectacled man nodded courteously at her, gracious in defeat.

Morgan was shivering with cold by the time the nice horse he had picked out was led into the ring by a young girl. The auctioneer studied his catalogue and reeled off the sales patter. He squinted at the crowd over the top of his half-glasses. "Who will start the bidding at five thousand?" He gazed around the ring for anyone who might be interested. The crowds stared back impassively, all hardly daring to move or cough. "Four-then-three-then-surely-two — surely someone will start me off for this gelding?" He sighed dramatically. Then a young blonde girl, accompanied by a fat balding man, raised her hand eagerly. The auctioneer gave a demonic smirk. "And two thousand, the lady's bid!"

Morgan, with his face impassive, raised his hand. The horse might make a nice hunter, he was handsome and well put together, there could be some money to be made out of him.

"Two thousand five!" shrieked the auctioneer, triumphantly.

Out of the corner of his eye Morgan glimpsed Derry lolling against one of the metal struts that supported the roof of the auction shed. As the auctioneer cast his eye over the audience, Morgan saw Derry raise his catalogue. Morgan gritted his teeth, determined not to be beaten by Derry. He was going to buy the horse, if only to take the smug expression off Derry's face. The bidding went slowly upwards. The Dublin dealer dropped out, shrugging his shoulders in refusal. Finally at four thousand pounds the blonde girl reluctantly spoke to her companion and they both shook their heads sadly. Morgan felt tension grip his stomach like a knot.

At five thousand pounds Derry smirked at Morgan and nodded his head.

"The bid is on my left," said the auctioneer, gazing intently at Derry. "Shame to lose him for five hundred pounds," he added, glancing at Morgan, his face deepened to a dark shade of purple and glistening with sweat from all the excitement.

Morgan lifted a finger in agreement to the auctioneer; this had to be the last - he could not go any higher, even to get one over on Derry. He could feel his breath coming in short gasps and felt weak at the knees with tension. He looked across the crowded ring at Derry.

Slowly Derry raised his eyes, met Morgan's and smiled. Morgan knew then without a shadow of a doubt that Derry had never intended buying the horse but had just been pushing up the price by bidding against him. Anger, raw and bitter, coursed through his veins.

The auctioneer, holding his gavel like a judge about to give sentence, gazed around the ring. "Any-more-bids-on-this-animal-very-cheap-at-the-price?"

Someone coughed and the auctioneer swung his gaze to them. The man dropped his gaze to the floor, hardly daring to move. "Going-for-the-first-time-going-twice-going-three-times - " he paused with the gavel suspended in mid-air and then suddenly banged it down hard on his rostrum. "Sold!"

Morgan felt anger flood through him. The bay horse was his. But how the hell was he ever going to make any money on it? That bastard Derry Blake had pushed the price up way above what he could realistically afford.

Now that he had bought the horse he suddenly realised that he was very hungry. After signing the documents and paying over the five thousand pounds, he went to the cafe. He ate lunch, a greasy pasty and chips with a tepid weak cup of tea. Sitting in the window seat he kept half an eye on the sales ring while he ate, reading the catalogue.

Suddenly he half-choked on the pasty as the scraggy grey horse was led into the ring by one of the handlers employed by the sales yard. He dashed out, wondering as he crashed into the tables and chairs in his haste why he was so desperate to get to the ring. He could not afford to buy it. He pushed his way through the people who were walking away, revulsion plainly etched across their faces at the condition of the horse who was shambling around the sawdust ring. Morgan clutched the rail surrounding the ring, dry-mouthed as the auctioneer's bull-face surveyed the buyers.

"Where-will-I-start-for-this-fine-looking-horse? Property-of-a-gentleman," he roared. There was a silence. Morgan spotted the knackerman leaning on the ringside looking at the horse.

"Come on, ladies and gentlemen. He has to be worth one thousand five hundred - well, one thousand - five hundred - please someone give me two hundred and fifty," he pleaded.

Seized by an emotion that he did not understand, Morgan waved his catalogue at the auctioneer. Deciding quickly that he was better off letting the horse go to the one bidder, the auctioneer banged his gavel down on his desk. "Going. Gone!"

Morgan sat down heavily, feeling sick. He wondered what on earth had possessed him to buy the horse. He went into the auction offices and unwillingly unfolded the money to pay for the skinny grey horse. The sick feeling still gripped his stomach as he spread the notes onto the table. The money should have gone to pay the farrier in the morning. A brusque redhead behind the counter hurriedly wrote out the documents that meant the horse was his. He must be mad.

As he left the office, wiping the film of sweat from his brow, he noticed the magnificent bay horse that he had admired earlier being led into the ring. Instinctively he walked over and leant against one of the pillars, interested in seeing who was going to buy him. The auctioneer was in full swing; now he had a truly magnificent horse to sell.

"Where -will-we-start-for-this-magnificent-bay-gelding-property-of-Maurice-Fawbert-ten-years-old-and-sold-through-no-fault-of-his-own-give-me-ten-thousand — nine-seven-six-five." One of the dealers stuck his hand in the air. "Five thousand," bellowed the auctioneer. Morgan saw Derry nod his head. "Six thousand," said the auctioneer slowly pausing in between each word for dramatic effect. The dealer stuck his hand straight in the air. "Seven," said the auctioneer, turning his gaze to Derry who raised his catalogue impatiently. "Eight," the auctioneer yelled triumphantly.

The dealer pulled a wry face and shook his head. "Sir, you don't want to lose him for a thousand pounds!" and he scowled at the dealer. The dealer shook his head firmly and walked away. Derry's triumphant laugh rang out across the hushed ring.

Almost before he was aware of it Morgan's hand was in the air, signalling a bid to the auctioneer.

"I-have-a-fresh-bidder-on-my-left-nine-thousand," the auctioneer said smugly, looking at Derry.

Morgan caught the look of raw fury that flashed across Derry's arrogant face. He knew that Derry was torn between the thought that Morgan could not possibly afford the bay horse and the doubt that just maybe he had a wealthy client he was buying the horse for. Scowling, he stuck his hand in the air. "Ten!" shrieked the auctioneer, his voice getting higher in excitement.

Knowing that he could not afford to pay for the horse if it was knocked down to him, Morgan began to play a dangerous game of cat and mouse with Derry. Anger at Derry for running up the price of the horse that he had bought earlier and hatred for his arrogant behaviour made Morgan reckless. He felt a film of sweat break out all over his body as he carelessly raised his catalogue as if the money meant nothing to him. "Eleven!" bellowed the auctioneer, the red colour of his face deepening to dark purple.

Derry shot Morgan a look of pure hatred across the ring and then raised his hand.

"Twelve!" screeched the auctioneer.

The bidding shot backwards and forwards from Morgan to Derry until it reached fifteen thousand to Derry.

Then, raising his shoulders in acquiescence and giving the auctioneer a smile of dismissal, Morgan turned his back and walked away. He giggled quietly as he heard the auctioneer knock the horse down to Derry for fifteen thousand.

CHAPTER TWELVE

Derry angrily shut the newspaper and rolled it into a tube. "Doesn't he know when to quit?" he exploded, slamming the rolled-up newspaper down forcefully on the back of the plane-seat in front of him.

The man sitting in the seat jumped violently and turned around to glare furiously at Derry, his pale blue shirt-front stained with the glass of red wine that he had just spilled down himself.

"Oy! Do you mind, old chap!" he said in clipped English tones.

"Not at all, old boy," Derry snapped back. He tossed the newspaper down in disgust and glared out ot the tiny window at the grey expanse of the Irish Sea far below them.

Tara unfolded the newspaper and glanced quickly through it to see what had offended Derry so much. There, in the column that gave out the Irish entrants in the English Grand National, a few horses beneath Derry's Music and Dance owned by Paddy Dalton, was a horse called Darkhound, trained by Morgan Flynn and owned by a man called Eddie Gallagher. Despite herself, Tara smiled — Morgan really had got under Derry's skin.

The elegant air hostess came forward down the aisle, smiling. She vaguely recognised Derry from his photographs in the newspaper and, not really knowing whether he was a famous actor or a pop star, was giving him five-star treatment on the journey. Tara was treated with cold politeness. "Can I get you anything else?" she asked pointedly. Derry shook his head, hardly acknowledging her presence.

Tara clutched nervously at the seat armrest as the concourse of Manchester Airport appeared beneath the plane's wing.

Then, after a few minutes, they were down, the plane wheels bumping jerkily onto the tarmac and the engine noise surging loud in her ears. She gave a small prayer of thanks as the plane began to taxi towards the terminal.

Derry leant against a pillar in the baggage reclaim with his mobile clamped to his ear while Tara retrieved the heavy leather bags that belonged to him and her own small, lighter one. Derry, ignoring the waiting people, jumped straight into a taxi followed by a red-faced Tara, leaving the remainder of the queue open-mouthed at his audacity.

It was dark by the time that they arrived at the hotel. A blushing receptionist, overawed by Derry, allotted them rooms. After a telephone call to Sarah who had flown over the previous day with the horse, Derry disappeared to his room, leaving Tara to arrange for his bags to be taken up.

The following morning, Tara and Derry breakfasted early and then made their way back to the racecourse. Sarah was already hard at work. She put the saddle and bridle on Music and Dance, and Derry legged her up onto the horse, which danced with excitement. Tara watched the easy way in which she handled the animal. She rode with a confidence that made Tara blow out her cheeks in awe of her obvious ability.

"Take him out onto the track," Derry ordered, shoving his mobile phone deep into the pocket of his jacket.

The racecourse was deserted except for the staff who were stocking the bars with beer and spirits and the catering staff who were unloading metal containers full of food. Still though, there was a buzz of anticipation. The Grand National was one of the biggest races in history, four miles over some of the toughest fences in the world. Some of the greatest horses in history had won the race over the years and now Derry's horse had a chance to compete in it. Derry had ridden in the tough race, but today was the first time that he had ever trained a runner.

The horse walked out onto the track and as his hooves touched the grass he began to prance, head high and ears sharply pricked. In the early morning mist that held all the promise of a fine, cold spring morning, the other horses entered for the race cantered around the track, the jockeys nonchalant, pretending not to be scared of the terrible fences. Tara shivered.

She was not part of all of this. She had no courage to be able to ride one of the horses at home, let alone on such a famous racecourse.

Then far away up the track she saw Morgan walking the course with his jockey. The two of them walked with their heads down, studying the ground, looking to see where would be the best place to gallop during the race. They came closer and Tara felt her heart leap. The memory of that night together, the feeling of his skin against hers, his body entwined around hers was still too painful and raw and still too close to the surface. As if he felt her watching him, Morgan glanced up and met her eyes. She looked abruptly away, feeling bitter tears prick at the back of her eyes.

Sarah rode the horse back to the stables. The day was spoilt for Tara. She wished that she had not come. It was a physical longing, a desperate need to be in his arms again. Yet it was impossible. He had betrayed her. And she had lost him his most important client. They would never be lovers again.

Spectators began to arrive. Loud drunk lads roared at her as she passed through the enclosures on her way to the parade-ring.

Sarah was leading the horse around the tarmac strip. Tara looked for Morgan, not wanting to see him, yet unable not to watch out for him. Someone that she did not recognise was leading his horse around. She recognised Kate, leaning against the guard-rail beside her.

"Hi," Tara nodded at the younger girl.

Kate returned the greeting stiffly, looking intently at the horses. Then suddenly she turned to Tara and spat, "I don't know how you have the nerve to be here after what your brother has done to Morgan!"

Tara, not knowing what to say in reply, moved away. Ducking under the guard-rail and wriggling quickly out of reach of the burly security guards, she sprinted across the grass to Derry, just as the bell rang to signal that it was time for the jockeys to mount their horses.

The jockeys rode one circuit of the parade-ring and then suddenly everything erupted into chaos. The ring stewards began to rush around like headless chickens, jockeys began to dismount and no one seemed to know what was happening.

"What's going on?" Tara said fearfully to a furious-looking Derry.

"There's been a bomb warning," he said. He looked at his horse in horror. The horse, ready to race, was like a coiled spring. Now the jockey slid from his back, making him plunge in fear.

All of the horses ready to race, filled with excitement and anticipation of the gallop, began to plunge, pawing the ground in confusion. Chaos reigned.

One of the ring stewards jogged towards them, a mobile radio buzzing in his hand.

"We have to clear the racecourse, quickly, please — take all of the horses back to the stables and leave as quickly as you can!"

"Everyone must leave immediately!" came bellowing over the loudspeaker system, the announcer's voice laden with terror.

The police hurried around, taut-faced, guiding everyone out of the course. Tara found herself swept out of the parade-ring on a terrified tide of bewildered spectators. As they moved slowly past the hospitality boxes, people spilled out of the doors dashing to join the mass exodus. Coats and handbags littered the ground, abandoned in the hasty dash to get out. Tara moved slowly, shoved along with the column of people. It was hard to breathe and she fought against the terrible panic that was threatening to overwhelm her. She had lost sight of Derry — she was alone.

In front of her two jockeys shivered in their racing silks. They had been on the horses, ready to go, and now they were cold and miserable, not knowing what to do. As they filed past the course a dozen drunken louts were jumping up and down on the fences, yelling and swaying in front of the cameras that were hastily and delightedly screening the chaos. A live broadcast of something so exciting made a change from filming the usual crowd of animal-rights protestors that usually had to be dragged kicking and screaming from in front of the horses at the start. Everyone filed out into the centre of the course where many of the cars were parked. Some sought refuge inside their cars, but many had left keys in the jackets that had been abandoned in the bars and hospitality boxes. Tara, glad that she had her thick coat on, felt sorry for those who had had to abandon theirs and were now shivering in the biting wind that swept across the racecourse.

Beside her a woman wearing only a thin dress cried pitifully — she had lost her husband in the crush to leave and her handbag, coat and telephone had been left in the bar where she had been standing. A chivalrous gentleman took off his coat and laid it around her shuddering shoulders.

Then, a short while later, the police came again and told everyone that they had to leave the whole course. Car doors were slammed regretfully as their owners struggled hastily out into the cold afternoon. Tara, shivering with fright and cold, followed a thin line of people towards the exit. The chivalrous man was now bewailing the fact that the woman who had been shivering beside him had disappeared with his coat. A jockey walked ahead of Tara, looking like someone from a fancy dress ball in the line of warmly dressed people. Someone asked him for his autograph and he signed it with a cheery grin and accepted a swig from the burly man's hipflask.

Tara, trying to keep the growing feeling of panic under control, wondered what on earth she should do. She desperately wanted to be with Derry and wished that she had kept with him in the initial chaos. He would know what to do; he was always in control and so sure of himself. Now she was alone. News of the bomb scare had been televised and, as they filed out of the course, house-owners with homes nearby invited people in out of the cold. Many who had left cars in the course had no way of getting home and just had to sit and wait until the chaos subsided.

Tara, along with many others, hovered on the pavement outside, unsure of what to do. Many had lost their partners and friends and did not know how to find them. Tara glanced at her watch. It was almost half past four. The race should have been over now and they should have been in the bar celebrating or commiserating with a drink. Instead she was alone, scared and shivering, outside the high redbrick walls of the course.

The police began to circulate through the crowds telling everyone to go home and to come back tomorrow. "No one will be allowed back into the course until tomorrow," said a burly officer, directing everyone away.

"What are we supposed to do?" bellowed a red-faced man wearing only a shirt and trousers and looking pinched with the cold.

The policeman shrugged. "Find yourself a hotel and come back tomorrow."

"There won't be a hotel for miles that has vacancies," wailed a woman who was clutching at her husband's arm and tottering slightly on very high heels.

Suddenly everyone seemed to have the same thought: they must find hotel accommodation immediately. Tara, realising that she had no hotel, now that she and Derry had booked out in anticipation of flying home that evening, wondered what the hell she should do. She was all alone in the dreadfully scruffy area outside the racecourse, virtually penniless. She fought the urge to sit on the pavement edge and sob. She had to find Derry.

Eventually she decided that the only thing to do was to return to the hotel and wait. Hopefully Derry would come back there or maybe she would be able to get a room there again.

She looked around bleakly, wondering how to get a taxi, but every one that went past was filled with pale-faced and shivering race people dashing to find accommodation before night came. All of the taxi drivers looked delighted at the huge fees that they were going to get out of the scared spectators desperate to find a bed for the night. With no prospect of a taxi she faced the long walk back to the hotel but had no idea of how to get there. A very competent-looking police lady pointed her in the right direction and Tara set off, not relishing the prospect of finding her way through the Liverpool streets on a cold and rapidly darkening Saturday afternoon.

She rounded a corner of the racecourse. Red brick houses stretched into the distance at either side of the busy road. In the distance a group of lads evicted from the racecourse, very angry and drunk weaved their way towards her. As they approached one of them nudged his companion and they lined the pavement in front of her.

"Lost from the races, are yer?" one of them leered, full of bravado in front of his mates.

"Yes," she replied, drawing herself up to the fullest extent of her diminutive size and trying not to appear afraid. There were plenty of people around, they would not harm her.

Hearing her accent, one of the lads shot forward out of the line. "It's your lot that bombed the races, you bloody Irish!" he yelled, his drink-reddened face inches from her. Tara cringed away, her heart pounding, as he seized the collar of her coat.

Then she felt herself being pulled by the shoulders from behind as someone lifted her away from the youths and pushed himself between her and them.

"Fuck off! Leave her alone!"

The lads, too drunk to fight, looked the man slowly up and down, considering whether to tackle him or not and then, as one, they turned and melted away, drifting nonchalantly down the pavement looking for another fight to pick with someone else. As they turned a corner and vanished into the gloom the man turned and Morgan Flynn was looking down at her, his expression of concern turning to dismay as he realised who he had rescued.

CHAPTER THIRTEEN

Tara and Morgan's mouths mirrored each other in perfect circles.

"I didn't realise that it was you," Morgan muttered stiffly.

"Obviously," she snapped back. "Otherwise you would have hardly have come to help me."

"How true." He shoved his hands deep into the pockets of his overcoat and walked off, then stopped a few yards away with his back to her. "I would hardly want to help the one person who is singly responsible for almost putting me out of business." He turned to face her, his expression bitter and contemptuous.

Tara felt herself flush with anger despite the bitter cold of the early evening. "You've got some nerve," she cried. "You were the one who took me to bed knowing full well that you had a girlfriend already!"

He was still and silent, his mouth clamped shut in a hard line, and then he turned and took another stride forward and stopped again. The set of his shoulders was as rigid and as impenetrable as a rock fortress. "Had it not been for you, your precious brother would not have stolen my best customer." He was speaking very levelly now, but she could feel the anger and emotion.

He strode off down the street away from her.

For a moment Tara watched him. Then realising that she was all alone in the middle of Liverpool on a dark and cold Saturday night she dashed after him, her feet ringing out on the pavement.

"Wait!" she yelled, pleadingly. "Don't go without me!" She caught up with him and for a moment they walked side by side, but his legs were far longer and he soon outstripped her. "What shall I do? I've nowhere to go." Her voice betrayed the fear that she felt.

He stopped and spun to face her. "Who gives a fuck?" Then he walked on.

Tara shoved her hand in front of her month to stop a strangled sob from escaping. "Morgan," she sobbed, watching him walk away.

Halfway down the street he stopped and came back. "I'm not having you on my fucking conscience," he said unwillingly. "I'm going back to my hotel — I suppose you'd better come with me."

They arrived at the hotel to find the place in complete chaos. Lost and frightened people hovered everywhere, sitting in the foyer or lying on the floor on makeshift beds with coats over them and using their arms as pillows. A tall man in a camel coloured overcoat was having a very loud and angry argument with the hotel manager who, seizing the opportunity to make a packet of money, had doubled his room rates and was even charging for people to sleep on old mattresses in the half-derelict ballroom at the back of the hotel.

Friendships had been forged in the spirit of adversity — two women shared a cigarette that one of them had bummed off a stranger in the bar. Another man had given his jacket to a gorgeous young girl who had been separated from her boyfriend and had neither coat or handbag or money with her. His wife was glaring at him in rage.

Tara, despite feeling relieved at the thought of having somewhere safe to stay, was aware that Morgan hated her being with him and resented her presence terribly.

"You must be hungry," she said tentatively. "Let me buy you something to eat."

He turned and looked at her as if for a long time he had forgotten that she was even there. "Great. Thanks."

He was so polite that he made her feel like a stranger. Impossible to believe they had been lovers. The morning Lynn Moore's high heels tip-tapped their way into their cosy love-filled world seemed like a dream.

The restaurant was crowded, but the restaurant manager managed to squeeze them into a corner by the window with a tiny table.

"I bet the hotel manager loves this," she ventured, looking around the packed restaurant.

Morgan looked around and snorted in agreement. "There's always someone who wants to make something out of someone else's trouble," he said, looking at the hastily written menu that a waitress had put on the table.

Tara swallowed; his comments were obviously directed at Derry. There was nothing she could say to him. Derry had taken advantage of Morgan's trouble, but she was not Derry. "Morgan, I'm not Derry. And besides which, you were the one who seduced me while you had another girlfriend." The bored-looking couple at the next table ceased their dull conversation to surreptitiously listen in.

"She was not my girlfriend," he whispered as loud as he dared, over the noise of the restaurant. "She just made me fuck her in order to keep her horses with me. I needed the money." The woman at the adjoining table choked on her soup.

"So why didn't you explain that minor point to me?"

"When I came to explain you wouldn't even come to the door to hear what I had to say," he mumbled crossly, shredding a bread-roll with his long fingers.

"What do you mean?" she asked in astonishment. "When did you come?"

Morgan stared. "Derry said that you wouldn't see me." They gazed at each other as they realised the Machiavellian workings of Tara's brother.

"Damn that man," snarled Morgan.

They ate a tasteless and hastily thrown-together meal of chicken and cold potatoes accompanied by a mash of congealed vegetables. They ate in silence letting the new revelations sink slowly in.

Tara wondered what she would have done if Morgan had spoken to her and explained about his strange relationship with Lynn.

"So is it over now with you and Lynn?" she asked as casually as she could, as they attempted to eat very soft ice cream that was passing itself off as dessert.

"Well, obviously," he snapped impatiently. "Her horses are now with Derry and presumably he's fucking her and he's welcome! She fucking wore me out." The last bit was more for the benefit of the adjoining couple who were lingering over their coffee, not wanting to miss a word of this thrilling conversation.

The waitress snatched away their coffee cups as soon as they had drained the final dregs of the awful brew.

"I think that we are not wanted in here," said Morgan, getting to his feet.

Tara got up and followed him out of the room, aware of the astonished gaze of the diners who had overheard their conversation.

"I'm going to bed — I'm worn out," Morgan said, stifling a yawn.

They stood together, aware of the fact that Tara had nowhere to sleep.

"Look," he began, "you can sleep in my room if you want." He raised his eyebrows quizzically.

Tara hesitated. "It's very kind . . . but I won't share a bed with you."

He inclined his head in agreement. "I never said that you could," he teased.

He led the way to the room.

"Bed or floor?" he asked as he opened the door.

"I'll have the floor," she offered generously but then was slightly miffed when he handed her a duvet out of the wardrobe and sat on the bed to pull off his shoes.

Tara woke in the middle of the night. There was shouting and screeching in the street outside — drunks making their way home. She pushed the quilt to one side, got up and padded softly to the window. She leant against the frame looking out over the cityscape of orange and gold lights twinkling in the dark.

A noise behind her alerted her that Morgan was stirring. She heard the quilt being pushed away and the creak of the bed as he got out of it, she even heard the sound of his footsteps as he came across the carpet towards her, yet still she started as he came to stand beside her.

"Isn't it beautiful?" she said softly, feeling her heart pounding horribly in her chest as if it was going to burst out through her ribcage.

"Yes," he agreed. "Though I must admit I much prefer to see the countryside and my horses." For a moment they stood side by side, quietly looking at the cityscape until Morgan's hand found its way into hers. "Come to bed," he said gently.

The 150th Grand National was finally run two days later. Morgan's horse finished tenth, two horses in front of Derry's runner. Tara had stayed with Morgan since the bomb scare, having managed to get Derry on the telephone and reassure him that she was safe. As the horses thundered across the finish line, Morgan enfolded Tara in a bear hug.

"Do you know something?" he whispered when they emerged from a breathtaking kiss for a gasp of air.

"What?" she stage-whispered back to him.

"I love you," he said slowly.

"Don't be silly," she told him. "It's far too soon — you hardly know me." But she was delighted.

Then, leaning against Morgan, she turned her head and looked straight into the icy glare of her brother, his face set in fury.

Later that evening they parted reluctantly. Morgan had to drive his lorry back to Ireland, while she was due to fly back home with Derry. She felt the pain of separation keenly, like a knife cutting through her heart. She tried desperately not to cry. It was ridiculous to feel this way; she had only just met him and she was going to see him as soon as she returned to Ireland, for heaven's sake! But still, as she watched the lorry trundle slowly away she felt as if she would never see him again.

Fear gripped her. Now she had to face Derry. He would be furious with her. He hated Morgan and the thought of her being with him would make him angry. She had seen his furious look when he had seen her with him. Taking a deep breath, she arranged her face into a brave smile and strode towards the bar. What could he say? It was her life. He might be her older brother but he had no right to decide who she could see or not see. She reached Derry who had watched her walk across the room.

"Tara!" he exclaimed in mock delight, reaching out as she arrived at the tight circle of people who were gathered around him. "Come and join us! I am so glad to see that you were well looked after during the awful bomb scare." His tones were clipped and icy. He was so slick, so professional, that no one would recognise the fury that he was disguising.

She began to wish that she had kept Morgan better hidden and perhaps not begun a relationship so publicly. Perhaps it really had been wrong to flaunt herself with the man her brother hated so much.

"Your horse did really well," she said to no one in particular.

Derry dipped his head in a parody of gratitude. "Thank you," he said, then continued in clipped sarcastic tones, "I'm surprised that you noticed — you seem to have been so busy."

Then he grabbed her arm and steered her out of the bar. She could feel furious tension coursing through every bone of his body. Once settled in the back of the cab he gestured at the floor where her bag was heaped with his own. "I brought your bag," he snapped.

Tara swallowed hard. Guiltily she wrung her hands together.

"Derry —" she began, but he silenced her.

"No need to explain," he sneered. "I'm so relieved you were well looked after."

She heard the double meaning plainly in his voice. He was brilliant at making her feel uncomfortable with his frosty, sulky silence. He was silent for the rest of the journey to the airport.

She sat, sunk in misery, missing Morgan and feeling so guilty about ever seeing him. How on earth was she going to have a relationship with him it Derry was going to be like this? She loved Morgan desperately, wanted every fibre of his body, felt so happy and comfortable and protected with him — yet was she strong enough to bear the force of Derry's disapproval?

Back to Ireland, they got the car from the long-stay car park and started for home. Derry drove faster than ever in his fury, taking his violent temper out on the car and the road.

Once at home, he skidded the car to a halt and, slamming the door, stalked off inside, leaving her to struggle with the bags. The hall was deserted when she got inside and she could hear his heavy footsteps vanishing upstairs to his bedroom. Maybe he would be in a better temper in the morning.

In this she was very mistaken. He was at breakfast when she came downstairs. She helped herself from the platter of bacon and sausage that Mrs McDonagh had laid out and sat down, wondering how on earth she was going to manage to eat.

"I don't believe you," he said suddenly, laying down his newspaper and looking at her sternly. "How on earth can you go off fucking the one man you know I hate?"

Tara gazed at his frozen face, his eyes like chips of ice glaring frostily at her. "I think that I should be allowed to choose my own friends," she said bravely.

Derry let out a roar of sarcastic laughter. "Hardly," he snorted. "If that's the sort of friend you choose, then I doubt if you can even demonstrate the skill of choosing your own breakfast. For heaven's sake, Tara," he sighed, trying to be patient, "don't see him again."

Tara glared at him. How dare he talk to her as if she was a child? She was surprised at the strength of her own feelings and at the courage that she found to stand up to him. "I love him," she said, feeling the words rush from her lips and regretting them instantly, as they slid by like naughty children darting past a schoolmistress.

"I love him!" mocked Derry. "You said that about the last one I seem to remember — and also how special he was!"

Something in Tara exploded. "Go to hell!" she stormed, jumping up from the table with such force that her chair fell backwards onto the carpet. She left it where it fell and dashed from the room, hot tears spilling down her cheeks. She ran outside and jumped in the Jeep. Like a fox running for cover she made for the one place where she knew that she could find safety: Radford Lodge and Morgan.

There, she flung herself crying into his arms and then later, when she lay with him in bed, she told him about Derry's awfulness.

Then he said to her the words that she longed to hear and that she had known he would say.

Yet she gasped in delight and relief when he said: "Move in with me."

CHAPTER FOURTEEN

Morgan came back from answering the telephone, hopping from one foot to the other and punching the air like a football hero. "Yes, yes!" he whooped, then seizing her around the waist he proceeded to smother her hair and face in kisses. "My Tara," he laughed delightedly, "I knew that you would bring me luck!"

"What's happened?" she said, disentangling herself from his embrace.

"A new owner wants to come and look at the yard! It's some guy that sings in a band and has made himself a packet of money and now wants to go all respectable. He saw my horse in the Grand National and reckoned that I'm the trainer he wants — so he's coming to have a look. He said he would be here in about half an hour — he was just visiting his granny in Nenagh." He glanced out of the window and suddenly saw the yard through the eyes of a stranger: the straw that had just been delivered and was now blowing all over it, the untidy doors that hung off their hinges, the sheds that had been made into stables.

"Shit!" he yelped.

"I'm going to go and fetch my things," called Tara to his back as he hurtled away yelling for Kate to come and help him tidy up.

Tara left the yard and drove slowly the few miles home to Westwood Park. As she drove up the magnificent drive to the glorious house she felt a tinge of regret. Was she doing the right thing? Leaving behind her home and Derry — she knew that he loved her and only wanted what was best for her.

She knew that by leaving him she would hurt him very badly. She gripped the steering wheel tight and manoeuvred through the final pair of gates into the house front yard. It was her life. Derry would have to accept it.

Derry came out of his office as she slammed the front door shut.

"So," he said, leaning nonchalantly against the door-frame, "you've calmed down now." A patronising smile lifted the corners of his lips into a sneer. "You'll thank me for this one day - he really was not the man for you. Go and get changed and we'll go out for something to eat."

Tara paused at the foot of the stairs and slowly spun around to face him. Then, with her heart in her mouth, she said: "I'm sorry, Derry, but I'm moving out. I'm going to live with Morgan." She watched as Derry's handsome face crumpled in disbelief, his mouth opening and closing like a goldfish gasping for air.

For a split second he seemed truly rocked by what she had said. Then he sighed, sucking m a giant breath of air and puffing out his cheeks as he exhaled. Then shaking his head in disbelief, he said, "well, Tara, I have done all that I can to try to look after you. This will always be your home - remember that when you can't stand that waster any more." With that he turned abruptly and retreated into his office, shutting the door with a quiet, controlled, angry click.

There was silence. Tara could sense Mrs McDonagh hovering close to the kitchen door listening. With Derry's words ringing in her ears she made her way sadly upstairs to her room. How was she expected to choose between the two of them?

There was not much to pack. She shoved her clothes and a few possessions into a suitcase and dragged it downstairs. Now that the exchange with Derry had taken place she just wanted to be out of the house and back to the safe haven of Morgan. She drove away without a sense of regret and was back at Morgan's a short time later.

A large and very ostentatious Mercedes with blacked-out windows was parked in the yard. The singer had obviously arrived. The yard however was empty. Morgan must have taken him inside. She went in. Morgan and a lad who looked about fourteen were sitting at the kitchen table with a bottle of whiskey between them, which they were drinking out of chipped glasses.

"This is Tara," slurred Morgan as she walked into the kitchen.

From the way he said it, she felt as if she should be accompanied by a fanfare of trumpets and a red carpet. "My girlfriend. Tara, this is Shane

McGrath!" He waved his hand to indicate the lad who was lolling at the kitchen table. As the pop singer stood up and extended his hand drunkenly towards her, Morgan added proudly: "She lives here!"

Shane sat back down. Tara had caught a fleeting glimpse of skin tight black jeans, very pointed cowboy boots made out of pony-skin, and a black shirt open almost to the waist to reveal a chunky gold emblem dangling on a chest covered in downy fluff.

"Hey, babe," he crooned, "Morgan's the greatest. I want him to find me horses, lots of horses, I want lots of horses!" He burbled on: "I'm buying a house near here and I want to see my horses, I always wanted lots of horses!"

"Oh right,' she said, looking at him wide-eyed in astonishment. There had never been any owners like him at Westwood Park.

A week later Tara knew she had made the right decision. She had never felt happier or more loved and secure. She and Morgan had settled into a routine in the yard and a loving and sexy relationship in the house. Life was glorious. Kate had accepted her presence with a glowering formality, but Tara was unfazed by the girl's anger towards her. The only cloud on the horizon was the forthcoming race at Punchestown when the two men in her life would meet head on for the first time since she had moved out. This she dreaded and had nightmares about the two of them clashing with her in the middle of them.

However, as with everything that is dreaded, the day of the Punchestown race soon came. Shane McGrath had been true to his word and Morgan had been busy buying him four brilliant new horses. Money was no object and Morgan had been able to buy him the very best, horses that he knew would be likely winners. Secret Lady was looking a picture as far as scraggy, tiny mares went and Morgan had that day seen a huge improvement in the handsome grey horse that he had bought in the sales, now called Carna Boy, after a seaside village where Morgan had spent a lot of happy holidays as a child. He had put on weight and had settled into the routine at Radford Lodge so Morgan was feeling on top of the world.

As they drove into Punchestown, Morgan grasped Tara's thigh and squeezed it in excitement. "I feel good about today — you have brought me so much luck!"

She leant against him and gave him a kiss on the cheek. The new lorry, which Shane had bought for them, was immaculate and so much easier to drive than the ancient one they had been to the races in the last time.

As the horses walked around the parade-ring Morgan stood with Tara in the centre, watching Kate lead Secret Lady around. The diminutive mare walked gingerly, her feet hardly seeming to touch the springy rubber tarmac. She looked a world away in size and class from the other horses in the parade-ring that were prancing around, pulling at their handlers and bucking back at the horses behind.

Then Derry walked into the ring with JT, the pair of them looking like gangsters out for mischief. They stood within earshot of Tara, and Derry said in a loud whisper that she was obviously meant to hear, "what the hell is that yoke?" He indicated the tiny mare who was walking gently beside Kate, her ears lolling to the side, her kind eyes half-closed. Suddenly Derry let out a huge guffaw of laughter. "I should have known! It's one from Morgan Flynn's enormous stable of racing stars! Bloody hell, it looks fit for a cat-meat can instead of a good-class race like this one!"

Tara glared at him. How dare he be so cruel? The mare might not look the prettiest, but she stood as much a chance as his horse did. Derry's horse, Saddler's Cross, was dancing about so much and getting so excited that it would be worn out before the race even started.

The jockeys mounted and rode out onto the racetrack. Tara clutched Morgan's hand as they walked in front of Derry to the owners' and trainers' stand. Derry's presence was really annoying her. She wished that they did not have to confront him every time that they went racing.

As soon as the race started Morgan was lost, watching intently through his binoculars. Tara stood on the step behind him leaning on his shoulders, breathing in the delicious smell of his hair, freshly washed that morning with a woody-smelling shampoo.

"Go on," he was muttering as the horses set off, riding the horse in his imagination. The horses ran as a bunch over the fences. One horse fell at the first fence and there was a collective groan of disappointment. She felt Morgan stiffen with tension and then relax as he realised that his horse was still running. The horses shot past the stand in a bunch of colour, moving as if in unison, the noise of their hooves loud, even over the roars of encouragement from the crowd. Then they were off again on the final circuit. Saddler's Cross began to pull away from the others, his long legs raking the ground, taking each fence with an easy grace, the jockey crouching impassively over his withers with the horse's dark mane whipping up into his face.

Derry spun around, caught Tara's eye and gave a demonic grin of victory. She looked at him and then turned away. The horses turned towards the final few fences, Derry's horse still in the lead. Tara looked away, not wanting to see Morgan's horse beaten. She looked at the people in the stand, at the rapt looks on their faces, the trainers moving slightly as if they were on the horses willing them towards the finishing line. She could ignore the race, but the commentator's voice went on. She tried to blank out his eager cries about Derry, the wonder boy of training, and his fabulous horse and then she heard his cries turn to astonishment as he said, "at the centre of the field the little mare, Secret Lady, is making up ground — she is finishing strongly!"

Tara turned. The two horses jumped the final fence a short way ahead of the others and then began the short run up to the winning post. Secret Lady nosed ahead, her kind face moulded into grim determination. Tara began to yell. Morgan, half-deafened by her cries, pulled himself up onto the step beside her and they yelled together, willing the mare home. Then Saddler's Cross, his long stride eating up the ground, came back, his nose edging in front of Secret Lady's brave little face. The horses charged over the finishing line together.

Derry turned as the horses began to pull up and yelled up the steps: "My horse won!" Then, with an arrogant grin, he turned and ran lightly down the steps with Lynn Moore tottering rapidly behind him.

Morgan strode down the steps in his wake. All around, as they made their way to the parade-ring, the bookies were beginning to put up boards with the two horses hastily scrawled on, wanting to bet on the outcome of the race.

"A photo finish," said the commentator who sounded so excited that he could burst at any second. The trainers waited in the centre of the parade ring as the tired horses were led back. Derry hovered by the winner's enclosure, holding Saddler's Cross's bridle triumphantly, convinced that he had won, while Lynn Moore clung to his arm while she blushed pink with delight.

Finally the bell rang to announce the outcome of the race.

"A dead heat," said the chief steward impassively over the loudspeaker system. In the stands the crowd went mad with excitement — it was a very rare occurrence for horses to dead heat.

Derry pulled his horse quickly into the winner's pen and Kate, glaring at him, shoved the mare in afterwards. Then the racecourse photographers tried to arrange the winning trainers and owners into a happy bunch for a photograph.

As they stood in the line-up Derry muttered, "you might have done well today, but I'd like to see you win the Gold Cup in Cheltenham!"

"No problem," answered Morgan. "I'll see you in the winner's enclosure."

CHAPTER FIFTEEN

Derry was furious. No one else in the crowded bar would have known it, but Sarah could recognise the signs, feel the fury and tension that he emitted, and quaked inside. There was trouble ahead. She sat in a corner of the bar sipping a Diet Coke. Another diet started. There were now only two pairs of jeans and one pair of jodhpurs in her wardrobe that fitted her - it really was time for a serious diet. If she didn't eat for the whole of the day tomorrow, it would give her dieting a great boost.

From her seat she could watch Derry unobserved. Lynn Moore was hanging onto his arm, laughing up at him coyly and touching his face as if she could not get enough of him. Sarah knew that Derry was like a trapped lion, angry and ready to lash out if anyone pushed him over the edge. Yet on the surface he looked totally in control, a perfect gentleman, delighted about his win even if he had to share it with his enemy, Morgan Flynn. Sarah took a long swig of her tasteless Coke. God, how she fancied a long glass of Guinness! It was what she deserved after such a long day. Derry was smiling now, submitting to the caresses of Lynn Moore who was getting drunker by the second. Sarah saw a flicker of disgust as he looked at the bumbling drunkenness of JT and his dizzy wife who was so drunk that she was trying to light the wrong end of her cigarette.

Sarah downed the last dregs of her Coke and, shaking off the advances of the spotty barman who was trying to give her another drink, she made her way across the room, weaving her bulk with difficulty between the crowded tables and milling people.

"Derry," she said, tugging lightly at his tweed jacket.

He spun around to face her, the fixed smile still in place, but his eyes were cold, looking at her like daggers that could pierce her heart.

"Derry," she said again, "I'm going to find Paul and take the horse home now."

"Grand," he said, clapping his arm around her shoulder and dragging her into the centre of the group. "This, ladies and gentlemen, is my head groom!"

Sarah blushed at the unusual attention.

"Isn't she gorgeous?" He laughed cruelly. "Now, darling Cinderella, take my horse home and be very careful with him. Lynn here would hate him to get damaged. Off you go now!"

He released her so abruptly that she stumbled against Lynn who let out an indignant squeal of rage.

"You clumsy cow!' she spat.

Sarah backed away from the group, all of whom were doubled up with laughter. How could he be so cruel? How could he lie in bed with her and then be so callous, making her just a figure of fun?

Exhausted, she dozed in the passenger seat as Paul drove the lorry back to Westwood Park. Once back in the yard Paul turned off the lorry, scrambled out of the cab and bade her goodnight. Sarah took the tired horse out of the lorry and put him into his stable. Then, pulling the collar of her coat up against the cold, she began the rounds of the dark and quiet stable yard making sure that everything was as it should be. She checked the horses, straightening rugs, refilling water buckets, giving a chunk more hay to those who whinnied pitifully at her. The horses all whickered at her, recognising the one who fed them and who showered them with love. With each horse she spent a moment, rubbing the silky hairs on their necks, feeling legs here and there checking for the tell-tale heat that could mean that something was wrong. One of the horses, Magnetic Attraction, began to bang impatiently on his stable door. "Hang on," she called to him, shutting the final stable door and then walking across the yard to his stable. Magnetic Attraction was her favourite horse. He belonged to JT. She let herself into the stable. The tall bay horse nudged at her pockets, seeking the treat that he knew would be there. In the darkness his white star glowed like a headlight. She fed him the treat and then, standing in front of him, put her arms around his neck. The big horse dropped his chin onto the small of her back as if he were giving her a hug.

"That's the best cuddle I'm going to get tonight," she whispered, drawing away from him, feeling hot salty tears spilling down her face.

She let herself into the silent cottage. Climbing the stairs she caught a glimpse of herself in the hall mirror. She stopped and went closer, looking at her face. Her face was blotchy from crying. She sighed and pressed her nose against her reflection in the cold glass.

"Derry has done this to you," she whispered.

The alarm-clock went off seemingly before she had even gone to sleep and Sarah rolled quickly out of bed and pulled on fresh clothes. There were dark circles of tiredness under her eyes and her face still looked blotchy from crying. She ran a comb through her lank hair and then, deciding that she could do nothing with it, scraped it back from her face in a harsh ponytail. She trudged miserably downstairs and out into the darkness of the early morning. The horses, with their acute hearing, heard the cottage door slam and began to whinny for their breakfasts.

Soon she lost herself in the work, supervising the yard and sending the horses out for exercise. At lunch-time she trudged back to the cottage. She was starving. Her stomach rumbled, she had a splitting headache and a heavy heart. Derry had really got to her. How, after all of this time, was it that he still had the power to hurt her? Why did she have to care about him so much?

Trudging into the cottage, she slammed the door shut and sank thankfully down on the sofa. She could rest now for a while. If she engrossed herself m the lunch-time chat shows then perhaps she wouldn't feel so hungry.

The door banged shut, making her sit up with a jerk. Derry bounced into the room, a wide beam across his face and two newspaper-wrapped parcels in his hands. She struggled to sit upright and for a second floundered like a fish out of water.

"Lunch," breezed Derry, marching straight into the tiny kitchen.

Sarah managed to arrange herself into a sitting position and pulled her sweatshirt hastily down so that it hid the bulge of flesh that crept over her waistband. A lot of banging and crashing of crockery and doors came from the kitchen and then Derry bounded back into the living-room, skilfully dodging the low beams. He carried two plates of fish and chips, soaked in vinegar and salt, and two big slices of bread thickly spread with butter.

These he put down onto the coffee table with a flourish and threw himself down onto the armchair beside her and proceeded to tuck into his plateful with relish. For a moment she stared at him, her mouth open at his nerve. How could he insult her so viciously and then just breeze in as if nothing had happened?

She reached forward and picked up the knife and fork he had perched on the edge of the plate. Perhaps he had no recollection of how he had insulted her. Perhaps he was just teasing her.

"Eat up then!" he said, waving his knife at her, in between huge mouthfuls of chips. Sarah, starving, fell upon the chips gratefully.

"Fuck that Morgan Flynn!" Derry said suddenly, his fork halfway to his mouth with a huge amount of fried fish teetering precariously on it. "He bloody goes off with Tara and then he had the frigging nerve to dead-heat with my horse yesterday and with a yoke like that bitch of a mare!" He shoved the fish into his mouth and chewed thoughtfully, glancing at her occasionally. "I'm going to show him once and for all who the best trainer is." He took a large bite of bread and barely chewed it before he continued, I bet him that he couldn't win the Cheltenham Gold Cup with that useless horse I sent to the sales that he was fool enough to buy." He roared with laughter. "And he accepted the challenge! Fucking idiot!"

Forking a mouthful of the greasy fish into her mouth, Sarah said nonchalantly,

"Which horse did you say you would run?"

He glared at her as if surprised by her stupidity. "Magnetic Attraction"

She stared at him open-mouthed. Magnetic Attraction was good, but the Cheltenham Gold Cup was one of the toughest races in the world.

Derry ate so fast that he had finished his food before she was halfway through hers. He pushed his plate away from him and stretched in the chair. Sarah cast a surreptitious glance at him. He was gorgeous - long slender legs encased in elegant moleskin trousers and a crisp cotton shirt beneath a well-cut tweed jacket that he wore with such an air. Quickly she looked away.

Pushing his arms behind his head, he yawned, stretching like a giant, elegant cat. "Do you know what I need now?" he smiled wickedly, but before she had chance to frame an answer he grabbed her hand, shaking the fork from it and heaving her to her feet.

Later, as they lay in bed, he rolled away from her. It was as if once he was satisfied he no longer wanted any part of her - she was just a convenience.

She felt his mood-shift so keenly and every time felt hurt by his après-sex dismissal of her. Yet, every time when he wanted her and while they were having sex she felt so desired and needed that she gave in to him always.

He rolled away, stood up and pulled on his clothes. "Party tonight at the house to celebrate Punchestown," he said, slipping his feet into his shoes. "Come when you're ready."

Then with that he nodded politely and spun around, ducking his head as he passed under the low door-frame.

She lay for a moment. He was like a whirlwind that came into her life, leaving her head spinning. She hated parties. What on earth would she wear that didn't make her look like the side of a house? But then if Derry had asked her to go he obviously wanted her there. She hugged herself in delight. Perhaps he really did want her to go.

She went into the yard smiling and happy. The afternoon passed in a blur. She couldn't wait for the day to finish, for the moment when she could lock up the stable yard for the night and get herself ready for the party. She would have to shave her legs — they hadn't seen a razor for weeks and must look like a hayfield — and she would blow-dry her hair — if she did it really well it fell into a pretty style that flattered even her moon-shaped face.

As the last of the grooms disappeared out of the yard, she trotted to the cottage and thundered up the stairs. There was plenty of water so she ran herself a deep bath and filled it with gallons of the lovely bubble-bath that one of the girls had given her for Christmas. She wallowed in the hot water, trying not to give in to the feeling of despair at the mound of flesh that defiantly swelled and moved over the water-line. With her legs shaved and her body scrubbed to a glowing red, she heaved herself out and dried herself on a towel.

With make-up carefully applied and her hair beautifully blow-dried even she was content with the results. Then came the problem of choosing a dress. Most of the things that she had were shapeless tent-things that were more suited to women twice her age, prim things in slimming dark colours with flouncy lace collars. Or there was the dress in bold pink with large flowers that she had once bought in a moment of madness when she had been feeling that she should be content with her size and flaunt it rather than trying constantly to be something that she was not. She pulled the dress out of the wardrobe and laid it on the bed, considering it for a moment. Then muttering, "I'll bloody wear it," she slipped out of her dressing-gown and into the dress. Wriggling to do up the zip, she went to the mirror and gazed at her reflection. The boldly coloured dress neither disguised her size nor made her look bigger. It just said, "this is me. Take me or leave me". She stared for a while. It didn't look like her. It looked like someone confident to be who she was, which was not how she felt. She slipped her feet into the high heels that she had bought at the same time and, deciding that she could linger no more, set off for the big house. The shoes were uncomfortable and the dress-hem was tight, making her walk in short tottering strides.

Every light blazed in the house as she tottered up the short stretch of drive to the front door, which was ajar. Music throbbed from the dining-room, eerie in semi-darkness, lit only by pale, coloured lights that flickered to the beat. She wandered in. The place was crowded with people, some that she recognised from the races and others she didn't. No one paid a blind bit of attention to her, although she did see some woman glance at her and nudge the man she was with. Sarah began immediately to feel out of place and wished that she had worn something a little less conspicuous. She decided to find Derry; he would talk to her since she knew no one else. She wandered through the rooms looking for him, and finally found him in the library. She stood in the doorway. Derry was opposite her, his back to the blazing fire, surrounded by a crowd of people. Standing beside him was a very gorgeous, tall, slender and well-dressed girl and his arm was possessively around her shoulders.

CHAPTER SIXTEEN

"Sarah!" cried Derry from the far side of the room. Everyone turned to look, gazing in her direction. Her dress felt uncomfortably tight and she felt dreadfully conspicuous. She went across the room towards the group of people surrounding Derry. He released the tall blonde and grabbed Sarah's arm as she arrived at his side, pulling her quickly into the circle.

"This is Sarah, my right-hand woman," he announced to the assembled people.

They were all staring at her. JT she recognised from the races and from being in the yard, a bumptious man with a fat cigar who blew an enormous puff of smoke in her direction. His wife, tottering slightly on the ridiculously high heels that she wore and from the enormous amount that she had drunk, smiled with glazed and uncomprehending eyes.

Derry indicated the tall blonde who was looking with undisguised contempt at Sarah.

"This is Ellen, JT's daughter."

Ellen would have made the prettiest and most glamorous woman in the room feel inadequate and she made Sarah fell as if she were a hippo in fancy dress. She was so tall, with the longest, most toned, slender and tanned legs that Sarah had ever seen.

She had a perfect oval face tanned to perfection and highlighted by a platinum waterfall of hair that set off her enormous cornflower-blue eyes and wide pouting mouth. "Do you help in the stables?" she asked disdainfully, looking for all the world as if she could not think why on earth Derry was bothering to fraternise with the hired help.

"Well, I run the stables," stammered Sarah.

"Ah," said Ellen, taking an elegant sip of her champagne, her eyes scanning the room over the top of her glass. There was an uncomfortable silence and then Ellen looked back at Sarah. "What an interesting dress you're wearing," she said, smiling cattily, before adding, "I do think it is marvellous that people who are challenged in the size department have the courage to wear something as bold as that." Beside her Derry almost choked on his drink.

Sarah felt herself blush to the roots of her hair. She felt her mouth drop open and her fingers itched to punch Ellen hard on her elegant nose. Ellen's mother saved the day. Blundering to get another drink she stumbled into a side table, knocking a priceless vase flying.

"Fuck!" roared Derry as with all of the grace of a rugby player he sidestepped and caught the vase before it crashed to the floor. The group burst into uproarious laughter, giving Sarah a chance to escape. She slipped away from the circle of people, close to tears and wishing that she had never bothered to come to the party.

How naive of her to think that Derry ever wanted her to come! She wished desperately that she had not worn this loud dress, wished that she could just disappear. She retreated back into the coolness of the hall. It was deserted — everyone had gone to get food or was dancing in the other rooms. The front door stood open. She could see the burning lanterns that lined the drive - lighting the way away from this hell, she thought. She took a deep breath of the cool air from outside, tinged with the scent of the summer roses and the smell of horses drifting from the stables. No one would notice if she just slipped away, she thought, moving quietly towards the door.

"Hey," said a voice behind her, "where do you think you're going?"

Sarah, recognising the voice, gave a cry of delight and spun around, leaping forwards to fling herself into the outstretched arms of Sean O'Rourke. Sean was one of the nicest jockeys on the racing circuit and definitely the best looking. All of the girls at the stables fancied him like mad.

"You weren't going to creep off without having a dance with me, were you?" grinned Sean, disentangling himself gently from her grasp. "You look great,' he told her, sliding his arm around her waist and dropping a flirtatious kiss on her cheek. He took her hand and led her back into the lounge. Sarah felt Derry's eyes on her as Sean steered her towards the waiter and grabbed two glasses of champagne off his tray.

"Cheers!" Sean grinned, chinking his glass against hers.

Much, much later as she danced to a slow number enfolded in his arms, Emer, one of the grooms, caught her eye and gave her the thumbs-up signal. She was delighted to see Sarah enjoying herself for once rather than mooning around hoping that Derry would give her some attention.

It was almost dawn when the party began to break up.

"Coffee at my place, I think," Sean said, steering her towards his car. "I've waited months to get you to myself."

Heady with champagne and delight at the attention, Sarah got into the passenger seat. She watched the early morning light send pale pink fingers of colour over the landscape as Sean drove her to his cottage. What the hell, she thought. Derry had Ellen now — it was obviously over between them.

It was late evening when Sean finally dropped her back at the stables. "I don't want you to go," he said, sliding his warm hand around the back of her neck and drawing her towards him. "I'll ring you when I get back from the races." He kissed her slowly, then as he drew away grinned with excitement. "I've got the ride on Legally Eagle for Joe Hegarty — he's a brilliant horse."

"Good luck," said Sarah, getting out of the car regretfully. She didn't want to see him go. Spending the last few hours with him had taken away the pain of Derry's brutal rejection. She waved him goodbye and then made her way across the yard.

Derry was standing in the tack-room doorway. Sarah had never seen him look so angry. His eyes blazed with the fire of a rage that threatened to consume him. He looked as if he was about to explode into terrifying violence. His lips, clamped into a tight, furious line, opened as he barked: "I've been looking for you all afternoon!"

Sarah stopped, all joy gone out of the day. A tremble of fear prickled her insides. Then, raking up a courage that she did not know she possessed, she retorted: "It's my day off!" She had never stood up to him before, but now, bolstered by the wonderful day that she had just spent, she would not put up with his tantrums.

For a second she had the satisfaction of seeing him deflate slightly, unused to her defying him.

But he soon recovered and spat, "you should be here! This yard is your responsibility!"

Still determined to stand up to him, Sarah drew herself up to her full height and said firmly: "It's my day off and I am going home now to enjoy the rest of it. I will see you at seven in the morning." And with that she turned on her heel and marched past him, feeling his eyes blazing with fury, glaring at the back of her head.

Next morning, everyone on the yard knew that she had finally got out of Derry's clutches and there were smiles and nudges of delight from all of the grooms. "Good night?" grinned Emer. The heady atmosphere soon disappeared when Derry arrived to find fault with everyone. The violent fury of the previous afternoon had simmered down to an evil temper that sent everyone running for cover. Sarah knew that this display of temper was because she had found herself a boyfriend. Well, why shouldn't she? He had just used her as a convenience and then flaunted his glamorous new girlfriend, Ellen, in front of her. Did he really expect her to put up with that, just hide on the sidelines until he wanted to have sex with her again? Well, no thank you, she mused, determined not to be intimidated by him. It was hard though — he was a glowering presence which was enough to scare anyone.

Finally the day was over and she escaped to the cottage. She was relaxing on the settee clad in her pyjamas and dressing-gown when Derry burst in. Frightened out of her life she leapt off the settee and faced the door.

He came into the living-room clutching a bottle of wine, which he had no doubt plundered from the Westwood Park cellars. He paused in the doorway waving the bottle as if it was a surrender flag and smiled sheepishly. "Drink?" he said and she knew that was as close as she was going to get to an apology for the way he had behaved all day.

She shrugged. "OK." She fetched two glasses from the kitchen, feeling very foolish in her pyjamas and tatty dressing-gown when he was so smartly dressed in well-fitting cords and a beautifully cut hacking jacket.

Derry rummaged around in one of the drawers for a bottle-opener. Sarah felt a prickle of annoyance at the way that he just made himself at home in her cottage. He quickly located the opener, expertly pulled out the cork and left the dusty bottle open to breathe.

As she put the glasses onto the table Derry crossed the room, pulled her into his arms and began to kiss her. She pulled back, fighting against his grip.

"Derry, I don't want this any more!" she said, wriggling out of his grip.

He released her abruptly and stood watching her.

"I'm seeing someone now and so are you," she said, pushing her hair back from her forehead. She felt a hot panic of sweat break out all over her body. Wanting him to go, his presence made her shake and she knew that she could not fight him off — the chemistry between them was too strong. If he kissed her again she would want him and she wanted to be rid of the black rot in her soul that was her passion for him. It was damaging her, making it impossible for her to be with anyone else. And now she had found Sean and he had made it obvious he was interested in her. It would be stupid to mess it up, especially for Derry who repeatedly made it apparent that he only wanted her for one thing.

"Come and sit down and have a glass of wine," he said. He led her slowly into the lounge and sat down on the settee, his long legs sprawling across the floor. She sat at the opposite end and accepted the glass of wine that he poured for her. "Here's to a new beginning," he said, touching his glass to hers.

She sipped the heavy liquid numbly. She was scarcely aware of Derry slithering closer to her along the settee until he gently reached out and took the glass from her and in one movement laid it on the table beside him, put his other arm casually around her shoulder and drew her towards him.

She let him kiss her, his mouth hard on hers, his tongue exploring her mouth, darting, probing. His free hand moved to her breast and she felt herself sliding relentlessly into his sexual power. He rolled away and began to tug at her pyjama bottoms, wrenching them from her in his haste.

Then something inside her snapped.

"Derry, no!" she yelled, wriggling upwards and pulling up her pyjama bottoms. "I won't do this any more! Go to your girlfriend! Leave me alone!"

Derry stopped abruptly and stood up, looking at her coldly. His eyes were like a shark's, impenetrable and violent. His mouth hardened to a thin line. Then without a word he spun on his heel and left the cottage. She heard the door bang and his footsteps crunching rapidly on the gravel path. She felt as though she had been violated. Hot tears spilled down her cheeks, a loud sob tore at her throat and she howled in anguish, desperately miserable and lost. Sobbing, she took the bottle of wine and poured it and the two full glasses down the sink and then ran the water until the heavy smell of the liquid had gone. Then she washed the glasses in scalding hot water, wanting to remove every trace of Derry from the cottage.

The following day only one horse was racing. Derry, curt and icily polite, told Sarah to stay on the yard — one of the stable lads would accompany him. Sarah was relieved - a day with Derry in his present mood would be no fun. Instead, she could watch the racing on the television in the tack room, while she cleaned the saddles.

Derry's horse was running in the third race. Sean, she knew, was riding in the same race. She watched, full of the excitement of seeing him on the television, yet terrified of seeing him race. Suddenly the television presenter announced that there was to be a jockey change. Sean was riding for Derry instead of Joe Hegarty A pang of anxiety clutched at her stomach. What was Derry up to? Why had he taken off the original jockey and given Sean the ride? Her heart thudded uncomfortably in her chest. She knew how Derry worked: he would charm Sean, have him in his pocket, make Sean think he was a nice guy, then use him to his own advantage. And she knew what he would do. Somehow Derry would turn Sean against her. Derry would never let her go.

The race began and she watched, pride tinged with a sense of fear as Sean rode the horse to a brilliant win. She was glued to the screen as the camera panned over the winning horse, the grinning jockey and delighted trainer walking into the winner's enclosure. Then the racing was over for the day.

Sarah switched off the television, unable to shake off the feelings of unease. Later, much later, she heard the lorry return to the yard. Sean should ring soon. The telephone remained ominously silent. The silence filled the house as she willed the phone to ring. She went to bed. Derry had worked his evil.

After three days she could bear it no longer. Sean hadn't telephoned. And Derry hadn't said a word about him. He didn't have to — she could sense the malice in his every movement. Finally she got into her little car and drove to Sean's house. She hammered on the door until it swung open and he stood there, looking at her silently.

"What's going on?" she exploded, brushing past him into the house.

"Derry told me that you're his mistress," he answered grimly. "I am not going to be made a fool of."

Sarah closed her eyes, trying to block out the expression on his face.

"I'm not. Whatever he told you." She prised open her eyes. "Sean —" she began and then in a harsh explosion of movement she shoved past him and bolted back to her car.

What was the use? Derry would never let her go. How could she have any other life than just being his mistress? Blinded by tears, she drove home. Skidding to a halt in the yard she stumbled into her cottage, wanting to lie down under the covers of the bed like a wounded animal and die.

But as she opened the door, Derry uncurled himself from the settee and laid down the glass of wine that he had been holding. She froze as he came towards her.

"Aren't you lucky that you have me?" he whispered, twining a strand of her hair in his fingers. "I will never let you go." Cupping her face in his hands, he drew her towards him.

CHAPTER SEVENTEEN

Tara could not believe that Morgan was pulling the bedclothes off her. It was the middle of the night for heaven's sake! The man was mad. Wincing against the light in the bedroom, which bored harshly into her eyeballs, she peered at the alarm-clock. Six o'clock. In her past life, the only occasion that she was ever awake at this time was when she came home from a party.

"I'll go down and make tea," he said and she listened, curled up under the bedclothes, as he thundered down the stairs whistling tunelessly. She rolled over again. It was impossible to get up. Nothing would move — she was exhausted.

"Tara!" he bellowed from the bottom of the stairs a few minutes later, jerking her awake again. "Your tea is here! I'm going to start doing the horses — hurry up!"

Then the front door slammed and the house was silent. She buried her head under the quilt.

Then, as Morgan went into the yard, the dawn chorus started. The horses, eager for their breakfast, began to whinny and bang on their stable doors, while Morgan was shouting at them to stop and banging stable doors and feed buckets himself. Tara groaned miserably. Grinding her teeth, she slowly pulled herself to the edge of the bed and swung her legs down onto the floor.

Still half-asleep, she dressed and went out into the stable yard.

Kate caught her eye and grinned. "Morning," she said, feeling very superior that she was so bright in the morning while Tara looked so bleary and tired. Tara wandered over to the stable where Morgan was looking at Carna Boy.

Tara scowled. Morgan seemed to spend more of his time with the big horse than he did with her. She and Morgan had a huge argument when she recognised the horse as the one that had escaped from Derry. Morgan had been furious with Derry because of Carna Boy's condition when he was sent to the sales. Tara had defended her brother, offended by Morgan's criticism of him.

She hated the horse. He had nearly killed her when they tried to catch him and she knew that she would always fear the brute.

The horse eyed her ruefully, sensing her dislike of him.

"There's something not quite right about him today," Morgan mused, running his hand over the horse's belly.

Tara only just stopped herself from saying "Good!"

Kate handed her a sweeping-brush and instructed her to sweep the yard. The brush felt heavy and unwieldy and the bristles kept getting stuck in the uneven concrete.

Kate's barely disguised titters of amusement irritated Tara as she struggled.

Then Morgan sent her in to cook the breakfast.

"Well, at least you're good in the kitchen," Kate later commented morosely, hungrily eyeing the bacon and eggs that Tara had prepared.

Personality, Tara decided, was not one of Kate's strongest points.

"You'll have to keep her chained to the kitchen sink." Kate hauled out a chair, sat down and helped herself to toast which she began to devour hungrily.

"I'd rather keep her chained to the bed," grinned Morgan.

Tara had the satisfaction of seeing Kate blush furiously and purse up her wide mouth in temper, with a dark scowl that brought her thick eyebrows together so that they almost met in the middle.

Breakfast eaten, Morgan and Kate took three of the new horses to the races. Tara leant on the gate and watched the lorry slowly lurch down the drive. How had she let Morgan persuade her to remain on the yard? He was worried that Carna Boy, his precious horse, was ill. Tara had shaken her head in amusement at his concerns. He was obsessed with the bad-tempered creature, convinced that it might one day prove to be a superstar. He felt that the enormous quarters, great barrel of a chest and long ground-eating strides would one day give the horse a terrific advantage over his rivals.

She seethed inside. Why did he want her to stay? Why did he not want her with him? Why did he want Kate to go? She had tried very hard to forget the Lynn Moore incident early in their relationship, but sometimes it was hard to trust him. Did he want to be with Kate? Was he just dumping her because he didn't want her around him all day? A myriad of insecurities bounced around in her head with the tiny insidious voice of her ego telling her that it was Kate that he wanted, that he was abandoning her.

"Why not leave Kate?" she had said, trying to keep the panic out of her voice.

Morgan had finished eating and pushed his plate away. "Simple," he smiled at her across the table, reaching for her hand and kissing each of the fingers in turn. "Because I can trust you to look after the horse. Kate would probably drop off to sleep in front of the television or ignore him even if he was lying on his back with his legs in the air. I need you to be here, because you are the one person in the world that I would trust with my horse."

She hadn't really believed him.

She turned away from the view of the lorry swaying down the drive and leant her back against the gate. The horses were all done and the yard tidy for the day. There was nothing that would really occupy the long hours until Morgan came back, sometime late in the evening. There were plenty of things that she could do, like giving the house a real clean, but somehow that did not seem a very inspiring way to spend the day.

Carna Boy, one of the few horses left in the yard, came to his door and looked out, a mouthful of hay between his huge lips. He proceeded to eat the hay like a child sucking spaghetti into his mouth, smacking his lips contentedly and nodding his head up and down.

"Oh yes," she said, crossing the stable yard and peering cautiously over his half-door. "You look really sick!" She jumped back in alarm as the horse tossed his head aggressively, laying his long ears flat against his scrawny grey neck. "Sometimes I think that he loves you more than me," she muttered to herself. She mooched inside. The untidy kitchen depressed her with the cracked draining-board and stained walls and the piles of racehorse paraphernalia. Bored and lonely, she decided to go into town.

We need some food and I really need a new dress, she decided, justifying the expedition to herself as she drove away.

As soon as she drove back into the yard Tara felt a sense of unease sweep over her. Carna Boy hadn't poked his head out of the door to look at who had come like the other horses had. His half-door was ominously empty. Slamming the car door, she sprinted across the yard. Why had she stayed so long?

Carna Boy to her horror was standing in the middle of the box, his eyes rolling in pain. His grey coat was darkened with sweat and he was kicking a back leg at his belly, trying to rid himself of the pain that knotted his insides.

"Oh fuck!" she cried and launched herself towards the house as fast as she could run. She dialled the vet's number, drumming her fingers on the table as it seemed an age passed while the phone rang. "Come on, come on!" she muttered, willing the phone to be answered.

Finally the vet's assistant picked up the phone. Tara explained who she was and that there was a horse sick at Morgan Flynn's yard. The vet's assistant quickly noted her details. "I'll get someone there as quickly as possible," she told Tara.

Tara shot back outside. The horses needed to be fed, but Carna Boy needed to be looked after. For a moment she circled the yard, darting towards the feed room and then back to his box. Finally she decided to feed the horses and then look after him. Hastily she shovelled feed into buckets and quickly darted into each stable giving sections of hay to the horses as she went. Then finally she grabbed a head-collar and went into Carna Boy's stable. The horse was rolling, trying desperately to rid himself of the pain. She stood, trying to stay out of the way of his wildly thrashing hooves, until he leapt to his feet and began to paw the ground looking for another spot to roll, maddened by the agony that tore his insides. Quickly she darted in and managed to drag the head-collar on over his nose. His nostrils heaved with the exertion and panic, his eyes rolling fearfully. She hung onto the head-collar, preventing him from rolling again. She knew from Derry and her father that the best thing that she could do was to walk the horse around until the vet arrived - that might bring him some relief from the pain. She tugged at the head-collar, forcing the horse to walk slowly around his stable.

After what seemed like an eternity she heard the vet's car swish into the yard and gave a gasp of relief.

"In here!" she yelled as she heard the car door slam.

She rushed to the door and saw the vet hastily donning his protective gear of waterproof clothing.

He jogged across the yard. "Bloody hell!" he exclaimed, peering into the box and seeing the state of the horse. He heaved the door open and came inside.

"It's colic," he said after a hasty examination, "and I would say," he added, listening to the horse's heaving belly, "that he has a twisted gut."

His words drove a stake of terror through Tara's heart. Even she knew that was the worst sort of colic and that it was usually fatal for horses.

The vet pushed his stethoscope back into his pocket. "I think the best thing that we can do, the kindest, is to put him down — the horse is in agony." Then, seeing her stricken face, he said, "the only other option is to take him to the Curragh and get him operated on." He stood back to look at Carna Boy. "But I don't think he will survive the journey in all honesty."

"We'll have to speak to Morgan," said Tara as she fished in her pocket for her mobile phone.

Morgan answered on the third ring. He was driving towards home. She could hear the noise of the radio in the background.

"Morgan!" she yelled tearfully over the noise of the bar. "Carna Boy is sick. The vet's here - he wants to talk to you!" Unable to bear the audible sound of his horror which came clearly over the phone to her, she handed the mobile to the vet. She felt tears pricking in her eyes as he explained what was wrong with the horse. Finally he clicked off the phone and handed it back to her. "He'll be here in about ten minutes and will take him to the Curragh straight away."

As he sped away to his next urgent call, Tara paced up and down the yard, waiting expectantly to see the headlights of the lorry coming up the drive. The vet had given Carna Boy a sedative injection and he was in less pain although he still rolled his eyes anxiously. She found sweat-rugs and put them on his steaming body. "Please let him live," she prayed, feeling guilty that she had left him. If he died it would be all her fault. She should never have gone off the yard. Morgan had trusted her and she had repaid his trust by abandoning his favourite horse.

It seemed like forever till the lorry came up the drive and then all hell burst loose. Morgan and Kate jumped from the cab and, pulling the horses from the back, led the stricken Carna Boy up the ramp and shut him in. Morgan told Tara to get into the lorry and then, curtly instructing Kate to look after the other horses, he spun the lorry around and belted back down the drive.

"When did he get bad?" he asked, wrestling the lorry at breakneck speed down the narrow lanes.

"Teatime," she said, justifying it to herself. She had not lied to him, just not told him the whole truth. It had been teatime when she had noticed that he was ill. For the rest of the journey he was silent, lost in his own world, concentrating on getting the horse to the vet's surgery, the only place that could possibly help him, in the quickest time possible.

Halfway there Tara, clutching at the seat to steady herself as the lorry lurched around the corners, ventured, "how did you get on today?"

"Won the three o'clock and had a place in the one before," he said distantly.

She was silent for the rest of the way and he barely seemed to notice that she was there. She was very glad when he finally reached across the lorry cab, seized her hand and squeezed it.

It was very late when they arrived at the vet's hospital and led Carna Boy slowly down the ramp. Tara let out a cry of horror as the great horse stumbled, seeming not to have the strength to support a body so racked with pain. The staff immediately put him on a drip to try to deal with his dehydration. The vet, alerted by his staff, had come back from a dinner dance much to the annoyance of his wife who rarely ever got a full night out as they were usually interrupted by some emergency. He took one look at the sick horse and shook his head.

"I'll do my best," he said, pulling on a surgeon's apron and looking at them with the seriousness of the situation clearly etched on his craggy face, "but I have to tell you I've never seen a horse as bad as he is that has survived."

Tara and Morgan were left in the waiting-room while a kindly vet's assistant took the horse's lead-rope and led him away.

"Oh God," groaned Morgan, sitting with his head in his hands.

Long hours ticked by. Morgan and Tara alternately tried to sleep and wandered around the waiting-room, picking up and then abandoning magazines, unable to concentrate on them.

Seemingly hours later the vet came back. "Well, I've done the operation, but we don't know if it'll be a success or not. Hopefully it will, because otherwise we have to repeat it and, in his condition, it is an absolute miracle that he survived the first lot of anaesthetic. 1 would be very loath to give him another dose."

Much later, as they dozed, the vet's assistant came back into the room. "The operation didn't sort him out — we're going to risk doing it again." Then, pausing by the door, he added, "I have to say I don't give him much of a chance though — he's very weak." Then he retreated into the darkened recesses of the surgery leaving Morgan and Tara alone.

As the first light of dawn threw grey fingers across the surgery waiting-room the vet came wearily into the room. He looked grey with tiredness, dark lines of concentration etched across his brow. Sadly he shook his head. Tara gave a gasp of horror but then he began to speak. "He's alive, but it's not looking good. He has only a fraction of a chance of surviving. I don't hold out any hope for him. We can only wait now."

Morgan sank into the chair, in despair.

The vet continued. "We opened him up and I've untangled the twisted gut and removed a good proportion of it." He shrugged wearily. "All we can do is give him time now."

Morgan and Tara drove onto the Curragh and watched the racehorses being worked and then went to a hotel and tried to eat something. The day passed slowly as they wandered around Naas, looking mindlessly at the shops, lingering for hours in cafes and staring blankly at newspapers. Finally Morgan's mobile telephone rang and he jerked it out of his pocket, fumbling in his haste, and put it to his ear. It was the surgery to tell them that they were wanted back there. Morgan was afraid to ask for news.

Silently they drove back to the surgery. It was deserted, all the mundane business of the day completed.

"This way," said the vet, fetching them out of the surgery and leading them through a long antiseptic-smelling corridor to an outer door that led into a yard. There, looking out over a half-door, looking very sorry for himself but alive nevertheless, was Carna Boy.

CHAPTER EIGHTEEN

"He's looking well," Derry mused, his eyes roaming over the horse's slender and well-muscled body Sarah watched his handsome face. His eyes missed nothing, looking at how the hard muscle was building up on the horse's back and quarters.

"But he's getting sour," he said, running a hand down the horse's front legs. "A few days' hacking out will make all the difference to him."

Sarah, picturing how the horse behaved on the gallops, bucking and cantering, quailed at the thought of him being ridden out on the road. The horse had too much energy; he was too fresh to cope with the discipline of hacking along a tarmac road with the myriad of things that would scare him — like lorries, dogs or plastic bags fluttering in the hedgerow. The horse would be better off with an afternoon in the field — that would improve his temper no end.

"But who will I get to ride him out?" she said patiently. There was no one on the yard other than himself who was capable of riding that horse out on the road.

Derry smiled at her. "You'll have to."

Sarah stamped across the yard in fury. She would lunge the horse before she rode him, which would take the edge off his energy and hopefully some of the mischief out of his system. The grooms were all swigging coffee in the restroom.

"Come on," she said, chiding them into action. "The sooner you get the yard done the sooner you can get off home."

Coffee was drained, cigarettes were crushed out and they went slowly back outside, retrieving sweeping-brushes and wheelbarrows from where they had hastily abandoned them when the clock had slipped around to coffee-break time. "Fetch the horses off the horse-walker, Sean," Sarah told one of the lads, "then bring the next six for their turn." A loud banging suddenly made Sarah jump and she went to the door to see an empty bucket being blown across the yard. The wind had got up and the sky over the woods above the gallops was black and angry-looking. She shivered. There was a storm coming. She went out into the yard to chivvy the grooms along and then sent them off for their lunch. If she was quick she could ride the horse and be back before the rain came. The thought of being caught in that storm was not appealing to her.

Hurrying, she grabbed a heavy nylon lunging head-collar from the peg, unfurled a long lunge-line and pulled a lunge-whip from the rack. She was just clipping the line onto the head-collar when Derry came into the stable, making her jump.

"What are you doing?" he demanded. "I told you to ride that horse!"

Fingers trembling and her mind the sudden blank it always was when he scared her, she spluttered, "he's a bit full of himself so I thought that I'd better lunge him before I take him out on the road. I would hate for him to injure himself if he messes about on the road — the main road can be very busy and he's not good in traffic at the best of times."

Derry let out a snort of impatience. "Well," he drawled, making her redden with indignation, "I would not have had you down as a coward, Sarah. Stop being such a wimp." He took the lunge-line out of her unwilling hands and seized the whip.

Grabbing the horse's reins, he pulled him out of the stable door.

Slowly Sarah followed, looking at the horse with apprehension.

"Come on then. Up you get!" he said, impatiently jerking the reins to make the dancing creature stand still.

She fumbled with the stirrups - the lad who had used the saddle before her had far longer legs.

At that Derry's short supply of patience ran out. "Give me your leg," he snapped.

She stood and faced the horse's saddle, the top of which was high above her head, and lifted her knee so that Derry could take hold of it underneath and give her a leg-up. Suddenly she was launched skywards and landed with a thud somewhat miraculously with a leg on either side of the horse. She just had time to gather up the reins and shove her feet into the stirrups before Derry let the reins go and the horse bounded forwards like a coiled spring being unleashed.

The wind was whipping up the avenue of trees down the drive and the horse marched jauntily forwards, excited and afraid. She gripped her legs hard into the saddle in case he would whirl around and want to bolt back towards the safety of his stable. His whole body felt full of tension and only her legs urging him on and her hands gripping tightly on the reins prevented him from any mischief.

Halfway down the driveway he suddenly spun around, deciding that he did not want to go out on his own — the wind whipped at his body and it was scary being alone. He was used to the comforting company of other horses, of being part of a line of horses who gave him confidence and the courage to venture out of the safe confines of his stable. This was not what he was used to and being alone in these conditions was beyond the limits of his tolerance.

Sarah clung to the saddle and brought his heady flight to a standstill. "Whoa, lad!" she said gently. "It's ok — it's only the wind." She turned the horse back in the direction they had come from and kicked him on. The horse walked unwillingly, every stride an effort.

At the bottom of the drive they turned onto the main road. Sarah felt her heart pounding. Her fingers were white with the effort of holding the reins and her knees trembled with the effort of gripping onto the saddle. Everything felt wrong. Her stirrups felt too long, the girth felt too loose, but she dare not stop to alter anything. The horse would feel her moving in the saddle and that could spark off the flurry of bucking that she was only just managing to prevent.

A car overtook them, making the horse shy into the side of the road and then a short way further on a bird flew suddenly out of the hedge making him shoot to the opposite side of the road. Sarah heaved a huge sigh of relief that there had been no cars coming. She pushed the horse into a trot — the work would make him concentrate and hopefully he would not be so busy looking at what there was to make him scared.

The horse trotted at an alarming speed down the road, his iron-shod hooves slipping and clattering on the shiny tarmac, but then he started up a long hill and the energy he put into the effort made him begin to behave. Sarah began to wonder why she had been so scared. She could manage the horse.

At the top of the long hill she slowed the horse to a walk. He felt calmer now, the tension in his back had gone and she began to enjoy the feeling of riding out on her own. She turned the horse onto a woodland track, riding him into the cool gloom created by the canopy of tall pine trees. The track stretched out ahead into the distance until it merged into nothingness with the trees. The forest stretched out at either side, a green tangle of tree-trunks and mossy rocks and the brown carpet of pine needles. She eased the reins a little and nudged him into a canter. He bounded forward eagerly, keen to stretch his legs, and plunged along the track.

She stood up in the stirrups, enjoying the feeling of his powerful legs pounding along underneath her and the thrust of his muscular quarters powering them along the track. The wind surged in her ears, whistling through her hair and whipping his mane up towards her face. Then, suddenly, seeing something scary, he whipped around like lightning. Standing in the stirrups, she was caught off-balance. The horse, sensing this, had immediately begun to buck and a second later she was off. She managed, through years of training, to keep hold of the reins and pulled him to a stop.

"You out-and-out bastard!" she raged.

Knowing that he was in trouble, he stood quietly. She dusted the mud from her backside; nothing was hurt except her pride. She looked in annoyance around the forest. There was a rock a short way ahead that had a flat top and was a few feet off the ground — that would give her the advantage that she needed to be able to mount. She led him to the rock and climbed on to it, pulling the tight jeans up over her thighs to give herself the ease of movement that she needed. The horse stood, his head up, looking at something miles away. Gritting her teeth, she shoved a toe into the stirrup and scrambled back into the saddle.

He was cock-a-hoop at his skill at getting her off and jogged down the track tossing his elegant head, feeling very pleased with himself. Sarah reverted to pushing him on at a smart trot, keeping her legs hard against his side and a tight hold of his head. He wasn't going to get away with that again. The end of the forest track brought them out close to the main road, which they had to cross to reach a road that brought them back to the yard.

Once they crossed the main road and started on the homeward route the horse recognised his surroundings and began to pull on the reins, eager to get home.

The wind, now that they had emerged from the woods, had got up again and was whipping the trees into a frenzy, making them sway, and the crops in the fields over the hedgerows were flattened, the flailing heads of corn dancing wildly. A storm was coming and the sky was black overhead. The horse could sense the tension in the air, waiting for the moment when the storm would be unleashed and the rain that hung so precariously in the dark threatening clouds would pour down.

With a crash of lightning the storm began and the clouds released the rain which came down in heavy torrents. The horse threw up his head, feeling the heavy drops sting his delicate skin, hurting his fine ears and getting into his eyes. Sarah urged him on into a trot - the sooner they were out of this storm the better. He dashed eagerly forward, plunging for home. Then as a roll of thunder rattled the sky above he reared. His iron-shod hooves danced on the tarmac, slippery with the long hot days and made into a treacherous ice-rink by the sudden rain. His hooves slid, trying to get a grip on the tarmac, legs splaying like a newborn deer. She could feel him sliding, feel that he was going to fall if she did not get him off the tarmac — and then, in slow motion, he fell sideways. They met the road with a crash, Sarah's leg in between the horse's rain-soaked body and the hard tarmac. She felt a spasm of agonising pain as her leg was crushed and she felt the bone break.

She felt the horse struggle to his feet, and a hazy bolt of pain shot up her leg as her foot stuck for a moment in the stirrup-iron. Then she felt a jolt as it slid free. She was aware of his legs above her flailing for a grip and then the sound of him galloping away before she slid into merciful blackness.

She was dreaming about someone asking her questions about when she last ate and a lorry, a man standing over her, his scared face, rain soaking her, an ambulance, sirens blaring, pain, pain everywhere, her leg being moved, bed, a comfortable haven and then peace and Derry looking at her. She smiled in her sleep. Derry was with her. Sighing, she opened her eyes. Derry was there. She blinked at the unfamiliar surroundings. A long line of beds, creamy walls, dull-painted doors and the unfamiliar smell of antiseptic.

Derry was sitting beside her, elegant as always, looking very dapper in creamy chinos and a navy blazer. He folded the racing newspaper that he had been reading painstakingly and then looked at her. "You had a nasty fall," he smiled gently.

Sarah blinked at him, wanting him to lean over and kiss her to show all of the people that were looking at him with open envy that she belonged to him. "He slipped on the road," she mumbled, her voice thick with anaesthetic. "The storm scared him and he slipped. He came down on top of me." She was feeling desperately sick and hoping that she would not be while he was there. It would not be very romantic. "How's the horse? Who found him?" A worried frown creased her face.

"After you fell off him he bolted back to the stable. He galloped up the drive and I heard him and went out and caught him. He has some nasty cuts and grazes all over his side and his legs are raw where he went down onto the road."

"How did I get here?" she asked, racking her brain for any recollection of being brought to hospital, then remembering her dream.

"Some driver found you and telephoned for an ambulance. They told me later that you told them where you worked." He tapped the newspaper on the bed impatiently. "Anyway," he said, "no point in putting this off. That horse should never have been out in that storm." He banged the newspaper on the bed in rhythm with his words. "You should have brought him straight home. I don't see how I can possibly employ someone who has no sense of responsibility and I am going to have to let you go." He got to his feet. "You can collect your things when you get out of here," he added.

The anaesthetic dulled the shock. Perhaps she was still dreaming? She watched him go, his arrogant back straight and proud. Then abruptly she reached for the buzzer that lay on the bed beside her to summon a nurse, "Quick," she gasped. "Can someone get me a bowl — I'm going to be sick!"

CHAPTER NINETEEN

This was a moment that Sarah had never imagined would arrive. She was looking at Westwood Park for the last time. She had asked the taxi that had brought her to collect her belongings to stop at the entrance to the great house and had got out to gaze at it, with the taxi-driver drumming his fingers impatiently on the steering wheel. She wanted to look at the house that she loved so much, the racing stables that she had grown to think of as her domain, her home, for as long as she wanted, now snatched away from her by the one man she adored.

The house in its late summer mantle of flowers and brightly coloured ivy stood at the top of a slight rise and looked out over the surrounding parkland. The beech trees in the avenue were wearing their summer coats of a myriad leaves coloured in every shade of green that in a few weeks would change to bronze. Away from the house she could see the walls that surrounded the stable yard. Her stable yard and her horses - her Magnetic Attraction, the darling horse that she loved so much. Now she did not belong here any longer. It was over; she had to face the reality that she no longer belonged to Westwood Park. That she would never again see Derry or Magnetic Attraction.

Derry had sacked her, in the cruellest way possible when she was lying injured in a hospital bed, because of his stupidity in wanting her to ride a dangerous horse that should never have gone off the yard. He had got his revenge for what he saw as a betrayal: finding herself a boyfriend. He wanted to punish her more in the cruellest way imaginable, by sending her away from Westwood Park and him. She fought back a sob of misery that tore its way up from her chest and began to constrict her throat.

Hampered by the unwieldy crutches that the hospital had given her, Sarah clambered back into the cab and slammed the door. The driver, looking at her in the mirror, frowned and hoped that she would not start crying. She looked so pale and wretched. He was tired and wanted to get home. The last thing that he wanted was a sobbing passenger. He shoved the car into gear and they shot off up the drive.

It was lunch-time when they pulled into the yard and all of the staff had gone home. Sarah had timed it this way to avoid seeing everyone and having to say goodbye. She could not bear their pity. It was best just to go. She directed the taxi-driver into the yard. He gave a low whistle of astonishment as he saw the beautiful surroundings. Sarah saw it all too from his eyes: the beautiful weathered stone and the immaculately kept stables with the forty elegant horses' heads looking out over the half-doors, their eyes alert and curious. Magnetic Attraction gave a low whinny that brought tears pricking once more to her eyes.

The taxi-driver came with her across the yard and into the cottage. There at the bottom of the stairs were her belongings, packed into her own battered suitcase and shoved into a selection of cardboard boxes. Derry must have got one of the grooms to pack up her belongings.

The taxi-driver, seeing her stricken face, said, "You go and sit in the car — I'll bring this stuff out for you. It'll only take me a minute." He shoved one of the boxes under his arm and heaved the suitcase upwards.

Sarah sat in the back of the taxi, fighting back the tears, determined not to cry. She would do that in private; no one would see her pain. Crying did no good; she knew that from the long years that she had been at home with her father, seeing him using her mother as a punch-bag. Now, she thought with dread, she was going back there. Back to the grim house and the rows that would rage long into the night when her father had been drinking

It took only moments to load up the remainder of her possessions and soon they were bumping back down the drive. The taxi-driver stole a look in his mirror and his heart went out to the chubby girl with her face set like an effigy of despair.

Out on the main road the taxi sped through the lanes of Tipperary, hurtling all too fast back to the noisy, smelly streets of Dublin.

It was dark when the taxi finally pulled into Dublin. Sarah wrinkled her nose in distaste at the cloying city smell of car fumes and stale air. Sarah was stiff and her leg ached horribly. She rested her head wearily on the back of the seat. The plaster-cast was digging into her leg uncomfortably, she could feel her toes throbbing and the broken bone ached horribly The lights and the antlike population slid by the window, going on forever, mile upon mile of civilisation and people and cars. Then they turned off the main road and slid into the housing estate where she had grown up. She sat up, her head feeling dull with exhaustion, to look at the familiar landscape. The bus shelter surrounded as always by broken glass, the pitiful stretch of grass in the centre of the houses. A diminutive shaggy piebald pony grazed in the centre of the grass, the rope that tied it to a stunted tree wrapped around its legs.

The taxi-driver slowed, looking at the numbers on the house walls. Most were missing as were the ones at her parents' house, but she indicated to him where he should stop. He pulled up and she sat, not wanting to get out, looking in horror at the house where she had grown up. A brown stunted hedge separated the house garden from the one next door. Buried in the hedge were the remnants of an old discarded washing machine and three bicycles. On the opposite side of the path was a car, propped up on bricks and slowly rusting to nothing. Her father had bought the car with some winnings he had won betting on a hurling match and then had done nothing with it. He had intended to do it up and then sell it for a profit - since then nothing had happened and it had remained in the garden like some shrine to his lack of ambition.

She rummaged in her handbag and pulled out the money to pay for the taxi. The driver manhandled her boxes and suitcase up the uneven path and dumped them against the peeling blue paint of the front door, leaving her to hop painfully after him on her crutches.

Before she had time to knock her mother burst out of the door, her pinched face wreathed in smiles, a bruise under her eye badly concealed with heavy make-up. "Jesus!" she exclaimed, stepping over the boxes to come out and cup Sarah's face in her hands and smother her in kisses. "God, what's happened to you? Come in now!" She heaved up the suitcase, at the same time shoving in one of the boxes with a slipper-clad foot. Sarah noticed that her big toe was poking through the threadbare fabric as she shoved the case onto the dingy carpet and dragged the rest of the boxes into the hallway.

Sarah hopped into the hall behind her mother who was nervously chattering. She trotted down the hall and into the kitchen with Sarah following, the rubber tips of the crutches thudding on the stained lino.

Her mother lit a cigarette and pulled on it nervously. "Thank God you weren't killed — them bloody horses — I'm glad that you're finished with them, so I am," she said, taking a long draw on the cigarette and puffing out the smoke as if her life depended on it. "You can stay here for as long as you want. This is your home." She sounded as if she were confirming the fact more to herself than to Sarah. Sarah noticed that her mother cast nervous glances at the kitchen door and knew that the bruise on her face was fresh. It was probably the result of telling her father that she was coming home.

"It's great to have you home," said her mother who was looking around the kitchen, her eyes unable to meet Sarah's.

Sarah looked at her mother. She was only eighteen years older than Sarah and yet she looked fifty years older. She was as thin as Sarah was plump, her pale faced pinched with tiredness and heavily lined from the amount that she smoked. She had let her hair go its natural grey and it hung in grey frizzy wisps around her high cheekbones with the enormous hollows under them.

"Why don't you get a nice job in a shop? There's a new Tesco's opening on the big estate up the road. They're taking on staff."

Sarah shook her head and gave a wry grin. "The horses are my life, and they're what I'm good at."

Suddenly the two women froze. The front door slammed and heavy footsteps echoed down the hall towards them. The kitchen door was shoved open and Sarah's father stood on the threshold.

He was a tall man, thickset with a heavily jowled face and deep-set, mean eyes. He was twice the age of her mother and twice the size and he bullied her mercilessly.

Any imagined misdemeanour was punished immediately. It was fairly obvious from the way that he was swaying in the doorway that he had been drinking. His red checked shirt and the jeans over which his belly protruded were stained with drink where he had spilled glass after glass of Guinness as he attempted to bring them to his flabby-lipped mouth.

Sarah, seeing him as if for the first time, wondered what her mother had ever seen in him. She had been painfully pretty in photographs of her as a young woman. She had deserved better than this drunken violent man, who terrified her.

"Thrown you out, has he?" jeered her father, drunken spittle flying from his flabby lips in his rage. He was looking for someone to take his temper out on and Sarah, always bearing the brunt of his anger because she tried to protect her inadequate mother, as always got the worst of it. "Them rich bastards always tire of rough trade like you and then they get someone else. So now you're out of a job and having to come back here sponging on me, you fat trollop!"

"She's had an accident - she's broken her leg," said her mother firmly, reaching for another cigarette to give her the bravery that she needed.

"It's OK, Mammy," said Sarah, spinning around to face her father. "Yes, I am back here, but I am not going to be sponging off you. I can pay my own way and I will be off as soon as I can, I can assure you of that."

"Wooo, quite the little madam now, aren't we?" he sneered, his dark eyebrows almost meeting with the scowl that darkened his face. "How did you break your leg? Did he throw you out of bed?"

"Noel," began her mother, her eyes wide with fear, "don't start on her — she's only just come back."

"Shut up!" he bellowed, taking a step forward.

Her mother shrank in fear, hunching her thin shoulders as if to fend off a blow.

Sarah struggled to her feet. "Leave her alone," she said to her father and then, putting a gentle hand on her mother's shoulder, she said, "I can fight my own battles, Mammy - you stay out of them."

Her mother leapt from the table and began to put on the kettle, wringing her hands nervously. Sarah leant on her crutches for support, thinking that if her father came for them she would give him a bash with one of them. She had tried it once before with a walking-stick that she had pinched from her granddad. She had not tried it again though; she carried the dark bruise-marks of the stick across her back for weeks afterwards. But she was bigger now and a lot stronger even if she was hampered by her broken leg.

"I had an accident on a racehorse," she snapped, "if it's any concern of yours."

Bringing herself to her full height, she faced her father, feeling her heart begin to pound. She had spent her childhood being terrified of this man. Old habits were hard to break — just a few years of peace away from him and then within a few minutes he was terrifying her again.

"Racehorse!" he jeered as if astonished by the idea that she could do anything so clever. "I'm surprised that they could find one to carry you!" Then he spat, "Don't stay here for too long, you fat bitch! You're not welcome here!"

CHAPTER TWENTY

Tara tried desperately hard not to laugh as Kate's body did a perfect arc through the air and landed in a heap on the muddy surface of the field. Kate, of course, had been showing off, trying to get Tzar to jump really well for Shane McGrath, the pop star, who was sitting in the Jeep beside Morgan. Kate had parted company with Tzar on the highest part of the jump and had landed with an audible thud.

"Wow," said Shane, peering over the top of his sunglasses.

Morgan was less than amused. Kate had ridden the horse so badly there was no way that he could have made the jump properly. "Fuck!" he snarled, wrenching the car door open and jogging across to Tzar who had stopped some way off and was contentedly grazing. He caught the horse and led it back to Kate who was red in the face with embarrassment and brushing furiously at a dark stain on her bottom. "I should bloody well kick you there," he snapped, pulling the horse to a halt. He legged her back into the saddle. "Do it properly now, for heaven's sake," he growled as she shoved her feet into the stirrup-irons.

He stalked back to the car, hands thrust deep into the pockets of his cord trousers as Kate trotted Tzar back down the field. They watched again as Kate turned him and let him gallop back up towards them, taking each of the three steeplechase fences perfectly, and then canter away into the distance.

Morgan nodded with satisfaction. "That's better," he said to himself, as

Kate slowed the horse to a trot and turned it back towards them. He turned to Shane. "The horse is as ready as he is ever going to be. He'll win you the Kerry National."

"Bold words," laughed Shane. "I hope that you don't have to eat them!"

Morgan began to regret having been so rash. In fact, he was in a frenzy of doubt, which reflected at home. On the yard with the horses he was as confident as he ever was, watching them and handling them with his casual confidence. But at home, he let the doubts surface and became short-tempered and snappy. He was unable to rest, watching the horses all of the time, dreading any recurrence of the illness that had laid Carna Boy off.

Tara was sick of it. She missed his attention and his confidence.

At last, however, the time came for them to leave for Listowel. Everyone was relieved that the moment of truth had arrived. Two horses were going: Wolfhound belonging to Gerry Walsh, which was entered in one of the early races, and Tzar. The racing newspapers had announced Tzar as second favourite. Derry's entry, Sloe Gin, was the favourite.

The Listowel racecourse was packed on the hot autumn day. Women wandered around dressed in short dresses with huge hats, as bright and colourful as butterflies, clutching the arms of the men that accompanied them, wilting in their shirt sleeves, jackets long abandoned.

Inside the weighing room, Josh Drake, the jockey who was to ride Morgan's horses, came out of the sauna as Morgan poked his head around the door.

Tara averted her eyes as he slammed the door shut on half a dozen other jockeys who were desperately attempting to sweat off last night's excesses, all dressed in nothing but towels.

The jockey came out towards them, looking like a skeleton in a horror film as he emerged from the steam, all bones and cadaverous sunken face, the result of constant dieting to keep his weight way below what it should be for his tall frame. He nodded at Morgan morosely.

"Still got some weight to get off," he moaned, shuffling from foot to foot. He had not eaten for three days and was as jumpy as a cricket, twitching with nerves and tension.

"Get back in the sauna then," said Morgan. "The horses are on top form — you'll only have to steer them to win."

Back outside it was time to get Gerry Walsh's horse ready for the race. Derry had just won the first race with Lynn Moore's horse and the press were clamouring for their photographs outside the winner's enclosure. Derry caught Tara's eye and grinned triumphantly. She waved briefly and then hurried guiltily after Morgan. Gerry blustered into the parade-ring, hat askew and shirt open almost to the waist revealing a huge expanse of red, bulging belly covered in dark curling hair that crept over his chest and into the sweaty recesses of his neck.

"Well," he demanded, taking off his hat and sweeping back a sparse head of sweat-dampened hair off his red face, "we have all heard enough bullshit about the pop star's horse - how is mine going to do?"

Morgan, diplomatic and not wanting to commit himself, replied, "the horse is in fine form — he'll do his best."

Gerry had a hospitality box at the top of the stands where he was entertaining a bunch of his business associates. Morgan was dragged unwillingly into the box. He hated this part of the job, but Gerry's horse was as important as Shane McGrath's horse in the big race and he had to spend just as much time entertaining him.

Tara found herself swept away by Breda, Gerry's wife, who was staggering from a tight pair of high heels and too much to drink. They all crowded out onto the balcony to watch the race.

From the beginning, as soon as the starter's flag went down, Wolfhound was in the lead. Tara watched with her heart in her mouth. Josh was going to burn the horse out - he could never keep up the blistering pace on the hard, deadly ground. She caught Morgan's eye across the balcony and he grimaced - she could see the panic in his eyes.

"What the fuck is he doing?" Gerry was roaring, looking one second at Morgan and then next back out onto the course where Wolfhound was lengths ahead of the others and still powering away from them. "He can't keep that pace up! What's the bloody jockey playing at?"

The other horses, unable to keep up with the pace, had fallen far behind. But, relentlessly, they began to gradually catch up with Wolfhound, and soon were breathing down his neck. Gerry, unable to watch, went into the hospitality box muttering under his breath.

"What does he think he's doing?" Morgan groaned. Wolfhound had slowed now and the other horses had caught him up and were galloping alongside him. Morgan gripped Tara's hand miserably and added, "he'll have to pull him up in a minute." But the other horses galloping alongside him seemed to give Wolfhound his second wind and he valiantly kept going — then, as they turned into the home straight, the little horse pricked his ears and began again to outstrip the other horses.

Tara shook her hand free and shot the door back. "Gerry, quick!" she yelled into the box.

Gerry puffed his way onto the balcony just in time to see Wolfhound battle up the home straight to finish where he had started the race: first. Gerry and Morgan let out a collective roar. Tara found herself beneath Gerry's sweat-smelling and very damp armpit as he flung his arms around the two of them and enveloped them in a huge bear hug. She disentangled herself as Morgan and Gerry began to dance a jig around the balcony.

Then the three of them made their way to the winner's enclosure where Wolfhound stood, his sides heaving, with Kate grinning from ear to ear and clapping him on the neck.

After a while, Morgan caught Tara's eye and gestured that they should leave. Kate pulled the horse out of the melee and they followed in her wake towards the lorry. "You had better get Tzar ready for the big race," Morgan told Kate as they reached the lorry. "I'll look after this one." He took Wolfhound's lead-rein and handed her Tzar's and she led him away towards the parade-ring.

After they had washed the sweat from Wolfhound, Morgan led him into the lorry. Tara shut the partition to keep the horse in and then, as Morgan tied his lead-rope, she slid into the section where the horse stood. "You were brilliant," she said, putting her arms around his waist and pressing herself against him, turning her face to his. He bent his head and kissed her, the adrenaline coursing through their bodies, turning them on very quickly.

"I want you," she whispered huskily, pushing her hips against his and feeling the push of his body as he responded to her touch.

"We can't, not here," he groaned as she slowly unzipped the fly front of his moleskin trousers and slid her hand inside. "Tara, I love you," he moaned and then shoved her so that she was against the wall of the lorry. She arched her back with pleasure and then moaned as he opened the front of her wraparound skirt and shoved his hands inside, sliding them around the back, cupping the buttocks left bare by the g-string knickers that she wore. "Oh fuck," he whispered hoarsely, pushing the crotch of the knickers aside and pushing himself up inside her. He lifted her leg and held it so that he could thrust inside her deeper and deeper. She moaned with the glorious sensation as he brought her closer and closer to the release that they both so desperately needed.

It was the most wild, passionate sex that she had ever had, her back banging against the side of the lorry that bucketed wildly in time with the loud groans of pleasure that escaped her lips when his mouth was not pressed against them, biting at them, his tongue halfway down her throat as if they could not get enough of each other. Then with one final thrust he came, lolling against her as if he was a dead weight.

Then, to her horror, Tara heard the sound of slow clapping from the bottom of the lorry ramp and then footsteps coming up towards them. Morgan jumped away from her and dressed himself hastily and she tidied her skirt-front quickly as Derry, looking very amused, appeared at the top of the ramp.

"What a performance," he drawled.

Tara felt an angry blush shoot right to the roots of her hair and felt Morgan bristle with anger beside her. "Half of the stable staff and jockeys were outside listening." "Fuck off," growled Morgan, ducking under the partition. With a laugh of amusement Derry retreated.

Morgan stood on the top of the ramp and watched the arrogant line of Derry's back as he marched back onto the racecourse.

"Come on," he said to Tara, who was feeling very deflated and embarrassed. "We had better hurry - the horses will be in the parade-ring."

He rushed off, making her feel as if she had distracted him from his job and had seduced him against his better judgement. Both of them, Morgan and Derry, had made her feel cheap. She wished that she had not seduced Morgan in the lorry. It was just that the excitement of the race had made her feel incredibly horny. She felt now as if everyone on the racecourse knew what she had been doing and was giggling in amusement at her.

Kate was sullenly walking Tzar around while Shane stood in the centre of the ring, watching the horse. He saw them and waved to them to come over. "'I thought that you had abandoned me," he whined. Like all stars he was horribly insecure and craved the attention that made him feel important.

"Sorry," Morgan said quietly. "I was delayed in the lorry park."

Tara felt awful and just wanted the day to be over so that she could go home.

The race set off, the horses plunging away from the starting flag eager to be off and galloping. Morgan went with Shane to watch the race from the owners' and trainers' stand. Tara felt he hardly seemed to notice whether she was there or not. Feeling very unwanted, she stood a little way away from them.

As the horses rounded the home turn, Derry's horse, Sloe Gin, was well ahead of the others having drawn ahead two fences from home. Tzar was amongst those following him. Sloe Gin was powering away, looking as if he was going to be a clear winner. Tara craned her neck around to catch a glimpse of Derry, whose face was enraptured as he watched his horse cruise home. The crowd went wild, cheering and roaring the horse's name as it surged over the final fence.

Then a stride further on Sloe Gin seemed to trip, his legs sprawling in every direction like Bambi on ice. The jockey, unable to stay with the horse, was pitched tumbling onto the rock-hard turf while the animal scrambled to its feet. The other runners surged past. Tzar shot forwards and just put his nose over the finishing line first.

There was a cheer of delight for the thrilling finish. As everyone surged forward to collect winnings or watch the horses parade for the next race Tara saw Derry, his face drawn with disappointment, begin to walk across the enclosure while everyone who knew who he was stopped to give their commiserations. Tara felt her heart go out to her brother, but Morgan grabbed her arm and pulled her along as he dashed delightedly to the winner's enclosure to claim his prize.

After spending a time in the bar with a delighted Shane McGrath and a frenzied Gerry Walsh, Tara and Morgan made their way back to the lorry. On the way they had to cross through a stream of lorries and horseboxes that were crawling slowly towards the exit.

"Hang on a minute," Morgan said suddenly and he dashed across the road and wrenched open the door of Derry's lorry. "At least this jockey didn't get unseated off the other Blake ride," he jeered maliciously at Derry, tapping his own chest.

He laughed delightedly all the way home about this witticism, but Tara was stinging with embarrassment and resentment.

CHAPTER TWENTY ONE

This was not, Tara thought miserably, her ideal way of spending a Saturday night. Morgan had gone to the races with Kate leaving her yet again with the enormous responsibility of looking after Carna Boy. The huge horse was turned out in the paddock beside the cottage to recover and could not have looked better. The vet had told Morgan that the horse would need months off before he could begin work again.

He was terribly phobic about leaving the horse unattended just in case something should go wrong, after his near-fatal illness. Tara heaved a huge sigh of annoyance. It was awful to be left alone while he went off enjoying himself at the races. After what had happened last time she had gone away she did not dare have a night out, even though she deserved one. There was evening racing on at the Curragh and that would not finish for at least another hour and then Morgan still had to make the long journey home. Having to stay here, bored and lonely, just to look after the malicious, ugly Carna Boy! She picked up the remote control to the TV and began idly to flick through the channels - channel after channel of awful films and mindless quiz programmes.

A dreadful quiz programme ended and the announcer came on to announce, with what Tara felt was a really malicious grin, that the film of the week was about to start. A real oldie in black and white. Tira gave a snort of disgust and zapped the set off.

Drumming her fingers on the settee she wondered what to do with herself for the evening. Finally she decided that a long bath and an evening spent pampering herself would be the best thing to cheer herself up.

The bathroom upstairs had been newly painted before the novelty of decorating had worn away, and had fresh brand-new curtains in billowing muslin floating from a very expensive pole that she had bought in an exclusive interior-design shop in town. She was pleased with the bathroom. It had come out exactly as she had envisioned it, very feminine and creamy and totally impractical for a man who spent his life getting muddy and covered with straw. A chaise lounge that she had found in one of the barns around the back had been dragged out and cleaned up and then re-covered. It now graced one of the walls of the bathroom with silk cushions in bright colours beautifully arranged along its back. Beside the bath a collection of expensive pots of assorted sizes and height were filled with bath salts and coloured pebbles. Morgan had already managed to break one of them with a clumsy boot.

Tara turned on the taps and, before drawing the curtains, looked out over the fields. She paused, admiring the gorgeous red sunset over the trees that crowned the top of Westwood Park which lay in a hollow, just out of sight. The whole sky was red, great swathes of red and black that seemed to move and sway against the dark above it. Then with a jolt of horror she realised that was not where the sun would set. Fear clutched at her stomach, making her mouth dry with horror. Something was terribly wrong. She ran downstairs to the telephone and quickly punched in the Westwood Park number. For long moments nothing happened, just the mocking ring of the telephone echoing into the silent hall. No one was there. Derry must have gone to the races.

Grabbing her car keys from the kitchen table, she dashed outside and wrenching the door open leapt into the driver's seat. With fumbling fingers, she shoved the key into the lock and turned it - the engine fired. She shoved the car into gear and it shot forward. She skidded to a halt outside the yard gate and leapt out, heaving back the heavy gate and then dashing back to the car. She shoved her foot on the accelerator too fast and stalled the engine. Cursing, she started it again and shot down the drive, onto the road, driving at breakneck speed towards Westwood Park. She hurtled up the drive. From the direction of the stables she could see smoke billowing down the avenue of trees towards her, long grey wisps that swirled amongst the tree-trunks in the gathering dusk.

The barn behind the stables was on fire. From behind the quadrangle of the stables came the smell of burning straw. Thick black smoke billowed over the stable yard, curling over the slate roof and sliding down into the stables where it lingered, making the air as thick as a fog. It was hard to breathe in the heat and smoke. With horror she realised that the wind was shifting, bringing the flames closer to the stables.

She ran to the far end of the stable yard. Where were all the grooms? Why wasn't Derry here? He would know what to do. The horses were pacing in their stables and the air was filled with their anxious whinnies. At the far end of the yard she could see the barn - what was once an open-fronted building piled high with hay and straw and shavings was being consumed by the grasping tongue of red and gold flames. The heat was stifling even from where she stood, the heavy metal supports of the barn warping in the heat. Huge fireballs of burning hay were billowing up into the air, taken by the wind, and landing all around the back of the stable yard. And she was the only one here to deal with it. She leant against the cool wall of the stable yard, gasping in the smoke, her heart pounding painfully against her ribs. She had to think. Had to do the right thing. Get the horses to safety.

Panting she ran to the tack room. The door of course was locked; inside she knew was the telephone. She wrenched at the door, sobbing in frustration, sweat beginning to trickle down her back. Where was the spare key? She hastily searched, harsh sobs of panic and fear slipping from her dry mouth, lifting the flower-pots that Sarah had quaintly arranged at either side of the door. Sobbing with relief, she found the key at last. She shoved it in the lock, her fingers clumsy with haste, then the key turned and the door swung back. She snapped on the light — thankfully it was still working — and dashed across to the telephone and dialled the emergency services.

She ran back outside. She had to get all of the horses out of the stables and away from the fire. The wind was stronger now, the flames visible high above the roof, flickering relentlessly closer. Soon it would begin to burn the age-old stables that had held generations of Blake horses. She pulled open the door to one of the stables, swung it back as far as it would go and darted inside. Smoke filled the stable and the heat was stifling. She gasped with the effort. The horse stood at the back of the stable, his outline clear in the darkness. He was quivering in fright, whinnying his terror, his eyes rolling in panic. "Get out of here!" she yelled, waving her arms and dashing at him, but the horse stood impassively, not wanting to leave the one place he felt safe.

Weeping with frustration she ran out of the stables. The horses would die if she could not get them out. She fetched an armful of head-collars from the tack room, and ran back to the stable. The horse let her put a head-collar over his head, but he would not come out of the stable. The smoke billowing around the yard and the noise terrified him, and although she tugged on the rope with all of her might he would not follow her.

Then with relief she saw the headlights of the Derry's car coming up the drive and heard sirens. Derry was home and the fire engine was following him. She ran out onto the main drive. Derry pulled the car onto the grass out of the way of the fire engine and leapt out.

"What's on fire?" he yelled at Tara.

"The barn!" she screamed.

He directed the fire engine to the end of the yard. "We need to get these horses out," he yelled above the roar of the fire.

Anna, the new groom, climbed from the cab, rubbing her eyes sleepily. "What's happening?" she said, looking around her. She was very drunk.

"Stay here," Derry snapped. She would be worse than useless in the crisis. He grabbed a handful of lead-ropes and head-collars from Tara and they ran side by side into the yard.

Everything would be all right now that Derry was here and in control, thought Tara.

Later they sat in the quiet kitchen of the house. The horses grazed in the paddock in the darkness, still in the rugs that they wore in the stables. They careered around, delighted to be outside and have the unexpected freedom. In case the fire flared up again and drifted towards the garden cottage Anna had been given one of the guest bedrooms to sleep in. The firemen were still outside, to damp down the fire and to check that it would not start again.

Derry sipped his whiskey and laid it down. He ran a distracted hand through his tangled dark hair, leaving a dark smudge of smut on his damp forehead. "Thank God you were here," he said, reaching for a cigarette out of a crumpled pack. He lit the cigarette with fingers that trembled. "Heaven knows what would have happened if you hadn't come — any longer and the whole yard could have gone up in flames." He shuddered at the thought.

"I just saw the fire out of the bathroom window," she said, adding, "Oh shit!" as she realised that she had left the bath running and the gate wide open. Morgan would be home by now and would be furious. "I must go," she said, pushing her chair back. Derry stubbed out the cigarette after taking only one drag of it and pushed it away with distaste. "Don't go," he pleaded. "I can't manage without you here! That bloody new groom is useless."

"Why don't you get Sarah back then?" said Tara, pouring herself another finger of whiskey to bolster herself up to face Morgan's wrath.

Derry snorted, "No way!" Once Derry had made a decision he stuck by it. He never changed his mind.

"I really hate the thought of you living with Morgan Flynn," he said, spitting out Morgan's name. "You deserve better than living in some hovel with a two-bit trainer like him!" His eyes scanned her face.

Tara looked at her brother. He looked pinched with exhaustion, his handsome face patched with dark smudges from the fire. She looked around the home that she loved and her brother, feeling torn between the two men that she loved the most in the world.

She set out to drive back to Radford Lodge, numb with exhaustion. It was almost two in the morning. The hay under the barn still glowed and crackled but the fireman sitting in his cab was keeping a watchful eye on it in case the fire billowed up again in the light wind that could fan the flames back into life. As she pulled into the yard at Radford Lodge the downstairs light still burned. Feeling guilty that she had not telephoned Morgan, she walked up the path and into the house.

"Where the fuck have you been?" raged Morgan, appearing suddenly in the doorway and startling her so much that she jumped back.

"There was a fire at Derry's," she said. "I had to go and help."

Morgan stepped back and she walked into the kitchen, looking in horror into the lounge. Morgan silently stood beside her, watching her take in the damage that had been done. The bath upstairs had overflowed and flooded the floor, which had collapsed, bringing water and plaster cascading into the lounge, covering the whole room in debris.

"I got back and you weren't here," he said peevishly. "The yard gate was open and then I came inside to this." He waved his arm in the direction of the damage. "I didn't know where you were."

"I just went to Derry's — I had to go — there was a fire," she said, seeing the cold hard look that had come over his face. He seemed to be slipping further and further away from her with every second. She wanted to take him in her arms and tell him how sorry she was but, tired and frightened now, she became angry and defensive.

"You must have known that was where I would be," she snapped, looking down at her filthy clothes, aware of the smell of smoke and sweat from her.

"You could have telephoned," he snapped, pouring himself a glass of whiskey. "I was frightened — I didn't know where you were or what had happened."

"Oh Morgan," she said softly, wanting to step forward and put her arms around him, but he seemed so cold, so unapproachable, as if his whole person had disappeared behind an impenetrable sheet of armour.

He snorted, knocking back the glass of whiskey. "You and Derry are so alike - you only ever think of yourself, never anyone else!"

Suddenly, something within her snapped. Tired and weary she flounced from the room. "That's not true and you know it!" she yelled, spinning around to face him as he leant impassively against the wall. She noticed that there was plaster in his hair — she longed to pick it out, to bath him, to wash his hair as she so often did, to wash every inch of dirt from him, to wash away the anger and make everything all right. But the bath was upended in the lounge, leaning incongruously against the soaking settee. On impulse she grabbed her keys from where she had thrown them as she walked in. "Well, sod you then," she snapped, and stalked back to her car. She assumed that he would follow, that he would kiss her and that later they would laugh about the incident. But he did not come.

She reached her car. Still he did not come. She had no choice but to get into the car and drive away. He would come around. She drove back to Westwood Park, still fuming. Derry was still awake. Unable to sleep, he was watching old re-runs of the Cheltenham Gold Cup. He lay on the settee, feet up on the coffee table. "Tara! How lovely to see you again," he said nonchalantly. "I told you it wouldn't last, didn't I?"

CHAPTER TWENTY TWO

Tara woke. She lay for a moment, thinking that the whole dreadful scene had been just a nightmare. But then she realised with an awful jolt, as the previous night swung into reality, that it was true. She groaned miserably and rolled onto her back. Derry of course, was delighted that she had fallen out with Morgan. She had heard him chuckling to himself as she had walked up the stairs when she had returned from that awful scene. Perhaps now Morgan would be missing her. Surely the whole miserable scene had been a result of fear and tiredness? She would go later and sort things out with him.

Derry was deeply engrossed in the pages of the racing newspaper and did not even look up when she went into the breakfast-room. Silently she helped herself to breakfast and sat down. Only then did he lay down the newspaper.

"Tara," he said in delighted feigned surprise, "how lovely to see you at breakfast time! Are you back for good or is this just a surprise visit?"

She had intended to try to be very cool and nonchalant, but she could feel her temper rising. Slowly she said with a fixed smile, "just a flying visit," then adding tartly. "Just a bit of a misunderstanding."

Derry's mobile telephone rang and he snapped it on. Tara listened as he arranged for a new barn to be erected. "I have a load of hay flying in from the States," he told Tara, snapping off his telephone. The fire-damaged barn and the loss of the hay had not even fazed him - he had merely ordered everything new. For Morgan to suffer a similar loss would mean complete devastation, but Derry always came up smelling of roses.

"Now where were we?" he said.

"I said it's just a bit of a misunderstanding — I'm going back to Morgan in a little while,'" she snarled, feeling that if Derry said any more she would thump him.

"I see," he said sarcastically and then picked up the newspaper and began to read again.

Tara glared at the top of his head with a mixture of frustration and hatred.

After breakfast she got into her car and drove to Radford Lodge, filled with longing for Morgan. They would soon patch things up, he would see how much he loved her and then everything would be all right again! They were so good together that he had to forgive her. Tonight she would lie in his arms and all of the unpleasantness would be forgotten. She drove into the deserted yard. Trepidation knotting her stomach, she went across to the house. How long would it take him to get over being mad at her?

As she walked up the path the front door swung open and Morgan stood in the doorway. He was silent, his face devoid of all emotion, and his dark eyes as cold and dead as a shark.

"Hello," she smiled. This was where he took her into his arms and told her how much he had missed her.

He looked at her wordlessly, his eyes roving over her face. Finally he spoke and it was as if she was listening to a stranger. Neither the voice nor the words seemed to belong to him. "Tara," he said in a hoarse voice, "this is never going to work."

"What?" she spluttered, the force of his words throwing her completely. This was a scene that she had never imagined in a million years. He was telling her that it was over.

"I love you to bits, Tara," he continued, "but we are too different. We are a world apart — you are spoilt, rich, you have no sense of responsibility. We have to end this before we hurt each other more."

"No!" she exclaimed, feeling all of the breath go from her body. "Morgan, no!" Then she looked past him and noticed her cases neatly-stacked at the foot of the stairs. He turned, seeing where she was looking and went and picked up the cases. He lifted them outside, laying them on the path. Then he straightened up. His eyes met hers and when he spoke his voice was harsh and cold. "I will always love you, but this will never work." Then abruptly, without giving her a chance to reply, he spun on his heel and went inside. The door slammed shut, leaving her outside with the cases.

For a moment she stood, her cases on the path where he had dumped them. He was gone. Only the horses looked over their half-doors, interested in seeing what was happening. She wanted to beat at the door with her fists, to make him see sense. What if they were a world apart? They still loved each other. It would work. Damn him for his pathetic excuse! He was too weak to even try to make it work. I can't help being Derry's sister, she thought peevishly, scowling at the peeling paintwork of the front door.

She returned to Westwood Park. Derry had gone to the races and the house was empty. She was relieved. The last thing that she wanted was to have Derry around crowing over her.

When Derry came home she was slumped in front of the television, miserably swigging her way through a bottle of wine that she had plundered from the cellars.

"Tara!" he yelled, grinning with delight, throwing himself down on the settee opposite her and reaching for the bottle of wine to read the label. "Hmm, I see that you have not lost your taste for the expensive." He wriggled to his feet and went to the cupboard to fetch a glass. "That is a seventy-year-old claret that you are swilling like children's pop!" He helped himself to a glass. "That would be about 200 a glass if you had it in a restaurant." He took a deep swig of the wine and rolled it around his mouth appreciatively. "Wonderful," he said dreamily. "Now what shall we drink to — my success today or your homecoming?"

Tara scowled; waiting for him to start making fun of her, but for once Derry was in a kind mood and did not mock her.

"My homecoming, I guess," she muttered.

"Ah well," he said generously, "that's how love goes, my dear!" He drank reflectively and then said, "Tara, since our parents were killed, you've been rushing around like a demented thing, getting into nothing but trouble, taking up with the wrong sort of people and doing yourself no good at all." He stopped to take another slug of the claret before continuing. "This is a suggestion, only that. Why not stay here? Help me with the stables and the horses. Let me find you a nice man."

Derry, true to his word, introduced Tara to every eligible bachelor that he knew. Time and again she found herself at a party, wedged in a corner with some complete dork who talked as if his mouth were full of plums.

At the Westwood Park Christmas party he wandered over with an arrogant-looking blonde glued to his side. "Tara," he announced with a smile, "I would like you to meet Ellen. She is JT and Sue's daughter."

Tara smiled a polite greeting to the icy blonde and wondered how two people like JT and Sue could have produced such a glamorous offspring.

"Now that you're home, you can look after the stables over Christmas," he continued, "I'm going to take Ellen away for a few days."

Tara was stunned into silence at his nerve. She had only just come home, he had told her how he was going to look after her and now he was announcing that he was going to take Ellen away for a holiday. She was speechless with shock and anger. That was typical of Derry — he didn't care for anyone else but himself.

Derry left a few days later with Ellen. Tara watched the car disappear down the drive and felt a huge wave of loneliness seep over her. Christmas alone.

Christmas Day came and went. Tara watched the television and opened her presents, shivering with a cold that seeped into her bones from the misery of being alone. How could Derry leave her when he knew how upset she was? How could she ever have let Morgan go? She should have fought harder for him, she should have begged and pleaded with him not to give up on the relationship but now it was too late.

Late on Christmas Night the telephone rang and she snatched it up, hoping that it would be Morgan telephoning to see how she was, to wish her a Merry Christmas. Heart pounding she put the receiver into her ear. "Hello?"

"Oh, Tara!" said a surprised voice. It was Sarah.

Tara was so disappointed that she could not speak.

"I was ringing to talk to Derry," Sarah said.

"He's not here."

There was a silence and Tara could feel Sarah's sadness at the other end of the line.

Then she heard her sobbing. "Tara, I miss him so much!" she wailed.

The following day, Tara was so miserable at being alone that she went off to watch the hunt that was meeting nearby. Everyone in the district had turned out to watch the spectacle. The meet was at the hunt kennels. Horses and riders jogged down the road towards the venue, abandoning boxes and lorries in every available spot where the road widened or where there was a safe spot of grass verge. Chaos surrounded the kennels as riders and lorries tried to cram into the courtyard and spectators pushed to get in to watch the hunt going off. The Hunt Master spotted her from his lorry and wound the window down, mouthing something, which she could not hear above the commotion of honking horns and clattering hooves.

Inside the courtyard, horses milled around as their red-faced riders, hot in the unexpectedly warm weather and full of yesterday's festive spirit, tried to control them and at the same time take glasses of hot port from one of the ladies on the committee who was handing them out from a precariously balanced large silver tray. The Hunt Secretary was shoving through the melee, her voice becoming more and more high-pitched as she tried to collect the hunt cap from the riders. Even the old Hunt Chairman was riding, perched dangerously on a black cob, looking like Humpty Dumpty, all big belly and tiny short skinny legs.

Tara accepted a glass from one of the ladies and found a mince-pie thrust into her hand. From beyond the courtyard came the sound of the hounds baying excitedly.

"The Huntsman's gone to let them out," said a tweed-dressed gentleman close to her.

The horses and riders parted like the sea as the Huntsman rode into the courtyard.

Cameras flashed as spectators grabbed the chance to take pictures of the famous Huntsman and his hounds framed under the arch that had been built by his ancestors a hundred years ago. Then through the courtyard they clattered, the hounds ignoring the spectators and making straight for the trays of drink and mince-pies, which they quickly upended and scoffed in seconds. The Whipper-in, looking harassed, cracked his long whip expertly and the hounds shot off in the wake of the Huntsman down the long drive, their sterns waving proudly.

Tara joined the spectators that were following the hunt on foot, telling herself that she would just watch for a little while. It was better than being in the empty vast house alone, even if it did mean tramping through fields of mud. At the top of the kennels' drive a small contingent of anti-hunt people was waving banners. No one took any notice of the smelly band dressed in brightly coloured baggy clothes with their hair mangled and knotted into bits of ribbon. Even the hounds lifted their arrogant noses disdainfully.

Tara trudged down the road in the wake of the riders and turned into the field gateway where the horses and riders halted while the Huntsman put the hounds into a small piece of woodland. The Huntsman galloped dramatically up and down the side of the cover shouting to the hounds, while the Whipper-in, equally dramatic, leapt his bay horse backwards and forwards over an enormous wall to make sure that the fox did not come out of the woods. Tara positioned herself on a small rise in the ground to watch the action. Suddenly the Whipper-in let out a shriek as he saw the fox slipping away from the woods. The Huntsman spurred his horse on, yelling to the hounds. The hounds spilled out of the wood and streamed over the wall. The Huntsman paused for a second to give them time to get over the wall and then charged his horse at it. The horse leapt over and then he was away galloping flat out over the fields.

The master charged after them, his horse leaping over the wall like a racehorse. The rest of the riders followed him. The Secretary's horse floundered into the wall levelling it to a heap of rubble. There was a collective groan of horror – some wanted to jump the wall, others were glad that it had been knocked down. Tara watched half-enviously half-glad she was not hunting.

As the riders disappeared into the distance she turned to go home. She was not, she decided, going to spend the day tramping through the fields following the footprints left by the hunt like the other foot-followers would do. One glimpse of the hunt was enough for her. She began to walk back down the hill and then stopped. A bunch of riders was joining the hunt late. They trotted through the field, smiling and calling out to the foot-followers. Then she saw the two riders at the back of the group, riding close together, laughing and smiling. A man and a woman. Tare saw the woman reach out to touch the man's thigh, to get his attention. He turned to look at her, smiling into her face. Then something made him look up the hill. Tara met his eyes. It was Morgan and his laughing companion was Kate.

CHAPTER TWENTY THREE

Sarah threw down the telephone receiver. Derry was a total bastard and she hated him with a vengeance. Yet even though she hated him so violently she still found herself thinking about him constantly. Even seeing her jodhpur boots gathering dust by the back door reminded her of him. Sometimes too, she found herself drifting off into her imagination seeing the beautiful house and stables in her mind's eye and worse still, when she lay in bed at night, she could almost feel Derry beside her, feel the length and hardness of his body, his thighs stretched along hers, his muscular arms holding her tight. That was the worst of the memories, and the most persistent, refusing to be erased.

It was the constant thought of him that had brought her irresistibly to the telephone, just to hear his voice. Stupidly she had expected him to be pleased to hear from her. Stupidly she had expected him to say that he could not manage the yard without her, that no one was as good as she was and that she must come back, that he had just been too proud to ring her.

Then finally the phone had been answered and Tara had said softly into the receiver:

"Hello, Westwood Park." Sarah could hear the hope in her voice that it might, just on the off-chance, be Morgan. She remembered from speaking to her weeks before, at Christmas time, how upset she had been that they had split up.

"Could I speak to Derry please?" she had said this time, after they exchanged pleasantries.

After a moment she had heard Derry coming to the telephone, his footsteps echoing on the stone flags of the long corridor, coming into the office and then the creak of his chair as he sat down.

"Hello," he snapped.

"Derry, it's Sarah," she had said, sensing his impatience and his unwillingness to talk to her, and she wished already she had not rung. "I just wondered how things were on the yard. How is Magnetic Attraction?" In the background she could hear the leather armchair creak and heard papers rustle as he reached for something to look at while talking to her. "Everything is fine here. Thank you for your concern," he said sarcastically.

She heard the chair creak as he stood up, ready to put the phone down.

"Magnetic Attraction is fine," he added cruelly. "My new Head Groom has got him looking in tip-top form."

Sarah just about managed to turn her snort of rage into a cough.

He continued, "Are you going to watch the Gold Cup at Cheltenham?"

She took that for an invitation, "Well, of course," she said excitedly. "Will you need any help?"

He laughed. "Well, if I find that I cannot manage without you I'll let you know." A moment later he said goodbye and severed the connection.

She sat by the telephone, wishing that she had not rung him. Wishing that she had the strength to just walk away and forget all about bloody Derry Blake and his horses. But it was so hard.

The front door banged shut with a force that made all the windows rattle and the curtains billow in the draught created. She heard her father stamping down the passageway into the kitchen and then listened as a row began almost immediately. The fridge door slammed and then he roared in temper, "Where's the bloody milk?" Through the paper-thin walls she could hear the tremble in her mother's voice as she replied, "Sarah and I just had the last for a cup of tea. She was going to fetch some more from the shop in a minute — she was just making a telephone call."

Then came her father's voice, raised in anger and Sarah trembled with the anticipation of another terrible row. "You lazy pair of bitches!" he roared. "Hanging around the house all day and you couldn't even get off your arses to get a drop of milk!"

She heard a chair scrape against the floor as he dragged it out of the way to get at her mother, who let out a fearful wail, and then she heard the dreadful sound of his hand slamming into her and then pitiful weeping.

Sarah could listen no longer. She stormed into the kitchen, not knowing what she was going to say or do, knowing only that she could not bear to have her mother treated in this way again.

As she went into the kitchen her father barged past her, pausing only to grab hold of her shoulder and drag her towards him so that her face was inches from his. She could smell the sour whiskey and smoke on his breath and all that she could see was the contoured form of his mouth as it opened and closed over a ragged brown row of teeth and a yellow-encrusted tongue, as he said quietly, "the sooner you are out of this house the better." He pushed her away abruptly so that she landed with a thud against the door and then he shoved past her and marched out of the house.

For a moment all was silence. Then Sarah looked into the kitchen with horrified eyes. The dinner that her mother had been preparing was strewn all over the worktop — potatoes ready to be cooked swam in water that dripped steadily off the counter and mingled with the frozen peas and the chops that had been smashed to the floor when he had lunged at her. Her mother was cringing, frozen to the spot against the cooker and then slowly she groped her way forward, pulled out a chair and sat down with her head in her hands. Sarah could see an ugly red bruise which she could not hide with her outstretched fingers, already colouring her high elegant cheekbones.

Silently Sarah knelt down, picked up the chops, washed them and put them back onto the grill pan. Then she scooped up the peas and potatoes, shoved them into the bin and threw yesterday's newspaper onto the floor to soak up the water. When finally she could do no more, she pulled out a chair at the end of the table and looked at her mother, biting back bitter tears. Her mother was only in her forties, but she looked like an old woman. Her hair was grey now that she had stopped caring about her appearance. She looked haggard and bent with worry, her once-beautiful face lost in harsh lines from the stress of living with a violent and aggressive bully.

"Why do you stay with him?" Sarah asked quietly.

Her mother raised her head, resting it on one open hand so that the fingers covered the worst of the bruise that she had just received. She looked at her daughter with sad grey eyes and, twisting her mouth into a grimace of a smile, said sadly, "I am too old now to have anything different. He is a good man under all of that - it's only when I get things wrong that he flies off the handle . . ." She rubbed absently at the bruise, which was now closing one of her eyes, before adding with a sad sigh, "It was all my fault - I should have got the milk so that there was some here when he came back . . ."

She reached across the table for her cigarettes, pulled one out and lit it with fingers that shook so much that it was hard to join the cigarette to the flame.

"I'll get the milk, Mammy," Sarah said, getting up from the table and feeling in her jeans pocket for money.

Then, as she turned to leave the room, her mother raised her head and looked at her, the livid bruise clearly visible on her face. "It makes it worse you being here — you just rub him up the wrong way," she said quietly, her voice breaking at the thought of telling her much-loved daughter that she had to go.

Sarah stopped in her tracks. She wanted to tell her mother to come with her, to pack her case and get the hell out of this life. The words formed on her lips, but instead, she said, "I'll sort somewhere out tomorrow and be off"." She knew that she had enough to do to make her own life — her mother was beyond help. She was like an addict, hooked on the violence that her father provided.

Later that night Sarah heard him return when she was in bed. She buried her head under the pillow to block out the sound of their making up, his words of apology, her mother blaming herself, apologising, telling him that she was useless and that she would try harder not to make him annoyed with her. And then the noisy reunion and their lovemaking, the bed squeaking, her mother's groans and his grunts of pleasure. Sarah felt sick. Retching, she shoved the bedclothes back and shot to the window. She wrenched it open and leant out, breathing in the night air, thick with petrol fumes and the smell of the city, but at least the noise outside of the traffic on the main road and barking dogs and wailing children on the estate drowned out the dreadful sound of their noisy lovemaking. She did not belong here; she could do nothing to help her mother.

She woke before the orange dawn crept slowly over the sleeping city and lay in bed thinking. As the first cars began to leave the estate when the early morning commuters headed off to their jobs, long before her parents were awake, Sarah shut herself into the lounge with her address book and began to make telephone calls. A few months ago she had been offered a job running a yard in England. A racing trainer called John McVie had seen how well she had done with Derry's horses and was very interested in her running his stables. He had given her his telephone number in case she ever wanted a job. This was this man she telephoned first.

"I'm sorry," he said, when she explained that she was looking for a job. "I've just set someone on."

Disappointed, she thanked the trainer and prepared to put the phone down. "Wait a minute though," he said. "I know of someone who's looking for a good groom. It's in a showing-yard though, getting horses ready to go to shows. Someone of your capabilities will find it a piece of cake. There's a mobile home to live in. If you're interested I could ring and see if the job is still vacant and call you back." Sarah tentatively agreed. Showing horses were not really her cup of tea, but it was a job, in England, far away from her parents and Derry. A chance of a new life.

True to his word John McVie rang back a few minutes later and gave Sarah a telephone number. "Her name is Lillie Marriott. She's expecting you to telephone."

Sarah thanked him and put down the receiver. She dialled the number he had given her. It was answered on the first ring, but then from the other end of the line came a lot of scuffling and yapping before a plummy English voice finally said, "Hello, Lillie Marriott here - get down, Tweezle, you naughty dog!"

Sarah explained who she was and a few minutes later Lillie had offered her the job.

"I desperately need someone — my last groomie walked out a week ago. I can't manage the horses and my darling doggies all on my own - it's just too much for me. Come at once," she begged. "There is a lovely mobile home for you next to the yard and the horses are all fabulous."

"Lovely," said Sarah, hoping that she had managed to keep the irony out of her voice as she wrote down Lillie's address. Then, wondering what she had let herself in for, she telephoned the airport to book a flight on the first available plane.

Her father barely concealed his delight that she was going and her mother seemed to glow with relief as she kissed her goodbye.

The taxi bumped up a rutted farm drive towards Wildfern House Farm and

Lillie Marriott. Sarah climbed out of the taxi in front of a bland-looking redbrick house surrounded by high rhododendron bushes. Behind the house she could see white painted railings and a row of redbrick stables with hanging baskets swinging gently in the breeze. Before she had time to look further a pack of yapping terrier dogs darted in a swirling mass of shaggy coats and snarling teeth from the house, surrounding her like a pack keeping their prey at bay. From a side door of the house emerged a woman who she presumed was Lillie, followed by a thickset, bald-headed man. She had, Sarah was grateful to see, even fatter thighs than her own. Lillie sauntered out, holding a snarling terrier dog that looked remarkably like its owner.

"Well, I'm glad that you finally got here," said Lillie in a voice that implied that Sarah was very late. "I will show you my darlings - you must be dying to see them." She strutted towards the side of the house where a path led down to the stable yard.

"This is Richard, my husband," she added, as an afterthought, waving an arm airily in his direction.

What I'm dying for is a cup of tea and a look at where I am staying, thought Sarah, trudging after Lillie.

At the back of the house was a sorry-looking lawn covered in bones and other debris from the pack of terriers and then beyond that, reached by a path of paving-stones that led across the lawn, was the stable yard. Five horses' heads gazed out over the green-painted doors, peering at her through the mass of greenery that hung from the hanging baskets beside their stable doors. Lillie led the way into each stable and insisted on pulling the rug off each of the overly fat show horses. Sarah made what she hoped were the right comments, comparing them unfavourably in her mind to the sleek slender thoroughbreds that she was used to looking after. She felt sick, dizzy and disorientated and longed to lie down and close her eyes.

"And I don't allow the horses' tails to be brushed," Lillie was saying. "Using a brush can break the hair. My horses' tails must be perfect when they go in the show ring — their hair must be combed out just using your fingers."

Oh, great, thought Sarah, rolling her eyes behind Lillie's back.

Finally Lillie closed her tour of the yard. "And this is your little housie," she cooed.

Sarah followed Lillie around the corner of the stable block. At the end of a gravel path was her new home: a long cream and pale green-coloured mobile home.

Welcome home, Sarah, she thought, climbing up the paving-slab steps and going into the damp-smelling caravan.

CHAPTER TWENTY FOUR

Sarah had just squeezed herself into the tiny hand basin-sized tub that was a sorry excuse for a bath in her mobile home when a loud rapping on the outside door disturbed her. Groaning she heaved herself out of the tepid water and snatched a towel off the rail. She swung back the door to find Lillie grinning at her with an embarrassed expression on her face.

"Sarah," she said, in a high wheedling voice, smiling meekly, "I was wondering whether you could do me the teeniest favour?"

"Erm," Sarah replied. Doing a favour for Lillie could mean anything from having to clean out the stables with a toothbrush to licking the horses' hooves clean with her tongue.

"It's about tomorrow," Lillie continued.

Sarah felt her heart sink. That was her day off and she had planned to leave early to go to the races. It was the Cheltenham Festival and tomorrow was the Gold Cup, the big day. She had planned to talk to Derry and see if she was ever going to get her old job back.

Lillie clasped her hands together and pushed them under her chin, looking at Sarah with a little-girl-lost expression. "Oh Sarah," she whined, "I've been so silly!"

Sarah sniffed. She could not imagine Lillie being anything else.

"I had forgotten all about your day off and I've arranged to go out to lunch with one of my oldest, my dearest, my very bestest friends." She looked at Sarah pleadingly, then continued in a rush. "Please, could you do the stables for me in the morning?"

Sarah groaned inwardly. Lillie had damn well known that it was her day off and she had organised this lunch regardless. "Well, I had arranged to go to Cheltenham," she said quietly.

The little-girl-pleading expression vanished instantly and Lillie's eyes became hard, belying the sweet smile of contrition that split her face. She knew full well that she was going to persuade Sarah to do the stables in the morning, by whatever means she had to. "I thought that I had done you such a favour giving you this job and now you can't do me the teeniest favour in return!" she snapped petulantly.

Sarah knew that she wasn't going to win. Lillie had made up her mind and she might as well back down. Lillie would only make her life a misery if she defied her and took the whole day off.

"OK, look," Sarah said, hoping that a compromise could be reached. "I'll do the stables in the morning and then I'll go off. Do you think that you could do the feeds in the evening?" If you are not too pissed, that is, she wanted to add sarcastically.

Lillie grimaced, then nodded reluctantly.

She woke in the morning already feeling grumpy. Now she had virtually a full day's work ahead of her to be done in the few hours that she could spare before she went off to Cheltenham, while bloody Lillie lolled in bed before getting up to go out for her ladies' lunch. She dressed and stamped into the yard. The horses began to whinny impatiently and Lucan, a big ugly black heavyweight hunter, began to bang impatiently against the football toy that Lillie had hung in the stable doorway, to give the little precious something to occupy him. The big horse was Lillie's favourite. Sarah thought he was grossly fat, pampered and spoilt. "Sod off!" she snapped crossly as he barged her out of the way in his hurry to get at the feed that she shoved in his manger.

Sarah rushed through her work, long years of working with racehorses making her fast and efficient at her job. She fed all of the horses, mucked them out and then shoved them all into their spaces on the horse-walking machine while she dashed in and had her breakfast. Lille had installed the machine to exercise the horses and avoid having to pay another groom to ride out all the animals.

After a rushed breakfast, Sarah pulled the horses back off the spinning console and jogged with them back to their boxes where she gave them all a cursory brush-over and spitefully ran a hard nylon brush through their tails in defiance of Lillie's no-brush regulation. Then, pulling a stray hair that would be evidence out of the brush, she chucked it into the grooming-bucket and fled indoors to change.

At last she was on her way, only an hour later than she had planned to leave. However, that one hour made all the difference to her journey as she hit all or the traffic that was heading to the racecourse.

She sat in a traffic queue waiting to get onto the course, fuming with impatience. Damn Lillie and her stupid lunch and her stupid horses! They were making her late for the one important thing in her life: Derry — and of course the racing. This was her one chance to see him again. He might not come to England again for months.

Walking into the course, she felt as if Ireland had been transported to England or as if the Irish had claimed a small part of the country for themselves. The enormous course enclosure was filled with tented bars and a rowdy festival atmosphere. The Irish flag and bunches of shamrock hung from every available spot and the whole area seemed to be a sea of Guinness. All around were excited cries of astonishment as Irish friends and neighbours found themselves face-to-face hundreds of miles from home.

Cheltenham is the course where dreams are made and shattered and all around was an atmosphere of frenzied excitement. A newspaper-seller wandered through the crowds shouting the name of his paper, the headlines giving Derry's runner, Magnetic Attraction, as the sure winner of the Gold Cup.

Sarah weaved her way towards the parade-ring, squeezing her way through the crowds at its edge.

Derry was in the centre of the ring. He looked dazzlingly handsome, his hair newly cut and sleeked back off his forehead, an electric-blue shirt under his tweed suit bringing out the tanned colour of his skin.

Then Sarah spotted Tara. Acting on a sudden impulse, she ducked under the guard-rail, wriggled past the security guard and dashed across the turf to Tara.

Tara, seeing her, grinned in greeting. "Sarah, what are you doing here?"

"I saw you in the ring and I didn't think that I would get another chance to say hello," Sarah lied. This was the only chance that she had to get close to Derry, to give him any chance to give her the job back. "I just want to say hello to Derry too," she said casually, moving away from Tara. She walked across the grass to Derry, towards the straight muscular line of his back. He was talking to JT, the owner of Magnetic Attraction, and his jockey. Sarah wriggled into the tight circle, breathless with excitement.

"Hello!" she said, her voice coming out as a frenzied squeak in her excitement.

Derry glared at her as if he could not believe his eyes. "Just a moment!" he snapped at the others. Then taking hold of Sarah's arm so tightly that she gasped with the pain, feeling his fingers close around her flesh in a vicelike grip, he led her a short way from the others. "Piss off, will you!" he hissed, his face very close to her so that she could smell the toothpaste on his breath and the shampoo scent from his hair. Then shoving her away so hard that she had to take a step backwards to keep her balance, he spun on his heel and stalked back to the others. Sarah, open-mouthed, caught a glimpse of Derry's ice-blonde girlfriend, Ellen, whose elegant eyebrows were raised in amusement.

Before she had time to rejoin Tara, the security guard, alerted by Derry's actions, shot across the grass. "You are in the wrong enclosure, Miss," he said, extremely politely. "You have to leave — this way please." He seized her arm making her wince with pain as he grasped her just where Derry's fingers had dug into her flesh and escorted her out of the parade-ring. She was shoved out onto the tarmac, her face red from embarrassment, tears of outrage standing in her eyes.

Miserably she made her way onto the stands to watch the horses. Magnetic Attraction looked fabulous. His coat gleamed in the spring sunlight. Sarah felt she wanted to cry again as she saw the horse she had spent so many hours preparing for this race.

The horses cantered down to the start line. There were nine of them in all - nine of the finest horses that could be found in Ireland or England, matchless in their skill and stamina. It looked as if the race could be won by any of them. Sarah managed to get herself in a position where she could see up into the owners' and trainers' stand. By moving her head she could peer through the crowds and see where Derry, Tara and JT had positioned themselves on the steps, preferring to get the atmosphere outside rather than to watch in one of the hospitality boxes on the close-circuit television.

Sarah felt a quiver of excitement as the starting-flag was raised and the horses walked forward to line up. Slowly, pausing for greater dramatic effect, the starter raised his flag and then hurriedly dropped it. The horses bounded away in one unified leap, charging towards the first fence as their jockeys battled to steady them.

Sarah craned her neck, trying in vain to catch a glimpse of Magnetic Attraction, but there were too many people ahead of her, blocking the view. Instead she had to be content with staring at the enormous television screen that had been positioned opposite the stands to relay the race. Magnetic Attraction was running well down the field of horses while one of the English horses, Dawn Raider, was powering away from the others. The rest of the jockeys let him go ahead, gambling that he would not be able to keep the vicious pace up for long on the hard ground. However, the horses strained to go with him, fighting their riders. At the third fence the only other horse from Ireland, Red Flash, took off way too soon, plunging at the fence recklessly. There was a collective gasp of horror as the horse somersaulted over the fence, sending the jockey flying through the air. Sarah shuddered as his tiny body hit the rock-hard ground and bounced and then rolled into a ball to get out of the way of the horses' hooves. Even so one horse could not avoid him and galloped straight over him. Sarah gave a gasp of horror. As the horses galloped on, the jockey scrambled to his feet and the last shot, before the camera panned away, was of him throwing his skull-cap and whip to the ground in disgust.

Red Flash, unharmed by his fall, was straight onto his feet and galloping after the other horses; riderless, he soon caught them up and began to outstrip them. Magnetic Attraction, carried along with Red Flash's speed, began to make up ground cruising easily to the front of the pack. Sarah found herself gripping the arm of the man beside her in excitement. He didn't seem to mind — everyone was so excited. The horses galloped past the front of the stand, a mass of muscle and straining legs thundering on the hard ground. There was a huge roar of encouragement.

Sarah stole a look across the stands to where Derry was standing. He was on the step above Ellen, his arms draped around her shoulders; his chin resting tenderly on the top of her blonde hair, his face was a mask of concentration as he stared out at the horses as they flashed by.

They shot off again into the countryside, a vague blur of colour on the horizon. The television screen, catching the sunlight, was no better — the horses moved as vague shapes and it was impossible to tell which was which. Then the screen cleared and then they came back into view. Magnetic Attraction was in the lead, racing against the riderless Red Flash. The crowd gave a huge roar of delight. The Irish horse was going to win! The man whose arm she had been grasping wrenched it out of her reach and began to jump up and down on the spot, delirious with excitement. There was only one fence left to jump and then the long, strength-sapping climb up the hill to the finishing line.

Magnetic Attraction could do it — Sarah knew without a doubt that he could win. Three lengths separated him and the riderless horse from the other runners. He was powering ahead, ears pricked, enjoying every second of the race, his legs pounding on the hard ground, as if he had wings. The two horses raced at the final fence, stride equalling stride. Sarah's heart was in her mouth as a riderless horse was every jockey's nightmare.

Then, as the horses went to take off for the fence, Red Flash suddenly veered off to the left, slamming straight into Magnetic Attraction, knocking him clean off his feet. He sprawled sideways over the fence, his legs flailing in the air as he rolled sideways onto the top. In the television screen above her, Sarah could see everything relayed in huge detail. The jockey was thrown to the ground beneath the fence and for one horrifically slow moment it looked as if the horse would topple slowly over the fence and land on him. But as Magnetic Attraction slowly rolled over the brushwood fence to land on the hard ground, the jockey wriggled out of the way. The horse lay still, his body stretched out.

The other horses flew over the fence at either side of him and powered up the hill to battle it out for one of the closest finishes ever seen at Cheltenham. For a second the camera panned back to the still form of Magnetic Attraction, lying beneath the fence, and then panned instantly back to the winner of the Cheltenham Gold Cup. The surprised jockey was standing in his stirrups punching the air in delight and slapping his exhausted-looking horse on the neck.

Sarah was still staring at the screen in disbelief when she caught sight of Derry dashing down the steps to go to Magnetic Attraction, his handsome face stricken with shock. As everyone surged forwards to welcome home the winner, she remained where she was, white-faced and dry-eyed, looking down the track at the final fence and the bulk of the horse that she had loved. From the distance Sarah watched as Derry jogged down the track towards his horse. "That's dead," said some sage beside her.

Then, as she watched, Magnetic Attraction suddenly rolled his head up and a second later scrambled shakily to his feet. Tears sprang to Sarah's eyes.

He had lost the Gold Cup, but had only been winded in the fall. He would live to battle another day.

CHAPTER TWENTY FIVE

The only tissue that Sarah could find in her handbag was now a sodden mess. As was her face, she realised, as she glanced in the car mirror. She had been so convinced he was going to win that the disappointment was now acute - like being picked up, thrown a great distance and then slammed into a wall. And Derry's face — the certainty that the horse was going to win and then the complete look of shock and horror and the fear that the horse was seriously hurt, or worse — was imprinted on her mind. Yet in a way she was glad. Rotten bastard. It served him right.

Cars began to pull away and finally she decided that she must make a move. She could not sit in the middle of Cheltenham racecourse all night. Her pale face stared bleakly back at her. She compared herself bitterly to the glamorous Ellen. There was no competition really; it was like comparing a Shire horse to a delicate thoroughbred. Ellen was glamorous, blonde and willowy, like a model stepped out of the pages of an expensive fashion magazine, while she — short, dumpy and badly dressed in unflattering cheap clothes — had nothing to offer. She had just been a convenient fuck, something to warm Derry's bed when there was nothing better. The sex had been so good though - he had made her feel that he cared and it was hard to comprehend that anyone could just turn those feelings on and off like a tap.

With her self-esteem and confidence at its lowest ebb she slammed the car into gear and, peering over her shoulder, reversed out of the parking spot. Suddenly there was an almighty bang and a screech of metal against metal. The steering wheel spun violently, burning her hands as it jolted away, and the little car stalled, jerking so that she was thrown forwards, banging her stomach on the steering wheel.

"Shit!" she exclaimed, looking around painfully, her neck sore from the jolt. Behind the passenger side of the car, embedded into the wing, was a large red Rolls Royce.

She turned back to face the front of the car and, resting her elbows on the steering wheel, buried her face in her hands. Now she was going to get shouted at by the owner of the priceless piece of machinery that she had just reversed into. Great. It would cost a fortune to mend her car and the damage on the Rolls Royce. There was another jolt as the Rolls Royce pulled away from hers and the grating screech of metal as her little car unwillingly released its back wing.

Then a car door clunked shut. Out of the wing-mirror she could see the driver coming towards her. She grimaced, hunching her shoulders in readiness for being yelled at.

Her car door was wrenched open and cold evening air rushed inside.

"I am most awfully sorry — are you badly hurt?" said a gentle male voice.

Sarah blinked and felt her mouth drop open in astonishment; she had not been expecting this at all. "I'm OK," she said, scrambling out of the car, "b-b-ut it was all my fault!"

"Nonsense," said the man. "I reversed straight into you."

Sarah managed to look at him fully for the first time and immediately was terribly conscious of how dowdy and scruffy she must look and ashamed of her blotchy tear-stained face. He was a handsome man, but a lot older than she was. He was tall with neatly cut, very grey hair and a clean-shaven face, lined and weathered, a lived-in looking face. But he was smiling at her and dusting her down with infinite care. Suddenly she burst into tears again.

"Don't - don't cry please," he was mumbling and through her tears she was aware of him fumbling desperately in his pockets searching for a handkerchief. He found one and pressed it into her hand. It was neatly ironed and smelt of clean laundry.

She dabbed at her eyes with it and finally managed to look at him with a faint smile. He was looking at her with a horrified expression from kind eyes that matched the green of the collar of his overcoat. "It was my fault," he was saying. "I'll get your car repaired."

She looked at the back wing of her car and burst into a fresh frenzy of crying. It had collapsed into the wheel. There was no way that she could drive the car. The Rolls Royce, she noticed, had hardly a dent in it.

"I'm sorry," she said. "It has just been a really bad day — my horse fell..." It seemed the only logical explanation.

"Blake's horse?" he asked, taking the crumpled handkerchief back gingerly and stuffing it quickly into his coat pocket. "Terrible shame that — I had my money on him too."

Sarah looked at the glamorous handsome man — what must he think of her, wailing and being hysterical? Then suddenly she felt terribly angry with him and the world — now she had no car, no Derry, no nothing.

"I'm Edward Dixon," said the man, handing her his card and gesturing to the crumpled back end of her car, "I'm going to put all of this right."

Sarah gasped inwardly - he was one of the biggest racehorse owners in England. She remembered too that he had lost his wife, and almost lost his own life when his helicopter had crashed on the way home from racing a few years previously. He was always in the expensive magazines that Derry left lying around — with a stream of glamorous beauties on his arm.

"Get in," he said, gesturing to his car. "I'll drive you home and get the garage to sort out your car." Then he smiled and added, "and maybe I could sort you out . . ."

She felt a surge of fury, hot and bitter, well up inside her. He was just like bloody Derry! Sort you out, she raged inwardly. She knew what that meant!

"I'll get home myself, thanks," she snapped. "Here's my address." She jotted it down on the back of a betting slip. She added sarcastically, "perhaps you would be so kind as to get the car brought back to me." Then she stalked away through the lines of parked cars towards the exit.

She had a nightmare journey home, first crammed on one of the many coaches that had been laid on to convey racegoers back to the train station, where she had to perch on a seat beside a very drunken man who spent the whole journey trying to light a cigarette and failing miserably. Then there was a horrifically long wait for the train to arrive. She began to feel terrible. She was freezing and shivers racked her body. She had the nauseous headachy feeling that accompanied the onset of a migraine. She longed to be back at the caravan, to crawl under the covers and wait until she felt better. She would feel better after a good night's sleep.

After a taxi ride from the station that took every penny that she had, she arrived back at the yard. The house was in darkness. No car stood in the yard. Lillie was presumably still enjoying herself at her "lunch". The horses were hanging their heads over their half-doors and neighing, impatient with hunger. Shivering and feeling as if her limbs were made of clay she was still outside, taking the muck out of the boxes and refilling water-buckets and hay-nets, when Lillie screeched to a halt in the house yard in her little sports car. Although it was dark, Sarah could hear that she was drunk and swaying, from the clack-clacking of her footsteps as she came across the lawn towards the horse yard — with every other step she wobbled off the paving-stones and there was a slight thud as her footsteps hit the muddy grass.

"Oh, aren't you a sweetie!" she exclaimed as she saw what Sarah had done. "I was just coming to do that," with enormous drunken emphasis on just".

I bet you were, thought Sarah, filling the last of the hay-nets. She felt truly rotten now and all that she could think of was crawling into a hot bath to try to get some warmth into her frozen bones, drinking something hot and then going to bed. Hopefully she would feel better in the morning.

As she shut the door behind her, she slowly surveyed the caravan. This was her life now. Derry really did not want her back; he had made that very obvious. Not bothering to eat, she climbed miserably into bed and pulled the covers around her, shutting out the world.

The following morning she woke with the flu. Every bone in her body ached and sweat poured from her and yet sire shivered uncontrollably. Dosing herself with hot tea and flu remedy she began to do the horses and had done the yard by the time Lillie came in, dressed beautifully in brightly polished boots, jodhpurs, a shirt and cravat. Staggering across the yard under the weight of the hay-nets that she carried, Sarah told Lillie that she was ill.

"I feel dreadful," she said, feeling a trickle of icy sweat running down her back.

"Oh, sweetie," exclaimed Lillie, taking one of the hay-nets off Sarah with her leather gloved hand, "you do look poorly — you must go back to bed! Richard will have to ride the horses, I really wanted them to have a good canter this morning," and she stamped off towards the house, screeching for Richard to come and ride.

Later as Sarah dozed she heard the big black horse, Lucan, canter into the yard and looked out of the window to see the horse jog riderless into his stable.

A few days later she felt better and was sitting on the bench that doubled as an extra bed when Lillie hammered excitedly on the door. "Sarah, sweetie, come and see what is here!"

Sarah got up slowly as she felt weak with lying in bed and from not being able to eat, but she was glad to find that, for the first time in a long time, the waistband of her jeans felt decidedly loose.

Lillie was outside on the porch step hopping from one foot to another, dressed in yet another one of her riding outfits with a neat hacking jacket and loud Hermes scarf. "Your car's back, sweetie!" she shrieked, unable to contain her excitement as she pulled Sarah out of the caravan. "Come and look!"

Scowling, Sarah followed her into the yard. Her car stood on the driveway looking as good as new.

The dented back wing had been repaired and the whole car gleamed a bright shade of red - the whole vehicle had been resprayed.

"But that's not all," said Lillie, heaving open the door. She reached inside and there on the passenger-side seat was an enormous bouquet of red roses in exactly the same shade as the car. "Look," she said, pulling the bouquet out with some difficulty because of its size and handing it to Sarah. "You've got an admirer, sweetie!"

Tucked into the flowers was a card. Sarah put the flowers down on the car roof and ripped open the little envelope. She pulled the card out. It read: "With my most sincere apologies. Please let me buy you dinner to say sorry properly, Edward," and then there was a telephone number. Sarah screwed up the card and chucked it on the ground and then, having second thoughts, retrieved it and stuffed it into her jeans pocket.

After Lillie had gone Sarah grimly surveyed the caravan. It looked like a funeral parlour. She pulled the crumpled card out of her pocket and picked up her mobile phone. She knew she should say thank you for getting the car fixed, but the flowers had annoyed her as did the dinner invitation. What did they mean? Did he think that she would be impressed by them? Men – they were all the same. Edward probably saw her as someone who would be so impressed by the dinner invitation and his wealth she would leap eagerly into bed with him. Sarah put down the phone. Stuff it, she would ring another day. He didn't need thanking. It was his own fault. He had backed into her car.

Quickly she got up and shoved the card into the bin. Stupid man, did he expect that she would be so flattered by the flowers she would rush to the phone and say, "Oh thank you, sir! Of course I will go straight to bed with you . . ."

Her decision made, she got up and began to make her dinner. Then a moment later she exclaimed, "Oh dammit!", retrieved the card from the bin and dialled his number before she could change her mind again.

He answered on the second ring. "Hello?" His voice was silky-smooth, like melted chocolate pouring slowly out of a saucepan.

"This is Sarah," she said curtly. "I just wanted to say thank you for the car." Then she added hastily, "and the flowers." Then hardly pausing to draw breath she said, "thank you. Goodbye."

"Sarah!" he almost yelled into the receiver.

"Yes?"

"I feel awful about inconveniencing you. Please, would you let me buy you dinner some night to make it up to you?"

"Really," she said quickly, "there's no need — thanks again, goodbye." She rang off, feeling shivery again and with a strange knot in the pit of her stomach. She wondered if she was getting the flu back again. Bloody men, she hated them, especially rich ones. They always seemed to assume that anyone would go to bed with them, just because of their money. She threw the card in the bin, shoving it right to the bottom where it nestled in the potato peelings and old tea bags, and felt satisfied. He had repaired her car. She had said thank you, end of story.

She rode the little show hunter around the edge of the ploughed field. A car was going up the drive but she did not pay it any attention — probably one of the many admirers who went to visit Lillie when Richard was away. She finished her ride and took the horse back. In the yard was a red Rolls Royce and there in the yard, leaning against the bonnet, looking terribly handsome in a charcoal-grey suit was Edward. Lillie was with him, flirting furiously, batting her eyelashes at him in unashamed admiration.

As Sarah rode into the yard he turned and smiled.

Fuck, thought Sarah, what the hell is he doing here? She felt disgustingly scruffy and ugly. She slid off the horse.

"Sarah!" he said in obvious delight, coming forward and offering his hand for her to shake. As she reached out to take his hand he pulled her towards him and kissed her lightly on the cheek. She breathed in the faintest smell of a delicious aftershave.

"Since you wouldn't accept my offer on the telephone, I thought that I would come and ask you in person to have dinner with me." He smiled, patting the horse while his eyes roved casually over it. "Nice animal," he added to Lillie who was pink with excitement and admiration for him.

"Of course Sarah will go," Lillie butted in, making Sarah cheerfully want to kill her.

CHAPTER TWENTY SIX

All of the girls in the yard suddenly began to stroke their hair back from their faces, wipe their filthy hands on the bottoms of their jeans, and surreptitiously apply lipstick. Tara smiled to herself, wondering if Derry ever noticed the effect that he had on the girl grooms. She doubted it. He never even seemed to notice them unless suddenly he singled one out for some sexual attention when the need arose.

Such was Derry's charisma and beauty that wherever he went everyone would stop and watch him and admire him.

"Tara!" he called, going into the tack room.

Tara abandoned her sweeping-brush against the stable wall and walked across to the tack room. Derry was sitting on the table holding the feed chart and studying it intently.

"Hi," she said as he looked up.

"There you are!" he said with a grin. "I have a little treat for you."

Her heart sank; she knew that Derry's little treats meant a lot of hard work for someone, usually her.

"Oh yes?" she said, hauling herself up onto the top of the work surface and banging her legs impatiently against the cupboard doors below her.

"Kings Newton, Paddy Kelly's old horse, has got some problems with his legs."

"Uhh, uhh," she said, wondering what was coming — probably a long drive up to the vet's to get the horse looked at or something.

"Well," said Derry, "I think that he would benefit from a paddle in the sea a few times a week, be nicer for him than going to the swimming pool, the change of scene would do him good. I want you to take him up to Silver Strand for me."

Tara's heart sank. The last thing that she wanted was to have to drive all the way to the sea just to paddle a horse in it. "Can't one of the others do it?" she demanded.

Derry screwed up his face in mock concentration. "Weeeell," he said, slowly, as if considering the options, "not really. I couldn't trust any of them to do the job right. Send any of them unsupervised and they would probably have the horse swimming off to America or leave it standing in the box while they sit on the beach getting a tan." He smiled at her, his lips curving softly over the row of white teeth. How could she resist?

An hour later a still-seething Tara was on her way to Silver Strand. She hated the thought of having to spend two hours driving a lorry alone. It gave her time to think about Morgan and that was the last thing that she wanted to do. As she passed through the little towns and villages, she found herself wondering what he was doing. Did he miss her ever? Or was he too busy with the new love of his life — Kate? The day became roasting hot and she stripped off to her tee-shirt and shoved on her sunglasses against the hot glare of the sun. Firmly she shoved all thoughts of Morgan to the back of her mind. It was great to be away from the yard, driving the huge lorry easily along country lanes with the window down, letting the breeze fan her hair and whip the sweat away from her body.

Despite the heat of the day Silver Strand was deserted except for two cars parked together — a courting couple meeting secretly, she supposed, seeing the two figures entwined in the front seat of one of the cars. She missed the physical contact of another person desperately.

She sat for a moment, finishing a drink, letting the cool breeze, with the tang of salt blown off the sea carry up the beach to her. Silver Strand was a beautiful spot. Reached only by a long narrow lane that ran off the main road down to the beach, the spot was known only by a few and "yet it was one of the nicest beaches that she had ever seen, a hidden gem. The beach itself ran forever in both directions away from the end of the laneway, a line of gold reaching out to the horizon where it blurred with the edge of the sea and the sky.

Finally she could sit enjoying the sun no longer and unloaded Kings

Newton from the lorry. He was a kindly old horse, seasoned by years as a top steeplechaser. His legs had taken more battering than most, but year after year he came back and performed at the top of his tree, winning race after race. He came down the ramp looking around him in surprise that he was not at the races. She led him to the sea wall, climbed up on that and then shoved her foot into the stirrup and got on.

The horse strode out as she rode up the little lane and then turned down the sandy slope that led onto the beach. He jogged as he felt the sand under his hooves in anticipation of being allowed to gallop on the glorious space that stretched ahead for miles. "Gently, old fellow," she said, easing the reins and patting his neck. "No galloping today." She rode down towards the sea, reflecting on how far her confidence had come since she had been working on the yard. Actually, since she had helped Morgan out at Radford Lodge.

She reached the sea and slowly rode along the edge of the shore, letting the waves gently lap against the horse's hooves. When he was used to the sensation of the salt water on his legs she turned him and rode him into the sea. Gingerly he went deeper into the water, snorting as the waves came billowing up at him and then broke, sending white cascades of foam over his legs and belly.

Up and down in the shallows she rode, getting deeper and deeper as the horse's confidence grew, until he was splashing through the water quite happily. The sun was baking hot and she could feel sweat trickling down her back and between her breasts as she rode. How inviting the sea looked!

Then on impulse she rode the horse back out of the sea onto the beach and cantered him up the sand back to the lorry. She slid off him and quickly undid the girth that held his saddle in place and led him back onto the beach. She was going to ride him into the sea and get him to swim in the delicious water. Sliding off her jeans so that she was wearing just her knickers and a tee-shirt, she kicked off her shoes and led him back across the beach to one of the rocky outcrops. Scrambling up the rock, wincing as the hot stone, sharp beneath her feet, dug in, she manoeuvred the horse onto the sand below the rock and then leapt and scrambled onto his warm broad back. She rode into the water, going deeper and deeper as she steered him straight out into the sea. Away from the beach the waves grew less and the ice-cold water crept up her legs. Beneath his hooves the sea was crystal clear. She could see the golden sandy bottom with shoals of tiny fish darting out of the way as they walked out into the icy water. Then suddenly the sea rushed over her thighs and waist making her gasp with the cold and she felt the horse begin to swim.

His body came up beneath her as she began to float. He moved gracefully, plunging slowly up and down like a giant roundabout horse on a carousel. His breath, coming from nostrils closed against the sea-water, came in great snorts as if she was riding some ancient sea-dragon. Then, he began to try to jump the sea, rearing his powerful front end high in the water, plunging and leaping, the icy salt water churning all around them. Tara laughed for joy at the pleasure of it.

They came out of the sea, water pouring from both of them. Tara was drenched, her beige tee-shirt wet to the level of her nipples, which jutted out with the cold. Then she realised that she was not alone. Way up the beach, parked next to hers, was another horse lorry. One that she recognised. Grey and green with a dark red stripe down the side underlining the words — Radford Lodge. Morgan.

Tara felt herself flush with emotion and embarrassment. The last person in the world that she wanted to see was him. What must she look like, with her drenched clothes clinging to every bit of her body? Damn him, what was he doing here?

She rode slowly up the beach scowling. She could see a figure leading a horse down from the lorry. A tall man, dressed in shorts and a tee-shirt, a mop of curly hair blowing in the sea breeze. The unmistakable figure of Morgan. Her heart leapt. She could not face him. Turning the horse away, she rode off. She rode to the far end of the beach and then turned back. Morgan was riding his horse in the sea. It caught her breath to see even in the distance his brown torso and the length of his brown legs wrapped around the horse. She cantered slowly up the dry sand and then trotted and finally walked the horse, sliding off as they reached the lorry and reaching inside to grab her shoes. Now she merely had to load up the horse and they would be away before Morgan returned. Fingers fumbling in her haste, she slipped the bridle off Kings Newton and replaced his head-collar.

She stole a glance down the beach. Morgan was still splashing in the shallows on his horse, seemingly oblivious to her. She turned Kings Newton and led him to the bottom of the ramp and walked up. The horse put his two front hooves straight onto the ramp and then stopped, stretching his neck out like a camel as she pulled the rope, refusing to go any further.

"Come on," she muttered angrily, tugging on the rope, remembering with a jolt that the last time this horse had been to the races they had a difficult time loading him into the lorry to bring him home. It had taken two of the yardmen from the racecourse to stand at either side of him with a strap that they had put behind his back legs to tug him in. Now she was alone with the stubborn creature that obviously had no intention of ever going into the lorry. "Not now," she hissed. He knew that she could not make him go in and was having a great joke at her expense.

Glancing onto the beach, she could see to her horror that Morgan was finished riding in the sea and was slowly riding back towards the lorry. "Oh shit!" she exclaimed in panic, tugging harder on the rope. Morgan had reached the car park. He rode towards her and smiled in greeting, nodding his head coolly in her direction, his expression icily polite. Tara ignored him. How dare he come here and spoil her afternoon! She pulled the reluctant horse back to the end of the ramp, where he stood looking at her with amused brown eyes filled with mischief. She stood on the ramp, watching out of the corner of her eye as Morgan slid off his horse and began to unsaddle him. He was tanned to a glorious shade of brown, his muscles hard beneath the sun, glittering with the dried salt from the sea. He put the head-collar on his horse which maddeningly followed him straight up into the lorry.

"Need any help?" he said finally.

"No," she said curtly, wishing that he would just go away. She was very conscious of his eyes roving over her body, of the line of wet that stopped just where her nipples jutted out against the cold fabric of her tee-shirt and of her bare legs with only the very tops hidden. He folded his arms and leant leisurely against the side of the lorry, barely concealed amusement written all over his handsome face. She pulled at the rope again and the horse shot backwards dragging her rapidly down the ramp, where she stumbled and was almost pulled off her feet.

Morgan let out a howl of laughter. "Are you sure that you don't want any help?" he laughed.

"Fuck off!" she snapped. Tears of frustration rolled down her cheeks and she dashed them away angrily, not wanting him to see her cry. Then in an explosion of violence that would have done Derry justice she slammed her fists into the horse's damp sides, so roughly that he jumped away, rearing straight up in the air in shock and fear. The lead-rope slid through her fingers like greased lightning, burning them as the nylon sped through and then reached the end. The horse shot backwards, spinning around, and for a moment stood, unable to believe that he was free, started to jog off down the lane.

Morgan deftly caught the dangling lead-rope as he passed. Turning the horse, he led him straight up the ramp, much to Tara's annoyance.

Tara staggered away, holding her burnt hands under her arms to dull the pain, tears of pain now mingling with those of sheer frustration. She leant against the side of the lorry as Morgan slammed up the ramp.

He came and stood in front of her. "Are you all right?" he asked gently.

"No, I'm bloody not!" she snarled, glaring up at him.

He took her hands in his, turning them over and looking at the red marks across her palms where the rope had burned her.

"Get off me!" she snapped, snatching her hands away. He was so close that his very presence made her feel weak. Then all the pent-up emotion exploded and she slammed her fists into his bare chest.

He took hold of her arms to still the flailing fists and very gently kissed her on the mouth.

CHAPTER TWENTY SEVEN

She loved him so desperately, longed so much to be with him, the raw emotion made it impossible to breathe. Then she could bear it no longer and wriggled away, fighting desperately to be free, panicking like a foal caught by a rope for the first time. Flailing her arms and legs, she shoved past him.

"Stop," he said softly. He moved forward, trapping her against the side of the lorry. The sun-warmed panels were hot behind her back and she could feel the searing heat that came off his body even though he was inches away.

"Go away. I hate you!" she stormed, flailing a fist across his body.

He caught her hands again with lightning-fast reactions and held them to her sides. He moved a step closer. "No, you don't," he whispered hoarsely.

They stood, his warm brown torso gently pressed against her wet tee-shirt. She was conscious of her nipples sticking into his chest. Then gently he tilted her chin and lowered his mouth onto hers. She felt herself turn to liquid with wanting him as their lips parted.

She broke again from his grip and stumbled away from him. "Please leave me alone!" she pleaded, stopping at the end of the lorry and turning to face him.

"I can't," he said desperately, kicking at a stone with the toe of his wet running shoes. "I think about you all of the time. I miss you. I wake up thinking about you and I go to sleep thinking about you. I'm in bits without you." His voice was strangled with emotion.

"You have Kate now, I saw you together at the hunt meet" she said, wanting to go to him, wanting to run her hands through his hair, to move her hands over the contours of his face, down the broad plane of his back, to feel him slide inside her.

"Kate?" he said, jerking his head around to look at her, his voice incredulous. "Kate is nothing to me! I took her hunting with me to give two of the young hunters some experience that's all."

Tara exploded into malicious laughter. "You said Lynn Moore was nothing to you as well!"

Morgan ignored the jibe. "I'm not seeing Kate — how could I be interested in her when all I can think about is you? I haven't been near a woman since you left." His voice sounded full of self-pity. Then he looked up at her, grinning. "I'm ready to explode!"

Despite herself, for a second she laughed, remembering moments when they had been together, when they had been so desperate for each other that often they did not even reach the bedroom.

Then she thumped the side of the lorry, wanting to kick out at everything and everyone. "You hurt me so much! I'm not going through that again!" And then she broke down, sobbing in desperation, sobbing out the emotion that she had kept so well-bottled for the last few months. She sobbed against the side of the lorry, wishing that he would just go away and leave her alone. He came to stand behind her; she could feel his body touching hers as he gently touched her hair.

"Don't," he whispered, stroking her hair. Gently he pulled her around and into his arms. "I love you so much," he whispered. He pushed her hair away from her tear-ravaged face and softly kissed her. "I was so afraid the night of the fire," he whispered hoarsely. "I thought that you had left me and then I was so angry that you had not called me."

Tara clung to him, unable to speak, weak with relief at being in his arms once more. He loved her and that was all that mattered.

She lifted her face and let her lips meet his. She felt as if she would explode with desire as his tongue softly explored her mouth, his hands roved gently over her body, gentle against the salty, damp skin, exploring under her tee-shirt, cupping her jutting shoulder-blades and pulling her closer and closer to him. Filled with longing she let herself fall against him. "I want you," she whispered longingly.

"I rather hoped that you might," he giggled, bringing a gentle hand around to cup one breast, his fingers playing expertly with the nipple, making her weak with wanting him. "Perhaps we should go inside," he said, glancing down the lane towards where the courting couple were gazing at them with extreme interest.

The large lorry was equipped to carry four horses. In the front was a section kitted out like a caravan with a cooker and table and bench seats, even a shower and television, the height of luxury, all padded and plush, in case they were travelling and had no accommodation. It was more often used when Derry wanted to shag one of the grooms. Above the lorry cab as a wide bed reached by a small ladder that dropped down. Tara led the way, scrambling up the ladder with Morgan caressing her bottom as she wriggled onto the high bed. He followed, heaving his long legs up and stretching out. Tara undid the narrow little windows, letting the fresh sea breeze slide in and caress their hot bodies.

"Come here," she said, stretching out her arms.

Morgan rolled into her arms, his body laid against hers, his long legs entwined around hers, drawing her closer and closer until every bit of her body lay against his. Then they kissed softly, tenderly and they made the slowest, gentlest love that she had ever experienced, entwining their bodies, gently, slowly, moving together.

Tara opened her eyes to see him looking down on her face, his eyes filled with such exquisite tenderness that she wept with pleasure and the ultimate feeling of love and protection.

"I love you," he whispered over and over again as they moved together, their movements becoming more and more urgent as she reached for and finally achieved a climax that seemed to go on forever.

Then they lay together, his arms wrapped tightly around her. He looked down at her while she stroked his face, unable to believe that he was really with her.

The horse stamping in the back of the lorry brought her jolting back to reality.

"Oh Christ," she said, reaching for hr bra, "I have to get this horse back home." She pulled on her damp and sticky tee-shirt and then stopped. "What now?" she asked, wondering how they were going to part, wondering if they were a couple again.

"I want you," Morgan said, pulling on his boxers and reaching for his shorts.

"You just had me," she grinned, dropping a kiss on his damp forehead.

"No," he said seriously, "I really want you. Forever. Will you marry me?" He looked at her with sincere blue eyes.

Tara felt as if she would explode with happiness. "Yes, please," she whispered putting her arms around him and kissing him with such passion that it made both of them gasp.

What on earth was Derry going to say, she wondered, shivering at the prospect. He would go off his head with temper. He hated Morgan with a vengeance and now she was going to marry him. She chuckled at the thought of him exploding, telling her that he had only sent her to exercise a horse and now here she was coming back bloody going to get married to Morgan.

All too quickly they were driving up the long and beautiful approach to Westwood Park. Tara had waited, parked on the side of the road, while Morgan had driven his horse home and then hurried back to her. Now they were together, heading towards the inevitable confrontation with Derry. On one side of the driveway the rhododendron bushes were in full flower, their pale pink heads waving in greeting, like flags to welcome a conquering hero. She pulled into the yard. All of the stable staff had come back to do the evening stables and the yard was a hive of activity. They all feigned disinterest when they saw who was with her, but she could feel them hiding around corners and peering through the dusty glass of the sheds, dying to find out what was going on.

As the last notes of the engine noise died away, Derry emerged from the tack room, his hands full of entry papers. Seeing Morgan, he snapped in a loud voice, "What the fuck is he doing here?"

The bustle of the yard was silenced as the staff stopped what they were doing and waited to see this exciting scene unfold.

"Derry, let's go inside," Tara said, amazed that she was able to speak at all. She was not going to have a scene with Derry, especially not outside, for all of the staff to witness and relate to the village for everyone to pick over and enjoy.

"Perhaps we had better," said Derry shortly, his face blazing with fury, his eyes like dark holes into hell glaring out at her, making her quake inwardly with terror at telling him that she was going to marry his most bitter enemy. Wordlessly he stalked past her towards the house without acknowledging Morgan. They turned to follow him with the staff nudging each other in excitement and trying to piece together what was going on. Tara reached for Morgan's hand and entwined hers into it for support. He looked white and his mouth was set into a determined line.

The house looked imposing as they followed Derry up the curved stone steps — even the wisteria around the front door seemed to shake its head at them in horror.

Derry went straight to his study, leaving the door open for them to follow. Morgan shut the door behind them and stood with his back to it glaring sullenly at Derry.

Derry moved around to the back of his desk and sat down in the armchair. The light from the window poured in behind it making it impossible to see his face and to read his reactions.

He drummed his fingers on the leather top of the desk, pausing before he asked coldly, "what are you doing, Tara, with this prick?"

"How dare you say things like that!" she raged. Then she took a deep breath. "We've come to tell you that we're going to get married."

For a long moment there was silence.

Tara stared defiantly at the sun-outlined shape of her brother until the silence was broken by the cruel sound of his laughter.

"Whatever next?" he said sarcastically. He shoved the chair back viciously and came around the table. For a moment Tara thought that he was going to punch Morgan. "For Christ's sake, Tara," he snapped maliciously, his fists clenching and unclenching with pent-up anger, "he's a useless nobody — you can't marry him!"

Tara drew herself to her full, diminutive height and raised her chin defiantly "I love him, Derry," she said calmly.

"I love him, Derry!" he mocked back at her, his words ringing out in the study. Then he shook his head sadly. "Well, you're a grown woman. I've done all that I can to help you. I seriously think that you need help — you're off your rocker. You've behaved like some cheap little tart going off like this — like a tinker's bitch — and coming back here smelling of sex. He's only after your money. Can't you see that, you stupid little bitch?" He was snarling now, rage oozing out of every pore.

Tara cringed back against the bookcase, feeling the shelves digging into her back as she tried to press herself away from his fury.

Morgan, unable to bear the scene any longer, stepped forward. "Stop it, you bastard!" he snarled at Derry.

For a moment the two men faced each other like two battling stags about to lock antlers in a battle to the death.

"Leave her alone!" said Morgan. "It's me you should be abusing, not her. All Tara has done is love me, and you, but she has made her choice — she's coming with me."

Derry shoved his hands deep into his pockets. "She's not fit to make any choices - she should be in a mental institute," he said nastily. "What sort of life is she going to have with a tinker like you? You aren't even a bloody racehorse trainer," he added, spitefully. "The few fucking owners you have are not enough to keep Tara in lipstick!"

Morgan's eyes narrowed and in a calm voice that seemed to infuriate Derry further he said, "well, I didn't see you do so well at Cheltenham."

Derry sprang forward like a cat, as if he were about to tear Morgan limb from limb, but Tara was quicker and leapt between them,

"Stop it!" she cried, facing Derry, defying him to hurt Morgan.

"We'll see who does well next year then," Derry muttered, backing away. "You'll be in rags by then, my dear. This will always be your home, but he is not welcome here," He turned away. "Don't forget — when you want to come back you can, but I am not having anything to do with him." He glared at Morgan with such hatred that Tara could feel the force of it.

"Come on," said Morgan, taking her hand and leading her out of the room. She let him lead her outside. As they shut the huge front door, she gasped in the rose-scented air as if she had been smothered. She was trembling, now that the scene was over. She clung to Morgan for support, wanting now only to go away with him — to put Derry and his awful anger behind them. Derry would get over it eventually, when he wanted something.

A few days later she was standing in an over-the-top chapel in Las Vegas listening as a priest dressed as Elvis recited the wedding vows. The chapel was painted all in white and decorated with enormous plastic flowers from floor to ceiling. Beside her stood a woman that she had never seen before who was grinning with amusement at being dragged off the street to assist in the ceremony. Tara wore a new dress that she had bought in the airport lounge as they waited for the flights to be called — a hideously expensive creation in a bright electric-blue satin, cut on the bias, with tiny spaghetti straps over her shoulders.

Morgan's hand caressed her bare back and slid tantalisingly down to where the dress plunged down almost to her buttocks. He looked stunning in a charcoal-grey suit and a blue tie that matched her dress.

As the priest said, "I pronounce you man and wife," hot tears of love and joy spilled down Tara's cheeks.

CHAPTER TWENTY EIGHT

Sarah pulled off the skirt roughly and threw it in a heap on the bed. "Oh fuck," she growled, feeling more and more angry. Why hadn't she just said no and told Lillie to shut up? It would have been so easy and then she would not have been hunting through her wardrobe for the last hour trying to find something to wear.

She unearthed her jeans from the bottom of the pile that littered the bed. She pulled them on — at least they were gratifyingly loose on the waist and bagged reassuringly around her bottom and thighs. She put on a shirt and stood back, peering into the tiny and rather useless mirror. Her face peered back crossly. Feeling tension begin to well up inside her, she pulled off the jeans and left them inside out on the floor. Finally she settled for a longish and baggy black dress. It was not too posh and yet she would not feel out of place if everyone else was dressed up. She found her high heels at the back of the wardrobe, cursing softly because they were covered in mud around the soles and halfway up the heels. Swilling the worst of the mud off, she added a loose low-slung belt to the dress which highlighted the fact that she now actually had a waist and then, grabbing her Barbour, she shoved it over the top and shot out into the darkness.

She was not looking forward to the evening. It was a long drive on a horrible night, to go to dinner out of politeness with someone she only vaguely knew.

The restaurant was in the centre of the village, a tall sandstone building glowing orange under the fairy-lights that festooned its every corner. There was a car park at the back but as she drove in there was no sign of the Rolls Royce. But he probably had so many cars if he was as rich as Croesus that he could be driving in any one of the Audis or Mercedes or BMWs that littered the car park.

She turned off the engine and sat, listening to a tetchy-sounding shower battering on the windscreen. Finally she got out.

Customers were two-deep at the bar, but she shoved her way through, ignoring the indignant glare of a tarty skinny lady in a skirt far too short for her age, and ordered a Coke which she took to a table close to the fire, pulled off her Barbour and sat down.

Then the door in the far corner opened, letting a welcome blast of cool air into the restaurant, ruffling the paper tablecloths and sending napkins fluttering to the floor. Edward came in looking very tall and elegant in a long camel overcoat with a brown velvet collar. Sarah took a sip of her drink, lowering her gaze as he weaved around the tables towards her. What on earth was she doing here? She had nothing in common with this man - they were a world apart. Then she told herself strictly to stop being silly. This was just for him to say sorry for breaking her car and her to say thank you for fixing it. That was all and then she would never have to see him again.

Finally she forced herself to look up. He was smiling and his face was lit up with delight at seeing her. She put the drink down with such a thud in her fear that he was going to kiss her that it almost spilled. She felt her face flush pink with embarrassment as she hastily righted the glass.

"How lovely to see you," he told her in his soft clipped English accent. "I hope that I haven't kept you waiting. There was an accident on the motorway."

"No," she said, wanting to be a million miles away from him.

He took off his coat and draped it over a chair-back — even the lining looked expensive. The waiter came up to the table as he sat down.

"Mr Dixon," the waiter enthused, "welcome back — good to see you again, sir."

"A pleasure to be back, Peter," Edward said.

Obviously he was well known in the restaurant. Sarah wondered if he brought all of his potential girlfriends and mistresses here and, if so, how many of them he took back in his Rolls Royce to bed. Was that what this was all about? Was he determined to add her to his list of conquests? Why would he want her when presumably a man like him could have anyone? He was wasting his time if he thought she was going to tumble straight into bed with him.

The waiter handed him a menu and then passed one to Sarah, hardly looking at her. He was obviously so used to seeing Edward in the restaurant with a string of women that one as plain and dowdy as herself barely rated a second glance.

Sarah scanned the menu. Most of it was in French and she couldn't understand it. In desperation she chose the steak, the only word that she could understand.

"Sir," bobbed the waiter coming back to take their order.

She welcomed his return to end the uncomfortable silence that had descended as they studied the menus. They ordered and then Edward invited her to choose a wine.

"Oh, you choose," she mumbled, blushing, and was glad she had left it to him when he immediately ordered a particular French red she had never heard of, without even referring to the wine list.

The waiter nodded approvingly and left.

"Is the car mended properly?" Edward asked, removing his glasses and shoving them into an inside pocket of his jacket.

He looked, she thought, like an older and even wealthier version of Derry, dressed in well-cut and very expensive but unobtrusive clothes. "It's fine," she said, feeling even more uncomfortable because she still couldn't think of a word to say to him — apart from 'fine'.

"How are you settling into England?" he asked politely, leaning forward so that she could hear him over the noise of the other diners. "I gather that you are from Ireland?"

"Fine, yes," she said, wishing that she could shake off her instinctive mistrust of him. He was so nice, but then so was Derry when he wanted his own way.

"Lovely country, Ireland," he commented and then proceeded to fill in the silence by telling her all about the Irish racecourses that he had been to.

Sarah could feel colour stain her cheeks red with embarrassment as she struggled to relax. She was as shy and tongue-tied as a small child.

"And how are you getting on in your new job?" he eventually asked.

"Fine," Sarah mumbled.

The waiter brought the food they had ordered. Sarah welcomed the intrusion. It was a relief to feel that she didn't have to talk. She stared hard at her plate as the French toast she had chosen crumbled when she spread pate onto it. Why the hell had she ever accepted his invitation? She cast a surreptitious glance at her watch. How long before she could make her excuses and leave? And why was 'fine', the only word she seemed to be able to say?

The meal dragged uncomfortably on but, as the conversation turned back to horses and racing, Sarah was able to forget her embarrassment as she spoke about her favourite topic. By the time they arrived at dessert, coffee and finally brandies she felt quite relaxed.

"Well, that was lovely," said. Edward, fingering his empty brandy glass contemplatively.

"Yes, I enjoyed it," said Sarah and found, to her surprise, that it was true.

He smiled. "Would you like to come for a drive? I've just bought a new yearling that I would love you to see. Her sire is the famous Clarkson."

Her heart plummeted. "No," she said, in total panic, in her mind's eyes seeing him bringing her off in the car and sprawling her along the lowered front seat down some dark lane.

"Oh," he said, the smile fading from his face.

"No, I must go." Sarah shoved her chair back and stood up, grabbing her Barbour.

"Surely you don't have to rush off so quickly?" said Edward, reaching across the table to put a restraining hand on her arm. "Stay. Have another drink."

Sarah shrugged his hand off, seeing the scowl of annoyance flash across his face. He was the same as Derry. All he wanted was to get her drunk, and then have sex with her. Sarah snatched up her handbag, thanked him curtly for the dinner and shoved her way past the other tables through the restaurant, feeling the annoyed glances of the other diners as she knocked against the tables.

She sat in the car, feeling totally foolish. Why had she bolted in such a way? That was really rude. Then she thought about the cheek of him, thinking that she would just happily get into his car and let him have sex with her — just on the strength of one meal, the cheeky bugger! Fury welling up inside her, she drove all the way back to the mobile home with the stereo turned up to full volume to block out the miserable thoughts that churned in her mind. Why did men only want to take her to bed? He was as bad as Derry. Just because she was plain and unattractive they all thought that she would be glad of the attention.

Lillie was in the yard very early the following morning, alive with curiously about Sarah's night out. "How did it go?" she asked, bursting into the stable that Sarah was cleaning out.

"Fine," said Sarah, sweeping a non-existent piece of dirt up very busily. She was not going to satisfy Lillie's longing for gossip and she certainly was not going to tell her that he had tried to get her to go for a drive with him in his car.

"Are you going to see him again?" Lillie was hopping from foot to foot with curiosity.

Sarah shrugged. "I doubt it. I don't think we'd be each other's type really, Lillie," she said, kicking the pile of dirt onto the shovel with her foot.

"Well, it looked to me as if you were his type," Lillie said, stooping down and picking up a piece of horse-poo that Sarah had missed with her leather-gloved fingers and very pointedly throwing it outside. "From the way that he was looking at you when he was here I would say that you were very much his type." She picked up one of the brushes and examined it for tail-hairs.

"Probably the type that he picks up for sex," snapped Sarah and then it all poured out about the awful evening.

"Oh God," laughed Lillie, "poor man! Must be getting too old to pull the dolly birds! He's probably so desperate that he's trying anyone now!" And she trotted off, obviously itching to get back into the kitchen to tell Richard all the gory details.

Sarah was miserable all day. She felt terribly guilty about the way that she had shoved off so quickly without saying thank-you properly. It was hardly as if he was some rapist — she could have just turned him down politely and gone on her way without bolting like some scared rabbit. What must he have thought of her? The thought went backwards and forwards all day, so much so that when the heavyweight hunter shied while Sarah was schooling it in the ménage she almost fell off because she was not concentrating.

Finally, at the end of the day, she could bear it no longer and plagued by guilt she picked up her phone and punched in his number. After ringing for ages it was finally answered. She could hear from the noise in the background that he was driving somewhere.

"Hello!" he yelled over the engine noise.

"Hello, it's me!" she yelled back.

"Hello, yes," he said in between the static, obviously not recognising her voice.

"Sarah!" she said.

"Yes?"

Hearing the note in his voice change and become cold, she quailed. Perhaps she should not have rung — perhaps she should have just let it be.

"I just wanted to —"

"Sorry," he said, "but I can't hear you. I'll ring you back in a while." Then the phone went dead.

It was ages before he rang back. Just as she was thinking that he was not going to, her phone rang and she picked it up.

"Sorry about earlier — I was in a really bad spot," he said. He sounded warmer now, his voice less impatient.

"I was just ringing to say thank you for dinner," she said. "I really enjoyed it."

"That's good," he said, and a note of dismissal came into his voice.

"OK then," she said. Unable to think of anything else to say, she wondered whether she should just say goodbye and put the phone down. At least she had done her bit and said thanks properly . . .

The pause lengthened and then he said, "do you fancy coming to the races with me next Wednesday? I've got a horse running at Worcester."

"Oh," was all that she could manage to say, surprised that after the uncomfortable dinner he wanted anything more to do with her. And he actually wanted to take her out to a public place, no danger of him having the opportunity to try to seduce her.

"Come on, say yes." His tone was persuasive.

Peeved, Sarah realised that she would have to work that day. She was not due a day off again for another week and there was no way Lillie would let her have time off just like that.

"I can't," she said, with disappointment in her voice — she missed the races and would love to go, even with him.

"Ah well, never mind," he said, in a coldly polite tone.

"I have to work," she said hastily, and then added in a rush, "I only get one day off a fortnight so my next one is not until the following Friday."

There was a long silence and then he said, "how about Southwell that day? I have a horse that should run there, all being well. I would love you to come."

"OK," she said and, after arranging to meet him at the course, hung up feeling very confused and strangely happy.

Her days were desperately busy and the time flew by. The following Friday came quickly.

She was on her way by mid-morning. Having gone to the races for years, she had a suitable selection of outfits to wear and set off feeling comfortable and looking forward to the day. She was going racing. She was going to be amongst racehorses and trainers and the sort of people that she knew and understood, not like these highly strung showing-people. She pulled into Southwell racecourse just after midday, having found it easily, and walked into the concourse. The ticket office had a pass waiting for her in Edward's name and the Security Guard looked at her up and down as he handed it to her with a grin. She knew she was looking her best. The suit, which she had bought years ago, suited her. Now that she had lost weight it was very flattering and Lillie had lent her a feminine trilby hat which set off its colours.

She had arranged to meet Edward in the owners' and trainers' bar, just beside the entrance, but it was obvious as she poked her head around the door that he was not there. He had explained that he was always late. It was never his fault — it was just that business kept him late, always dragged on his time. Seeing that the bar was empty she wandered back outside and sat on one of the benches that overlooked the paddock, watching the horses going around. A helicopter flew in and landed in the middle of the course. She watched it idly and then sat up in shock as Edward got out and ran across the course towards her.

CHAPTER TWENTY NINE

Sarah felt her heart jump into her mouth and begin to pound with horror. What on earth was she doing spending the day with someone like Edward Dixon, or more importantly what on earth was he doing, wanting to spend the day with someone like her? What could they possibly have in common? He was wealthy beyond anything that she could imagine, years older than her and a world away from anything that she knew.

Then, deciding to make the best of things, she stood up, straightened the skirt of her suit and walked across the grass to meet him.

He was, as always, impeccably dressed, in the now familiar camel coat underneath which he wore a charcoal-grey suit and a lilac shirt with a tie dotted with racehorses. He looked very glamorous and as he leant forward to kiss her cheek in greeting she caught a whiff of his expensive aftershave.

"You look lovely," he smiled, looking her up and down appreciatively.

Sarah scowled. Why did he have to pretend that he thought she looked nice?

"Come on," he said taking her arm. "We're just in time for the first race. Let's see how good you are at picking the winners." He smiled, thrusting a race card into her hand.

Sarah leant against the guard-rail and immediately was lost. Gazing with great love at the horses she was oblivious to everything else. She let her eyes rove over them. She opened the race card and ran her eyes down the list, feeling for the first time relaxed in Edward's company.

"What do you think?" he said, bringing her back to reality.

She glanced down the card again for a final time and then closed it and straightened up. "Boy Scout," she said decisively.

"Why him?" asked Edward, a frown drawing his eyebrows together.

Sarah opened the race card and turned so that he could see it. He peered at it as she ran her hand down the list until she found the running form for Boy Scout. "Look," she explained, running her fingernail along the list of the places that the horse had come in his last few races: fourth, fourth, second. "He's really coming into form and look at his pedigree!" She waved the race card in excitement. "The horse is by Red Maguire and his mother won seven races all at this distance — he has to be worth a bet!"

"Come on then," said Edward as the jockeys began to spill out of their weighing-room, their colours bright against the grey day. "Let's put our money where your mouth is." Once the bet was on he tugged at her arm. "Let's go and have a drink and watch the race inside."

She followed him to the owners' and trainers' bar beside the entrance and was soon sitting beside a roaring fire with a hot cup of coffee in her hand, glued to the television set as the horses cantered down to the start of the race.

As they set off along the sand track she got to her feet and moved closer to the TV. She stole a glance at Edward out of the corner of her eye. He really was a most attractive man and she knew that she had to be careful of him. He was just another heartbreaker and there was no way she was going to become another rich man's play thing.

Boy Scout romped home three lengths ahead of anyone else. As the jockey trotted him arrogantly over the line Sarah gave a whoop of delight.

Edward let out a roar of laughter. "Beginner's luck, I bet," he said, snatching off his glasses and beaming at her. "Let's see if you can double your money."

They collected the winnings from a very disgruntled bookie and then walked back to the paddock to look at the horses for the second race.

"What do you think in this one then?" he asked, opening his own programme and studying the horses. He ran a hand distractedly through his grey hair, scowling at the programme.

Sarah picked out the horse that she thought would win: Gold Trinket.

"Well," he said, rolling up the race card and stuffing it into his pocket, "you put your winnings on him. I'm going on something different - I'm going on Raving Rosie." With a decisive nod of his head, he handed her the winnings from the last race, "go on then, put your money where your mouth is," he joked.

A short while later she was laughing with delight as Gold Trinket beat Raving Rosie by a very short nose on the winning line after a battle that had gone on for the final two furlongs.

Edward inclined his head, conceding victory to her. "go and collect your winnings," he said, his mouth pouting into a sulk, but his dark eyes danced with amusement. Sarah found herself strangely drawn to this handsome and charming man but every fibre rebelled against the attraction.

They leant against the rail to watch the horses parade for the last race. "I'm going to have my money on that horse, Another Promise," he said, waving his race card to indicate a wiry-looking grey gelding wearing number four on its number cloth.

Sarah opened the race card and looked at the details of the horse. "Another Promise should do well," she said reading the horse's form, and then pulled a face, impressed with the horse's parentage. "God!" she exclaimed suddenly, making Edward jump, "I remember seeing the sales report about this horse! It was sold for an absolute fortune at Tattersalls in Ireland."

"Well done," he said, impressed by her memory,

Just then the bell rang and the jockeys spilled out of the weighing-room, their long limbs and pale faces contrasting with the healthy, grinning faces of the girl grooms who leered at them hoping for a date afterwards.

Sarah recognised the colours that Edward's horses ran under, yellow and blue, and watched, wide-eyed in astonishment, as the jockey went straight to the horse that they had just been discussing and was legged up.

"Bloody hell!" she exclaimed, forgetting where she was. "Another Promise is your horse!" The old feeling of determination not to like him prickled in the background of her mind but she fought it down. It was a lovely day and she was going to enjoy herself. What did it matter if he was a multi-multi-millionaire and she was just a plain penniless groom? There was no way that he was going to get her into bed and use her like Derry had, so what the hell? She was enjoying his company and it was a lovely way to spend a day.

The horses were shoved into the starting gates at the far end of the course. Edward ran lightly up the steps onto the stand to watch the race. He pulled the binoculars that had been slung over his arm up to his eyes and was lost, watching the race intently. Sarah could feel the tension he was emitting as his horse refused to go into the confining-box of the starting-stall and had to be shoved in by four skull-capped handlers. Finally all of the horses were loaded up, the gates shot open and the horses burst out, a rapidly moving centipede of colour and flashing legs beneath the white guard-rail. Edward was oblivious to everything except Another Promise, his glasses trained intently on the animal. "Come on, come on," she could hear him muttering as the horse ran down the middle of the field seeming to be swept along by the others. Then as they rounded the home turn Another Promise moved to the outside of the track onto the better, less churned-up sand and shot for home, outstripping the others as his grey legs pounded as fast as he could. As he shot over the line a length clear of the other runners, Edward let out a great cry of delight and dropped a sudden kiss on Sarah's forehead. She jumped back defensively and instantly regretted doing so. Maybe he was different from Derry.

"Now let's go and celebrate!" Edward said exuberantly, slipping under the guard-rail and heading off towards the owners' and trainers' bar. Sarah scurried after him, her strides two to each of his long ones.

"Let's have some champagne." Edward waved his arm at the barman to attract his attention. Sarah took tiny sips of the heady liquid, as she was conscious of the effect of the alcohol making her face pinker than it already was and conscious also that her resistance would be lowered.

There was no way he was getting her drunk and getting her to join the mile-high club in a helicopter over Southwell racecourse.

Then Edward, relaxed by the champagne, turned suddenly to her and said, "You're a real person, Sarah." And when she frowned quizzically he went on to explain, "a lot of the women that I keep company with are with me for what they can get out of me. You are different — you are so real." His eyes were looking into hers.

She looked away quickly, afraid of what she saw there.

She was saddened when the races were over and the barman began to clear the glasses away, hinting that they should all clear off, it was early evening and he wanted to go home.

"Will you come for dinner?" asked Edward, shrugging on the coat that he had draped over a chair-back.

Sarah smiled sadly. "I can't," she said, torn between wanting to go for dinner with him and her suspicion and fear that he merely wanted to take her to bed. "I must go — I have a long drive."

"I wish that you didn't have to go," Edward said, a tight smile turning up the corners of his mouth. "I enjoyed spending time with you."

Sarah felt herself waver. He looked so genuinely disappointed. She had to go, quickly, before he persuaded her to stay.

"Thanks for a lovely day." She kissed him shyly on the cheek and left. It was best to go now. She needed to get away from him. His charm was starting to chisel away her defensive shell. And besides, heaven knew what havoc Lillie would have created in the yard.

She was halfway home when her phone rang. She snatched it up, half-hoping it would be Derry. It was Edward.

"Thank you for a lovely day," he said. She could hear the noise of his car as he drove home from wherever he kept the helicopter. "Would you have dinner another time?"

She accepted, unable to keep a huge smile of delight from spreading over her face. She had enjoyed his company at the races.

Lillie was still in the yard when she got home, hovering around trying to find something to do until Sarah got back, itching with curiosity as to what had happened.

"Did you have a good day?" she smiled, her beady prying eyes intent with curiosity.

"Oh, it was OK," Sarah said airily. "I won five hundred pounds." She could feel the wad of money in her suit pocket.

Lillie's mouth opened and closed like a goldfish. "He's one of the richest men in the Midlands," she said and then added spitefully, "I don't know what he sees in you."

Sarah ignored her and headed for the caravan.

"Well, but are you going to see him again?" Lillie called after her, dying of curiosity.

"I don't know — maybe," Sarah said nonchalantly over her shoulder.

In the caravan she lay on the settee and stared at a television programme sightlessly, her mind still at the races.

Sarah was riding one of the horses out on exercise when her mobile phone shrilled in her pocket. She fumbled with the zip, holding the reins in one hand, and finally managed to extract the phone from the depths of her pocket. "Hello?" she said, struggling to hear over the noise of the wind. "It's Edward."

A broad grin broke across her face of its own volition much to her annoyance and she felt a huge knot of excitement churn her stomach. "Can I interest you in dinner this week?"

"Lovely," she agreed and a few minutes later snapped off the telephone having arranged to meet him at a restaurant one night after work.

Later she was extremely annoyed with herself that she was looking forward so much to meeting him. He was only a man and look at what they did — just hurt you, like Derry who had charmed her and then used her for sex. There was no way she was going to let this one do that.

He was waiting for her at the entrance when she arrived at the restaurant, and she felt very proud to walk in to dinner on the arm of such a handsome man. Who cared if most of them thought that he was old enough to be her father? He looked very handsome in a pair of green moleskin trousers and a casual shirt, worn beneath a smart jacket which brought out the colour of his green eyes. The dinner was delicious and for once she did not pull away when she felt his knee brush against hers under the dinner-table.

After dinner he turned to her and asked tentatively, "Are you in any great rush?"

"Well —" she began, determined that she was not going to fall for that old cliché.

Reading her mind, he grinned. "I only want you to look at a horse that I have bought."

Then feeling her cheeks flush at her presumption, and a little miffed that he wasn't trying to get her into bed, she laughed in embarrassment, and shrugged. "OK."

She followed the Rolls Royce in her little car. At last they arrived at a tall pair of iron gates, operated by a remote control, which opened soundlessly and they drove up a wide tarmac drive flanked by tall bushes and elegant flowerbeds, lit up in the darkness by ground-level lights that cast eerie shadows all over the lane. After what seemed like miles he pulled into a wide yard flanked by four enormous sheds. Security lights came on as they drove in and the yard was lit up like daylight.

He led the way into one of the sheds, pulling back a sliding door of enormous proportions. Sarah felt her eyes widen with amazement. The shed stretched into the distance with stables at both sides of a wide passageway. Elegant thoroughbred heads looked out over every half-door as far as she could see into the gloom.

"Wow," she whispered.

Edward took her hand and she did not resist. His hand was cool and smooth with long fingers that wrapped easily around hers as he led her down the long line of stables. "He's over here." He led her to a stable and laid his hand on the dark neck of the beautiful horse. "County Cousin," he said proudly, "a full brother to Sunset Rock, the winner of the Derby three years ago."

"Wow," she breathed again, mad at herself that she could not think of anything more constructive to say, but the enormous wealth of the place had tied her tongue into a thousand knots and her brain felt as if it had turned to jelly.

"Do you want to look around?" asked Edward, seeing the look of wonder on her face. It gave him great pleasure to share the stables that he had designed himself with anyone that appreciated them. Since he had made his money through sheer hard work he could easily remember the very hard times and it was nice to be with someone who was interested just in the horses and the stables for their own sake rather than for what they could get out of him. He took her on a guided tour of the yard, watching and loving the look of wonder on her face.

Finally, when the tour was over, he asked, "I know that this sounds like a cliché, but would you like a nightcap?"

Sarah nodded her head, dumbstruck by the place.

She followed him m the car down more darkened private lanes until they pulled up outside a magnificent house, lit by powerful lights. She followed him inside; it reeked of immense wealth and power.

After coffee she stood up, regretfully. She had been enjoying his company and was suddenly reluctant to leave. He followed her to the door. She let him take her by the hand.

"Sarah," he whispered gently, touching her face as if he thought that she was made of china, "Sarah, I'm not the womanising bastard that you think I am. Give me a chance to show you that. I've kept my distance so I wouldn't frighten you off."

Slowly Sarah raised her eyes to meet his. They were kind, boring into hers as if he could look inside her and see her fears. The spectre of Derry and the destruction he had wrought over her for so long hovered close by.

Gently, as if he were afraid that she would vanish, Edward lowered his lips onto hers. She froze, her body tensing against his. Then, feeling the tenderness in the way he held her and the gentleness of his lips against hers, she began to relax, returning his kisses, feeling his need growing as urgently as her own.

"Give me a chance to show you how much I care for you," he whispered against her neck.

He led her silently upstairs her to a vast bedroom, dominated by a huge bed, where she let him undress her. She revelled in his joy as he explored her voluptuous body and cried out in sheer delight as he skilfully brought her to a climax.

Much, much later she lay in his arms, basking in the rosy afterglow of sex.

"I must go," she said, looking lazily at her watch and seeing that she only had time to get home before stables in the morning.

He followed her downstairs after she had dressed, and leant against the door as she went. "I have to go away to the States for a month," he said, kissing her softly on the mouth. "I will ring you when I can."

She turned abruptly and ran down the steps.

She wrenched the car door open and threw herself in.

She was seething with anger and disappointment. That was a brush-off if ever she heard one. Cursing her own stupidity, she slammed the car door shut and drove away.

CHAPTER THIRTY

"Well, now, Mrs Flynn," said Morgan, pulling the duvet from Tara's naked body and ejecting her forcibly onto the cold floor with a shove of his leg, "how about getting up and making your husband a cup of tea?"

"How about you getting me one?" she laughed, scrambling back under the cover and running her fingers over his warm torso.

Giggling, he groaned, "mercy, mercy, you harlot you!" as he rolled over and pulled her into his arms.

They were roused a while later by Kate hammering crossly on the front door.

"Come on, for fuck's sake," she snarled when Morgan leant out of the bedroom window wearing only his boxers and shirt. "We've got races to win."

Tara giggled as the garden gate slammed in temper. "Ooops," she said, huddling back under the duvet.

Morgan pulled on his jeans and buttoned his shirt hastily. Then as he left the bedroom he grabbed the duvet and pulled it off her warm body, "come on. Get up and get your husband's breakfast!"

The yard was a hive of activity when she arrived, having dressed and made them all cups of tea. Morgan was busily shovelling droppings into a battered wheelbarrow. She handed him a cup.

"Big day today," he said, wrapping his long sensuous fingers around the cup. "Three of our horses are running."

Kate scuttled past shoving an even more battered wheelbarrow laden with horse-tack and rugs ready to load up into the lorry. "Thanks," she said, pausing to grab the cup of tea from Tara, and then very pointedly hurried on, spilling most of the tea over the yard as she tried to push the wheelbarrow and carry the cup at the same time.

Tara shook her head in astonishment at her rapidly retreating back, with her mane of curling red hair cascading down, already escaping from its clasp.

Leaving them to get the horses ready and load the lorry, Tara escaped back to the silence of the house to cook breakfast and get the passports ready for the horses in case the officials needed to check that they had their injections up to date. She made bacon sandwiches and wrapped them in tinfoil ready to be eaten on the long drive to the racecourse.

Then, once they had all changed into decent clothes, they set off with the horses for the races.

They were standing in the paddock with Shane McGrath, watching the first of his two entries go around the ring when Eddie Gallagher blustered towards them.

"Is he worth a bet?" interrupted Eddie Gallagher, not wanting to be kept out of the action.

"Course he is!" snapped Shane, his black eyes blazing at Eddie through the dark lenses of the sunglasses.

Eddie shrugged, his thick skin hardly dented by the pop star's anger.

Tara ran across the grass to join them. Chancer, Shane's horse, looked brilliant. He walked around the ring looking like a prince amongst the other horses, his coat gleaming with health and his ears sharply pricked as he marched, tugging Kate who was walking as fast as she could.

The jockeys filed out. Morgan's jockey, Josh, had just come out of the sauna. His skin was an odd greenish shade; not having eaten or drunk for two days now he felt decidedly sick with fear, and lightheaded and weak from the sauna.

Morgan legged Josh up on Chancer. As Tara watched, the jockey bent over, leaning down to listen intently, nodding his head, as Morgan gave him the instructions on how he wanted the horse to be run.

"I hope that you told him to keep up the front," said Shane, taking off his sunglasses and scanning the faces in the crowds leaning around the parade-ring, in the hope that someone would recognise him.

"Course," lied Morgan. He had told the jockey to run the horse at the back, and then bring him through towards the end of the race, otherwise the horse would run too fast and tire himself out.

Shane spent most of the race peering through his binoculars and bellowing, "what the fuck is he doing?" until on the home turn the jockey pulled Chancer to the outside of the others and, with two fences left to jump, let him power towards the finish, easily outstripping the others and leaping the fences as if they were nothing. He cruised into the finishing-line a horse's length ahead of the others. Josh punched the air, as did Morgan and Shane.

"That's one in the bag!" Morgan yelled, kissing Tara. "Maybe it will be our lucky day!"

Kate walked Shane's second horse, Rock Star, around the ring, glowing with pride. He was telling everyone that would listen that this was his second horse and that it was a certainty to win. Morgan became short-tempered with the tension. The horse had only won once in his life, before Morgan had bought him for Shane. Morgan had liked his pedigree and he had won superbly that one time, but since then he had done nothing and had come to Morgan's yard sullen and unresponsive. Morgan had given up trying to get him to work on the gallops and instead had sent Kate out hacking around the lanes and galloping him in farmers' fields in order to get him fit.

Josh came back, clutching his stomach and looking greener around the face than the trampled grass that he was standing on, longing to be sick. He was racked with the most awful stomach-ache which made it hurt to straighten up. He winced as Morgan legged him up onto the horse. Then as Kate led him around the ring, he snapped, bad-tempered with the pain, "what the bloody hell is this fucking donkey?"

"It's the winner of this race," she snapped back. She had grown fond of Rock Star as she hacked him around the lanes and was the only one on the yard who was convinced of his capabilities. The little horse cantered down to the start. To Josh he felt like something that would have been more at home in a riding school. He had no interest in the other horses and never even batted an eyelid when a child standing on the guard-rail suddenly let off his toy gun with a loud bang making all the other horses shy and buck with fear.

The horses lined up on the start, fourteen of them in all. The starter lifted his flag and then dropped it as they walked forwards. Thirteen of the horses bounded away, leaving Rock Star standing on the start-line watching with interest as the others galloped away from him. Dumbstruck in horror, the jockey lifted his whip and gave the horse an almighty slap down on his skinny quarters whereupon the horse set off sullenly after the others.

"I thought we had a horse that was going to refuse to start," laughed the commentator, maliciously, "Morgan Flynn's horse has now joined the race although he already looks completely outclassed."

Tara felt Morgan seethe with anger and, putting her hand into his, squeezed it gently. But he did not seem to notice as he was glaring intently at the television screen overhead. Shane, having forgotten his superb win in the first race, was ranting and raving about the dumb horse in her other ear. While Eddie, who now considered himself to be a real expert where racing was concerned, was telling the man who was standing next to him that the ground was too soft for the horse. The leading horses were now beginning to tire; the initial first blast of speed gone, they slowed to a more sedate pace for the long run home. Rock Star, seeing the quarters of the last horse over the next fence, put on a spurt and began to catch up with them. Then as he outstripped the last horse he pricked his ears, seeing another pair of quarters ahead of him that he wanted to get to. As the final fence came into view Morgan's little horse had worked his way up the field to fourth place.

"We've caught him up! He's still on the first circuit!" laughed one of the jockeys, making a grab for the Josh's whip as a joke. Josh snatched it out of his way and brought it down with a crack on the horse's shoulder by mistake. Rock Star, furious at such treatment, surged forwards, finding acceleration that would do justice to a Ferrari. He charged past the leading horses, put in a magnificent leap over the final fence and romped home to tremendous cheers ten lengths ahead of the others.

The television cameras hurried to catch a glimpse of Morgan as he shoved his way through to the winner's enclosure to greet a delighted horse and an exhausted-looking jockey. Then he shoved his way back to the paddock where Kate was leading the last entry, Brackley Gate, around for the third race.

The pressure on Morgan was incredible. He had won two races, one with a real no-hoper. Now if he could pull off a third race, it would be an incredible feat. Punters would want to come to him to have him train their horses. Pull this one off and he was made.

Tara went into the parade-ring where she tried to calm an overexcited Eddie Gallagher and keep a very tetchy Morgan calm as he watched his horse being led around the ring. Kate was flushed with delight and chattered to the horse, unable to keep silent. She looked like a small excited child, delighted to have so many Christmas presents. Derry had a horse in this race, but the two trainers stayed at opposite ends of the parade-ring and Tara stayed well away from him. But even at this distance she could sense his intense disapproval.

The jockeys came out of the weigh room. Josh looked completely washed out, having only just managed to make it to the toilets after the last race. He had sipped a cup of very sweet tea and hoped that he would make it onto the horse without being sick again. He had won two races on the trot; it would be an achievement like no other to win three races.

Morgan went up to Eddie's hospitality box as the runners cantered down to the start. Eddie had just bought himself a huge pair of very powerful binoculars which he was dying to try out. All of the guests that he had with him squeezed out onto the balcony. Tara found herself shoved away from Morgan, wanting desperately to be beside him to offer him comfort from the stress she knew that he was feeling now. She could see his face, etched with tension as he glared out over the racecourse, trying to make out his horse amongst the others as they circled at the start of the race. His lips were pressed into a determined line and his dark eyes blazed with desperation as he glared out over the course, willing the jockey to do a good job and bring the horse home in the lead and safely.

"All I'm concerned about is that the horse comes back safely - he's like a family pet," Eddie Gallagher had lied to the television cameras, making Tara smile in wry amusement. He barely knew the horse's name and certainly wasn't worried about its safety. All that he was concerned about was it coming back in the lead and lining his very deep pockets with prize money.

The race set off. With only five runners in this highly competitive race, it was easy to tell them apart. These were some of the best horses in racing and there was even one flown in that morning from England which was completely outclassed by the powerful Irish chasers. Brackley Gate ran in second place, his long legs pounding on the rock-hard ground, vying with Derry's runner, which swept into the lead and then dropped back for a fence before taking the lead again. Morgan was silent, lost in his own thoughts, willing the horse forward, riding it in his imagination, and gathering it before the fences. Tara watched him surreptitiously, seeing how he winced as the horse took off too soon, his eyes never leaving the race. They powered past the stands, carried on a tide of screaming from the crowds. Brackley Gate outstripped Derry's horse as they headed back out into the country and seeing the open track in front of him began to gallop faster, relishing the ground and eating up the fences. The English horse slowed as he went past the stands and then turned in, totally outclassed and exhausted.

The horses went off into the country becoming tiny dots bobbing in the distance. Tara strained her eyes to see what was happening. Derry's horse was trying to keep up with Brackley Gate, breathing down his neck as they powered away from the other horses. They rounded the home turn, coming suddenly into proper view again, and leapt the second last fence together. Then Brackley Gate, inspired by the roar of the crowd, pricked his ears and bounded forwards leaving Derry's horse behind him. He leapt the last fence, put in a short stride before it getting it completely wrong and landed in a sprawling heap, pitching the tired and weak jockey out of the saddle and onto his neck. He scrambled to his feet with Josh clinging on. Derry's horse, taking advantage of the stumble, took the lead, powering away to the line, but Brackley Gate, not wanting to be beaten, charged after him. Josh -weak, seeing stars and hearing a rushing noise in his ears - feared that he was going to faint but valiantly wriggled himself back into the saddle and, with his long legs dangling, booted the horse over the finishing line to win by a short head.

The crowd shouted and cheered to welcome the brave horse and jockey home. Still leaving his legs dangling, Josh smiled weakly at Derry's jockey who saluted him. "Fair play to ye," said the other jockey, trotting the horse away. Josh just managed to take off the saddle and sit on the weighing-scales before he staggered to his seat and passed out in a faint.

Tara, walking behind a delighted Morgan who was being mobbed by autograph hunters and the television cameras, found herself walking beside a scowling Derry. "Congratulations," he sneered sarcastically. "Amazing what can be done with a three-legged donkey and two nondescript horses." He turned to face her as they walked to give her the full benefit of his temper and black scowl. "Must be the luck of the Blake's rubbing off on him." Then with a curt nod he sauntered away to catch up with his horse.

CHAPTER THIRTY ONE

They drove home at almost midnight, all on a complete high. Kate had been in the owners' and trainers' bar with the jockeys and was completely pissed. She spent the whole journey home alternatively singing tuneless and unrecognisable songs and hanging her head out of the window complaining that she was going to be sick.

As they rounded the final bend before the entrance to Radford Lodge Morgan suddenly exclaimed, "what the fuck?"

Tara sat up tiredly. She had been asleep, her head lolling onto this shoulder. She peered out of the windows. Fires were burning at the side of the road and a crowd stood beside the flames, cheering and waving banners.

Morgan stopped the lorry as one of the local people came to the side of the lorry. "Well done!" said the man who they all recognised from a local farm. "I had a bet on you winning all three races – I've won a bloody fortune!"

"So have I!" called someone else and the cry was echoed the length of the road. "Brilliant!" grinned Morgan and then, still laughing, put the lorry into gear and rolled slowly forwards to the cheers and congratulations of the villagers.

He stopped the lorry in the yard and pulled Tara towards him,

"You were brilliant today. You deserved those wins," she said tiredly, lulled into dozing against his warm chest in the cosy fug of the cab.

"Go in, you," he said, pushing her gently upright. "Kate and I'll do these horses – I won't be long."

Tara scrambled out of the cab. There was a full moon and it was as light as day, the whole yard looking gorgeous, washed by the silver rays which hid all of the battered imperfections that were so glaringly obvious in the daylight.

She woke with a start a while later. Morgan was not in bed. She glanced at the clock, the hands visible in the bright moonlight. Two o'clock in the morning. Where the hell was he? Had he gone to sleep downstairs, she wondered, nerves making her hands fumble as she dragged on her dressing gown.

The house was deserted. Fighting against the fear that was rising in her heart she wrenched open the front door and peered out into the yard.

"Morgan!" she yelled, hearing the panic in her own voice as she ran out into the yard. The yard was deserted, the lorry covered in mist and the horses gazing out in amazement at seeing someone in the yard at this time.

"Here!" she heard him call back, relief flooding into her at the sound of his voice.

She headed to where the sound had come from. He was leaning over the paddock fence, which was bathed in the silvery light of the moon, casting long shadows where the trees stood.

"What on earth are you doing?" she said crossly.

"Just looking," he answered.

She went up to him and leant against the fence with him. "Looking?" she said sharply, thinking that he had gone off his rocker. As she spoke she saw what he had been looking at: halfway down the field, grazing unconcernedly was Carna Boy, his head to the ground eating as if his life depended upon it, the sound of his munching carrying easily across the dark field towards them. He looked like a huge carthorse, his grass-filled belly rounded and his massive quarters plump and fat, completely healthy again after his near-fatal illness.

"He's ready to start work again," said Morgan, his voice filled with the dreams of a thousand racehorse trainers, that this was the horse who was going to win the biggest race in history - the Cheltenham Gold Cup — and prove once and for all that he was one of the greatest trainers in Ireland.

To celebrate, Morgan decided that they were going to have a day out. Tara scowled when he announced they were going to the races. Just as spectators. But at least it was a day out. Together. A rare luxury nowadays.

She was very much mistaken if she thought they were going to manage to spend the day alone. Morgan's wins had made him famous overnight and they were mobbed from the moment they walked onto the course, everyone wanting to get his autograph. They spent the whole day being dragged from one hospitality box to another by eager owners wanting to bring their horses to Morgan for him to train. Tara wished they had spent the day away from the races; it would have been lovely to take a picnic somewhere and spend a lazy afternoon making love in a secluded spot instead of being mobbed and fought over by jostling autograph-hunters and eager newspaper reporters wanting the story on the three wins.

Morgan went off to talk to a businessman who wanted to buy a few racehorses and Tara found herself wandering alone through the crowds, feeling miserable that the day out together had been spoilt.

Suddenly hot chubby fingers grabbed her arm and she spun around to face JT, his face purple with the heat beneath a straw hat.

"Good wins for Morgan," he leered. "You must be bringing him luck."

Tara smiled politely; JT was only interested in her because of Morgan's wins.

"Come and watch my horse running," he said, hooking his arm through hers and giving her no choice but to accompany him back to the air-conditioned luxury of his hospitality box.

It was magnificent inside – cool, with waitresses dishing out ice-cold glasses of champagne and smoked salmon on slivers of soda bread, which melted in her mouth. "Come out onto the balcony," he said, pulling her into the bright sunlight where she felt her smile die. Derry lolled against the guard-rail looking as dangerous and handsome as a leopard. He turned to face her when he heard the doors slide back and she saw the look of anger cross his handsome face as he straightened up to greet her. "Tara," he said, kissing her politely.

"Derry," she said equally politely, before taking a place beside JT as far away from Derry as she could.

"They're off!" yelled JT in excitement as his horse, Eagle Eye, bounded out of the starting stalls. The horse thundered up with the leaders as they shot towards home and then JT let out a howl of annoyance as he suddenly dropped out of the running and cantered home to go over the line the last of all of the runners. Derry glared down the track white-faced in anger, as JT, wordless in his fury, shook his head in temper.

"What the bloody hell is going on?" JT snapped a moment later, suddenly recovering his voice. Tara wished that she were a thousand miles away. "You said that Eagle Eye was going to win," he snarled at Derry, his face flushing a darker shade of purple. He wrenched off his dark-blue jacket and flung it down on one of the chairs. Sweat had darkened huge rings under the arms of his pale blue shirt.

Derry, recovering his legendary icy charm, shrugged nonchalantly. "He's still a young horse, JT. These things happen. He seemed to tire quickly — maybe he's got a bit of a virus."

"I think that I would be better off going back to a trainer that is in form instead of messing around with you," JT snapped irritably and then, just to acid insult to injury, the tannoy crackled into life and it was announced that there was to be a steward's enquiry and would the trainer of Eagle Eye go to the steward's office please.

"Fuck, that's me," fumed Derry. He shoved past Tara, shooting her a look of pure hatred.

When he had gone, JT gave her a malicious grin. "Do him good to keep him on his toes!" He smiled with all the complacency and danger of a cat about to spring on an unsuspecting mouse as Ellen glided into the terrace looking very elegant in a cream silk dress embroidered with flowers that crept from the hem to the shoulder. "I couldn't leave him. Ellen would kill me, wouldn't you, darling?"

Unable to bear being with the horrible man any longer, Tara made her excuses and fled, looking desperately for Morgan.

A few days later the postman barged into the kitchen as Tara was making sandwiches for lunch. The mail had increased since the day when they had won the three races. Cards had come from all over the country congratulating them. She sifted idly through the letters as Morgan came in.

He seized some of the large envelopes. "Great — these are the brochures for the new stables," he said perching on the edge of the table and ripping open some of the envelopes. "Christ," he exclaimed a moment later looking at the prices of the sheds. He slumped down against the table munching a sandwich distractedly. "What am I supposed to do," he moaned, taking a bite. "I've got new owners wanting to bring horses and nowhere to put them. I can't afford to put up new stables until I have new owners and I can't have new owners until I have new stables." He moaned, grimacing at the complexity of his problem.

"We'll just have to mortgage this place," said Tara gently, pulling out a chair and taking his hand.

"What?" he exclaimed. Then he put down the sandwich and shook his head. "I don't want more debt, Tara," he said miserably.

Tara picked up the sandwich and then got up and fetched a pile of paperwork from the office table. "Look at these," she said. "I was working on them today." She opened one of the files and spread the neatly typed papers in front of him. "You can't expand without new stables. I've been doing some cash projections for you. With even a few of the new owners that want to come, we can easily afford to put up new stables and a horse-walking machine."

Morgan pulled the sheets towards him, studying them intently for a moment, munching his sandwich. Then finally he said, "Mrs Flynn, you're a genius. We had better make an appointment to see the bank manager."

Tara grinned. "I've already done that — it's at two o'clock tomorrow."

The new stables seemed to go up overnight. One moment there was a field and an old tumbledown shed surrounded by the crumbling remains of old farm machinery and a battered horse-trap and the next moment a digger had driven in, levelled the lot, and a few days later a raft of concrete had been laid that would be the floor of the new shed. The telephone never seemed to stop ringing with eager people wanting to put horses with Morgan and wanting to know when they could bring them over. He was hot property — when it was not eager customers on the phone it was news reporters wanting to come and interview the new golden boy of racing.

After everyone had gone home, Tara and Morgan wandered around the new yard. It was fantastic, a long low shed that could house forty horses.

"This is what I've dreamt about for years," said Morgan, standing in the doorway of the silent shed and gazing dreamily at the empty boxes. He kissed her softly. Then he pulled away. "There is one thing that we should do now," he said, lighting up with excitement.

Tara felt her eyes widen: they were going to christen the stable block! Then she frowned in disappointment when he grabbed a head-collar from the yard where it had been abandoned by Kate.

"Wait there," he said and jogged off across the yard.

A short while later the sound of an unshod horse's hooves thudded up the yard and Morgan appeared with Carna Boy dancing on the end of the lead-rope beside him.

"Now," he said, pulling the fat horse into the first stable and slipping the head-collar off his head, "we have our first guest."

After the old stables had been done and Kate had cleaned out Carna Boy's stable, she put the saddle on his fat body and led him into the yard. The big horse walked beside her as docile as an old dog. Morgan came out of the house where he had been talking to some new owners on the telephone, arranging for the new horses to be delivered.

This would turn Radford Lodge into one of the biggest training centres in the county.

"I have some new horses coming this afternoon, so you can take him out for a bit of roadwork — twenty minutes of just walking," he said, legging Kate niftily into the tall horse's saddle.

She gathered up her reins with a grin and, shoving her feet into the stirrups, booted the horse forwards. "I think that twenty minutes is all he is fit for with this big belly," she laughed, kicking the horse.

Suddenly, with a massive leap and squeal of temper, Carna Boy jumped forwards, twisting viciously in the air. They parted company and Kate landed with a thud in the dusty yard. Then before Morgan could grab the horse's reins, he had shot around, leapt the yard fence and disappeared in the direction of Westwood Park

"Fuck!" yelled Morgan.

"Oww!" moaned Kate.

"Oops!" cringed Tara.

Morgan threw down the head-collar that he had been holding. "You stupid bugger," he snarled at Kate. "Don't ever kick a horse like that again," and then, casting her a glance that would have frozen anyone, he set off in the direction that the horse had gone. Only a trail of footprints marked the dusty soil.

Tara followed him, bleakly hoping that the horse would stop before he reached Derry's. Morgan marched silently, his hands deep in his pockets, his body set in anger. Both were hoping that the horse would stop soon, but as they followed his tracks over fence after fence it was obvious that he had no intention of doing so.

Then, as the hoof-prints disappeared over a huge hedge and ditch, Morgan stopped, examining the ground, muttering, "he can't have."

Then, as no prints veered oft at the hedge, he climbed over a low bit of fence and they scoured the ground the other side of the hedge and found where the horse had landed. "He bloody jumped that," said Morgan in delight and then renewed his efforts to catch the horse.

A few minutes later, as they crossed onto the gallops at Westwood Park, they both froze in dismay when they saw that Carna Boy had been caught and was being led back by Derry on his smart skewbald trainer's horse.

They walked towards him, speechless in their dismay at the horse being caught by Derry of all people. He reined in Carna Boy and tossed the reins to Morgan. "Why don't you just forget doing anything with this horse, Morgan?" he drawled, looking very cool beneath a leather cowboy hat and regarding their red faces with amusement. "He's a complete rogue. You're wasting your time trying to train him for Cheltenham. Why don't you give up now before you make yourself look an even bigger fool?"

CHAPTER THIRTY TWO

Morgan was so angry, Tara did not dare to talk to him; instead she trudged miserably after him as he led Carna Boy back toward Radford Lodge. The horse walked gently beside him, his huge fat quarters swinging in rime to the rolling of his tangled tail which almost touched the ground. From the solid set of Morgan's shoulders and the bow of his head, it was easy to see that he was still furious and in no mood to talk to the horse or her.

Tara wished desperately that she could reach him but he was at that moment lost to her, deep in his own anger.

When they finally led the horse into the yard Kate was sitting on the outside water trough. "Oh, you've found him!" she cried, leaping to her feet and throwing her arms around the horse's neck.

"On Derry Blake's gallops," said Morgan grimly, leading the horse towards the hosepipe.

Kate undid the horse's saddle and pulled it off his fat back. The hair underneath was dark with sweat. Morgan gently played the hosepipe over his legs and then finally over his hot body. The horse pawed at the water, delighted to be getting a cool shower. "You should have seen the enormous hedge he jumped Kate," he grinned, shaking his head at the memory of the horse leaping over the hedge. Then suddenly he became morose again. "He's probably knackered his legs though," he moaned, crouching down and feeling the horse's legs gingerly. At last he stood up with a sigh of relief.

There were no signs of damage.

Then when Morgan led him into this stable he lay down, groaning in mock tiredness, hoping to get sympathy.

Tara was woken from an exhausted sleep by the sound of the bed creaking. She rolled over, blinking against the bedside light which shone its pale glimmer in her eyes. Morgan was sitting on the side of the bed pulling on his socks.

"What are you doing?" she groaned, her voice thick with sleep.

"I have to check Carna Boy," he whispered. "I can't sleep. I'm worried that he could have damaged himself with all that galloping and jumping."

"Oh, Morgan!" she said crossly, rolling over and shutting her eyes tight as he stomped out of the room. She heard him come back later and when he climbed back into bed again and wrapped his cold body around her for warmth she feigned sleep, annoyed that he should want to go checking the horse in the middle of the night. He was completely obsessed with the bloody animal. He and Derry were as bad as each other and this ridiculous challenge had driven them both mad.

He was gone again when she finally awoke to the raucous sound of the alarm-clock and when she dressed and went into the new stable yard with a cup of tea for him, he was leaning on the open half-door looking in at Carna Boy.

"Has he survived the night then?" she said softly, making Morgan jump.

He spun around to face her. "Looks that way."

He took the tea from her and sipped it thoughtfully. "The Gold Cup is the race that every trainer dreams about. It's not the prize money, it's just the glory, seeing your horse powering up that hill in front of all of the others and knowing that all of your hard work and faith have brought you to that victory. This horse can do it. I know it and he deserves us to have the faith in him."

Tara looked at the horse, wrinkling her nose, and said ruefully, "but he's nothing but a nasty old bastard. He could have killed Kate yesterday, and the only reason that he was sold from Derry's is that Derry thought he was no good."

Morgan drained the rest of his tea and threw the dregs towards the drain in temper. "We'll see," he snapped. Then he stalked away to start the yard work, leaving Tara and Carna Boy to glare at each other.

A few days later Morgan announced that he was going to ride the horse again. Tara followed him into the barn to Carna Boy's stable.

"Are you sure that he's ready to be ridden?" she said doubtfully, standing well back from the door, not wanting to get close to Carna Boy's daring teeth and hooves that could fly out as quick as a flash.

"Soon find out," grinned Morgan, fastening the chin-strap on his hat.

Since Morgan very rarely wore a riding hat she began to worry immediately - things must be serious if he wanted to wear it. She moved forward to undo the bolts that shut the door.

"Leave them," he said quickly. "I'm going to ride him in here first - then if he does buck at least I can control him."

Tara watched wide-eyed as he vaulted lightly into the saddle and shoved his feet quickly into the stirrups. He had scarcely time to do that when the horse erupted into a frenzy of bucking.

"Wow," breathed Kate, coming into the barn and peering awestruck over the door. "For God's sake," wailed Tara, "will you stop? The bloody horse is mad, and I think that you're as bad for wanting to try to ride him!"

But Morgan only laughed. Now Carna Boy, realising that he could not get his rider off, walked sullenly around the stable, his ears glued back, his eyes rolling in temper as he tried to work out a way of getting Morgan off.

After a week of lunging the horse with his saddle on and riding him in the confines of the stable, Morgan was finally satisfied that he was ready to be ridden outside.

With Kate's assistance he rode him first in the stable and then quietly told her to open the door. She opened the door and he rode out into the relatively large space of the stable walkway towards the bright daylight of the yard.

"This is where I'll get trouble if I'm going to get any," he said as he passed through the large sliding door into the vast open space of the yard.

If the horse began to buck here Morgan would have had no way of stopping him until he either tired the horse out or, more likely, was bucked off. The horse now, with all of the work he was having, had lost the huge belly and looked like the fit and well racehorse he was. But his eyes glared with hatred at everyone and Tara looked at him with dislike as he marched proudly into the yard, casting her a disdainful look.

Halfway across the yard towards the sand school, he suddenly stopped and hunched his back, trying to buck, but Morgan was ready for him and clamped his long legs around his belly and kicked him forwards. "Get on," he growled, forcing him into a trot. Grumpily, with his ears flat back against his neck and his eyes rolling maliciously, Carna Boy trotted unwillingly around the sand. After twenty minutes Morgan slowed him to a walk and rode him grinning back to where Tara and Kate were sitting on the fence.

Then suddenly, as Morgan relaxed on him, the horse, sensing his momentary lack of attention, leapt skywards, rounding his strong back and lashing out with his strong back legs. Morgan, caught by surprise, sailed straight over his head and landed with a thud in the ring.

Kate exploded into gales of laughter and Tara shoved her hand in her mouth at the look of indignation on Morgan's red face. Then, as he got up and went to catch Carna Boy, their laughter turned to cries of horror as the horse flattened his ears against his lowered head and then, waving his head like a malicious snake, shot across the sandy ring towards Morgan. Morgan stood still and then at the last moment leapt forward, yelling at the horse and waving his arms in the air. Carna Boy lost his courage at the last moment and shot away, going to sulk at the end of the school like a naughty schoolboy.

"Please, will you just forget this horse?" begged Tara, watching through her hands as Morgan walked calmly down the sand-ring to catch the sullen-looking horse. He led him back to the stable and remounted him, going through the whole procedure again.

"I think that will do him for today," he said tiredly as the horse trotted a circuit of the ring. He slid off his back and handed the reins to an impressed Kate.

Tara, however, was less than impressed. "What if he breaks your back or worse?" she said, as they ate supper later. "It's just a horse, Morgan! Can't you see that it doesn't matter if he wins or not? I don't want you to be injured by a horse that isn't worth anything!"

Morgan shook his head, his face set in hard determined lines. "I have to, don't you understand? I have to beat this horse just like I have to beat Derry. I have to win."

Tara came into his office a few days later to find him filling out race entries; he was going to enter the horse for his first race in September, at the meeting at Listowel. "You're completely mad," she said crossly, looking over his shoulder as he filled in the form.

"Mad about you," he murmured, grabbing her wrist and pulling her down so that she lay on the table in front of him. Gently he began to unbutton her shirt. "I wonder what the stewards would say if they knew what we had done on these entry forms," he murmured, easing her bra up over her breasts and lowering his mouth to one of her rosy nipples.

The time seemed to fly until it was September. Carna Boy had finally settled down enough to be ridden properly and, although he occasionally exploded and bucked his riders off or launched himself at unsuspecting visitors to his box, he finally began to settle down and was fit for his first race. The yard began to fill with horses, eager customers keen to have their horses with the new golden boy of racing. The run of luck continued with Morgan notching up more and more wins every time he went racing. The yard grew rapidly with more horses coming in and more staff being taken on.

Carna Boy completed his training programme and looked a picture of health for his first race. The only blot on the horizon was that Derry's horse, Magnetic Attraction, was running in the same race. Having been off all summer, he too was ready to start the long and perilous campaign on the road to Cheltenham.

Another factor making everyone tetchy that morning as they drove down to Listowel was the fact that the press were saying that Magnetic Attraction was sure to win. Morgan glanced at the headline and threw the newspaper down in disgust. "Bloody newspapers," he groaned, as the horse began a fresh bout of slamming and banging against the sides of the lorry in his excitement. Kate wore a huge plaster on her arm where he had bitten her right through her coat as she plaited his mane, making a nasty bruise.

As soon as the horse left the box and felt his feet touch the ground he began to mess about, barging at Morgan and trying to pull away. It took all three of them to get his saddle on, Tara hanging very uncertainly on to the bridle as he danced from foot to foot while Kate and Morgan hastily did up the saddle.

"Hopefully he'll be too interested in seeing what's going on to buck the jockey off," whispered Morgan as Kate led the horse out into the parade-ring.

Derry was standing in the parade-ring with JT, watching Magnetic Attraction walk around.

"Got that dog going again?" he sneered, nodding in the direction of Carna Boy who was now dancing uncontrollably. Sweat darkening his neck and foam splattering his broad chest as it flew from his mouth; he champed on the bit, hauling Kate around the ring.

"I wouldn't give him much chance," Derry jeered in amusement. He yelled with laughter as Carna Boy, now with Josh on board, gave an almighty kick backwards just missing the old lady who had awarded Derry's horse the prize for Best Turned Out.

The race to everyone's relief was started quickly and Carna Boy galloped off with the leaders. Tara reached for Morgan's hand and squeezed it gently, feeling the pressure of his fingers as he returned her grip. They stood in the stand listening intently to the commentary. The horse was running well on the inside, close to the rails. Then at the fourth fence the commentator announced that the jockey had fallen off. Morgan gave a gasp of horror. As they peered up the track, they saw Carna Boy running back towards the stand, no doubt trying to get back to the stables. The whole stand gazed in fixed horror as he galloped towards the public enclosures and, gathering himself up, took a flying leap straight over the guard-rail, scattering people before him like confetti.

"Let me through!" bellowed Morgan, shaking Tara's hand off and bursting through the owners and trainers who were watching, immobilised with horror, as the horse ploughed on through the spectators.

"Well, I hope that he doesn't do that at Cheltenham," drawled a voice close to Tara.

She spun around to face her very amused-looking brother who cocked his ear towards the tannoy as the announcer said that Magnetic Attraction had just won.

"But I expect my horse will do that," he grinned.

Tara ran after Morgan, feeling bitter tears begin to pour down her face. The horse meant so much to him — why did he have to be so wicked? She caught up with them in the lorry park where the horse had let himself back into the lorry and was pulling unconcernedly at his hay-net.

Just then the tannoy close to the lorry crackled into life and the announcer said in stern tones, "would Morgan Flynn, the trainer of Carna Boy, please go to the stewards' offices immediately?"

CHAPTER THIRTY THREE

Sarah was still smarting from the treatment that she had received from Edward. How could she have let herself be so stupid as to fall for him? He had charmed her, made her like him and relax in his company, taken her to bed and then in the morning just given her the brush-off. Very clever of him and very stupid of her — how could she not have seen that was what he was all about? Wasn't that what all of them were about? Just wanting to get you into bed. It had not cost him anything, just a day at the races and two evenings of dinner and she had gone to bed with him, easy. That was all that she was, easy and stupid.

She had been in such a temper that when she arrived home she got out of the car and slammed the door hard. Lillie's little terrier dogs set up such a cacophony of barking that the bedroom light snapped on and Richard roared loudly at them to shut up. She had glanced at her watch — only a few hours till she had to get up and start work. It hardly seemed worth while going to bed. As she opened the caravan door the mobile phone shrilled in her pocket. She pulled it hastily out and glanced at the number. Edward. She switched on the phone and lifted it to her ear.

"Hello," she said, quietly sulking, hoping that her voice would be full of the complete betrayal that she felt.

"It's me," he said unnecessarily, not yet picking up on the coldness in her voice.

"Oh, hi," she said nonchalantly, sitting down heavily.

"I'm missing you already," he said. "I just wanted to say that I had a wonderful time last night and that I will see you when I get back."

After the call, she felt more confused than ever.

Later on in the morning, while she was working and trying not to betray to Lillie how tired and miserable she felt, he rang again.

"I'm just about to get on the plane. I truly miss you."

Thrown totally into confusion and loneliness, Sarah began to look backwards with longing, desperately missing the security of her job at Westwood Park and the difficult but predictable nature of Derry. At least she knew where she stood with him. She telephoned Westwood Park, just to hear the sound of his voice. Sometimes if he did not have anything to do, he would talk to her. He would discuss the horses and how they had done in the races, seeming to enjoy her conversation; other times he was short and snappy and made her wish that she had not bothered — made her wish that she could just have walked away instead of torturing herself with him.

As the weeks crawled by she found that she had learnt to live without Edward, and no longer felt that she had been used, or felt anything. It was just something that had happened. Derry occupied much of her thinking and most of her phone bill. When Edward rang it was just a pleasant phone call between two people who vaguely knew each other, nothing more. He was busy, distracted with his work, and she was busy and distracted with Derry. They drifted slowly apart.

Lillie was becoming increasingly uptight. One of the big county shows was coming up and she had entered an important event. She had entered one of the big ladies'-hunter classes, which meant that she had to ride her horse side saddle. Lillie had absolutely no talent for the class and the horse had become more unruly, sensing her fear — fear had made Lillie tetchy and picky, finding fault with everything.

They were due to leave at some unearthly hour the following morning which meant that Sarah had a desperately busy day ahead of her, getting all of the stables done to Lillie's exacting standards and then exercising all of the horses so that they would be well-behaved when Lillie hauled them around the ring tomorrow. She had to get them going so nicely that they would tolerate Lillie's appalling riding — her fat body heaving itself around like a sack of potatoes and her heavy hands hauling on their mouths — and yet with enough energy to show themselves off to the judges, not an easy task by any standards. And then, after all of that, she had to bath the horses so that they would be immaculate when they went in the show ring, get all of the tack ready and load up on the lorry, ready for the five-thirty start in the morning. Not an easy job, especially when Lillie spent the whole time wandering around after her, wanting to make small talk, upsetting the horses and making them jumpy.

Sarah hated the show set; they were all completely self-obsessed and whoever had the most money was going to win and whoever crawled the most to the judge would come off the best. It was a world away from the down-to-earth people that she had dealt with in the racing world where everyone knew that the horse was a great leveller. Anyone could spend an enormous amount of money on a horse and still have it fall at the first fence, leaving you looking like a fool.

At four in the afternoon the phone rang. Sarah, who was in the middle of washing Bittersweet Boy's tail, scowled and tried to ignore the insistent ring. They would leave a message. The ringing stopped and then started again. Sighing, she picked up the receiver. She was short of time and there was still so much to do before she finished for the night.

"Hello," she said impatiently, hoping that whoever it was would realise that she was busy and hadn't got time for small talk.

"It's Derry," came the cracking and disjointed voice at the end of the receiver.

"Derry," she heard herself breathe and was annoyed at how pleased she must sound.

"Sarah," he said dramatically, "I need you!"

She knew it was probably just that he was having trouble getting a good groom and so had decided he had punished her enough. She was always there when he called her, like a faithful dog that clings to a brutal master, refusing to see the bad in him. He would reel her back to him. And he knew that she wouldn't refuse.

Nevertheless, knowing all this, she still felt her heart give a huge leap and her face flush with pleasure.

"Please come back. I need you here," he pleaded. "There's no one that can run the yard like you — I need you back here!" He didn't apologise for the way in which he had sacked her, but then that was not Derry's way. "How soon can you get here?" he asked, without even waiting for her to reply.

And Sarah, not even noticing that yet again she was at his beck and call said: "As soon as I can get a ferry."

Lillie, of course, was less than impressed, even though Sarah had hastily organised her own replacement from an equestrian employment agency, "How can you leave me in the lurch like this?" she mouthed, slumped against the kitchen table dramatically. "It's the biggest show of the year and you just waltz off and leave me!"

Sarah could see her mouth opening and closing, but her mind was elsewhere. She didn't care about Lillie or the big show. Derry needed her and that was all that mattered. Lillie was still following her around, screaming abuse, as she packed up the small caravan, furious that Sarah was leaving her, it was hard to find someone who was such a pushover when it came to working hours and conditions.

"Richard won't give you a reference — I will see that you don't work again on the show circuit!" she was screeching breathlessly, her face puce with temper, her fingers white where she clenched them.

But nothing mattered. Sarah shoved her clothes into her suitcase, put all of the bits and pieces she had brought from Ireland into a cardboard box and shoved them all in the car, haste making her rough.

And then she was in the car bumping for the final time down the track away from the farm, with Lillie standing in the middle of the lane watching with indignation.

She drove straight to Holyhead, getting caught in the rush-hour traffic, impatient to be on the open road and on her way back to Derry. He needed her and she was going back to him, back to the beauty of Westwood Park and the racehorses that she loved and the man that meant so much to her. He was a bastard. He had abused her, but now he had realised what an asset she was to him, things would be different. Now he realised that he needed her.

Gradually the traffic cleared as the commuters went home and she finally drove onto Anglesey with the evening sunlight ahead of her. She stopped for something to eat in a cafe that overlooked the sea. She supposed that she should telephone Edward and tell him that she had gone, but he was still not back from America and so she decided she could ring some other time. Refreshed, she got into the car and carried on, excited that every turn of the wheels on the dual carriageway was bringing her closer and closer to Derry.

The ferry was quiet. Most of the holidaymakers were not yet travelling and it was filled with lorry-drivers eager to sleep the journey away. Sarah curled in a corner of one of the lounges and lost herself quickly in a racing magazine. Then as tiredness overtook her she slept, waking only when the tannoy announced that they were docking in ten minutes.

She stretched, easing away the stiffness of being curled up cold and in such a strange position, and then wandered out onto the deck to watch the wonderful sight of Ireland coming into view — a sliver of green on the horizon growing closer and closer until finally they slid into the docks and she shot excitedly down to the car and was soon trundling down the ramps and on into the busy thoroughfares of Dublin.

She hurtled through the streets of Dublin, wanting to get out of the city onto the road towards Westwood Park, never once considering a visit home. That part of her life was gone now — she would probably never go back there again. Then eventually the busy smelly streets were left behind, finishing abruptly, and she left the urban sprawl and headed south into the countryside.

It was lunch-time when she arrived. Turning up the long drive of Westwood Park she felt a broad grin split her face. This was home, more home than the place where she had spent her childhood. This was where she felt that she truly belonged. She crawled at a snail's pace up the drive wanting to savour every second, loving the way that the trees and the bushes seemed to enfold her in their gloriousness, welcoming her back, like a lost child. She felt all of the tension drift out of her body. She was home.

The yard was deserted as she drove in. She gasped with horror. The place was in a terrible state. Straw littered the once-immaculate yard, blowing over the grass. An abandoned bucket rested where it had been blown in the last storm. The unoccupied stable doors were empty and, when she got out and looked inside, the beds were dirty. Even the tack-room door had been left open — anyone could walk in here and help themselves to the valuable saddlery that she had so lovingly cared for.

Derry, hearing her car pull up, came from the house, walking softly up behind her as quiet as a cat. "Welcome back," he drawled, making her jump.

She spun around to see him standing a few feet away from her with the familiar malicious supercilious smile on his handsome face. He looked tired, as if he had had a long night on the tiles.

"Thank God you're back," he grinned, waving a careless hand as if to take in the whole of the yard. "As you can see, it needs your loving care and attention."

She looked around the yard and smiled, glad that she was needed.

"And so do I," he said, moving swiftly forwards to slip a hand hastily inside her shirt. "Christ!" he exclaimed. "Where have you gone? Didn't they feed you in England?"

Sarah set to work a short time later, getting the yard straight, and was still hard at work when the staff came back and then left again for the night. She worked long into the night getting everything back to how it should be, feeling cross at one of the grooms who had told her that the only reason that Derry had wanted her back was that Tara had left him to get married to Morgan and there was no one else to supervise the work on the yard.

Finally the yard was done to her satisfaction and she crawled tiredly back to the cottage that she loved. She had barely bathed and changed and shoved her tangled clothes back into the drawers when she heard the door open and Derry's voice from downstairs called her name. Frozen into inactivity she listened as he called again and then, feeling her stomach knot with a frenzy of butterflies, she shot downstairs, her face split with a huge grin that she could not prevent. She had wanted to play it cool, but it was impossible.

"There you are," he grinned, holding out a bottle of champagne and two glasses. "I thought that we had better celebrate."

She slunk into the lounge feeling very sexy in the clingy dress that she could now wear. He poured two glasses and handed her one. The bubbles fizzed out over her hand. He seized her hand and slowly and very sensuously licked the liquid where it had trailed over the skin. Then equally slowly he dipped his finger into her glass and trailed the champagne over her lips and then very gently, in a way that made her toes curl with the pleasure, he touched her lips with his tongue. "What do you want to do now?" he breathed, sliding his hands over the slinky satin fabric and lifting the bottom of the skirt tantalisingly up over her hips so that he could slide his hands around to cup her buttocks.

"Take me to bed," she gasped, clinging onto him for support.

The sex made missing him and being apart from him for such a long time worthwhile. She had forgotten quite how good he was, rough and fast, very different from the gentle tender lovemaking with Edward.

Later she lay propped up against the pillows while his head was buried between her legs. Suddenly he looked up, and reached for his glass that had been abandoned on the bedside table.

"I almost forgot," he said, chinking his glass against hers. "Our toast." He took a long swig. "To Ellen, my fiancée — I got engaged yesterday."

CHAPTER THIRTY FOUR

Tara darted to the side of the stable and threw up. "Oooooh!" she moaned, as her stomach tried to turn itself inside out, as if to rid itself of the nothingness that was left in it. She had barely made it to the toilet this morning after Morgan had brought her a cup of tea first thing. Now she felt dreadful. Sick, shivery and completely exhausted in a leaden way that made every task a seemingly unachievable ordeal.

"See you later!" yelled Morgan, riding past the open stable door as they took the horses to the gallops. If he had noticed how ill she was he had not said anything.

Somehow she managed to finish mucking out the row of stables that she had to do and decided she felt so ill she would have to go inside.

She leant against the kitchen sink. She would feel better in a while. "Ohhhhhhh," she wailed, groping her way from the kitchen to the lounge to sit down. She lay on the settee and was instantly asleep, until the noise from the horses returning woke her. She sat up guiltily. She had to get on — there was so much to do. She felt marginally better now and made a cup of weak tea and took it into the little room that served as an office and began to work her way through a pile of paperwork that needed doing.

The thought began as a tiny insidious one way at the back of her mind. She did not know where it had come from, but it grew and grew until she could not ignore it. She pulled the desk diary towards her, scowling in concentration. Counting back, weeks and weeks had passed since she had last had a period. She could never remember if it was every 21 days or 28 - and was that from the day that it started or the day that it finished? But she knew, even as she flicked through the pages, that she was long overdue. She had to be pregnant.

A whirlpool of feelings spun around in her mind. A child. She was delighted, terrified, furious. She was not ready for motherhood — a child — demanding, expensive, noisy. But then a child, made from the most incredible and tender love that she felt for Morgan, something that was part of her and part of him. Morgan would be a brilliant father.

Morgan burst into the kitchen. "Where's my lunch, wench?" he called, slamming the door.

"I'm just coming," she yelled, folding up the paperwork that she had barely touched and pushing it in a drawer. She could not tell him, not yet. She wanted to know for sure and then to come to terms with the knowledge herself.

"You will be in a moment." said Morgan, slinking into the office and enfolding her in his arms. "I missed you all morning," he moaned, "and I was thinking about this for the last hour." He led her upstairs.

As he pulled off her jeans and gently lay her on the top of the quilt, she ran her hands over her flat, almost concave stomach. What would it feel like when it was full of a child? And then as he hastily pulled off his shirt and lay beside her, his skin against hers, his mouth meeting hers tasting faintly of coffee and mints, she forgot everything except how much she wanted him.

Afterwards, he quickly shrugged on his jeans. "I've got to go. Got to take Carna Boy to the tooth specialist in Cork. I'll be back sometime." He pulled a face that said, 'and I don't know when.'

She lay listening as he banged around in the kitchen, then she heard the door slam as he went out into the yard. She got up and stared at her reflection in the mirror. She looked awful. Her hair, despite having been washed the night before, hung limp and dull at either side of her face which was white and pasty, her dark eyes staring back at her from sunken hollows. Morgan had not noticed how ill she looked, how she could not eat, how if she did she was violently sick, or the fact that she was so tired that she fell asleep every evening in front of the television as soon as they came in from the yard. He didn't seem to notice anything; he was so obsessed with his bloody horse.

Now he was driving away, leaving her to cope with the yard, while he swanned off for the afternoon bringing that useless and extremely nasty animal to yet another specialist. Since the incident at the races he had become obsessed with trying to cure the animal. The stewards at the races had given him a real dressing-down. The horse had behaved in a completely dangerous way and they were all on for banning him from running again, but somehow Morgan had managed to persuade them that he would sort him out and reluctantly they had agreed to give him another chance.

It had turned out that Josh had not actually fallen off Carna Boy - the horse had first of all leant against the rail badly and then become so uncontrollable that the jockey had leapt off him in mid-jump rather than continue riding him any longer. And now Morgan was carting the horse to and from every back-specialist, horse physiotherapist and equine dentist in the country, trying to find out what had made him behave in such an uncontrollable manner.

The yard was deserted, the lads all gone home for lunch. The new stables were already half full and there were promises of more horses to come in after Christmas. The empty spaces seemed to mock her, making her tense. They were now in debt and could not afford for anything to go wrong. They needed those horses, needed to keep winning to convince customers that they were right to place horses with them. Sometimes the pressure seemed insurmountable. And all that Morgan was doing was messing around with that stupid Carna Boy, determined to get him right for what? To prove to Derry that Morgan was a better trainer.

Tara got into her car and drove to the village. The sour-faced assistant in the chemist tried not to look curious when Tara selected and then finally bought a pregnancy-testing kit. Then she drove home and dashed to the toilet. Two minutes later there it was. Two blue lines. She was pregnant. She threw away the kit, stuffing it all right down to the bottom of the bin. She wanted to get used to this idea herself and tell

Morgan when the time was right. She quaked inside; heaven only knew what his reaction was going to be.

However, when he got home it was very late and he gave her no chance to say anything. He shot into the house, slamming the door. "Tara, Tara, we've found out what was wrong with Carna Boy!"

She stood up stiffly from where she had been curled on the settee close to the fire waiting for him, too tired to do anything, even go to bed, and yet too tired to stay awake and do anything useful. "What was it?" she said, valiantly trying to be interested.

"A tooth, a bloody abscess under his tooth!" He shoved his hand in his pocket of his jeans and triumphantly held up a large square-shaped horribly brown horse-tooth. "The pain of this was making him hang hard on the jockey's hands and run against the rail! Poor horse, poor brave horse that he managed to do anything," he said proudly putting the tooth in pride of place on the mantelpiece above the fire.

What about poor brave me, thought Tara bitterly, managing to run this place while you are off and I feel so terribly ill? Can you not notice that, you thick-headed idiot? She went and picked up the tooth, running her fingers over the sharp surfaces.

"The tooth-specialist pulled it out so that the abscess can drain. He'll be all right now," said Morgan delightedly.

After a few days the horse was put back to work. Morgan was delighted with him. There was no sign of the abscess now and the horse was working properly on the gallops. He looked magnificent: his quarters were huge with muscle and his belly taut, his coat shining with health, his eyes bright with pride and mischief.

"I will run him at Limerick after Christmas," Morgan told Tara excitedly.

Christmas Eve was wet and windy. They booked a room in one of the hotels close by and held a huge party for the customers, which went down very well. Tara, feeling tired and tetchy, was very annoyed by Eddie Gallagher telling her how rough she looked. Morgan had just looked at her, put his arm around her shoulder and drew her to him, hugging her close. "She looks gorgeous," he said proudly. That annoyed her all the more. She knew that she did not. Her hair was desperate, hanging lifeless and falling out in handfuls and her body was now skin and bone from not being able to eat. She was living on cups of tea and a handful of biscuits - that was all she could keep down.

When they got home it was the early hours of Christmas Day. They got into the house to find that the power had gone off in the gales. She stood in the hall and broke down, sobbing uncontrollably.

"What on earth's the matter?" asked Morgan, coming back with a candle, the flame flickering uncertainly in the gales that blew under the door. For a long while she sobbed against his chest, feeling safe there.

"What is it?" he asked again, pushing her away so that he could look at her tear-ravaged face. He pulled a handkerchief out of his pocket and rubbed at her face rather roughly, not knowing quite what to do with her.

"I'm pregnant," she managed to say eventually, when the constricting lump had gone from her throat.

Morgan looked as if someone had knocked him over the head with a brick. His mouth opened and closed and she was suddenly very afraid. He was mortified, he was going to be furious, how could she have got pregnant at this time, they were too busy, they could not afford a child . . .

"That is the best Christmas present I could ever have," he whispered, looking at her as if she had suddenly turned into some sort of Madonna. He led her slowly to the lounge and sat her down as if she was made of cut glass.

Relief made her feel light-headed. "I've been mucking out and riding the horses," she laughed, forgiving him everything in an instant. "It's too late to treat me like this now!"

Limerick was beginning to fill up as they drove onto the course. It was one of those bitterly cold but clear days with a blue sky that held the promise of a hard frost later. But now the sun made everything warm and the atmosphere was bright and cheerful. Everyone was glad to be outside and to have an excuse to get away from being trapped with boring relatives and the onslaught of unwelcome friends.

Carna Boy was settled as they led him down the lorry-ramp. He walked beside Kate with a proud stride and a professional look in his eye. He knew now what all of this was about and the racecourse held no fears for him any more. He was impeccably behaved as she led him around the paddock. Aware of the admiring glances that he was getting he held his head up high, pricked his ears and walked out calmly. Tara went with Morgan to the weigh room to find the jockey. Josh was in a worse state of nerves than usual. Prior to Christmas he had been drinking and had been out for a meal and since then had been popping laxatives like sweets in order to get his weight back down. Now, with them and the slimming pills he illegally shipped in from America that quickened up his metabolism, he was as jittery and nervous as a wild pony. He came out of the sauna, sweat dripping from his painfully thin body to get the low-down from Morgan on how well the horse was doing. He looks more ill than I do, thought Tara, noticing the way he shivered like a leaf and hopped from foot to foot, unable to keep still even for a second.

Josh had stars in front of his eyes and the effort of standing up in the weigh room had made him feel dreadful. Once the race was over he would have a sweet cup of tea — that would make him feel better. Then he would be in fine form to take his new girlfriend out for an evening's drinking.

Carna Boy began to dance with excitement as they put the saddle onto him, but he was not as naughty as he had been the first time that he raced. Kate grinned proudly at the jockey; it was one of her friends he was going out with. Morgan legged him up and helped him shove his feet into the irons.

"He looks well, sir," said Josh, running his hand down the horse's short mane.

"He is well," Morgan said proudly. "Let him make his own race today and then we can decide how best to run him next time."

The jockey nodded. "Right." He gathered up his reins, standing in his stirrups as the horse hunched his back with excitement and gave a tiny buck.

Kate let go of the lead-rope as the pair went through the gates out onto the racecourse. "Bring him back safe," she called to the jockey, watching the horse's muscular quarters power away up the course with the jockey's pert bottom high in the air as he crouched over the horse's withers.

The race went off. Carna Boy started with the leaders.

"Josh's giving him a good run." Morgan watched through his binoculars, giving Tara a running commentary.

Over the first fence they went, like a colourful centipede humping into the air and then down again. Then at the second fence Morgan gave a gasp. He watched horror-struck as the horse seemed to hit the fence wrong, as if he had not seen it, and then plummet to the ground. "Fuck! He's bloody fallen!" He saw the jockey fly through the air and land heavily.

"That looked bad," commented someone unnecessarily.

The race carried on with Carna Boy staying rider-less with the leaders until he finally galloped off the course and was caught by a steward. Morgan watched as the ambulance that followed the race stopped to attend to Josh. In the distance they could see the nurses bent over the prone form. The jockey looked very tiny against the ground.

Josh was placed in the ambulance and it shot away from the fence, its sirens wailing. Angry and afraid, Morgan went down to the entrance to the course to retrieve the horse from the steward.

"How's the jockey?" he asked, taking the tired horse's reins from the fluorescent-coated steward.

The steward shook his head sadly. "I don't know," he shrugged, "but he didn't look very good to me."

Morgan took the horse and they walked back to the box, aware of the hostile stares of everyone they passed and listening to the cheers as one of Roger Drake's horse hurtled over the line to win for the third year running. They were halfway home when Morgan's telephone rang.

"Hello," he said putting it to his ear and straining to hear over the sound of the engine. "What?"

Tara looked at him in horror as his handsome face seemed to crumple before her.

"I see, thanks for ringing me, doctor." He switched off the phone. For a moment he drove on. Tara looked at him, fear gripping her insides. Numbly she reached for his hand. He gripped hers back and then said quietly: "Josh is dead."

CHAPTER THIRTY FIVE

Tara grasped Morgan's hand and held it tightly as he sobbed uncontrollably. The lorry juddered to a halt.

"Poor Josh," he said eventually when he was able to speak. "What a fucking awful thing to happen! The horse just fell — he should not have been killed!"

Tara was dumbstruck. Usually Morgan could deal with every situation, good or bad, with his calm control and courage, but now he was completely devastated. She held his hand and watched the traffic rushing past the lorry cab.

"You had better let me drive," she said, shaking his hand slightly to try to get his attention.

Meek as a child, he slid out of the seat and sat on the box-seat in the middle while she slid into the driving seat and took the steering wheel. She restarted the engine and crawled rather jerkily home while Morgan sat silently, staring morosely out of the window with unseeing eyes. When they got back to the yard he jumped down out of the cab and went into the house without another word. Tara watched numbly as he walked away, the weight of the world on his hunched shoulders. He seemed beyond her help.

She climbed down out of the cab, feeling uncertainly for the footholds while manoeuvring herself around the big steering wheel. Then she lowered the ramp and led the horse back to his stable. Carna Boy of course had no notion of the devastation that he had caused and was delighted to be home.

He walked jauntily beside her, his head high and his ears sharply pricked, calling out a greeting for the horses that looked out over their half-doors at him. She put the extra rugs on him that he wore in the stable and pulled his head-collar off. Mischievous as ever, he could not resist lowering his head quickly and nipping at her thigh. "Fuck off!" she roared as the stinging pain shot through her leg.

She checked the rest of the yard, slowly. Putting hay into the stables, refilling water buckets, anything to keep her from having to go into the house to face Morgan. When finally she could put it off no longer, she went into the house. Downstairs was silent, the lights all on and the door half-open. She closed the door, turned off the lights and went slowly upstairs.

Morgan was curled in a foetal position under the duvet. He was not asleep but lay, his eyes open and unblinking, as he stared at the dark hole of the window. She slipped into bed and wrapped her arms around his shivering form, holding him tight until she felt him relax gently into sleep. Then she lay awake thinking about Josh.

Sleep restored Morgan to something like his usual calm confidence.

"It was a terrible tragedy," he told her as he made breakfast, "but people die every day. We all know the risks of being around horses. At least he wouldn't have suffered. He wouldn't have known a thing about it." He sounded as if he were trying to convince himself.

"Damn," said Tara, getting up from where she was crouching, peering into the fridge, "we're almost out of milk — I'm going to fetch some." She got up slowly to avoid the waves of nausea that would hit if she got up too quickly.

She escaped into the pale winter sunlight and drove to the village where the shop was just opening. She grabbed a carton of milk from the fridge and took it to the counter, then gazed in horror as she noticed the headlines of all of the newspapers lined up there: Killer Horse; Flynn's Horse Kills its Jockey.

Mrs Carroll, who served in the shop, did not meet her eyes as she took the money for the milk. Then, as Tara turned to leave, the door opened and Derry sauntered in to collect his racing paper.

"Well, well," he said, pushing the sunglasses he wore up over his forehead, so that she could see the icy glare of his eyes, "your husband's chickens have finally come home to roost, haven't they? I told you he was a failure as a trainer, but you wouldn't listen — now he's gone and killed someone!" His lips curled in contempt.

"Leave me alone," she cried, shoving past him, knocking half a dozen tins of beans onto the floor in her haste to get away from him. She ignored them and shot out into the fresh air, her breath coming in painful gasps.

Thinking that the day could not get any worse she drove back to Radford Lodge, only to find Morgan sitting in the kitchen surrounded by paperwork and bank statements, white-faced, his mouth set in a tight grim line. "Two of the people that were bringing horses in have pulled out," he said bleakly, shifting the papers.

Tara pulled out a chair and sat beside him, twining her legs into his beneath the table. "We'll be all right," she said, laying her hands over his. "I know we will." The terror that she felt belied the conviction in her voice.

The doctor from the Turf Club phoned and told Tara that Josh's funeral was to be held in Adare, his home village, in two days' time and that a post-mortem had discovered that the fall had severed a vein that led into his heart. Nothing could have been done to save him.

Tara desperately wanted to avoid the funeral. She and Morgan felt responsible for Josh's death and did not want to face the bleak sight of his coffin being lowered into the ground. But it was unavoidable. They had to go.

They drove silently to Adare a few days later. The street was lined with cars, and crowds of people were hovering, standing outside the Dunraven Arms with glasses of whiskey to stave off the icy cold of the bitter final days of the year. Morgan managed to squeeze into a parking spot just outside the village and they walked down to the church. Everyone turned to stare at them as they walked down the aisle towards a vacant seat. The service was heartbreaking; the pain of Josh's death had sent shock waves through the little community where he lived. The priest tried to make his voice heard over the loud sobbing of Josh's mother and girlfriend. As the funeral service ended, the coffin was shouldered down the aisle on the skinny shoulders of four of his jockey friends. His family filed out in the wake of the coffin. His mother, who had lost her husband and three older children in a car crash shortly after Josh had been born, was now alone. Her tiny frame was huddled in a vast black overcoat that she has borrowed from a neighbour. Her heavily lined face seemed to have crumpled and collapsed in on itself with the shock and devastation his sudden death had caused. She shuffled slowly up the aisle, weeping loudly and leaning heavily on the arm of his girlfriend whose pale face contrasted sharply with the bright red lipstick that she had mindlessly scrawled across her lips.

For a second the dead jockey's heartbroken mother looked up and from the depths of her torment saw Morgan and Tara, their faces frozen and white with the pain that they had caused. Like a wildcat unleashed from a cage she sprang forward, her face twisting with fury as she launched herself at Morgan, her thin bony hands clawing at his face as she shrieked like a demented animal. "You killed him. You killed him!" she wailed over and over again, spittle flying from her mouth. Morgan made no effort to protect himself, seeming to find release from his own torment in the pain that she inflicted on him. He stood impassively as the blood from a fingernail scratch oozed slowly down his face and dripped onto the collar of his white shirt. "You have no business here!" she screamed at him as some of her neighbours clutched her arm and pulled her resisting away, her harsh sobs echoing around the damp ancient stone walls of the church.

In bed that night they clung together, needing the comfort of each other like lost children.

When she woke in the morning, Tara was alone in the bed. She came around slowly, waiting expectantly for the waves of nausea that accompanied the first few moments of wakefulness, and then darted hastily to the bathroom.

Then she heard Morgan run into the house, screaming her name. The nausea forgotten, she hurried downstairs. He was punching a number into the telephone. "Answer, answer!" he begged, turning to look at her in wordless horror. Something terrible had happened — it was written plainly over his face.

She stood in the doorway, icy fingers of fear clawing at her stomach and making her heart pound painfully against her ribcage. Then she heard a faint voice at the other end of the phone as it was picked up.

"Morgan Flynn at Radford Lodge," he snapped into the receiver, looking directly at Tara as he spoke, his lips tight, his eyes blazing from his white face. "I need a vet here immediately! It's an emergency! Please come at once!"

She could hear panic close to the surface, barely kept under control as he spoke. Then as the voice replied on the other end of the line he replaced the receiver.

"It's the horses in the new stable block," he whispered as if the pain of speaking was too much for him. He gripped the side of the table while Tara felt her heart pound as if it was going to break out through her ribcage. "They're all dying."

"What?" she exclaimed — he must surely be exaggerating. But as he pushed past her in his haste to get back to the yard, she caught the rank smell of fear rising from his body.

She followed him into the stables. None of the horses looked out over the half-doors. There was nothing to be heard, just the faint and pitiful sound of breathing. Then she realised it was the horses she could hear, their gasping breathing rolling into one fearful sound. Kate sat on the mounting-block, pulling on a cigarette, blowing the smoke fiercely from her mouth like a dragon as if she could dispel the fear and pain that lay over the yard like an almost visible mist. The other lads hung around her, leaning against the pale stone wall of the old stable block, looking at their boots, scuffling them in the mud, puffing frantically on cigarettes, wordlessly.

Ignoring them all and following Morgan, Tara went to the first stable and stood back as he opened the door. She froze as the door swung back. Inside, prone on the straw was the horse. Yesterday the animal had been gloriously fit and healthy, its coat shining with health and vigour. Now it lay on the straw, all four legs outstretched and limp, moving compulsively as if it was galloping. Sweat darkened its coat and stained the straw and the straw behind its tail was a pool of dark liquid as the animal churned out its insides listlessly, so exhausted and in such pain that it did not even lift its tail as another stream of shit shot out.

"What's wrong with him?" she gasped, her voice scarcely above a whisper.

"It's not just him," Morgan said tonelessly, turning to face her. "Every one of the horses in the new stable block is like this."

By the time the vet arrived into the yard a short while later, Morgan had sent Kate and the lads home. The yard was eerily silent. The car stopped and he jumped out, nodding at them in greeting.

"What seems to be the matter?" he said patiently, well used to racehorse trainers and even pet-owners who flew into a panic every time an animal so much as sneezed.

"You had better come and look," Morgan said tonelessly, not looking at him.

"OK," he shrugged, pulling on a plastic overcoat and Wellingtons over his ordinary clothes.

Morgan led the way to the first stable where Tara crouched by the horse, stroking his steaming neck.

"Bloody hell!" swore the vet, looking at the horse. "Are there any others like this?"

Morgan let out a hollow laugh. "They all are," he said, the laugh beginning to sound like hysteria. "Bloody hell," said the vet again.

He crouched down and began to examine the horse, peering into its mouth, looking at its gums, pulling down the inert eyelids and finally shoving a thermometer into its rectum. Then he stood up shaking his head, his mouth set in a grim line. "On first glance I would say that they have been poisoned - probably something in the water," he said, striding across the stable and dipping a finger into the horse's water-bowl. He smelt the finger and then touched it tentatively with the tip of his tongue, screwing up his face at the bitter taste. "Weedkiller, for a guess," he shrugged. "Put into the header tank in the roof."

Tara saw Morgan visibly reel. The water system that they had installed to make life easier for the lads had been used to kill the horses. How simple it had been for whoever had done it! All they had to do was climb up the steps into the storage area in the roof and tip weedkiller into the water tank. The deadly poison had run into each of the horses' water-bowls. That explained why the horses in the old stable were unharmed. Their water was hauled into them every day in buckets run from the tap.

By lunch-time they had done what could be done. The horses were all on drips to rehydrate them and had been given painkillers to help their systems cope with the shock of the poison. Tara, unable to stay in the yard with the devastation wrought around her, wandered inside. She tried to eat, but the food stuck in her throat so she abandoned it. How on earth were they going to pay the mortgage and the huge bill that would inevitably accompany this latest disaster? She wished that she was a thousand miles away. Nothing in her life had prepared her for dealing with trauma like this. She went to look for Morgan in the stables. The door stood open and she could hear the sound of his wretched crying, loud across the yard.

Morgan was kneeling by Brackley Gate, the horse's head cradled in his lap, his unseeing eyes staring towards her, his lips flaccid. "He's dead," he whispered. "Brackley Gate is dead."

She went back towards the house. She could not stay in the yard, could not witness his pain, or see the gorgeous horses like this. She closed the front door and leaned against it, needing the release of the sobs she wanted to come and yet that would not. Then she winced as an electric spasm of pain racked through her body. She bent double, clutching at her stomach.

Not this, please. Not the baby.

CHAPTER THIRTY SIX

Sarah had hated Ellen Healy on sight. And now that she was engaged to Derry she hated her even more. She was one of the most glamorous women that Sarah had ever seen. She stood in the centre of the parade-ring with her arm linked possessively through Derry's, and looked at him with her haughty face full of love and admiration. Magnetic Attraction, catching her out for inattention, caught Sarah's arm with a sharp nip, ripping the sleeve of the hacking jacket that she wore.

Ellen wore a long cream coat with a fur collar. Even at this distance Sarah could see that the coat was of the softest wool and that the collar was real fur. She also wore a large cream hat that would have looked ridiculous on anyone else in the bitterly cold wind of a January afternoon, but on Ellen it merely heightened the pale blonde of her hair and her gorgeous perfect oval face with its perfect make-up and her perfect white teeth.

The jockeys trooped out of the weigh room, looking pinched and tense, silent, the dead jockey close to their thoughts, knowing that such an accident could happen to any one of them at any time. The commentator suddenly announced that there would be a minute's silence for Josh Drake. The jockeys huddled together, wrapping their arms about their scrawny chests with childlike thin arms to conserve some warmth, and shivered, the chattering of teeth audible in the hush. The horses stood impatiently; not used to the unusual change of routine, they stamped and jangled their bits in temper. Sarah glanced across the ring to Derry's party. Derry's eyes were hidden behind the sunglasses he wore in spite of the pale sunlight and Ellen had eyes only for him.

The silence ended and the jockeys drifted away out of their huddle to the horses. The normal chatter and sarcastic banter that accompanies the start to a race was gone. No one was in the mood today.

As she let the horse go onto the course Sarah turned and found that she had to walk across the parade-ring with Derry and Ellen.

"How are you?" said Ellen, with a small and polite smile on her face that did not quite reach her eyes. "You look as if you have put on a bit of weight." She smiled again, sugar sweetness coating the bitter words.

Sarah shrugged, determined not to let Ellen see that she had wound her up. She had lost even more weight since she had been back at Westwood Park, not put it on. She followed them sullenly up onto the stands. It was so crowded that she had to stand on tiptoe to see over the heads that crammed the stands around her. Ellen, noticing this, turned and smiled. "What a disadvantage it must be to be short!" Sarah moved away, further up the stands. She could not bear to be near Ellen — at any second she felt that she would explode and want to thump her. Below her she saw JT pushing his way through the stands towards Derry and Ellen, Sue trailing miserably behind, tottering on her high heels and clearly pissed. Ellen looked away. JT had made a lot of money and had pulled himself up from his original working-class level of poverty. The wealth sat as easily on his shoulders as his dark fur-lined long overcoat. Sue was still the poverty-stricken cat-fighter that she had been when they married. She had been born on a rough estate in the centre of Dublin and mentally she had remained there. JT's wealth only made her louder and because she felt socially inferior she drowned her inadequacies in drink. Sarah watched her struggling up the high stone steps, inadequately dressed in a tarty short skirt under a fluffy fur coat and high heels that only accentuated the scrawny muscles of her calves which were clad in shiny black tights.

"They're off! Woopeeee!" Sue's high-pitched slurring voice carried back to Sarah over the heads of the spectators as the starter's flag fluttered down and the horses bounded forward. At the far end of the track it was hard to differentiate between them, the colours of the jockeys bobbing and merging into one mass, so Sarah concentrated on the racecourse television just over her head. Derry's horse, Magnetic Attraction, was loping along at the back, his ears lolling at the side of the head as he galloped. Sarah winced; he did not like the ground, sticky with the recent rain on top of inches of frost. For painful lengths he trailed miserably at the back of the field. Sarah glanced down the stand. Derry had his long field glasses trained on the horses and she could tell by the solid set of his shoulders that he was furious. He would give Tony Slattery a real dressing-down for letting the horse set off at the back and trail so far behind. When a horse began to lose ground it was hard to keep him motivated and running. The jockey might as well have pulled him up now.

The horses thundered past the stand, mud flying up behind their frantically churning hooves. The crowd let out an almighty roar, and when it had died down Sue's voice could be clearly heard roaring, "Go on, you fucking lazy bastard!" Sarah bit her lip to stop herself giggling as she saw JT and Ellen pretend that they had not heard her. Someone close by, a man, let out a loud bellow of raucous laughter. "That's it, darling, you tell him!" Behind the main bunch of horses trailed Magnetic Attraction, looking thoroughly miserable.

The horses rounded the bend in the course and headed away from the stands, disappearing rapidly into the distance. On the screen Sarah could see the jockey give Magnetic Attraction a belt down his shoulder with his whip. The horse pricked his ears and began to surge forward, slowly making up the ground that he had lost. Then the horse in the lead fell causing two horses behind to refuse, shocked at seeing the horse ahead sprawling on the ground. On the television screen, Sarah could see the jockey shortening up Magnetic Attraction's reins and holding him, making him jump. He hit him down the shoulder and the horse made an enormous leap over the fence, just as the fallen horse leapt to his feet. Magnetic Attraction shot sideways, sending the jockey sprawling down his shoulder, holding on only by magnificent balance, sheer determination and with superb balance Tony righted himself, gathered in the washing-lines of his reins and urged the horse forwards.

"Two fences to go," yelled the commentator, "and Magnetic Attraction is now making up ground! He's coming up fast on the outside!"

On the screen Sarah saw the jockey steering the horse to the outside of the track, onto the better ground and away from the danger of the others falling or refusing. He powered forward and at the last fence, when he was four lengths ahead, he made a careless leap and clipped the top, dragging his back legs through the brush and screwing his back end around. Tony, with the agility and balance of a circus acrobat, sat still until the horse righted himself and then thundered on. The bad jump seemed to have cost him the race as the second horse put in a magnificent jump and surged ahead. Magnetic Attraction put his head down and, as the jockey slapped him twice on the shoulder, redoubled his efforts and just managed to put his nose in front of the other horse as they reached the finishing line.

The crowd went mad at such an exciting finish. Hats were thrown in the air and the course echoed with a roar of victory as winning betting slips were punched into the air. Ellen had thrown her arms around Derry and was smothering him with kisses as Derry, looking very embarrassed, tried to disentangle himself. JT was slapping him on the back from the other side, leaving him well and truly trapped between them. Finally in a move that would have done justice to a fish escaping from a line, Derry put in a hasty sidestep, dodged both of them and shot down the stand steps to retrieve his horse.

Sarah hurtled after him, reached the gate before him and slipped her lead-rope through the delighted horse's reins.

"He's amazing," Tony was saying, grinning as Sarah led him through the crowd that surged forward. It was impossible to tell where to go, as there were so many people around them, all wanting to pat the exhausted horse and shake the jockey's hand.

In the winner's enclosure Tony climbed up onto the horse's back, stood upright and, as the stewards frowned at him in dismay, leapt skywards in a Frankie-Dettori style dismount, caught by the delighted crowd.

A photographer surged forward. "Can you line up, please? I want the horse and the trainer, his handler and the owners, please," he roared trying to focus his camera and direct them into an orderly line. Derry shoved his arm around Ellen and drew her beside him and JT squashed beside her, while on Derry's other side was Sarah, all crowding around the horse.

Once the cameras had finished whirling, a reporter shoved his way forwards and shoved a microphone under Derry's nose. "What a magnificent win for Magnetic Attraction," he bellowed over the noise of the crowd, glaring angrily at a young lad who was still trying to get Derry's autograph. For the benefit of the camera Derry took the race card and hastily scrawled his name and rubbed the lad's hair, before turning back to the reporter with a smile. "Well, he's just coming into his own now — he'll be on top form for Cheltenham." Then he added, "hopefully", knowing that it did not do to appear too cocky in front of the camera — one's words had a way of coming back to haunt one.

"And what about the future?" said the reporter, peering at the camera to read the autocue which the director was frantically trying to wave in front of him in between the bodies of the spectators.

"The only thing on my mind at the moment is this woman," said Derry, turning to look in admiration at Ellen, who beamed beautifully at the camera.

Sarah, standing beside him, felt his other hand creeping slowly underneath her jacket and sliding over her bottom as he spoke. Stiffening with annoyance at his deceit, she was horrified to realise how desperately she still wanted him. "This is my fiancée — we are to be married just as soon as I can get a day off."

Later, in the owners' and trainers' bar Derry announced that he was going to have a celebration party back at the house.

"I've got a lot to celebrate," he said proudly. "I've got a gorgeous woman who has, very luckily for me, agreed to marry me and I have had a great win today with a horse that is destined to become one of the greats in racing history!"

Sarah sat in the lorry with Paul to take the horse home, helped the lads to do the yard and then went slowly to her cottage. The last thing that she wanted to do was to go to a party with Derry and the supercilious Ellen. She loved Derry and she could not bear to see him with Ellen. Slowly she bathed and then shoved on the black dress that she had bought to go out with Edward. As she put it on she could still faintly smell the perfume that she had worn that night and it brought the memory of him back painfully. Then at last she could put it off no longer: she had to go across to the house.

The hallway was full of jockeys raucously drunk, swigging out of cans, and holding the necks of bottles — one was already sliding down the wide, polished curving banister. Sue wandered out of one of the rooms holding a bottle of vodka, a fixed smile below her glazed eyes. Sarah felt a surge of sympathy for her.

Then Ellen came towards her, looking fabulous in a long bias-cut dress that left one shoulder sexily bare and skimmed her hips and waist before plunging to the floor in gentle folds that accentuated rather than hid her willowy frame. She held a silver tray of oysters and slivers of smoked salmon.

"Sarah!" she smiled. "How lovely you look! Aren't those loose dresses just so easy to wear?" She cruised past.

Then Sarah spotted Derry, his eyes undressing her as they roved leisurely over her body.

"I need to discuss something with you," he said, taking her arm and steering her towards his office, holding the door open to let her walk in. "Now," he said, leaning against the door and turning the key in the lock, "we have some very urgent business to deal with."

Sarah turned to face him. He looked gloriously handsome in his black dinner jacket and oozed sex from every pore.

"What?" she asked curiously.

"This," he said taking a stride forward. He took hold of her arms and turned her so that her bottom rested on the edge of his desk. She felt herself melt inside. Oh God, what was she doing? She threw her arms around his neck and pulled his head towards hers, hungry for him as he slid his hand slowly up the length of her thigh lifting the long folds of the dress and plunging his hand inside the crotch of her knickers. He lifted her roughly onto the desk and pushed her legs apart. She wrapped her legs around him and gasped with the forbidden passion and desperate longing of a deprived mistress. It was over in a few quick, violent minutes.

Derry withdrew abruptly, straightened his clothes and ran a hand through his hair, grinning at her. "We needed that," he smiled wickedly. Then as she hurriedly pulled down her dress he unlocked the door and they wandered back outside into the hallway.

"Come with me," he said, seizing her wrist. 'I have to do something." He dragged her through the rooms until he found Ellen and then, dragging her too by the wrist, pulled the pair of them into the hallway and onto the stairs.

"Listen everyone!" he bellowed, as the guests surged out to see what he wanted,

"These are the two women that I am most proud of! Sarah here for doing the horses so well and Ellen, my darling, for agreeing to be my wife. Oh and by the way, we have set a date! Next Thursday!"

CHAPTER THIRTY SEVEN

Sarah hated weddings. They always made her bitterly aware of how terribly lonely she was. Derry and Ellen's wedding was the most awful one ever. It was made worse by the fact that Derry had come to her cottage the previous evening and spent the entire night in her bed, only getting up when it was light and jogging back to his own house to get himself ready for the nuptials.

Now she stood at the back of the crowded University chapel on St Stephen's Green watching for the arrival of the bride. The doors opened. As one the congregation rose and everyone halt-turned to stare at the bride as she made her appearance. Ellen glided in with her arrogant model's sashay, on the arm of her proud and flustered-looking father. She wore a long dress of cream silk, tightly fitting to show off her slender figure and falling in a long, long train that slid along the floor. As she passed the only sound was the whisper of her silk dress caressing the aisle as she stepped forward to become Mrs Derry Blake.

Sarah wished that she had not come, but there had been no reason for her not to. Even at the last minute she had gone around the horses, peering over their half-doors hoping that one would look minutely off colour and give her the excuse to stay away. She felt cheap and dirty. He did not love her, he never had, but she was a convenient way of curbing his enormous sex drive. She should have had the strength not to submit to his whims, but every time, once he began to kiss her she was lost, wanting him so desperately. She knew that he would be back; Ellen would never hold him. He was a man of tremendous sexual appetites which needed satisfying and Ellen was far too glamorous, far too high maintenance, to be shoved into a corner for a quickie.

Then it was all over. To a loud round of applause and great cheering from the congregation, they were announced as man and wife. Everyone craned their necks for a view of the bride and groom as they stood on the altar steps. Sarah did not bother.

She spent the reception sitting at a corner table, pushed into obscurity with half a dozen jockeys who rode occasionally for Derry. Ellen had obviously done the table plans. Once the meal was over, the guests pushed away from the tables and began to sidle to the bar, relieved to be able to escape from people that they had fallen out with twenty years ago. Sarah made her escape from the hotel, dashing out into the icy air of St Stephen's Green.

Feeling decidedly oppressed in the dark city she hurried to her car and then headed for home. She was in charge now while Derry honeymooned in the south of France. She felt a huge buzz of excitement grip her as she thought of how she would look after the yard while he was gone. She would make sure that everything was immaculate when he got home. There would be a mistress at Westwood Park now and not of the extra-curricular variety. Ellen would be the real thing, Derry's wife and now part-owner of the house, and the stables. While she, Sarah, was the true mistress. With no status, only that of an occasionally desired quick fuck, to be played with or discarded at will. Sighing, bitterly unhappy, she began to cry. She still had Derry and always would as long as he wanted her, and she still did the job that she loved, but she felt cheap and used and that was heartbreaking. She should never have come back; she should have gone free while she could.

Derry came back from his honeymoon in a terrible temper. Away from his racehorses and confined to spending all day wandering around the shops carrying bags of clothes and shoes and cosmetics for Ellen, he came back like a caged tiger, furious at everyone and everything. Minutes after their car had cruised up the drive, he was in the yard.

Sarah was busy putting ice-packs on Mountain Man, another of the horses that belonged to JT. She had felt some heat in his legs when he came off the gallops earlier.

The lad holding the horse glanced out of the open stable door. "Here's the boss," he said, "and he looks fucking wild." He nodded in the direction of the courtyard.

Sarah turned her head to watch as Derry walked along the tarmac strip to the tack room. His face was set and his shoulders stiff with tension: there was trouble ahead. She finished bandaging the Mountain Man's legs and stood up. "Thanks, Mac," she nodded at the lad who took the head-collar off the horse and went outside, walking quickly in the opposite direction from Derry. They all knew to keep their heads down when he was in a temper — he could turn on anyone and give them a vicious lashing of his tongue.

Suddenly the air was rent with a bellow of "Sarah!"

Sarah swallowed hard. She was obviously going to get it in the neck for something. She walked across to the tack room, aware of the stares of the lads.

Scowling, she went into the tack room. She had tried so hard to get everything right for him and yet she had known that he would come back and find something wrong. He always did. But it still hurt.

Derry was standing by the work chart that was pinned onto the wall. She had painstakingly worked out which horses needed to be worked hard, which gently, which were being rested after a season's racing, which were getting fit after a lay-off. "What is this?" he spat, punching a finger at the chart. He turned to face her. His face was red with temper; it clashed horribly with his newly acquired tan. She peered at the chart. "This!" he demanded, stabbing at Mountain Man's name on the chart — the horse she had just been bandaging.

"There was heat in one of his legs so I decreased his work," she said sullenly.

"I decreased his work!" he said, mocking her defiant tone. "That horse is due to run in a week's time and you decrease his work, you fucking stupid bitch!" His voice grew louder and louder.

Exploding into action he shoved past her and marched across to Mountain Man's box, with her trailing miserably in his wake. He banged the door open, sending the frightened horse rushing to the back of his box. "Get a head-collar," he demanded. She held the horse as Derry crouched by his legs, ripped the bandage off and ran his hand down the damp hair.

"There's no heat here at all," he snarled furiously.

"I have been ice-packing him and hosing his legs with cold water," she protested, tears of frustration and anger pricking the backs of her eyes.

"Put him back on full work," Derry snapped, straightening up and tossing the bandage into a corner of the stable.

He stalked off across the yard. Sighing, Sarah picked up the soiled bandages. As she was stuffing them into the washing-machine in her cottage, her mobile rang. She pulled it out of her pocket and slipped out of the door into the silence of the yard.

"Hello?"

"Hello, stranger," said a voice that she instantly recognised.

"Edward," she smiled, cradling the receiver to her ear. It was good to hear his voice.

"I got back a few days ago to find you gone," he said, his voice tinny over the airwaves.

Sarah sighed quietly. How could she explain to him? "There was a crisis at Westwood Park and Derry begged me to come back," she exaggerated.

There was a moment's silence on the other end of the phone as if he was getting his thoughts in order before he spoke again. Then he said, "I'm sorry that you won't be around any more. I was looking forward to seeing you again."

Sarah suddenly regretted that she would not have the chance to get to know him better. "Me, too," she replied truthfully, wanting to tell him that she was sorry and that she would miss him, but somehow she did not know him well enough for that, "Ah well," he sighed. "We'll have to go out for dinner if I'm ever in Ireland."

Sarah nodded, wordlessly, her throat filling with emotion. Then she felt a presence close by her and turned slowly. Derry was watching from the doorway.

"I would like that," she managed to say. "Very much."

The carefree days of Derry's bachelorhood were long gone. Ellen had taken over with a vengeance. The dogs had been banned from the house and were now sleeping resentfully in the tack room. Derry appeared more and more in the yard, moving his paperwork into the tack room and making his phone calls from there.

"She's going to bloody bankrupt me," he moaned one morning, slumped into the armchair in the tack room looking moodily over a pile of quotes from interior designers and decorators.

Much to the amusement of the lads and lasses Ellen occasionally put in an appearance in the yard. The lads were all highly amused when one day she arrived in a dazzling white suit that she had bought to go to the races, and one of the horses that she had been gingerly stroking at arm's length suddenly threw up its head and covered her in brown spit. She had screamed so loudly that Derry had rushed out of the tack room, frantic that one of the horses had been injured.

JT, though, had no qualms about coming into the yard. Now that Derry was his son-in-law he constantly turned up, watching his horses work, expecting to be entertained. One day he turned up while Derry was checking the horses, telling him in no uncertain terms that he had clients from abroad coming to the races and that Derry had better put on a good show for them.

"Stupid fucker," Derry moaned as his father-in-law drove away. "He thinks that they just win when he wants. Doesn't he, Mountain Man?" He slapped the horse on the neck. "You had better win now, or your owner will be pissed off." Then he hissed into the horse's ear, "And so will I!"

After Derry left, Sarah felt the horse's front leg — there was heat in it. There was no point in saying anything. When Derry thought that he was right that was it; no one could change his mind.

JT invited Derry up to his hospitality box to watch the horse run, and since Sarah was beside him JT was obliged to ask her too. Mountain Man ran well. From the vantage of the high balcony it was easy to pick him out. Then at the fourth fence from home, while he was lying in second place, he suddenly dropped out of the race. He cantered on for a few strides with the horrifically bobbing stride that every trainer dreads. The horse had injured his leg.

"What's bloody going on?" demanded JT, slamming down the glass of champagne that he had already poured in expectation of a good win.

Derry, looking out over the racecourse with a stricken face, was beyond words.

"He has probably damaged a tendon," Sarah told JT.

JT lowered his head, shaking it slowly like a bull about to charge. "I don't know what to fucking say," he said in furious tones.

Derry suddenly sprang into life, shooting off to get the horse. Sarah shot JT a sympathetic smile and darted after him. She felt a grim sense of satisfaction about the horse. She had known that there was something wrong with his leg. If Derry had listened to her this might never have happened. Now the horse would be off for at least a year, maybe forever.

The following morning Sarah was grooming one of the horses, enjoying the relaxing rhythm of the brush sliding over the glossy coat while the animal pulled gently at his haynet. From the tack room next door she heard the sound of JT walking in and Derry's greeting.

"How's Mountain Man?" snapped JT.

Even through the wall she could hear Derry sigh. "I am taking him to have the leg scanned later today, but looking at him I would say that he had damaged a tendon." There was a silence and then she heard JT speak again. "I'm divorcing Sue. I can't stand her any longer."

Sarah stopped brushing the horse and listened shamelessly.

Then JT continued, the malice in his voice clear as was the veiled threat. "Your wedding cost me a fortune, a bloody fortune," he said in deep, threatening tones. "I need you to make me a packet of money. I'm nearly skint and the divorce is going to cost me every penny that I have."

She leant against the wall, her heart pounding. What was going on?

Then Derry spoke again. "What are you saying?" he demanded.

"A big bet on the second favourite in Magnetic Attraction's next race," said JT, his voice so quiet that Sarah had to strain to hear what he said.

"What!" Derry" voice was high with shock and temper.

"I want Magnetic Attraction pulled. He will be the favourite and I'm going to put a packet of money on Carna Boy."

"Fuck you!" Derry's reply was so loud that Sarah jumped back from the wall.

"With Magnetic Attraction pulled up, Carna Boy will win," JT said determinedly.

"No way," Derry exploded, then dropped his voice to an angry whisper that Sarah had to strain to hear. "I have never had any part in that sort of thing and I don't intend to start now — not for you, even if you are my bloody wife's father!"

"Fuck you then!" JT roared and then strode off, slamming the tack-room door viciously behind him.

Sarah sighed in amazement. What a scene that had been!

Derry came to the cottage that night, for the first time since his wedding. He sat down heavily in the armchair, silently looking at Sarah.

"He's got no money," he said miserably, shaking his head in horror. "JT penniless!" Then he gave a hollow laugh and buried his head in his hands. "I only married the stupid cow because I thought that he had plenty of money. I was going to tap him up for money to renew the gallops and put up a new block of stables." He roared with laughter, mocking himself, then slapped himself on the forehead as if he had just discovered something vital. "Now I discover she's married me for my money!"

He pulled Sarah down on the armchair so that her legs were astride his and pulled her towards his belly so that she pressed close to him and could feel very clearly where they would be heading next. "At least you can be sure it's not your money that I'm after," he said, beginning to unbutton her shirt.

CHAPTER THIRTY EIGHT

Tara lay listlessly on the settee looking bleakly at the chaos that surrounded her. The floor beside her was littered with empty cups and dust lay thick on the furniture and dulled the silver cups that Morgan had won. And because the door was open into the kitchen she could see the piles of unwashed plates and pans that were stacked up on the work-surfaces.

The doctors had told her that she had to rest, that she was having a threatened miscarriage and that she had to go home and lie quietly and not let herself get stressed out. That had been a joke. Morgan had barely taken in what was happening when she had told him about the pain that she was in. Of course he had to stay and look after the horses.

So she had driven herself, crying from the pain and the exhaustion and the worry, to the hospital. She lay on the bed in casualty clutching her stomach protectively as if her very doing so could protect the unborn baby. She prayed silently for the safety of the baby, bleakly unaware of her surroundings except for the dim background of noise.

A nurse rubbed gel over the tiny bulge of her stomach and began to slide a cold and slippery instrument against the flesh. Then as the machine moved backwards and forwards over her stomach she heard for the first time the sound of the baby's heartbeat, clear and loud in the silence of the room. She gave a gasp of pleasure. The baby was there, safe and alive.

"Everything seems OK there." The nurse put away the equipment and shoved a lump of tissue into Tara's hand. "We'll get you back to casualty now. The doctor will talk to you there."

It seemed ages before he came. Tara lay back against the lumpy pillows wishing that she could stay here forever. Here it was safe, and quiet. The money worries and the trauma of the poisoned horses all seemed to have faded into the background. If only she could stay here in peace until the baby was born and then go home to find that everything had been a bad dream, that the stables were full again, the horses majestically restored to life. Morgan would be caring and attentive, and they would be happy again.

Then finally the curtain was shoved right back and the doctor came in. Tara could see out into the ward, at others whose curtains had not been closed: a man, his face covered in blood clutching a patch on one eye, and another, rigged up to a heart-machine that bleeped restlessly. The doctor clasped his hands together like an athlete who has just won a big race. Then he flung them apart in a gesture of dismissal.

"Well," he said, sitting down gently on the bed, "the baby is safe at the moment, but you are having a threatened miscarriage." A plaintive bleep from the pager in his top pocket interrupted him. He pulled it out and stared at it intently for a few moments before turning back to Tara, looking as if he could not remember what she was there for. Then he seemed to remember. "Ah yes," he said, "rest is the only thing — you must rest completely and just live quietly. No stress."

She had laughed about that as she drove slowly home. How the hell was she supposed to live without stress?

She had pulled into the yard and Morgan had come out of one of the stables, looking for all the world as if he had not even known that she had gone out. He looked frantic with worry, his face etched with the tired numbness that she had seen on the faces of doctors in the hospital, as if he was beyond pain, beyond feeling any sort of emotion any longer, as if what he had seen was so traumatic that he had shut down from it all.

"The baby's OK," she told him, climbing out of the jeep. She felt light-headed with relief, the trauma of the horses somehow paled in comparison with the joyful knowledge that the baby was safe, alive and growing, inside her.

"Good," Morgan hugged her briefly. She felt a shift in his emotions as she swam hazily into his thoughts. "Thank God for that," he said, the relief evident in his voice as if what could have happened to the baby had only now occurred to him.

She sighed, holding his face and clinging to him, wanting to feel the solid warmth of his body. He slipped his arms around her and she could feel the relief slide through her body. They clung to each other.

"I have to rest though - just lie on the settee for a good while," she told him.

Ignoring the chaos behind him, Morgan held her hand as they went into the house. Tara let him put her onto the settee, hand her the television remote-control, make her a cup of tea, and find a doggy-smelling blanket out of the press upstairs and wrap it around her solicitously. Then he perched on the edge of the settee and wrapped his arms around her, holding her close. For a while they stayed like that, silent, listening to each other's breathing and the distant sounds of the yard outside.

"How are things out there?" she whispered, not really wanting to know, hoping that he was going to tell her that everything was all right again.

"Another one died," he said bleakly and she could hear the tears choking his voice as he dashed his hand across his eyes. "Jealousy," he said, and she pictured the enormous black gelding that had come into the yard only recently. It had been a wild-eyed rough horse when it had come, but it had just started to relax, responding to the gentle routine of the yard and the care of the staff. "He had just died when you came back."

Tara closed her eyes, trying to blot out the awful things that were happening, but when she opened them again they were all still there. "How are the others?" she asked, taking his hand and sliding her fingers into his. His hand was icy cold and the fingers curled around hers as if to draw the warmth from them.

He shrugged and sighed bleakly. "They seem better, but then so had Jealousy and then he just died." His voice was breaking again with the harsh emotion.

"What about Carna Boy?" she asked, quietly.

She hated the animal so much that it was almost a disappointment when he replied, "not bad - he responded to the treatment faster than any of them." Then as if unable to bear to be parted from his precious horses, he shoved away from her. "I had better go back." He stumbled from the room, clumsy with exhaustion.

She spent the night alternatively dozing and staring bleakly at the television.

247

She woke with a jolt in the morning. A tepid cup of tea lay on the floor beside her. She must have slept through Morgan coming in. She drank it quickly and was strangely relieved when the familiar wave of nausea gripped her. Tossing the blanket hastily from her legs, she dashed to the kitchen and just made it to the sink before she was sick. When she finally straightened up, she looked out of the kitchen window to the stable yard. A strange lorry that she did not recognise was in the yard. Scowling, she looked as two horses from the old stable block that had escaped being poisoned were loaded up into the box. More being taken away. Could things get any worse?

As she watched, the ramp was shoved up and the lorry drove away. Then Morgan came towards the house. Tara felt her heart catch at the sight of him; he was, even in the depths of the trauma that they were going through, so strong and handsome. He looked, she thought as she watched him come towards the house, better, calmer, more together, like someone who has witnessed the end of the world and survived it and now knows that they can survive anything. She went hastily back to the settee and rearranged her rugs as he came in.

"Two more horses have gone home," he said in an almost conversational tone, as if a business collapsing around them was an everyday occurrence, "at least Shane has said he will stay, so we still have his horses – what's left of them."

Tara could not think of anything to say that would give comfort. Anything that she could say would only make them more aware of the dreadful financial situation that they were facing and somehow by not saying anything it made it seem less real, "how are the other horses?" she said eventually after he had kissed her on the forehead and then gone into the kitchen. She could hear him opening the fridge and putting strips of bacon on the grill for his breakfast. "Better," he said and she could hear the relief in his voice. "Most of them are up now. The vet came a short while ago and there is only one on a drip still. Carna Boy is actually eating again."

Tara lay her head back against the high arm of the settee. That bloody animal!

Morgan clattered around in the kitchen and the smell of bacon cooking wafted into the lounge making her feel dreadfully nauseous, but by the time that he came into the lounge with a bacon sandwich for her she had begun to feel better and picked at it to please him. He sat at the far end of the settee and she rested her feet on his lap as he ate and read the racing paper.

The air of normality was strange.

"How are we going to cope?" she muttered finally, unable to bear the uncertainty any longer.

He shrugged, almost nonchalantly. "We just will. We can just afford to pay the loan for the new stables and once I start to win again things will improve — owners will come back. Racing is a very fickle business. This thing about Josh's death will blow over soon, you'll see." He finished his sandwich, stood up, and went back outside.

She lay back feeling safe because of his strength; he was so certain about the future, so unafraid.

The telephone was ringing. She stood up to answer it, the dull pain still low in her stomach as she walked uneasily to the office to answer it.

"Hello, Radford Lodge," she said into the receiver, propping herself on the edge of the desk in order to find a way to stand that took the pain away.

"Hope that you're having a good time with the dead horses," said a voice quietly on the end of the phone.

"What?" she snapped, her heart pounding suddenly at the quietly threatening tone of the voice.

"Dead horses today — it will be Morgan and you next." With a peel of loud vicious laughter, the phone went dead.

The shock had made her stomach tight. Her breath came in fast loud gasps. She needed Morgan. He would know what to do. The pain gripped her again - she must lie down. Had to rest. Must get to the settee. The room began to swim hazily and there was a furious pounding noise in her head, as if she were far below the surface of the sea. She groped towards the lounge. As her hand reached for the settee, there was a heavy leaden feeling far below her stomach and when she looked she was covered in blood.

It was gone. The baby did not exist any more. The little boy that she could feel, imagine, had gone. She was empty, miscarried. She had lost him in the globs of blood that had poured from her as if they would never stop, soaking up the towels that Morgan had found when he had run in response to her screams.

Morgan had telephoned for the doctor who had come quickly. She had only been vaguely aware of him examining her, of Morgan taking away the bloodstained clothing. It was a complete miscarriage, she heard the doctor announce, no need for her to go to hospital. The bleeding would stop eventually and then she would have to go and be checked over before she tried again, no reason why they should not have more children, just the pressure and trauma of everything that was happening. One of those things.

Now she lay in bed upstairs, alone, listening to the muffled sounds from the yard. Morgan had gone to the Curragh to the Turf Club to be interviewed about Josh's death. Kate was running the yard outside. Tara lay alone, wanting the release of the tears that would not come, lying dry-eyed staring at the shifting patterns of the clouds in the sky through the window.

Later she heard him come back. He came slowly and tiredly up the stairs. She listened as his feet trod on the carpet and watched as he came into the room. She resented him for going to the inquest, resented him for leaving her alone to cope with the death of their baby, hated him, hated the horses, hated everyone.

"Hi," he said quietly, sitting on the bed and stroking her hair off her forehead, pushing away the matted strands.

She smiled bleakly. "How did you get on?"

"There's no blame attached to me," he said. "Just a dreadful accident."

"That's good," she said faintly. Frankly at the moment she could not care less about anything. She just wanted the baby back. "Do you want anything?" he asked.

She could hear an impatient ring in his voice, as if he thought that she should not really be lying in bed. She shook her head and closed her eyes, wanting to blot everything out.

"OK," he shrugged and went out, closing the door quietly behind him.

After a while she got up. She wanted to be near him even though at that moment she hated him, hated his preoccupation with the horses, hated the way that he could not comprehend how she felt about the baby. Hating to be with him and yet needing to be near him to cling to his strength. She pulled on her dressing-gown and went downstairs. He was in the office on the telephone.

"OK, I understand. No problem," she heard him say as he replaced the receiver.

She went into the office and sat in the armchair watching him. His hair was untidy, ruffled at the front where he had been running his hand through it distractedly. He picked up the receiver again and she listened as he spoke to one of the jockeys' agents, trying to get someone to ride for him. She watched his hand clenching and unclenching as he spoke. Finally he put down the receiver and looked at her with a tight smile and a sad shake of his head.

"No one will ride for me," he sighed.

CHAPTER THIRTY NINE

"Fuck them, fuck them all!" Morgan exploded, slamming his fist down on the table. He leapt to his feet as if he could no longer stand the confines of the chair and began to pace the room in fury. Tara looked at him fearfully; she had never seen him so angry before. "No one will ride for me," he said through gritted teeth.

Tara waited, looking around the office, the now-familiar cream walls covered with the photographs of Morgan winning races, holding trophies, grinning delightedly at the camera. Tattered remnants of days that were lost and that now looked as if they would never be retrieved. Tara could not bring herself to look at him, did not want to see the misery that she knew would be etched on his face. They had suffered so much over the last week, but this would mean the end for them. If they had no jockeys they had no runners, it was as simple as that and then Morgan could not prove that he had ability as a trainer.

"The cowardly rotten bastards!" he raged coming back to his chair and slumping down on it. He sat, gazing at Tara, one elbow on the table, his chin resting m his cupped hand. Finally he said decisively, "sod it. I'll ride them myself. I am not giving up!"

Tara felt her eyes widen in shock.

"I'm only a few pounds over my racing weight. I can easily lose that. I'll bloody do it!"

"But you always said that you would never ride again," Tara said quietly, not wanting to remind him of the time that he had confessed to her that he was terrified of racing again. He had suffered too many falls, too many broken bones.

"I know that I did," he said, looking at her with a confident smile which lit up his handsome face. He suddenly looked stronger and happier than she had seen him for days, despite the dark tired circles under his eyes. "But this is different. I have to do it. Otherwise, what else will I do? I train racehorses and now, if I have to, I will ride them. Carna Boy is going to prove to the world that he is the best horse when he runs at Cheltenham and I am going to be the one sitting on him when he goes up that hill!" He stared into the middle distance, as if in his imagination he was already at Cheltenham, hearing the roar of the crowd, feeling the strength of the horse as he pounded towards the finishing line.

Tara got up and went out of the room. He was mad, completely bloody obsessed. She felt miserable, neglected. He should be looking after her, crying with her about the baby, telling her that they would have more, helping her to mourn for her lost child. But all that he could think of was the bloody horses and her nemesis, Carna Boy.

The telephone rang again and Tara jumped. What if it was that maniac again that had threatened her? She had not told Morgan about it. She could hear him talking on the phone and then he came into the kitchen, his face wreathed in smiles.

"That was the vet," he said, crossing the room in a rush to sweep her off her feet and smother her in kisses. "The horses were definitely poisoned. Somebody put weedkiller in the header tank. And he said that he had seen a newspaper and the headlines said that I was exonerated from all blame for Josh's death at the inquest. Hopefully now things will start to get better again."

Tara smiled. "Brilliant — I hope so," and wriggled out of his grip. She felt too numb about the baby to even begin to contemplate anything else.

Tara's body recovered from the miscarriage, but the damage had gone deeper than that: the pain of the lost child was raw and at times unbearable. There were pregnant women everywhere, full of life, proud of their bulging bellies. The pain was incessant, making her short and snappy, but Morgan was so involved in himself - watching every mouthful that he ate, running for miles each morning to get fit, working the horses - that he barely seemed to notice her feelings. He seemed only to have thoughts for himself and the great prize — the Cheltenham Gold Cup. Tara saw herself going through the motions of everyday life, feeling as if she was watching herself living her life from the end of a great long telescope.

She sat in the Jeep, trying to look interested, as Morgan worked Carna Boy on the gallops. Both of them looked fit and happy. The intensity of training the horse and himself had occupied Morgan, taking his mind off the tragedy of the dead jockey and the awful aftermath that had wreaked such havoc in their lives. Tara watched as the horse galloped towards her, Morgan crouched low on his withers, Kate riding the horse beside him, matching stride for stride, eating up the ground for the sheer joy of it. Kate's long red hair streamed out behind like the chestnut horse's tail, her face was split in a broad grin and her cheeks red with the bitter wind.

Morgan gave Carna Boy his head and the powerful horse surged ahead of the other, his feet churning up the turf as he pounded up the field with Kate's horse's legs flailing desperately, trying to keep up. He reined in the horse at the end of the gallop and rode him down to the jeep.

Tara opened the window as he rode alongside her, his face shining with the thrill of the ride.

"Getting fit, isn't he?" he said breathlessly.

She nodded. "Yes."

"Watch him jump the chase fences," Morgan said proudly, turning the horse and trotting him away.

Kate caught up and came to stand her horse beside the jeep. Her horse was breathing hard with the exertions of trying to keep up with Carna Boy. "Isn't he brilliant?" Kate bellowed into the window.

"Yes," said Tara again. She was sick of the horse. She wanted someone to ask how she was, instead of just assuming that she had lost the baby and that was that, just get up and go again. She wished that it was like that, but it wasn't — a dark cloud hung over her that she couldn't escape making her listless and exhausted with no energy or interest in anything. Just this deep resentment against Morgan for his lack of concern about her and his obsession with the bloody horse and bloody Cheltenham and his damnable desire to beat Derry and win the Gold Cup.

The Turf Club granted Morgan his jockey's licence. Tara watched as he filled out the forms and sent in his entry, saying his name proudly over the phone as he declared a few days before his first race. Then it was done. There was no backing out. He was going to ride Carna Boy in his next race and Derry's horse Magnetic Attraction was entered as well.

The newspapers were full of the story about Morgan riding his own horse again and that increased the pressure on him. He spent the morning of the race in the toilet being sick with nerves while Kate had to do the horses.

When they arrived at the course he was mobbed by news reporters. A reporter made a beeline straight for him, thrusting the microphone straight under his nose as soon as he slid down from the lorry cab. "What do you think about your chances in the race?" he asked making Morgan step back as the microphone was shoved in his face.

Morgan shrugged noncommittally. "I don't know — as good as ever I suppose." Then he shoved past and made his way to the steward's room to declare the horse and weigh in.

Tara stood in the middle of the parade-ring, watching Kate proudly lead the horse around. Derry came into the ring, looking elegant and arrogant with the haughty Ellen glued to his side, hanging onto his arm, as they watched Sarah lead the horse around. Magnetic Attraction looked fit and full of energy, jerking his head trying to bite Sarah's arm.

Out of the corner of her eye, Tara saw Derry disentangling himself from Ellen and coming towards her. She half-turned as he reached her. "Derry," she nodded at him, a slight smile turning the corners of her lips.

"Tara," he said, reaching down to kiss her cheek.

She could smell the woody scent of his aftershave as he stood close to her. She felt herself prickle with annoyance at his presence.

"Horse looks well," he commented, looking in the direction of Carna Boy.

"Thanks," she replied, shortly.

"Shame about his jockey though. I just saw him in the weigh room- he looks as white as a sheet." He laughed. "He'll never be able to ride that horse in an actual race!"

Ellen, obviously lost without Derry, sauntered over, her long legs clad in black trousers over very high and unsuitable heels that sank into the grass as she walked. She gave a smile that did not reach her eyes and kissed the air at the side of Tara's face. "You look awful," she said in her particularly catty way of going for the weakest spot that anyone had -she seemed to home in on it like a ferret sniffing out something to kill.

The bell rang and the jockeys trooped out. Derry and Ellen rushed off to meet their jockey. Tara watched for Morgan coming out. He was taller than most of them and looked a lot older. Most of them looked like skinny young schoolboys who should have still been behind their school-desks, not making a living doing one of the most dangerous sports in the world. Morgan saw her and gave her a brave grin; his face was white above the red and dark blue colours that he wore. Tara's heart went out to him. Her own malaise forgotten, she hurried over and hugged him. "You'll be fine," she said, wanting to go on holding him.

She legged him up, an undignified scramble because she had not the practice or the strength that he had, while Kate tried to calm the excited horse. Then finally somehow he was on the horse, thrusting his feet into the irons, sorting out his reins and grinning down at her, suddenly confident now that he could feel the brave horse and its raw power beneath him. Tara reached up and put her hand on his long hard skinny thigh.

"Good luck," she breathed.

Kate led him down to the gate and then let the horse go, darting out of the way as he kicked up his heels for the sheer joy of being able to gallop and the excitement of remembering what this job was all about. She grinned weakly at Tara, and gave her the thumbs-up sign. Then the two of them went silently up to the stand to watch the race. Tara was terribly aware of the stares of all the people who knew who she was and what had happened in her life. She peered through the binoculars that she had borrowed from Morgan, watching intently as the horses arrived at the start and began to circle around, the stewards checking their girths, checking shoes and chatting to the jockeys. She could see Morgan but he was too faraway to make out his expression. She wondered what he was thinking, hoped that he would be safe, longed for later when she could hold him in bed and forget the dark days that they had just gone through.

The horses lined up at the start and the flag dropped. The horses charged forwards as one, a mass of colour pounding towards the first fence. Tara took the binoculars away from her eyes, unable to watch, and they were snatched away by Kate with the cord still around her neck. Tara looked everywhere but at the race, unable to bear seeing Morgan risking his life for the sake of the reputation of that damn horse. Then as the horses thundered past the stand she looked. Morgan was up in third place, grinning broadly, loving every second. The horse was going well beneath him, looking full of power and courage. She snatched the binoculars back from Kate, staring through them as the mass of horses surged over the fences, strung out now, some tiring and beginning to fall behind.

At the third fence from home a horse in the first bunch fell. Tara felt her heart drop momentarily until she could make out Morgan's colours; he was all right and was galloping alongside the leader, Magnetic Attraction.

Then Magnetic Attraction began to pull away, leaving the rest behind. Carna Boy remained with the rest galloping in second spot as he powered away. Then, at the final fence, Magnetic Attraction seemed to lose ground and the gap between the horses closed again. Carna Boy surged ahead and then, as Morgan slapped him down the shoulder, he redoubled his efforts and shot into the lead to finish first — a length ahead of the other horses.

As Tara shot down the steps to meet Morgan and Carna Boy she caught sight of Derry, his face full of disappointment. She met his eye. There was something more in his face, more than just the upset of seeing his horse fail. Something was wrong, she knew it instinctively. Just then the tannoy crackled into life, demanding that Derry go to the stewards' offices.

Now was not the time for finding out what was wrong with Derry, thought Tara. She dashed to Morgan's side. He was panting with the exertion, his face mud-splattered and delighted. He turned the horse into the winner's enclosure, slid off him and hugged her tightly.

"I did it! We won!" he gasped. "What a horse!"

Later, much later, they were at home lying on the settee celebrating, a half-bottle of champagne lying empty on the floor beside them. The phone rang.

"I'll get it," Tara said, scrambling to her feet. If it was the malicious caller she did not want Morgan to hear, not now - she didn't want to spoil the glory of the day.

"Hello," she said nervously, picking up the receiver.

"Tara, it's Sarah," came a shaking voice.

"Yes?" she said, hardly able to keep the annoyance out of her voice. What could be so important that Sarah should ring at this hour?

"Tara, I've just found out that the race was rigged. I heard JT rowing with Derry. JT bribed the jockey to pull the horse."

Tara's heart sank Morgan would be devastated when he discovered that Carna Boy hadn't won the race fair and square. "Bloody JT!" she exploded, seething with anger.

"How dare he jeopardise Derry's reputation!" Sarah was ranting furiously on the other end of the line. "Everyone will assume that Derry had placed a huge bet on Carna Boy and told the jockey to make Magnetic Attraction lose the race!"

"It's OK, Sarah," said Tara, trying to calm the other girl down. "Don't worry - I'm sure the stewards will clear Derry." For once she didn't care about Derry's feelings or his precious reputation. All that she cared about was Morgan and how he was going to feel. And with a dreadful sense of foreboding, she knew that he was going to be devastated when she broke the news to him. Magnetic Attraction should have won the race. Maybe Carna Boy wasn't the wonder horse that Morgan thought he was.

CHAPTER FORTY

Sarah had never seen Derry so worried, or miserable. He lay, sprawled across her small settee, his feet hanging off the far end, his head propped against the arm, grimly nursing a glass of wine.

"I have never been so fucking humiliated in my whole bloody life," he said bitterly. "I had to stand outside the door of the stewards' offices, while everyone went past." He took a long slurp of the wine. "I felt they all knew why I was there."

Sarah stood, looking out of the window at the old walled garden, flowerless now in the pale spring sunlight. The bare earth looking dark and rich and full of promise for the summer when the borders would be filled with the flowers and herbs that would waft their scents into the cottage. Poor Derry! He was so arrogant he hated to be made a fool of.

"It was like being at school." he moaned irritably, "being lined up to see the headmaster. I did plenty of that." He smiled at himself for the first time since he had appeared at the cottage. "I had to stand in front of the stewards," he went on, "while they sat at a desk staring disbelievingly when I said I had nothing to do with the horse being pulled."

Sarah smiled and bit her lip to stop herself from spluttering with laughter. She had a clear picture in her mind of Derry grovelling in front of the stewards, pleading that he had nothing to do with rigging the race, fighting desperately for his livelihood. Good, she thought, it would do him good to be on the receiving end of an injustice for once.

She turned and leant against the windowsill. "But you managed to convince them that you had no part in it," she said, watching as he sat up and drained the rest of the glass of wine in one gulp.

He nodded, bleakly. "The jockey admitted that he had been bribed to pull the horse up to make him lose, but he wouldn't say who it was that had bribed him. Except it wasn't me." He leant forward and poured himself another glass. "Bloody fool — of course the stewards spotted what he was up to. Now he has had his licence suspended for three months — all for the sake of a few thousand pounds!"

The following morning the newspapers were full of the story, accusing Derry of being crooked and devising a scam with the jockey. Sarah thought how quickly anyone could turn from hero to villain. The media, it seemed, were only too keen to tear down the hero that they had created.

Derry's temper had not improved overnight, having had time to mull over the stupidity of the jockey whose involvement would now mean that he would have to miss Cheltenham.

The race seemed to have terrible repercussions for Derry at home as well. He was furious with JT for being so stupid. JT, of course, was delighted with himself. His scam had come off and he had made a packet of money on off-course bets. He had a team of men, paid to put money on Carna Boy in betting shops all around the country, and he had cleaned up, making enough money to pay Sue off. She had been delighted to have a large settlement which meant that she could buy herself a nice little house close to the rough estate where she had come from and spend the rest on lashings of drink.

When Derry had tried to reprimand JT, he had just laughed. "You could have been part of it and made yourself a tidy little nest-egg," he said when Derry tackled him about his stupidity.

Derry took all of his temper out on Ellen. "I can't stand her around me," he finally confessed to Sarah. "She reminds me of bloody JT She has the arrogance to tell me that I shouldn't be horrible to her father as he is one of my best customers."

Derry almost seemed to gain some sort of sadistic pleasure from hurting Ellen. He was coming to Sarah's cottage more and more at night, and was staying longer and longer. This gave her no sense of satisfaction — it only served to make her feel cheap.

Now everything that Ellen did annoyed Derry, like when she had come bothering him while he was on the phone trying to get a jockey for the forthcoming races. It was deadly important to get the right jockey. Magnetic Attraction had to be ridden right at Cheltenham and there were very few jockeys that he felt had the ability.

At length he put the phone down. He had got the services of a jockey he did think would be able to ride the horse. He had seen Pat Harris ride before and had admired his style. Hopefully he would be able to get the same song out of Magnetic Attraction that the bold riding style of the banned jockey had.

Sarah was helping Paul load the horses into the lorry - Magnetic Attraction who was having his last but one race before Cheltenham, and Lippy Lad, Lynn Moore's horse.

She wished that Derry would hurry up. They were going to be late but he was shut in the tack room arguing with Ellen. The sound of raised voices drifted unintelligibly across the yard, punctuated occasionally by one of her high-pitched yells. Then there was the sound of crying. Sarah threw the last of the tack into the locker at the side of the lorry and leant against it with a sigh. Now what?

The door opened and Derry exploded out into the yard, with Ellen hot on his heels, screeching at him, her pretty face contorted with rage. Her mascara had run and lay in black rivulets down her usually immaculate face giving her the odd appearance of a clown.

"You bastard!" she shrieked, immune to the curious and amused stares of the lads who stopped working to watch the side-show, leaning on their sweeping brushes.

"How dare you say that about my father! He could buy you out any day!"

Derry stopped suddenly and turned around slowly like a big cat about to spring on some gentle gazelle. "What did you say?" he exploded.

Sarah could only see his back, but his arms, pinned by his sides quivered with rage and his hands clenched and unclenched as if to punctuate his words. "Your father only got you to marry me because he thought that I had enough money to keep you in bloody clothes and fucking make-up!"

Ellen's face twisted with anger before she spat, "yes, and you only married me because you thought that I was some poor little rich girl you could push around and take all of her money to spend on your horses! Let me tell you," she folded her arms aggressively across her body, "my father has been trying to get another yard for his horses — he's looking for another trainer! And when he gets one, you will be finished!"

Derry laughed suddenly, the loud sound ringing and echoing in the stunned silence of the yard. "I know that he has, my darling! And I also know that no one will take him because he is as crooked as they come, sweetheart!" With that he spun around on his heel and marched towards his car, leaving Ellen mouthing wordlessly in rage.

The yard erupted back into movement as all of the lads scuttled back to their jobs, not wanting to be caught eavesdropping.

Things did not improve when they got to the races. As they led Magnetic Attraction to the parade-ring some wit bellowed, "are you going to pull him up again today, Derry?" Sarah saw Derry's face close with black temper.

The bell rang and the jockeys trooped out.

The new rider, Pat Harris, was a jockey that she had seen before. He was tiny and skinny with a cherubic face that belied the aggressive way he rode. He nodded courteously at Sarah before shaking Derry's hand. "Sir," he drawled.

Sarah instinctively disliked him; he was far too cocky. "Let him run his own race," she heard Derry tell him. "He'll get you round."

Sarah turned away, running her fingers through the horse's girth to check that it was tight enough. He was wrong. The horse needed to be ridden so that he thought that he had a horse to beat all of the time; let him run his own race and he would shoot off and tire himself out too quickly. Derry was being a fool.

Derry legged Pat up onto the horse. "Come on," he said to Sarah as the horses went out onto the course. Sarah followed him up onto the stands.

"That's the trainer who was in the newspapers," she heard someone whisper and hoped that Derry did not hear them.

She peered upwards at the course television. Magnetic Attraction looked miserable with a new jockey on him. The horse was sensitive and was used to the gentle hands and careful touch of his usual jockey. He pulled his head up and down as if trying to wrench the reins that were holding him too tight. Pat Harris did not have the assured confidence of the horse's usual jockey who was happy to sit quietly on him.

The race went off and Sarah could immediately see that something was very wrong. The horse was galloping with his head high almost as it he was panicking, while the jockey hauled at his mouth trying to get him to run with the other horses. He shot ahead, blundering over the first fence, his back end brushing through as the jockey tried desperately to stay on.

"Well, he'll need to jump better than that if he's going to tackle Cheltenham!" came the high-pitched tones of the commentator, maliciously going for Derry's jugular.

Beside her Derry stiffened with rage. "What the fuck is he doing?" he said, gazing in horror at the television screen.

"He's afraid of the horse," Sarah whispered, "and so he won't let him go."

Derry, if he even heard her, made no reply, staring grimly upwards as the horse ran raggedly, blundering over every fence and eventually trailing in at the back of the field.

"I'm not letting that little prick Pat Harris ride my horse again!" Derry raged, watching the horse trot in behind the others.

Sarah took Lippy Lad to the parade-ring. He was a handsome horse, a big bay with four long white socks and a blaze that made him easy to spot while he was galloping on the course, especially with Lynn's loud red and green striped colours. Derry stood with Lynn in the centre of the parade-ring. She clung to his arm possessively, gazing at him through her mascara-caked eyes. Like a bitch on heat, thought Sarah miserably, as she led the horse around. She longed to stride across the ring and punch the tarty woman.

The ancient steward who always was there, doing the rounds of all of the races, indicated that they should take the horses into the saddling stalls. Sarah led Lippy Lad in, holding the horse with one hand as she reached for the pile of saddlery that lay on the floor. Saddling up was not a difficult job but it was vital that it was done properly and that the tack was checked. Any strap that was weak could break under the strain of the tough racing conditions and a broken rein or stirrup could cost a race. Or a life.

"I'll do that," Derry told her, flinging the saddle onto the horse's back and roughly shoving the straps into place, pulling at the buckles. He was still angry about Magnetic Attraction and Sarah stood by the horse's head, not daring to speak to him. "Go on, lead him out!" he snapped finally, stepping back to let her leave the stall.

She led Lippy Lad into the parade-ring.

Derry had found a new jockey for the horse, by pinning Joe Neilan into a corner so that he had no choice but to agree to ride Lippy Lad. He came towards Sarah and the horse resentfully and stood silently raising his leg from the knee to let Derry leg him up. Joe was silent as she led him down to the course and then did no more than nod briefly at her as she slid the lead-rein from the bridle and let the horse gallop away.

"At least he should give him a better ride that the last fool," Derry commented, watching as the horse cantered down to the start. As the other horses turned and galloped past him, he put in an enormous buck that would have unseated any rider but Joe just sat still, undisturbed.

The race started. Sarah stood on the stand beside Derry watching on the television. It was easy to tell the horse with his distinctive colours and markings. Lynn stood on Derry's other side squealing with delight as the horses lined up for the start of the race. Sarah stole a glimpse at Derry. His face was impassive, professional as ever, but she knew that inside he was cringing with embarrassment at Lynn. As the horses thundered past the stand for the first time Sarah gazed with increasing horror at Lippy Lad. His saddle was slipping backwards. Derry in his temper had not done the girth up tight enough. She watched speechlessly as fence after fence the saddle slid back towards the horse's hindquarters. She stole a look at Derry who was open-mouthed with horror. Eventually the jockey had to slip his feet out of the irons and ride him bareback, his legs trailing as he leapt the final fence and thundered home to win. Joe, grinning, rode the horse into the ring. Fortunately Lippy Lad was too tired to protest at the strange position of his saddle.

But as Joe slid off in the winner's enclosure he scowled and he snapped at Derry, "don't ever ask me to ride for you again! You can't even get the horses turned out properly!" Then he snatched off his saddle and marched away to weigh in.

Derry glared at Sarah, white with fury, as the cameras turned on him in amusement. "You fucking stupid bitch!" he roared, hardly seeming to care that the scene was being filmed for the delight of thousands of racing spectators. "You forgot to tighten his girth!"

CHAPTER FORTY ONE

Sarah saw the whole awful scene replayed again on television that evening. She sat numbly watching the screen, watching Derry turning on her in front of everyone and calling her a fucking fool, telling her that it was her fault that the saddle had slipped back when it was him who had put it on in the first place. She watched Derry, his fury evident on the screen, his eyes blazing, hating her, yelling at her, not caring who saw - and then her own face, tired and frightened, stepping backwards from him in shock and horror.

She put her head into her hands and wept bitterly. He had betrayed her in the cruellest and most public way possible. "You stupid bitch!" That was what he had yelled. Well, now she knew that she was - very stupid. She had always forgiven him for being horrible to her, given up her new life and a fledgling relationship in England to come running when he asked her, taken him into her bed whenever he felt like it — and how had he repaid her loyalty and trust? By making her look a total fool in front of thousands of people. She hated him with a bitter loathing that clawed at her heart and made it feel almost impossible to breathe.

She made herself something to eat but, after pushing the food around her plate, finally abandoned the idea and scraped it into the bin. Wanting distraction she wandered upstairs and began to run a bath, pouring in bubble-bath that one of the grooms had given her for Christmas. Stress relief, it said on the bottle. Smiling to herself at the ridiculous suggestion, she turned off the taps, then suddenly heard her mobile phone begin to ring.

Uninterestedly she followed the sound to where she had thrown the telephone on the bed and snapped it on.

"Hello?"

"It's Edward," said the voice at the other end. She felt herself dissolve into tears, longing all of a sudden for his maturity and strength, for the comfort that she had felt with him. "I've just seen the news."

A sob escaped her. She stretched out on the bed, tracing a pattern of a rose on the cover.

"Sarah?"

She made an effort to control her tears. "Derry saddled the horse, not me," she said, giving a hollow laugh. She wished that she were with Edward. He would make everything seem all right. At that moment she realised what a dreadful mistake she had made. She must get another job and go back to England, pick up the pieces of whatever relationship she had with this kind man — if he still wanted her — break away from the influences of Derry Blake and Westwood Park.

"Well, I did rather think you were too much of a professional for that, but whatever did happen he was totally out of order to behave like that in public. The man is a menace."

Sarah let a long sigh slide through her lips; she felt unable to speak. Edward was so kind.

"Are you all right?" he asked.

She could imagine him in his office, surrounded by the rows and rows of books and paintings of horses and hunting scenes. She nodded silently and then managed to squeak, "yes". Half of her wished that he had said, 'come back. Come and work for me,' but that only happened in the ridiculous Mills and Boon books that her mother had lost herself in periodically.

"Listen," he said, "if things get rotten, if you need me, just ring."

A loud banging noise woke her later; she sat up, sleepily fumbling for the bedside light. It was almost midnight. The banging continued. It could only be Derry. Furiously she wriggled out of the duvet and put her feet onto the floor. She felt half-asleep, her eyes leaden and the beginnings of a furious headache beginning to pound behind her eyes. She opened the window. She could see Derry, looking up, his face in shadow in the darkness.

"What do you want?" she snapped.

"Open the door," he said. He sounded calm, but there was an underlying menace in his voice and he sounded very drunk.

"No!" she said, leaning back to pull the window shut.

"Sarah!" he yelled, his voice pitched higher, and he slammed his fist against the door, making a bang that seemed to echo around the cottage and the silent garden. "Open the door." he repeated, "or I will stay here banging on it until either you open it or I knock it in."

Anger coursed through her. She would go down and open the door and tell him to get lost, to go away and never to bother her again. She would hand in her notice there and then, get rid of him and then leave straight away. This life had come to an end. Finally she had really seen Derry for what he was — a nasty malicious arrogant thug. She shot down the stairs, pulling the sides of her dressing-gown together, tying the belt roughly, and threw open the door.

Derry lolled in the trellis porch holding out a bottle of champagne. "I thought that we could celebrate Lippy Lad's win," he grinned, twirling his wrist so that the bottle swung to and fro.

"Oh? And shall we celebrate you subjecting me to a public row for not doing what you should have done? Or shall we celebrate the fact that I'm leaving?"

He staggered past her and threw himself down on the settee. "Oh Sarah, Sarah," he sang, suddenly springing up and beginning to throw logs and pieces of turf onto the embers of the fire. He watched as they sprang into life, flames consuming the dead wood. "I was only messing around — I wasn't telling you off!" He smiled up at her, kneeling in front of the fire while she stood at the other side, fighting an urge to kick him very viciously while he was on his knees.

"It didn't seem like that to me!" She watched the flames flickering over his face, casting strange dark shadows in the half-light, making his handsome face look like that of a stranger, a suddenly very menacing and dangerous stranger. "I have had enough of this, Derry. I'm handing in my notice."

"You can't leave," he said sullenly. "You are the best head groom I've ever had. I won't let you go." He smiled into the fire and then turned to grin up at her. "You know that you haven't got the guts to go — who would ever give you a job, especially after you failed to tack the horse up properly?"

"Get out of here!" she cried. She shoved past him to open the door but as she passed he grabbed her wrist, holding her roughly as she squirmed to get away from his cruel grip. "Get off me!" she snarled, wincing as his fingers gripped harder. "Derry, you're hurting me!" She pulled away roughly, jerking her wrist so that he overbalanced. She darted away, bounding up the stairs, taking them three at a time. She pulled her suitcase off the top of the wardrobe.

She heard him coming up the stairs, panting, his breath loud as he came towards her and she felt the first prickle of fear. She shot to the door and bolted it, then leant against it, feeling her heart pounding roughly in her throat. The latch lifted and he discovered that the door was locked.

"You bloody fool, what do you think you're playing at?" he snarled at the other side of the door. "This is my house - you can't lock me out!" He shoved his shoulder on the door, the flimsy bolt gave way and he stumbled into the room.

"Derry, go away. Please leave me alone!" she pleaded now.

He advanced slowly, crossing the room towards her. Then, with a suddenness of movement that took her by surprise, he lunged forwards and she found herself flying sideways, landing in a sprawling heap on the bed, the breath knocked out of her. Before she had time to move, he had scrambled onto the bed and sat astride her, his bottom pressing on her belly, making it hard to breathe as she squirmed beneath him.

Then fear gave way to an inner strength. She felt nothing beyond wanting him to go, but she had to be polite, to stop fighting, to make him think that he was winning. Then he would go away and leave her, then she would be able to make her escape.

"OK, you win," she panted, smiling at him. "I was only joking! I wasn't going to leave. How could I? You're my greatest lover — I was just mad at you!"

"I know that you were," he said smiling down at her. Then he leant forward and kissed her hard, forcing his tongue into her mouth.

"Derry, I'm so tired — why don't you come back tomorrow?" She smiled up at him, her voice pleading.

He undid the buttons of her pyjamas top, then pulled it open and sat above her looking at her breasts, slowly stroking the skin, fingering the nipples that rose in betrayal of her and in response to his touch. He gave her a malicious smirk. "You know that you want this!" he hissed.

"Of course, but not now when I'm exhausted," she whispered back, hoping that her voice would not betray the fear and loathing that she felt.

"Well, I want it now," said Derry, not fooled for an instant by her. Gripping her arms, he shoved her pyjamas down, the fabric sliding along her legs as he tugged, then pushing her legs apart with his he thrust himself hard into her unyielding flesh.

She reached for the telephone. Her fingers trembled so much that she could hardly press the numbers. It was early, only four o'clock in the morning, she noticed bleakly, but she really needed to talk to Edward.

Derry had gone and she was alone. She had bathed, scrubbing the smell of him off her, and thrown her pyjamas and the dressing-gown in the bin. She could never have worn them again, not even if she had washed and washed them. The memory of Derry and the look on his face as he removed them meant that she would never ever be able to wear them again. And then she had sat, numb, not able to move or think until finally she had reached for the telephone wanting nothing more than to hear the soothing voice of Edward rang the number of his mobile.

The phone began to ring, and for a moment she panicked. What would she say? How could she explain to him what had happened? The ringing stopped and his answer phone kicked in. She listened to his calm very English voice apologising for not answering the telephone and asking her to leave a message. She listened for a moment and then put the phone down. She felt silly for even bothering him. He was nothing to her and she nothing to him -it had been a foolish thing to do. What if he had answered the phone? What would she have said? How would she have explained what had happened? The phone shrilled, making her jump. If it was Derry she would not answer it, but on the display face she recognised Edward's number.

"I woke you, by calling you didn't I?" she said as she picked up the phone.

"It doesn't matter. I didn't get to answer it but it woke me and when I looked at the last-number display I saw that it was your number. Are you all right?" The tone of his voice revealed his concern.

"I . . . " She didn't know what to say. How could she tell him that she had to leave, that Derry had come here and had virtually raped her? Or was it even rape? She had not fought. He had not hurt her. Had she given in or deep down had she actually wanted him to do it? She could never resist him and even before when she had said no she had always given in, been seduced by his touch, by the gentleness of his kisses and the feeling of his hands playing a tune on her body.

"Something has happened, hasn't it?" Edward asked.

Then she began to cry, a huge choke in her voice making it impossible to do anything other than sob, wanting to speak but being unable to do so.

"Do you want me to come?" he asked, "I'm in Dublin on business, I can be with you soon."

She could hear his fingers drumming on his desk as he tried to contain the frustration at not being able to get a proper answer out of her. She continued to sob pitifully. "I—I c-can't tell you ..."

"Look," he said after a long pause, "do you want me to come to you?"

"No...," Sarah whispered, "I'm fine, I'm sorry I bothered you." She ended the phone call, leaving her cradling the receiver, as she curled up unable to move, too tired to be able to fight any longer.

The alarm clock woke her. It was pitch black. She sat up. She felt better, stronger, more able to cope. She would pack up her things and then as soon as it was light she would be on her way. She felt annoyed at herself for bothering Edward. What must he have thought? She would ring him as soon as it was a more reasonable hour and apologise. He would be glad, of course, and relieved at being let off his Sir Galahad duties. What on earth did she think that he was going to do? Drive all the way over here and give Derry a punch on the nose? She packed, shoving things roughly into some suitcases and a battered hold-all and then, after a final look around the cottage, she opened the front door.

She went into the stable yard. It was a long walk with her overloaded suitcases. With difficulty she heaved them to the end gate. Her little car was just beyond, parked just outside the main entrance to the big house. The horses began to whinny, hearing her and scrambled to their doors, surprised to see anyone awake so early. Faltering, she began to look around the yard and then went back to stroke Magnetic Attraction's elegant nose. How could she leave this horse? But she had to. Magnetic Attraction did not care, as long as he was fed and watered.

A lorry was driving along the main road, the engine noise carrying across the dawn fields. As she moved around the stable yard, patting the horses, the noise grew louder and a light shone in the sky.

Then with a sudden realisation she gave a cry of joy and ran to the yard gate. A helicopter was swooping in over the trees at the edge of the park and then dropping lower and lower until it landed in the field in front of the house. A figure emerged from the passenger side and, crouching under the still spinning blades, began to come towards her. Edward. She yanked open the yard gate, closing it solicitously behind her, and then grabbing her bags she went to meet him.

CHAPTER FORTY TWO

A loud noise penetrated her dreams. Tara rolled over, grimacing, and slowly prised her eyes open. The room was still in semi-darkness; outside through a gap in the curtains she could see the first slivers of a silver-grey dawn spreading its tentative fingers over the stable yard. The telephone was ringing, loud and insistent. Tara was awake in an instant, fear clutching at her stomach. Please don't let it be another malicious call! Beside her Morgan slept on, oblivious to the noise, and as she reached over him to grab the receiver he did no more than pull the bedclothes tighter around his shoulders.

"Radford Lodge," she whispered, her voice croaky with sleep. For a long moment she listened to the sound of silence, fear clutching at her again.

Then, as if from far away, came Derry's voice. "Tara ..." He sounded numb, his voice dead and expressionless.

"Derry, what is it?" She had only heard him sound like this once before, when he had phoned to tell her that their parents had been killed. "Tara, I need you — can you come?"

Morgan hated Derry; the last thing that he would appreciate was her rushing off to him when he asked her to.

"Why, what is it is it? Ellen? One of the horses?"

"Come, please," he said and the connection was severed.

She sat in bed holding the receiver, listening to the dull buzzing of static, until finally she reached over and replaced it.

"Morgan," she said quietly, laying her body along his back and leaning over him so that she could whisper into his ear. "Morgan," she said in a louder voice.

He sat up, instantly alert. He rubbed his eyes and pushed back the tangle of hair from his forehead. "What?" he blurted, blearily.

"I've got to go to Westwood Park," she said, calmly, though her fingers kneaded at the sheets fitfully.

"What?" he snapped — the suggestion that she was going to Westwood Park was so bizarre.

"Derry has some sort of problem and he needs to talk to me."

Morgan shook his head slowly, trying to get to grips with what she was saying. She watched him, not wanting an argument, not wanting to have to choose between either of them. Morgan was her husband, but Derry was her brother. They hated each other, but both loved her. How could she choose between them?

"For fuck's sake, Tara," snapped Morgan, flinging back the bedclothes in temper and sliding his feet onto the floor.

She watched silently as he dressed. He opened the curtains, drawing them back slowly, his back to her, stiff with unspoken anger, and looked out over the stable yard as the dawn slowly broke.

Eventually he turned and stared at her, his face dark with anger, his lips turned down in a harsh grim line. "I don't understand you," he said, leaning his hands back on the window sill. "Derry has been an absolute bastard to you and yet one word from him and you go running to him!"

"But he . . . he needs me ..."

He gave a harsh laugh. "Yes — well, Tara, I need you too!" He turned again and looked out of the window. "I need you, Tara. We have a business tailing around our ears, sick horses everywhere, no money — and you have to go dashing off to Derry!" He turned and walked out of the room. "You should have a look at your priorities," he said, closing the door firmly behind him.

Tara lay back on the pillows with a sigh. She hated this, the confrontation between the two men, the feeling of being torn apart by them as if she was some prized toy that they were squabbling over.

She dressed, looking at her tired pinched thin-looking face in the mirror. She seemed to have aged ten years in the past few weeks.

The door opened and Morgan came in with a cup of tea as a peace offering. "Look," he said putting the cup down on the bedside table and slopping some of the liquid over the edge, "I can't stop you going."

Tara watched the spilt tea slowly spread out and trickle over the edge onto the floor.

"I would rather that you didn't go, but you have to make your own choices, sort out your own priorities."

She smiled weakly at him and nodded, "OK."

He left and she listened, sitting on the bed, as he went back downstairs and then she heard him go out into the yard and the noise of the hungry horses begin, clamouring for their breakfast.

She had to go to Derry He had sounded so desperate. He needed her and besides which, she thought, the bitterness still very much present, Morgan had not had much time for her when she had lost the baby. So it was no good him talking about priorities — it was easy to see where his lay, with the bloody horses and his bloody precious Carna Boy. She sipped her tea, sitting on the edge of the bed pondering. Morgan would be cross, but he could get over it. She was getting over the loss of the baby - she had to; he would have to get over this.

Morgan was in the stables banging feed into buckets.

"I'll see you later," she said and received a grunt of agreement in reply. Then, knowing that there was no point in saying anything further, she turned and went.

Westwood Park always looked beautiful, no matter what the time of year. The garden and the parkland that surrounded the long drive were always immaculate, trimmed and cared for by the housekeeper's husband. The rhododendron bushes swayed busily in the keen wind and the beech trees moved in unison as she drove along the avenue and pulled up on the sweep of gravel in front of the house. She went up the stone steps. The office door swing open and Derry came towards her.

"Thank you for coming," he said courteously as if she was some visitor who had gone out of her way to pay him a call rather than his sister here on a family emergency. She walked towards him. He looked dreadful. His face was grey beneath his normal tanned pallor and his eyes were bloodshot and red-rimmed with tiredness. As he reached out to hug her to him, she could smell the aftermath of whiskey on his breath. He obviously had an enormous hangover. "Coffee?" he said, releasing her, and as she nodded he marched ahead to order some from the kitchen, indicating that she should go into his office with a sweep of his arm.

When he returned a few moments later with coffee cups and a jug of coffee, milk and sugar on a large tray she was seated in the padded window-seat that had been her favourite as a little girl. He sat down at his desk and busied himself with the ritual of coffee.

"What's happened?" she said, looking at him intently.

Finally he looked up, framing the words that he had been so far unable to say. "She's gone. She's left me," he said bleakly.

"Ellen?" exclaimed Tara.

"Not Ellen," he snapped as if the suggestion was ridiculous. "Sarah."

"Sarah?" she said, unsure that she had even heard him right.

Derry stopped fiddling with the coffee cups and looked up, his face bleak, staring at her with unseeing eyes and she looked with increasing horror at the pain that she could see there.

"But you were always horrible to her," she frowned, trying to think of any clue she had missed that Sarah had meant anything to him. He was married to Ellen — surely he loved her?

"I never meant any of it," he said. "It was just a way of stopping her really getting to me." He shrugged and took a sip of coffee, wincing as the scalding liquid burnt his lips. He gave a half laugh at himself. "Unlike with Ellen - I'm horrible to her because she drives me nuts."

Tara stared at the rain that had now begun to fall in squally sheets against the windowpanes.

"She left this morning — with bloody Edward Dixon. He came for her in a helicopter." He gave a snort of laughter. "Like some fucking scene from Pretty-bloody-Woman." He ran his hands through his hair. "Christ, my head hurts!" he winced.

"But you have Ellen!" Tara said, feeling impatient with him. If he cared so much, why the hell had he married Ellen? Why not marry Sarah? She stared at her brother. She knew why. Because Ellen had money and status and looks. He would have kept her as his showpiece wife while he carried on loving Sarah and treating her as if she was his wife.

"Ellen!" he said contemptuously, giving another snort of derisive laughter. "She and her bloody father are nothing but crooks - she only married me for my money and he — he —" Derry paused, trying to form the words, as if he was so angry that he could barely speak, "he pulled the bloody scam, pulling the horse that nearly lost me my licence." He sighed bitterly. "How am I supposed to manage without her?" he said miserably. "I've got to think of a way to get her back, but first I've got to find myself a jockey. Now that that bloody idiot is banned and Joe Neilan won't ride for me again, I don't know who's going to ride for me." Abruptly, he picked up the phone.

Tara took her coffee and went back to the window seat, curling her legs beneath her and pulling the curtain halfway across to give him the impression of privacy while he phoned jockeys and their agents, trying to get someone suitable to ride the horse.

At last he slammed down the phone. "I'll bloody have to ride the damn horse myself! No one is out there that I would trust with him and Liam Healy, the champion jockey, won't ride for me after the fiasco with the saddle slipping backwards!"

Tara watched him with a faint smile.

"I'll make the weight easily enough," he said, patting his concave stomach, "if I don't eat for the next two days. And I still have my licence."

A car pulled up onto the gravel outside. Tara craned her neck to see who had arrived and saw JT getting out of his car. He wore a dark suit and a dark overcoat with a thick lambskin collar over it that gave him the appearance of a gangster. All that he lacked was a violin case carrying a machine gun as he swept up the steps. Tara watched from the window as Ellen departed from the house and shot into his arms, wobbling down the steps on ridiculously high heels and an equally inappropriately short skirt.

A short while later, the door to the office swung open and Ellen and JT came into the room, oblivious of Tara in the window seat.

"I'm on the telephone," she heard Derry snap.

"Well, get off it then," said Ellen rudely.

Tara heard Derry slam the phone down and an oppressive silence filled the room. She wondered whether she should come out from behind the pulled curtain, but then as JT began to speak it was too late. She had to remain, an unwilling eavesdropper to a bitter row between husband, wife and an over-protective father-in-law.

"Stop taking our row out on Ellen," JT fumed. "I arranged for the horse to be pulled - it was nothing to do with her."

"Maybe," Derry snarled in reply. Tara could hear him tapping a beat on the leather cover of the desk with his pen. "But she knew about it - she should have stopped you. The pair of you are just greedy little crooks!"

"How dare you speak to my father like that!" Ellen shrieked, her voice rising to a fishwife's pitch in her anger. "He only did it to make money for us!"

For a moment there was silence and then Derry spoke again, his voice quiet with pent-up anger. "He did it because he had no money of his own — he had gambled it all away and he wanted you to marry me because he thought that I could give you the money and prestige that you wanted."

Tara sat back against the wood panelling, wishing that she were a thousand miles away.

"Well," she heard Ellen's harsh voice, "you're stuck with me now. You would never go through the embarrassment of betraying the sham that our marriage is — and even that tart of yours has gone now!"

The office door slammed again and she heard the sound of Ellen's high heels tapping along the corridor and the sound of her raised voice and JT's trying to pacify her as they retreated into the depths of the house. Slowly she pulled back the curtain and looked at Derry. He was slumped over his desk, his shoulders seeming to carry the weight of the world on them.

"What the hell have I done?" he groaned.

Tara stood up; she wanted to go home to Morgan. "I have to go," she said. "If you want to talk things through again you know where I am." Stopping to drop a kiss on the top of his head, she went out and ran down to her car. He would be all right; Derry was tough and arrogant. He would soon find himself another mistress. He would get over Sarah and his marriage would carry on under its veil of convenience. She should not have come.

She drove quickly home. Morgan was out with the horses so she let herself into the house and began to tidy up, shoving the dirty plates into a bowl of hot soapy water and washing up furiously, angry with her brother and angry with herself for letting him convince her that she was needed. It was just a bid for sympathy and to get one over on Morgan, she knew that now. She listened as horses' hooves clattered into the yard.

Some time later Morgan came into the house. "You're back then?"

His tone put her back up immediately. She had wanted to apologise to him for being so silly, dashing off at Derry's beck and call, but something about him made her angry. "Looks like it," she snapped back.

"Terrible crisis, was it?" he said sarcastically, snapping on the kettle to make tea.

"Nothing to concern you," she said, sick of his jibes, sick of being tossed between Morgan and Derry.

"Tara," he said finally, "you're going to have to choose once and for all between me and Derry."

CHAPTER FORTY THREE

The atmosphere felt as if she could cut it with a knife, thought Tara, looking at Morgan as he roughly shoved tea bags into the pot. He had barely spoken to her since she had gone to help Derry and she felt decidedly like a small child, sent to stand in the corner for some misdemeanour.

The evening stretched onwards like a black cloud rolling in on the horizon bringing; with it a thunderstorm. Tara glanced at the clock. It was only six o'clock, and already it was pitch-black outside, icy cold with a frost that would come later hanging in the air. The yard was all finished and now there was no excuse to keep busy. All that remained was to sit together for the evening, waiting for one or the other to apologise or for another argument to break out. Morgan lit a fire, plonked himself in the chair beside it and poked listlessly at the embers while Tara watched him over the top of the book that she was reading.

Finally he stopped poking and sat with his elbows resting on his knees and his chin resting in his cupped hands. "Look," he said with an embarrassed shrug, "I'm sorry. 1 shouldn't have acted like that. It wasn't fair."

She put down the book and looked at him with a half-smile of forgiveness.

"There's just so much pressure at the moment," he continued. "Everything is going wrong and Derry is like a thorn in my side."

"I know," she said, looking hard at her fingernails. There was dirt engrained in one of them and she picked at it fitfully as she replied, "I shouldn't have gone, but I feel so torn between the two of you."

"Come here," he said, holding out his hand across the room.

She reached forward and their fingertips touched. He pushed back the hair that had fallen over her face and then lowered his face to gently kiss her. She felt herself turn to liquid, she wanted him so much.

"Bed?" he said brushing his lips softly against hers so that she could feel her toes curl with delight.

"Mmmm," she whispered dreamily as she nuzzled his neck, suddenly longing to have her skin pressed against his and her legs wrapped around his while they made tender and gentle love.

She wriggled to her feet and held her hand out to him. She pulled him to his feet, then fingers entwined they went slowly up the stairs.

"It's a bit early for bed, isn't it?" she said as he shut the door.

He turned to her with a grin. "I don't intend to go to sleep," he said wickedly, beginning to unbutton her shirt, "for a very long time."

She stood still as he undid every one of the buttons and then slid the shirt away and gently ran his outstretched hands over her skin.

With aching slowness he unbuttoned her jeans and slid them down over her legs and then led her gently to the bed where he lay and held her tight as if he felt that she was the most precious thing in the world. Then gently he rolled onto one arm and looking at her with a tender smile began to kiss her softly, his lips like a whisper of breath on hers.

Then the telephone rang. With a groan he rolled over and snatched it up. "Yes," he said, barely concealing his annoyance at being interrupted. Then heaving himself furiously out of the bed, he tossed the receiver into her hand. "Derry," he snapped, marching out of the room.

Tara was glad that she and Kate were going to the races in the car rather than in the lorry with Morgan. He had left hours ago to get to the crowded racecourse, leaving them behind to do the horses.

Carna Boy was ready when they arrived at the course and Morgan handed his lead-rein to Kate to bring him off to the parade-ring while he went to change. Derry was riding too, looking unfamiliar in JT's silks. It had been a long time since he had ridden in a race and Tara felt it was very strange to see him dressed as a jockey once more.

Tara shot him a shy smile and tried to stay well away from him, to avoid winding Morgan up further. Morgan looked like a coiled spring and she felt a pang of fear for him. He had lost so much weight that he hardly looked like himself any more. His face was etched with the stresses of the past few weeks and dark with shadows under his eyes. His mouth had vanished into a hard bitter line.

The horses jogged past, Carna Boy shooting her a look of distaste. Big nasty brute, she thought, staring at his enormous grey quarters as he jogged past, kicking back moodily at the horse behind. Magnetic Attraction on the other hand looked like a prince among horses. He shone like a conker and walked politely beside the young handler who was leading him around. Ellen and JT stood at the far side of the ring, smiling for the cameras that were filming all of the Cheltenham hopefuls, presenting a unified picture to the world for Derry's sake.

The bell rang and the jockeys trooped out, the handlers pulling the horses into the centre. With an effort Tara managed to get Morgan onto the tall horse and then watched out of the corner of her eye as JT legged a grinning Derry onto Magnetic Attraction.

Tara watched the horses cantering down to the stand, Derry grinning for the benefit of the cheering crowds as Magnetic Attraction cavorted like a gentle rocking-horse beneath him, obviously delighting in the crowd's acknowledgment. Carna Boy on the other hand behaved badly, leaping upwards and trying to buck as Morgan, tight-lipped with nerves and tension, hauled on his reins to keep his head up,

Through the binoculars Tara watched the horses line up at the start, Magnetic Attraction pulling a face at an unruly horse which barged into him. Carna Boy messed around at the back, ignoring Morgan's frantically thumping heels by refusing to join the other horses. Then suddenly one of the young jockeys, getting overexcited, let his horse leap away from the start and the line descended into chaos. The horses bounded forwards with the exception of Carna Boy who ran backwards, knocking one of the starting stewards out of the way as he flailed his whip.

The furious starter called all the horses back into line and finally the race went off again. The steward who had been knocked out of the way cracked his hunting whip loudly at Carna Boy and was rewarded by the sight of his hooves lashing out angrily inches from his head. In the powerful binoculars Tara could see Derry grinning as he launched his horse at the first fence and then, after the first bunch of horses, came Carna Boy galloping alone with three other horses trailing after him. She could see the firm set of Morgan's face as the horse made an enormous leap over the fence and made up ground towards the leading bunch. All that Tara could hear in the commentary as the horses thundered past the stand was Magnetic Attraction and how well Derry was doing and what a shame it was that he had ever stopped riding

Ellen watched impassively, a small smile playing on her lips. JT beside her watched, his lips moving as he whispered encouragement to his horse. As they went past the stand Carna Boy motored up the inside, his long ears flapping sideways and his huge hooves churning up the mud as he shoved his nose through the other horses to gallop alongside the leaders. As they went away from the stands Tara could see Derry glance sideways to see where Carna Boy and his rider were and then saw the look of sardonic delight on Morgan's face as he flashed a look of triumph over his shoulder at Derry.

As they went away Carna Boy seemed with every stride to get better, gallop stronger, as if he could go for miles and miles relentlessly eating up the jumps and the spongy turf. Above him the loudspeaker was ringing out the news that Carna Boy was going like a fresh horse as he cruised away from the others. Tara saw Derry give Magnetic Attraction a vicious lash of the whip down his shoulder and the shining horse put on an extra spurt.

The fast ground was telling on the horses and the race became strung out as if each horse was going around the track on his own. Carna Boy rounded the turn for home and the crowd began to go wild, cheering him on, willing him forward to the finishing line, hoping to see the outsider coming home alone way ahead of all of the others. He jumped the second-last fence alone, putting in a huge bold leap like a fresh young horse. The crowd redoubled their cries, until Tara thought she was going to go deaf. She joined in jumping up and down, clutching Kate's arm. He only had one jump to go and he was alone. Derry and Magnetic Attraction were so far behind that he only had to jump the last jump and then he could nearly walk home to the line.

Then, as they watched, Carna Boy put in a short stride before the jump, and before their horrified eyes turned a huge very slow cartwheel in the air, sending Morgan sprawling down the track to land in an untidy heap with his whip fluttering to the ground behind him. The crowd let out a loud collective groan of shock and disappointment. Morgan got to his knees. Carna Boy lay flat out, his sides heaving, as Morgan got up and walked unsteadily over to him. He leant over the horse and patted his neck while the crowd held their breath, hoping that he was alive.

Then with an audible groan of disgust the horse put his huge head in the air, then rolled onto his side and shot to his feet. Morgan patted his neck in obvious delight as the crowd let out a huge "Ahhh!" Tara looked and saw Morgan glance with dismay at the sight of Magnetic Attraction thundering towards them, approaching the fence. Squinting into the binoculars, she saw Morgan gather up his reins and brace himself ready to spring onto the horse. Then Derry s horse give a huge leap over the fence and with one stride was on top of Morgan and Carna Boy.

As he shot past, Carna Boy lurched forward and galloped after him. Morgan, unable to keep his balance as the horse shoved away from him, fell backwards, landing on his bottom in the mud. Tara saw Derry turn his head and his arm flash out, waving goodbye to Morgan as he got angrily to his feet.

The crowd roared in delight as Derry cantered slowly over the finish line, waving his stick in the air in triumph. Kate ran down to catch Carna Boy, leaving Tara still looking through the binoculars at Morgan as the crowd dashed down to the winner's enclosure to welcome Derry home. Morgan was trudging miserably up the track to the entrance, swishing his stick miserably beside him. Tara put down her binoculars and closed her eyes, trying to blot out the picture of his devastated face.

She didn't know where to go; she wanted to go to him and comfort him but she knew that he could be furious at her because of Derry winning the race. Yet again she was stuck between the devil and the deep blue sea.

After the race they found Morgan at the lorry. Tara smiled sympathetically, but received a scowl in return. She rubbed her hand along his arm. "What a bloody awful thing to happen!"

"What do you mean?" he snarled irritably. "Falling or the way your brother made the horse bolt while I was trying to remount?"

"What is that supposed to mean?" she snapped, fed up with him.

"Derry booted the horse in the bum!" he blazed. "That was what made him shoot off, otherwise I could have got back on. I might not have won but at least it would have been fair. Your brother is a shit!"

Tara turned on her heel. She was sick of him, sick of being stuck between the two of them.

She had finished the horses when Morgan got back to the house, and she left him and Kate to bring Carna Boy off the lorry and put him away while she stalked inside. She began to make the dinner, shoving chops under the grill and peeling potatoes, scraping at them as if she could scrape the anger away from herself and Morgan. This was not fair; there was too much pressure on both of them for their relationship to survive.

Eventually Morgan stomped into the house and went up for a bath. She listened to the sounds of him splashing in the water — maybe later he would be in a better mood. When he did come down however he went straight into his office and she fiddled with the chops and prodded the potatoes, trying to keep herself busy, anything rather than sit at the table and wait for the inevitable storm.

He came into the kitchen brandishing a piece of paper. "Here, you had better read this," he said, thrusting a piece of paper under her nose.

She took it and sitting down at the table began to read.

She barely took in what she was reading, finally she looked up.

"What does it mean?" she frowned at him.

He stood at the opposite side of the table, drumming his fingers on the wooden surface. "You can read," he said bleakly. "We have no money, the bank haven't been paid and they want to close us down and sell this place to get their money back. Simple as that."

CHAPTER FORTY FOUR

Tara watched as the chops exploded into tiny violent fires under the grill, sending plumes of smoke dancing around the kitchen, carried on the draught from the open window. She had not got the energy to take them out from under the grill. After all the hard work and heartache they were going to lose Radford Lodge. It was going to be taken away by some bureaucrat for whom the place meant nothing other than just a red mark on a balance sheet.

Morgan idly shuffled the piece of paper with his fingers.

"There must be something we can do," Tara raged, maddened by his stillness. She would have been happier if he had been throwing himself around the kitchen, pulling things off the walls and smashing plates on the floor, anything but this stoical acceptance of the situation.

"It looks pretty clear to me," he said quietly, picking up the letter. "Foreclose on loan — they want their money back and are sending in the bailiffs to repossess."

"But what will we do?" she said, desperation in her voice. She felt as if she was going to drown, falling into a deep, deep pit of despair with her hands tied.

Morgan shook his head slowly and shrugged his shoulders. "Fucked if I know," he muttered.

Tara wanted to shake him, to raise him out of this dull acceptance.

She was silent, glaring at him, leaning against the sink, feeling the water that had slopped over the edge earlier seeping through her jumper wetting her back. Angrily she turned off the grill and shoved the chops onto plates - she could not see them eating these tonight.

Morgan shook his head as if wakening from a long sleep. "I suppose get a job on a yard somewhere," he said bleakly. "What's the bloody point in all of this anyway, working like a dog all day every day, day in day out, rain or shine, for what? For some prick to take his horse somewhere else when it won't win, while the bloody thing's useless because he could not buy decent blood. They all make me sick!" Getting up quickly he pushed his chair out of the way.

Bitter tears trickled slowly down her face. She shoved the remains of the potatoes that had boiled to mush, into the oven. Then she pulled out the chair that Morgan had vacated, feeling the warmth of his body still in it, and buried her face in her hands and let the pent-up tears flow.

Life was so unfair. She loved it here. They had such plans turning Radford Lodge into a magnificent training yard, rebuilding the old mansion - it should have all been so easy. The yard should be a hive of activity by now, she should be still pregnant, life expanding everywhere, blossoming, all of their plans coming into fruition. Instead all around was barren waste. Thank goodness the malicious calls had stopped, the poisoning of the horses and the owner of the icy cold threatening voice had been identified as one of Josh's friends. Devastated by the loss of his friend he had lashed out in the only way he could at Morgan, Tara and the horses. He had walked out of court with a suspended sentence and a large fine. His Solicitors had assured the jury that his actions were due to his trauma and he was horrified at what he had done.

Crying seemed such a useless emotion — what on earth would it change? But it seemed to help — the tightness at the back of her throat had gone when she finally wiped her eyes.

She went upstairs and bathed and then, feeling better, went downstairs in her dressing-gown and curled up on the settee. Neither of them seemed to have any appetite for food. As she lay, lulled into to a half-sleep by the heat of the fire, the telephone rang. It was Sarah.

"Hi," Tara said, her voice husky and full of sleep.

"I saw the races today," Sarah said, her voice sounding as full of joy as Tara's was of misery. "Derry is an out-and-out bastard! He made Carna Boy jump out of the way so that Morgan couldn't get on him, otherwise I reckon that Morgan would have won!"

"Well," said Tara bleakly, "it's all hypothetical now." She asked Sarah how she was getting on in England and listened enviously as Sarah told her about being fetched by Edward in the helicopter from Derry's and taken to his place in England. Her whole life had taken on a dream-like quality, ever since his helicopter had swooped in to land in the front paddock in the dawn light. The rescue of a damsel in distress. As soon as Sarah had realised who it was she had run headlong into his arms. The bemused pilot had grabbed her bags and heaved them up into the helicopter as she had stood with Edward in front of Westwood Park with the wind from the rotary blades whipping their clothes and hair into a frenzy. She had let Edward gently guide her up the metal rungs into the plush inside of the helicopter. As the helicopter had taken off and swooped at an alarming angle over the house she had looked down and her eyes had locked onto Derry's, standing in his bedroom window, stark naked, gazing with fury at them. And then the house and the stables and the immaculate gardens and her cottage and the horses grew smaller and smaller as she was carried away. Edward reached across her and fastened a seatbelt around her middle and she lay back in the thickly padded creamy leather and closed her eyes, wanting to scream with delight.

Then as quick as a flash they had reached the English coast and after what seemed to be moments he was pointing out the boundary of Finis Cross, his home. She gazed down at it: green rich grass and lines of immaculate brown timber fencing with trees and rows of huge sheds — and then the house, more beautiful than she remembered, an elegant building of red brick.

And then down and into the house and the rooms that she recognised from her first visit there when she had left so crossly, thinking that he had only wanted a quick one-night stand. Now she knew that things were different; now she was here to stay with him.

"We haven't been apart since," she gabbled excitedly. "In fact, even now he is lying with his head on my lap!" She went on, making Tara envious of her obvious happiness and security. "And guess what?" she added, her voice rising to a shriek. "We're getting married and I've been given the best wedding present ever!"

Tara listened enviously as Sarah recounted the previous evening when she had gone out to dinner with Edward.

Once their desserts had been cleared away he had taken hold of her hand with a smile. "Do you think it would be a nice thing to do to get married before we go to Cheltenham?" he had asked conversationally as if he were asking her whether she could like more coffee.

Sarah had felt her face spilt into a broad grin as she squeezed his hand. "Yes, oh yes," she had breathed.

"Good." He had reached into his pocket and pulled out a small box, which he slid across the table to her. "I rather hoped that you would say that."

Sarah opened the box, inside which lay a beautiful and ostentatiously large diamond solitaire ring. "Wow!" she breathed, sliding it onto her finger and holding it up, watching it catch the light.

"Oh yes, one other thing —" He grinned broadly. "I met JT Healy at the races a while ago and I told him that I would be interested in buying some of his horses if he ever wanted to get out of racing. Seems like he has had enough of Derry. He telephoned me tonight just before we came out wanting to get rid of his horses, turns out he's bought a hotel on the Cayman Islands and he's going to live over there. Anyway I have bought Magnetic Attraction for you." He smiled at Sarah's gasp of delight. "He will stay with Derry until after Cheltenham. Derry doesn't even know who the new owner is — as far as he is concerned it's a syndicate from England."

Sarah, crying and laughing at the same time, had thrown her arms around him "I love you Edward," was all that she could manage to say.

"Oh Sarah, I am thrilled for you," Tara heard herself say, while in truth she felt completely differently. Everything was going well for Sarah while for her the world was coming to an end.

"So, how's life there?" asked Sarah, unprepared for the storm that she had unleashed with the question.

Tara suddenly began to cry, bitter tears of sheer misery and hopelessness. "We are going to have to leave here. We can't afford to pay the loan — after the accident and the horses dying, everyone has gone. Carna Boy will go to Cheltenham and then that's it."

After a night's sleep the picture, although looking bleak, seemed less frightening, "We can start again somewhere," Tara told Morgan as he nodded in reply to her. "People will come to you once you start to win again." They would get Cheltenham over and then think what to do.

But the one thing that drove Morgan was the desperate need to prove to everyone that Carna Boy was the best in the world.

Tara was bitterly annoyed by the way he seemed to have shelved the worry about the bank repossessing the yard. Every bit of his concentration went into the horse — he spent hours working it, brushing it, watching it, just standing gazing over the stable door watching the bloody thing as if willing it to get faster, stronger, fitter, as if he could will it over the fences at Cheltenham. It was as if Morgan had a mistress whom he flaunted in front of her. Everything came second to the horse. She had just lost a baby and she was about to lose her home and livelihood, if it could be called that, and Morgan did not seem to be even aware of the situation. She felt more and more resentful.

She felt trapped in a limbo. He would not talk about what they were going to do. Everything, he said, had to wait until after Cheltenham. She knew they could come home from Cheltenham with a dead horse, an injured rider and find that they had been evicted in their absence. If only he would do something rather than just moon about with the flipping horse!

The telephone rang in the office and she went to answer it. The ringing nowadays was something to fear. Once it had been interested enquiries, people wanting to bring horses for them to train; now it was feed merchants wanting money immediately or a snotty-nosed bank clerk making impossible demands on them.

"Hello," she said, gingerly picking up the phone. "This is Edward Dixon," said the voice from the other end. "Sarah's fiancée," he added proudly.

"Hello," Tara said bleakly, taken by surprise.

"I wonder if I might be able to help you," he said and she could hear the twinkle in his voice.

"Oh?"

"I am looking to buy into an Irish training establishment and I wondered if you could help?"

"Oh," she said stupidly again, her mind a blank. "You mean, where is there a training stables that would want a partner?"

"Yes," he said again, in patient tones. "I wondered if it would help the two of you if I came in as a partner, paid off the debts, things like that . . ."

"Oh," she repeated, feeling like a parrot, mouthing desperately and not knowing what to say. This was the answer to their prayers! Edward could save them from having to leave.

"I'll fetch Morgan," she breathed, dropping the receiver on the table where, abandoned, it slid slowly off and clattered to the floor. She ran to the front door and yelled his name into the yard.

He came to a stable door at once, a look of fear on his face. "What?" he yelled back.

"Come quick!" she shrieked and he shot out of the stable door and dashed across the yard.

"What's wrong?" he said, the panic clear in his voice, making her realise how close fear lay to the surface, making them live their lives on tenterhooks. He had been refusing to see the oncoming eviction, feeling somehow that a miracle would happen and make it all go away and of course that had all seemed rubbish. Until now.

"Phone. It's good news," she said, seeing the frantic expression on his face.

Morgan went into the office and she could hear him talking to Edward on the telephone. Now everything would go back to normal. With a partner Morgan could afford to expand even more — with the pressure from the banks gone they would be able to concentrate properly on the training. Life would have a security that it had never had before.

Morgan came back out of the office. "What the fuck do you think you were doing telling Sarah about our problems? You bloody Blake's think that you can just manipulate the world to suit yourselves. If it's not your fucking brother rigging races to suit himself, it's you trying to run my business!" He spoke so quietly that for a moment she thought that he was joking.

"What?" she smiled, thinking that in a moment he would laugh and fling his arms around her and dance for joy that the yard had been saved from the clutches of the bank.

He was silent, leaning in the doorway with his arms folded aggressively and she realised with a sinking heart that he was not joking. He was really mad that she had said anything to Sarah. A thousand thoughts flashed through her mind. How could he be so cross? What did it matter? Sarah was a friend — it was not as if she had written a banner and paraded it through the streets of Tipperary for everyone to see: Morgan Flynn is going bankrupt! Look everyone!

"How dare you go broadcasting our problems all over the place! How could you?"

"Morgan!" she almost shouted, trying to penetrate the angry fog that dulled his mind. "What does it matter? He wants to buy into the business. To help us — we could even expand!" Edward was going to help them, for heaven's sake! He had clawed himself up from nothing - he knew all about being penniless - what on earth had got into Morgan?

"No!" he raged, and she watched his mouth opening and closing in temper as he spat the words out. "I won't have charity from anyone! And I'm damned if I'm going to take anything from Sarah's new sugar daddy!" He shoved roughly past her in his haste to go.

Tara remained where she was, her fingers clutched around the back of a chair, staring at the empty doorframe where he had just been standing. In those seconds something inside her had changed. She could not live like this any more. She had tried to do what she could, tried to help, but she was wrong. Now something had altered in her feelings; this had to end. Her marriage was over. She was going home. Derry had been right all along.

She dragged her case downstairs and out into the yard. There was no sign of Morgan. He was probably consoling himself with that bloody Carna Boy, she thought, yanking open the car door and shoving her stuff into the back seat. Then with a final brief glance around the yard, she got into the car and started the engine.

As she pulled out of the yard, Morgan shot out of one of the stables.

As she drove away she could see him in the mirror, standing in the yard, bellowing her name.

CHAPTER FORTY FIVE

Derry began to laugh as he read aloud from the racing newspaper. "Mick Cassidy and Tommy Keane banned for three days for jumping a hurdle on the way to the start of a race," — he paused with a mouthful of food hallway to his mouth — "bloody idiots." Tara glanced up smiling at her brother, trying to ignore the frosty feeling emanating from the far end of the dining-table.

Ellen was picking pointedly at her food, cutting it very deliberately into tiny pieces, putting them delicately into her mouth and chewing as it she thought that the food was going to poison her. She looked up with a tiny and very forced smile turning the corners of her small mouth. "What plans have you made for the future, Tara?" she asked, making it very clear that Tara's presence in the house was not something that she could tolerate a moment longer.

Tara opened her mouth to speak, but Derry spoke first. "She has plans to stay here for a while to recuperate from the terrible marriage that she has just managed to escape from." He threw a challenging look at his wife, a half-smile playing on his lips.

"What about my terrible marriage?" snapped Ellen and, getting to her feet, she threw her napkin down petulantly on the table and then stalked from the room.

Tara sighed. Returning to Westwood Park had definitely been a very bad idea. While Derry had been delighted when she had turned up, Ellen had been furious and had made her feelings very obvious. The unpleasant atmosphere had hung around the house for days although Derry seemed blissfully unaware of it. Tara felt every half-hidden jibe and double meaning in everything that Ellen said or did.

It did not help her either that Morgan kept turning up at all hours of the day and night, pleading with her to listen to him, telling her that he had been a fool to ever let her go, that he had spoken to Edward and was going to let him come in as a partner, that things would get better. At first Derry had gone out and told him to buzz off and that she would not see him, but then he had started to sit outside the house for hours on end, just sitting in the jeep with his head in his hands — which had driven her mad. Eventually she had seen him, let him into the official-looking surroundings of Derry's office where she had listened impassively to his pleadings. Somehow she felt that she had slipped beyond caring about him; she had suffered so much pain that there was nothing left, nothing to grasp at and to let regrow into the love that she had once felt for him. It was all gone, dead, like the baby that he seemed to have shown so little interest in. She had felt nothing for him, not even a faint stirring of compassion when she saw how tired and thin and shaken he had become. His clothes hung off him and he sported a dark growth of stubble on his chin but he hardly seemed aware of anything except the pain that he was going through and the longing for it all to be put right again. But she could not go back; she just wanted to be left alone to heal the deep wounds he had caused.

And then, when she had told him firmly that it was over, he had stopped coming around. He had driven away and she had watched him go, watching the headlights picking up the dark bushes of the rhododendrons and making long shadows in the beech trees as he crawled down the drive. And still she had felt nothing. She wondered if she would feel better if she did, if she could cry and scream and pummel her fists on the ancient stone of the house, to draw blood and find solace in physical pain. Anything would be better than this empty dead feeling. It was as if the love that had been inside her had been sucked out and nothing left in its place but a dark, cold void of nothingness.

Except for Ellen's hostility, she felt safe at Westwood Park, safe to regroup her forces and to gather her thoughts so that she would eventually be ready to move on from this dark time. The house seemed to reach out and nurture her and she drifted about, feeling rather like a wilting Victorian heroine, without the strength to do anything other than get through the days. She spent her time wandering in the gardens, watching the rebirth of the plants, ready to blossom with the summer flowers that would appear with the warmth and sunshine.

Ellen however, bitterly resenting her sister-in-law, was bad-tempered and snappy with everyone, ignoring Tara except to dart viperous comments at her, and with Derry she was just bloody-minded, ranging from savagely aggressive to icily polite or ignoring him completely. Tara would lie in bed at night and hear her bitter voice screeching indignantly at Derry long into the early hours. Derry usually switched off from her completely, laughing at her, which seemed to make her angrier. Tara, drifting around the house 'as if she owned the place", drove her completely bananas. It did not help when Derry tried to tell her that in fact Tara did own half of it.

Tara and Derry sat compatibly beside the fire. With the curtains drawn and the winter weather shut out it was blissful. Tara curled up on the settee and read a book while Derry gazed sleepily at the television.

"Where's Ellen?" Tara asked. The atmosphere was so nice without her, but it had been such long time since she had flounced out at dinner-time that Tara wondered where she was.

Derry shrugged nonchalantly. "Fucked if I know," he mumbled unconcernedly, turning back to the programme that he was watching.

A few moments later the door was flung open and Ellen flounced into the room, her usually pale face ablaze with unspoken anger. "I have had enough, Derry," she said through gritted teeth, coming to stand in front of him.

"Uhhh uhh," said Derry, peering around the side of her where she was blocking out his television screen.

"I can't stand any more of this!" She was yelling now, her slender body rigid with tension. She turned and snapped off the television.

"Oyy!" moaned Derry. "There's a good bit coming in a second!"

"There's a good bit coming now," Ellen said quietly, her mouth pursed up into a tiny prune shape. "I am leaving you! I have had enough of living with a man who is such an unpleasant bastard! And I have just come to say goodbye."

"Goodbye," said Derry, getting up and switching the television back on.

For a moment Tara thought that Ellen was going to explode in temper and start hitting him, but she remained where she was, still and silent.

She glared at him until finally she turned her attention to Tara. "I hope that you two will be very happy!" Then turning on her high heels she marched from the room, slamming the door with a satisfying thud.

The incident might never have happened for all the notice that Derry took of her flouncing out. In fact he never even so much as raised an eyebrow when the front door finally slammed shut and Ellen's sports car raced away down the drive.

"Ah well" he said eventually, rising from his chair and giving a stretch like a cat getting up after spending an afternoon in the sunshine, "I think I'll go to bed — I've a couple of horses running tomorrow." He began to walk out of the room and then paused beside Tara and looking down said, "why don't you come? It will do you good."

"OK," she nodded slowly.

Derry stooped to drop a kiss on the top of her head. "See you in the morning," he said. Tara wondered if she was ready to go the races — maybe it was too early. Morgan was bound to be there. But then again, racing was in the family and Morgan could either take it or leave it but she had every right to be there.

She slept fitfully for the night, dreaming of dead jockeys and screaming horses and woke, feeling miserable and un-refreshed and wondering if she could plead sickness to get out of going, but Derry was giving her no chance to cry off. And fairly quickly she found herself in the car with Derry while Paul drove the lorry with Floozie, the new groom on the yard who had taken over from Sarah when she had dashed off with her hero. Floozie lived up to her name very well, having done the rounds of most of the jockeys and many of the trainers. She was tall and very curvaceous in a way that just oozed sex, with short very red hair and a blatant come-to-bed smile.

"This time next week," Derry said, "it will all be over. We leave for Cheltenham the day after tomorrow. By this time next week Magnetic Attraction could be the winner of the Gold Cup." He backed the lorry expertly into a parking spot and switched off the engine.

Tara wandered off into the racecourse while Derry and Floozie got the horse ready for the first race. The course was windswept, bitterly cold, and miserably empty. Everyone seemed to be staying at home saving their money before Cheltenham. The whole atmosphere seemed depressing —

without the hordes of people to cheer it up the whole place seemed dowdy and abandoned. Shivering, Tara went into the cafe to warm herself with a cup of tea.

In a corner, staring miserably out of the window, was Morgan. "Tara!" he exclaimed, looking up as she turned to bolt. He leapt to his feet and, shoving tables and chairs out of the way in his haste to get to her, grabbed her arm while the restaurant staff looked on with amused eyes. "Come and sit with me," he begged.

"Morgan," she said firmly shaking her head, "leave me alone, please."

Morgan reached out to a table close to her and pulled out a chair. "Sit down," he pleaded, "please."

Tara sat down. Why on earth had she come to the races? This had been an enormous mistake. She stared at the chequered pattern on the plastic tablecloth, at the damp stains creeping up from the tilting floor and climbing up the walls, at a chip in her nail polish and finally at him.

He looked awful: there were dark shadows of grief under his eyes and his cheeks were hollow with anguish. He had aged twenty years. "Come back," he said and, resting his elbows on the table, buried his chin and mouth in one hand as if to stop himself from crying out like a child. "Please, I can't bear to be without you . . ." His words trailed off and he stared past the dingy lace curtains at some point far beyond. Tara looked sullenly at him. He looked broken. Pathetic. He had discarded her when she had needed him and now it was payback time. It was too late for them.

Firmly she shook her head. "I can't," she said. "You were never there when I needed you and now it is too late for us." He shifted his gaze slowly from the lace curtains as if every movement was painful and looked at her. "Too late," he whispered, "too late." Slowly he got up and pushed his chair away. Then he said with quiet intensity, "I will always love you and I will never forgive myself for driving you away."

She went back outside to where Derry was in the parade-ring with Lynn Moore standing beside him shivering like a whippet, badly dressed for the bitter cold in a pink summery suit that billowed about her slender frame. Clutching Lynn's arm as if he thought that she was going to blow away was a very tanned and very muscular and very, very much younger man dressed in a smart suit.

The race began and Lynn's little mare, Frottage, swept home twenty lengths in front of the rest of the field, to wild applause from Lynn's toy boy who swept her off her feet and spun her around as she beat at him in mock anger with her fists.

Morgan's only runner of the day, Tzar, trailed in miserably at the back of the field, looking as unhappy and as unwell as its trainer and rider. "Morgan Flynn's yard looks well off form," announced the commentator. Derry and Lynn and the toy boy were in the owners' and trainers' bar yet again downing half a bottle of champagne each and came back for the last race of the day looking decidedly pissed. Floozie, who had been drinking champagne from Derry's flask, looked decidedly wobbly as she led the final runner of the day around the parade-ring. The owner, a dour-faced ancient English lady, gazed on the scene with a look of pure hatred on her face as Floozie took another swig of the flask.

The horse romped home, a brilliant second place after running at the back for most of the race. Floozie led the horse away while Tara led the still prune-faced owner to the bar for a celebratory cup of tea. After a while Tara realised that Derry had not returned from helping Floozie to get the horses back into the lorry.

Suddenly she looked across the bar to see Ellen obviously searching for Derry. Tara's heart gave a lurch of horror. Ellen coolly surveyed the bar, her pretty face immaculate but impassive. She saw Tara and her eyes narrowed with dislike as she turned towards her. "Where's Derry?" she asked coolly.

"I have no idea," Tara managed to say.

Ellen glared at her and then with an arrogant swing of her long blonde hair swung around and marched out, her cream wool coat billowing behind her.

Derry returned a short while later with a very red-faced Floozie clinging for support to his arm and frantically trying to pick the straw out of her hair and off her jumper.

"Did you see Ellen?" Tara asked when she met Derry at the bar later.

He snorted with laughter. "Kind of," he said. "She came into the lorry while I was in there with Floozie, took one look at my bare arse and went out again."

CHAPTER FORTY SIX

Tara looked at the party remnants, the drunks laughing and falling around, Floozie quite unrepentant lolling against Derry, her chin and neck reddened where his stubble had grazed her skin. The English lady had woken up and was drinking tea rapidly in an attempt to sober up.

Tara felt strangely out of place amidst the merriment and thought that Derry was really horrible. He did not care one bit that Ellen had seen him having sex with the groom. All the love and promise that had seemed to be there at his wedding had vanished like a summer mist and what remained was only hatred and loathing. He was, Tara thought, very cruel. Even if their marriage was over it must have been awful for her to see that scene.

Tara put down her drink, shoving discarded glasses out of the way, and then gave one final glance around. No one would miss her for a while anyway. She eased her coat gently from behind the stiff back of the Englishwoman and went outside.

The bitter wind whipped her coat, sending it billowing around her legs. The course was almost deserted now; abandoned betting slips danced and blew in the wind like leaves blown from a tree. A few lorries still remained in the lorry park, trainers and stable lads that had runners in the final race were rugging up their horses and feeling anxiously at their legs to make sure that no harm had come to their precious animals.

Tara moved between the lorries, looking for Ellen. Maybe she would have gone, driven off in a huff, but maybe she would still be there, upset and needing comfort. Tara, although she had never really liked Ellen, felt her heart go out to the prissy girl. No one deserved to be treated as Derry had treated her; it was not fair, it was inhuman. And she felt that just maybe she could offer some comfort to her.

The trainers nodded in greeting to her as she mooched through the lorries as she searched. Then she stopped abruptly, her eyes widening in astonishment. She had found Ellen. And Morgan had his arms around her.

Tara stayed where she was, as if frozen to the ground, not wanting to see what she was looking at, wanting to turn away and walk back to the party, but she remained, watching unseen in the growing gloom and the shadow of the lorry as Morgan stood with his arms wrapped around Ellen, stroking her hair, holding her head to his chest as she clung to him possessively. Morgan and Ellen. On the rebound from herself and Derry they had found each other. Tara angrily dashed away hot tears of fury and despair. They would find comfort in each other. While she had no one. She had lost the one man who she had felt true happiness with. From her concealed spot she watched as they drew apart, Morgan taking Ellen's face in his hands and speaking softly to her. And then gently helping her up into the cab of the lorry. There was a long moment until he started the engine. Tara imagined them kissing in the cab. Morgan was the most tender and gentle of kissers and she still missed the feel of his lips on hers. She shrank back as he reversed out, the headlights shining close to where she stood — but she was concealed, they would not be able to see her. Then as they passed her she could see that Morgan was driving with one hand, the other was possessively around Ellen's shoulders, holding her against him.

Tara walked slowly back to the owners' and trainers' bar, feeling her shoulders hunching as if she had the weight of the world pressing down on them. Everything felt awful. She wished that she was a thousand miles away, that she had never met Morgan Flynn. Every breath seemed to hurt and the bar seemed so far away that every step was an almighty effort. She wanted to curl up in bed like some wounded animal and howl and wait until this dreadful feeling had passed.

Finally she reached the bar door and shoved it open. The party was just breaking up and Derry was manhandling the English lady out of the door while Floozie propped up his other arm. Tara gazed beyond him to where Lynn Moore, her pink suit askew revealing a long length of tanned thigh, had her tongue very firmly down her toy boy's throat.

"Derry," Tara said, her voice feeling as if it was coming from far away, it was such an effort to speak, "Derry!" It was a plea for help as stars danced in front of her eyes and the room began to swim.

She sobbed hysterically all the way home. Finally exhausted with crying she let Derry carry her up the stairs and put her to bed. He sat on the edge of the bed, and ran a cool hand over her burning forehead. Her eyelids felt as if they were made of lead. She wanted to close her eyes and sleep for a week.

"I think that you are just worn out with all of this messing with bloody Flynn!" He spat out the name as if he could not bear to say 'Morgan'. Then he added more gently, "stay here and rest so that you will be well enough to come to Cheltenham."

Tara closed her eyes. Bloody Cheltenham! She never even wanted to hear the name mentioned, let alone go to the races there. She did not care if she never even saw a horse again. What were they, only trouble and heartache? They had wrecked her life, her marriage, everything. She felt a tear slide slowly down her cheek. Derry, never one for dealing with emotional scenes, got up abruptly. "Derry," she whispered.

"Uhhuhh?"

"Morgan was with Ellen," she said, aware of every syllable of their names sliding over her tongue. "I saw them."

Derry let out a great gale of laughter. "Well, I'm going to open a bottle of champagne! We are well shut of the pair of them and how well they suit each other!" Then still giggling to himself, he patted her gently on the hand and went out.

Tara slept fitfully, replaying the scene over and over of the two of them in the lorry cab, leaning against each other tenderly.

The next day, sick of her pitiful weeping and sitting virtually comatose around the house, numb with the pain, Derry steered her towards his Jeep and instructed her to go shopping — saying a bit of retail therapy was good for the soul. Just to please him she went into town and mooched around, half-heartedly looking into the shop windows. Then when she could reasonably return home she went back to the car and headed back to Westwood Park.

A few miles out of town a pair of headlights flashed in her mirror. She glanced into the mirror to see a car whizzing up behind and Kate behind the wheel mouthing angrily at her, gesturing wildly. Tara scowled, what on earth did she want? Kate carried on following, headlights flashing wildly. On a long straight spot in the road Kate swerved out, passed Tara's car and began to slow, forcing Tara to brake and finally to stop.

Kate jumped out of her car and jogged back to stand at the side of Tara's car. "Open the window. I need to talk to you!" she yelled, knocking on the glass ferociously.

Tara wound down the window a fraction.

"I only want to talk to you," Kate exclaimed, putting her fingers on the window as if to force it down by sheer willpower.

Tara lowered the window a little more. "What do you want?" she snapped, her nerves jangling.

"It's Morgan," said Kate, looking earnestly at Tara. "He found Ellen in a state — she saw your fucking brother shagging his groom. But now she's got her claws into Morgan — he's always got his arms around her."

"I know. I saw them," Tara snapped. "What do you want me for? Did you want to rub salt into my wounds?"

Kate looked at her with ever-widening eyes. "It's you he really loves," she said, her voice coming out as a whisper as she was close to tears. "Don't let him go!"

Tara revved the car engine. "Let me go! Morgan's made his own decision. He didn't fight for me when I needed him," she let out the handbrake and the car rolled slightly forwards. She turned the steering wheel and pulled out.

"He misses you so much!" Kate yelled as she drove slowly away.

Tara threw the plastic shopping bags down on her bed and sat, numbly examining the clothes that she had bought. What on earth had she been thinking of? Lacy lingerie, the sort of thing that Morgan would have loved to peel off her. And a pretty dress. When would she ever get the chance to wear it? She hated Morgan. Hated the way he had neglected her when she had needed him. She would never go back to him. But why did she miss him so much? She threw the purchases into her wardrobe and wandered downstairs. Derry would be coming in for dinner soon.

They ate and then went into the lounge where a fire blazed in the hearth.

Derry poured himself a glass of whiskey and settled down in front of the fire. Tara curled onto the settee and pointed the remote at the television. Derry was soon engrossed in a sales catalogue while Tara was idly staring at a television programme, her mind a thousand miles away.

Suddenly the front door slammed and they both sat up in surprise. They looked at each other.

"What the fuck was that?" said Derry, getting to his feet.

The lounge door was jerked open abruptly and Ellen exploded into the room, her eyes wild and triumphant, her hair tousled as if she had just got out of bed.

"Well, Derry," she said, taking in the scene with eyes that glittered maliciously, "I have come to tell you something that I'm sure will make you very happy!"

"Really," said Derry in an almost conversational tone, a slight smile playing on his broad mouth. "What's that then?"

Ellen pushed herself upright and marched into the centre of the room, glaring at Derry and ignoring the fact that Tara was there. "I want a divorce, darling," she smiled, her fingers twisting at the wedding ring that she wore, in a attempt to wrench it off. "I am sick of you — you are nothing but a bastard!" She succeeded in getting the ring off and held it out for Derry to take.

He ignored the ring and just stood, his hands deep in his pockets, looking at her with great amusement.

For a long moment she glared at him, then drew her arm back and flung the ring as if it was scalding hot into the fire where it clattered against the back with a resounding noise before tailing between the red-hot chunks of turf. "Best place for that!"

"My pleasure," said Derry, sitting down again as if he was dreadfully bored with the whole scene. "And the sooner the better for the divorce."

Then seeing that she was going to get no great reaction out of Derry, Ellen rounded slowly to face Tara.

"I'm very happy now" she smiled. Her eyes glittering with unspoken malice she waited, watching the increasing look of horror spread across Tara's face. "I have a lovely new man. We have just gone into partnership with the new Mrs Edward Dixon, your brother's last lover. Morgan is going to make Radford Lodge into one of the greatest training stables ever."

Then, seeing a wedding photograph of herself and Derry propped on the sideboard she moved slowly across to it and picked it up. She looked at it for a moment, then with a snort of derision carried it over to the fire and dropped it in, the glass shattering into a thousand pieces. They watched silently as the photograph caught fire, the paper bubbling and then exploding into flames.

"You were a fool to let Morgan go," she told Tara watching as the flames consumed the photograph, "I won't be such a fool."

CHAPTER FORTY SEVEN

Tara sat in the car ready to take Derry to Shannon where he was to get on a plane to England. Magnetic Attraction was being flown over on an earlier plane. The yard throbbed with life. Derry dashed backwards and forwards, checking and rechecking that all of the equipment needed was loaded up. Finally Floozie brought out Magnetic Attraction. He looked wonderful, clad in the blue wool rugs with the red binding, and the leather head-collar with a red rope and matching bandages on his legs and tail. He bounded up the ramp straight into the lorry as if he was glad to be on his way. Floozie climbed into the cab beside Paul and drove away.

"Thank God Ellen has gone," Derry said, settling down to drive. "I would have hated to have her bugging me all through the Cheltenham meeting." He heaved a sigh of satisfaction.

There were four other horses going to Cheltenham and the jeeps and trailers and lorries stood in the cargo area of the airport waiting for the plane. Derry settled down to sleep while they waited, while Floozie went off to see who was around that she knew.

Tara felt strangely uprooted now that she knew her marriage was truly over and that Morgan was with Ellen.

A hundred yards from them a vast commercial plane landed and a few minutes later the handlers appeared, ready to load the horses. Floozie put the ramp down while Derry stretched as languidly as a big cat and then, still yawning, got out of the car. He pulled out his big leather bag, ready to go on the passenger plane. The other lorries and the trailers were unloading their precious cargo of Cheltenham hopefuls. A handler took the lead-rope from Floozie and led Magnetic Attraction into a tall narrow container. Soon all of the horses were loaded and the paperwork completed. Derry reappeared from behind the lorry where he had been kissing Floozie.

"Are you sure that you won't come?" he said, kissing Tara goodbye. "You could get a plane tomorrow."

Tara shook her head. She had no heart to be in the midst of the merriment — her wounds were too raw and unhealed.

Tara watched them go and then went back to Derry's car and drove home slowly.

The days stretched ahead aimlessly. She passed Radford Lodge. No doubt Morgan was there with his new girlfriend getting ready to take Carna Boy to Cheltenham.

Suddenly seized by rage at the thought, she slammed the brakes on and wrestled with the steering wheel, spinning the car round into the gateway and driving rapidly up the house. She had to tell him that he was a rotten bastard for taking up with Ellen, even if it was only for revenge.

She drove into the stable yard, catching sight of Ellen peering out of the window to see who had arrived.

A second later Ellen came dashing out of the kitchen door, her long hair done up in huge padded pink rollers and her bare legs covered in pink wax as she shot down the path, her face pink with fury. "What the hell do you want?" she yelled, her mouth wide with rage, revealing a row of very even very white teeth.

"I want to see Morgan," said Tara swinging herself out of the cab and dropping lightly to her feet in the muddy yard.

"You leave him alone," raged Ellen. She wore a pink frilly dressing-gown and pink mules that looked ridiculously out of place in the mud of the yard.

"Bugger off," said Tara, shoving her out of the way.

She left Ellen mouthing with fury and jogged across the yard. She pushed open the tall sliding door of the stable building. She waited for a second, letting herself breathe in the familiar scent and letting her eyes grow accustomed to the dim light. Then she walked forward slowly down the wide aisle between the boxes. He was where she had instinctively known he would be, in Carna Boy's stable. The door was half open. She went slowly forwards and peered in.

Morgan sat with his back to her on a bale of straw, contemplating his beloved Carna Boy. The ugly horse glared at her. She stood in the doorway. Morgan was completely unaware of her presence, lost in his own thoughts. As always.

It was hopeless. She should not have come. She would get over the pain of his betrayal, eventually. She turned, wondering if she should make a bolt for the door, but just then Carna Boy gave a low whicker of recognition and took a stride forward. Morgan spun around to see who had come.

"Tara," he exclaimed in delight, getting quickly to his feet. "I can't believe you're here!" He strode towards her, holding out his hands.

"Fuck off away from me, you prick!" she cried, her anger rushing back in again. She backed away from him.

"Tara!"

"You didn't waste any time finding someone to replace me, did you?" Carna Boy shot to the back of his stable in alarm as she gestured wildly at Morgan.

"You left me," he said quietly, turning back and sinking tiredly down onto the bale again. He gazed up at her. "Ellen was upset about Derry." He paused, shaking his head. "I'll always love you." He looked at her, his eyes filled with mute pleading.

Tara felt nothing but fury. How could he be such a fool as to think she would fall for that rubbish? "Yes," she snarled, "and that fucking horse!"

Morgan got to his feet slowly as if he had aged a hundred years. His jeans hung in folds around his legs and his cheeks were pinched and dark in the hollows under his high cheekbones. "That's not fair," he said quietly, taking hold of the rail that divided the stables, as if to support himself.

Tara snorted in disgust. "Isn't it? You always put everything before me. You were never there for me through the baby and everything and now you've moved someone else into the house just like that! And it just happens to be my brother's wife! I'm better off without you!" With that, she spun on her heel and marched out.

"Tara!" she heard him call as she shoved the sliding door open and marched back into the yard towards the lorry.

Fortunately Ellen was inside the house and so she just got into the car and drove away, wishing with her whole heart that she had not come in the first place.

Tara lay on her bed. The house was silent, she was alone and had never felt so lonely. Her head was pounding, filled with a myriad of thoughts that refused to leave her. They churned around and around, making her feel sick and giddy. She hated Ellen and Morgan with a vengeance and the feeling had left a bitter taste in her mouth that would not go away. Morgan was a fool and Ellen was a conniving bitch. Her marriage was over. She would wait until after Cheltenham and then decide what she should do with her life. It was a life that stretched barren on to a listless horizon, a path that she must trudge alone.

She drifted slowly into sleep, her head still pounding.

She snapped back to wakefulness to an almighty ringing. At first she couldn't understand what the noise was and then she realised that it was the insistent sound of the telephone. Scrambling to push back the warm quilt and struggle out of the warm nest that she had made for herself, she snatched up the phone. "Westwood Park," she snapped crossly into the receiver.

For a long moment there was silence and she was about to slam the receiver back down when there was the harsh sound of sobbing coming from the other end of the line. "Who is this?" she asked, holding the receiver away from her and glaring at it as if she could see who it was on the other end.

"Tara," said a female voice between enormous gasps of sobbing, "Tara, I don't know what to do — Morgan has gone." It was Kate.

"It's not my problem," Tara said harshly.

"It is!" cried Kate. "It's because of you! Ellen said you turned up while I was in the village getting my lunch. He had loaded up the lorry for Cheltenham and was ready to go but, when I came back, he got in his car and just drove away! Ellen went berserk at me — she said we were all mad. She's going to her father's — please come, please! I'm frightened that he's hurt himself and I don't know what to do!"

The last thing Tara wanted was to go back to Radford Lodge. But poor Kate sounded desperate.

"OK," Tara sighed. "I'm on my way."

She put down the receiver and swung her legs onto the floor. What the hell had she let herself in for, she wondered, slipping her shoes on and standing up. The headache had receded to a dull ache behind her eyes.

She stamped sullenly downstairs. She was being a fool. If Morgan had gone, what the hell did Kate think that she was going to do — magic him out of thin air like a conjurer with a rabbit?

But deep down worry gnawed at her. How could he go off just before the most important race in his life? He must have been out of his mind. Then a horrifying thought crept in: everything in Morgan's life had gone to pieces — what if he had finally snapped? What if — in despair - he killed himself? Her final words to him echoed in her mind: 'I'm better off without you!'

She let herself out of the house. The heavy winter dusk was laying its cloth of darkness over the house and grounds, sending the rhododendrons into heavy oppressive shadows, and the wind whipped the spindly branches of the beech trees. Sighing, she let herself into her car and drove over to Radford Lodge.

As she drove into the yard the headlights of her car shone brightly on the open boot of Ellen's car and the open doors. As she bumped slowly over the yard and drew to a halt, Ellen came out of the garden dragging a suitcase which she humped slowly into the back of the car. Then she tottered back on very high heels for another which she had left beside the gate. Cases and boxes were crammed into every space inside the car. She slammed the boot shut. She was, as usual, immaculate in a pale suit with a long coat over it that swung open to reveal a long expanse of her elegantly clad legs. Tara shoved open the door and got out.

Ellen stood and faced her, glaring straight into her eyes with a face like thunder. "I'm going," she said, adjusting the strap of her handbag. "You're all mad! You, Morgan and Derry with their bloody racehorses! They have wrecked their lives and yours and they aren't going to wreck mine! You can have the two of them and welcome! Morgan's good for nothing but moping about you anyway!" She spun on her heel and picked her way delicately across the yard, stepping around the puddles on her high heels, her coat swinging arrogantly around her thin calves as she walked. Then she got into the car, started it up and drove away.

Tara watched Ellen's car bump away until the red tail-lights turned off onto the main road and she disappeared. Kate came out of one of the sheds in tears. Her heart filling with compassion, Tara turned and put her arms around the younger girl.

"Where has he gone?" Kate sobbed as if her heart would break. "He just came out of the house with a hold-all and got into the jeep and drove away."

In spite of the awfulness of what had happened, Tara sighed with relief.

Surely he wouldn't have packed a bag if he intended killing himself? She pulled the girl's head onto her shoulder and stroked her long hair gently. "I don't know where he could have gone," she whispered, looking around the yard at the lorry, which stood in readiness, the ramp open, the paraphernalia for the horse all packed neatly inside it.

"He was all ready to leave for Cheltenham," Kate sobbed, her tears soaking through Tara's jumper.

Sadly they wandered into the big shed where all was calm and normal. The horses pulled eagerly at their hay-nets, glancing with disinterest as they walked past them. In the middle of the row they stopped at Carna Boy's stable. The horse looked up from his haynet with calm intelligent eyes. He looked a picture. Tara recalled the scraggy delinquent that had arrived so long ago and shook her head in amazement at the transformation Morgan had wrought on him.

"He looks wonderful, doesn't he?" Kate whispered. "Morgan was convinced that he was going to win ..." They looked at the horse for a moment in silence before Kate continued quietly, "He was in bits after you went."

Tara shook her head sadly. "I was stupid to leave him, we could have worked things out. I loved him so much. But now I've lost him. All because of Cheltenham, this horse and bloody Derry!"

Tara moved away from Kate. Her marriage had been sacrificed to this horse and now it was all such a waste: the work and the hours of toil that had gone into shaping Carna Boy, long hours day and night in rain and sleet and snow forming him into this, a pure racing-machine that glowed with life and power. He could be one of the greatest horses that ever raced and now he would never have the chance to prove himself, because she and Morgan were such fools — fighting when they should have been pulling together. Everything had revolved around Cheltenham. And now everything was lost.

She smiled bitterly. It was time that she grew up and stopped running away from problems. She was going to get Morgan back. Prove to him how much he meant to her.

"It's OK, Kate." Even her voice sounded more positive. "Don't worry — he'll come back. He just needs some time on his own. But for now we have to run the yard."

Tara leant on Carna Boy's stable door, staring at the horse that had meant so much to Morgan. Cheltenham was his dream. It should have been a shared dream. She should have understood more instead of behaving like a spoilt brat.

The horse had to go to Cheltenham. She would bring Morgan's dream to life. She would prove to him how much she loved him.

"Can you get someone to look after the yard?" she asked quietly.

Kate shrugged. "Yes, easily."

"Well, find someone now and then get your stuff. We're going to take the horse to Cheltenham," said Tara.

CHAPTER FORTY EIGHT

They reached Rosslare just before 9am. "Oh fuck!" yelled Tara, hurtling down the roadway towards the ferry. A uniformed man was shoving the huge iron gates shut. She slammed her foot harder on the accelerator and the powerful lorry surged forward. The man, seeing them coming, pulled back the gates in horror, fearful of being mown down.

"Thanks!" screamed Kate out of her open window as the man stared after them, outraged.

A short time later, they were following the line of people making their way onto the deck — businessmen and racing people on the way to Cheltenham.

"I need a cup of tea," groaned Tara as she emerged from the narrow stairs onto the wide corridors of the ferry. "This way," she said, seeing an arrow directing them. Even as they drank their tea Kate was unable to settle, squirming in her chair, eager to be off the boat and on their way. Spending three hours on the ferry would be unbelievably boring.

"You're doing the right thing," she said, taking Tara's hand over the table and squeezing it reassuringly.

Tara looked at her and gave a small uncertain laugh. "I wonder?" What on earth did she think she was doing? Where on earth were they going to find a jockey who would ride the horse? They could be on a total wild-goose chase and have to just turn around and come home.

"We'll find someone to ride him," said Kate, echoing her thoughts.

"You'll see."

The thoughts however refused to vanish, nagging insistently at the back of her mind. What was she doing bringing the horse all this way, with no rider for him? She must have been mad to even consider doing it! But now that she had made the decision, somehow she was committed and had to see it through, right to the bitter end, whatever that end would be.

"God help us," moaned Tara, fighting to see through the rain as they crawled along a motorway with rain spraying up from under the tyres of the lorries that thundered by, seemingly oblivious to the treacherous conditions.

Kate, her excitement giving way to worry at the horrific drive, was silent, peering intently through the windscreen with anxious eyes.

Halfway across the sea it had begun to rain, a huge gale that lashed at the boat, sending it rocking and reeling, with all of the cups on the tables spinning to the ground and everyone dashing for the toilets to be sick.

The rain was still pelting down as they drove onto the racecourse a few hours later. The afternoon's racing was in full swing, the horses battling valiantly against the rain and the increasingly horrific conditions of deep mud and slippery going. The racecourse was battered by the wind. Rain was forming huge lakes on the car parks, The hospitality tents with their banners and flags flapped furiously in the gale as stewards, wrapped against the weather in waterproof coats and trousers, battled to retie ropes and flags that had come undone and were billowing in the wind. The spectators darted by, dashing for the shelter of the tents and the more solid stands, huddled in waterproof coats, holding hats onto their heads as the water ran in rivulets down their arms.

A steward directed them into a parking spot, holding onto his hat with one hand and waving vaguely in the direction that he wanted them to go, bent almost double against the rain.

"Well," fumed Tara, "they say that it rains a lot in Ireland, but this is bloody ridiculous!"

Sliding and skidding on the slippery turf they managed to park the lorry without it getting stuck.

"Right we had better do what we came for," said Tara, reaching behind her seat for her waterproof coat. She slid her arms into the cold stiff fabric. She zipped the coat up as high as it would go and tied the hood tight beneath her chin. She grinned at Kate. They had made it. They were probably both certifiable, but at last they were here. She pushed open the door, battling as the wind whipped it out of her hands, threatening to rip it off its hinges. She slid out, feeling the wind catch at her coat, whipping it around her legs. Grimacing she slammed the door shut. They opened the lorry ramp. Carna Boy gave a deep whinny of recognition as they scrambled up to him. Tara undid the partition as Kate untied the horse and led him outside. He came unwillingly down the ramp, laying his ears back against the wind and trying to turn around so that he had his quarters to it.

"Come on. Let's get you inside!" yelled Tara, her voice lost against the rush of the wind.

The paperwork seemed to take forever before finally they were allotted a stable and could lead the horse through the security gates into the stable complex. There were horses and trainers and stable lads everywhere, rushing around desperate to be inside out of the fierce gale.

They led the horse through the walkways to the stable.

"Here we are!" cried Tara, heaving the door open and shooting inside in front of Kate and the horse. Carna Boy charged through the doorway, almost knocking Kate out of the way in his eagerness to get out of the storm. Inside it was amazingly quiet. A deep bed of straw had been put down in readiness. Kate slipped off Carna Boy's head-collar and the horse sank thankfully to his knees, then rolled with joy at being out of the confines of the lorry at last.

They could safely leave him to rest.

"What the bloody hell are you doing here?" said a familiar voice as Tara shoved the final bolt into place to secure the door. She straightened up and turned. Derry was glaring out over the adjoining stable half-door, contempt pasted all over his face. "I don't believe it! You've gone running back to that loser again!"

Tara faced her brother, hating him suddenly. Why did he always have to put her down?

"Carna Boy's entered in the Gold Cup," she said sullenly.

Derry gave a snort of derision. "Where's his trainer?" he sneered, drumming his long fingers impatiently on the top of the stable half-door. "In the bar with my wife while you act as his groom?"

Tara shrugged, trying to feign nonchalance. "Actually I don't know," she said, as if it was the most normal thing in the world for a trainer to simply vanish just before the biggest race of a horse's career.

"He's gone — he cleared off," announced Kate making Tara wish that she could kill her; somehow it was the last thing that she wanted to tell Derry.

Derry let out a roar of laughter, rocking backwards and clinging onto the door for support. "Bloody coward," he said. "The bloody horse is such a nail that he couldn't even bring it to the races and you, Tara, my stupid little sister, are going to let him make you look like a fool instead." He straightened up and looked at her reflectively, wiping a trickle of rain from his forehead. "Can't you see that? Take the horse away now before you make yourself look a complete idiot!"

Tara seethed with rage. "This horse is as good as Magnetic Attraction any day!" she stormed, shoving her hands deep into her pockets and glaring at him from beneath the stiff fabric of her hood — amazed to find herself defending the horse she had always hated.

"So who's going to ride him?" asked Derry. Then, as they hung their heads, comprehension dawned and a delighted grin spread over his face. "You have nobody to ride him, have you?" He laughed softly and then, shaking his head slowly in a very irritating fashion patiently said, as if Tara was mentally deficient. "You'll never get a jockey for that horse, don't you know that?"

Tara couldn't bear to be near him any longer. She turned on her heel and matched away.

"Fuck off, you prick!" was Kate's retort as she dashed after Tara.

"Come on," snapped Tara miserably as Kate caught up with her. "We've got to find a jockey."

The last race of the day was just about to start and already spectators were starting to drift away, eager to get away before the bulk of the crowds, suddenly worried about retrieving their cars from the muddy car parks. A steward directed them to the weigh room and Tara waved her owners' and trainers' pass at a bored-looking security guard who was fed up with standing by the door all day watching the tiny rain-soaked jockeys come and go. "OK," he said with a jerk of his head, swinging the door open for her to pass.

"I'm with her," snarled Kate, darting past him before he had time to stop her.

Total chaos reigned in the changing room. All around on the bench seats were discarded clothes and exhausted jockeys, lolling naked apart from towels draped nonchalantly over their thighs. They grinned and cheered to see two pretty young women entering their lair. One, just out of the shower, towelled down his naked body, careless of the wide-eyed gaze that Kate was fixing on him.

"I'm looking for a jockey," announced Tara and there was a loud collective roar of laughter.

"Well, you came to the right place, darling!" yelled a voice from the back of the room. Tara gave a small smile; this was not going to be easy. "I'm Morgan Flynn's wife and I need a jockey to ride Carna Boy," she said, her voice sounding horribly loud amidst the steamy room full of sweaty rain-soaked jockeys, dripping racing silks and mud-splattered boots and tack and helmets.

One of the jockeys who sat close to them leant forward, putting bony elbows on even bonier knees. "I thought that Flynn was riding the horse himself," he said slowly, looking up at her, scowling.

Tara opened her hands in a gesture of defeat. "He should have been but he . . . ," she paused, fumbling for the words.

"He just can't now," butted in Kate, trying hard not to stare at the naked and very pert bottom of the jockey who was now turning sideways to rub at his crotch with the tiny towel he had.

"Can't or won't?" snorted one of them from behind a pillar of clothes.

"Look, love," said one of the jockeys, dressed and ready to leave the course, "with the reputation that yard has got, no one will ride for you. You're wasting your time here." He steered her to the door of the changing room and opened it for her politely. "Sorry, but there you are."

Tara glared at him for a moment, but he looked at her with an unrelenting gaze, a slight smile of amusement playing at the corners of his lips and dancing in his pale eyes. He gestured towards the door and finally she had no choice but to admit defeat and leave.

"Well, now what are we going to do?" moaned Kate unnecessarily.

"I have no idea," snapped Tara in reply. The last race had finished and the jockeys were trooping back in, muddy and drenched, their breeches clinging transparently to their legs. Seeing one that she recognised, she grabbed his arm. "Tommy," she pleaded, "I need a jockey for the Gold Cup."

The lad shrugged. "Sorry, Tara, I've got a ride. Try boyo here." He gestured over his shoulder at the jockey that came in behind him but he in turn shook his head as she turned her gaze to him. Then one by one they trooped past. There was no one.

"Oh Kate!" Tara said, slamming her fist against the sickly-coloured wall decorated with the pictures of the past Gold Cup winners, their triumphant gazes staring back at her. "What am I going to do?" She closed her eyes, wanting to block out the horrors of the day and when she finally opened them again she shook her head. "Someone will ride him," she said, looking at the pictures on the wall. The horse had come this far against all the odds — he had fought against everything and everyone — he had to have his chance to prove that he was the best.

Kate went off to give the horse his final feed while Tara went back to the lorry to make them something to eat. The luxurious lorry had everything in it including a television, cooker and shower so that they could spend a comfortable night. Tara made them both an omelette from the stuff that Morgan had filled the fridge with and it was ready when Kate came back in.

"Some of the lads said that there will be loads of jockeys here for the Gold Cup and that there's bound to be one without a ride that will take the horse," said Kate, her face pink with excitement and the pounding that the rain had given it. She pulled off her waxed coat and dumped it carelessly down on the quilt and sheets that Tara had found to make up the bed later. Tara removed it pointedly and hung it on the peg beside the door.

"Those were just a cowardly bunch of jerks," Kate continued bitterly, smothering her omelette in tomato sauce and tucking into it hungrily.

"I hope so — otherwise I don't know what we will do," Tara muttered miserably, watching with a growing feeling of distaste as Kate piled huge mouthfuls of food onto her fork.

"Go home, I guess," said Kate, with a shrug of resignation.

Tara sighed, wondering for the thousandth time what the hell they were doing there.

They finished eating and Tara washed up while Kate stretched out on the padded seat and switched on the television, yawning comfortably. When she had finished, Tara made up her bed in the tiny area above the cab and lay on it watching the television until she saw that Kate had fallen asleep. She slithered off the bed and covered Kate with the quilt, tucking it around her in a motherly way. Then finally she scrambled back onto her bed and turned off the lights, watching the flickering pictures of the television with unseeing eyes.

She found her thoughts drifting relentlessly back to Morgan, wondering where on earth he was and hoping that he was all right. "Morgan, come back!" she pleaded silently, tears sliding slowly down her checks. "Oh, please let him come back! I love him so much. Please make everything be all right!"

CHAPTER FORTY NINE

Sarah realised that she was awake and let herself slide gently back into consciousness, relaxing in the luxurious feeling of having Edward curled around her back, his legs tucked into the backs of hers like spoons, warm and contented.

Mrs Dixon — she rolled the name over and over in her mind listening to the sound of it and imagining herself saying it, writing it. She was his wife. They had married in a simple ceremony a few days before and were going to honeymoon later, after Cheltenham. Life was wonderful. She rolled slowly away from the warmth of his body, untangling her hand from his where it had lain all night, the fingers entwined. Slowly she slithered out of the warmth of the bed, put her feet into her slippers and stood up, smiling with happiness. She turned to look at the man that she loved so much, the man who made her feel more loved and cherished than she had ever felt in her life before. He slept on, his face relaxed, his grey hair tangled against the thick linen pillow.

Silently she padded across the room on the thick creamy carpet and pulled her silk dressing-gown off the peg at the back of the door where it hung against Edward's. And looked back to where he slept. It was a magnificent room and she never tired of the novelty of waking in such luxurious surroundings. The bed dominated the room, a massive four-poster with huge carved pillars draped with a dark canopy that gave the room a heavily seductive and luxurious feel. Everywhere there was space, acres of cream carpet, lit from the tall windows that looked out over the magnificent gardens.

She opened the door silently and padded off down the wide stairs with its antique carpet and dark wood panelling, holding onto the banister.

Downstairs it was silent; the housekeeper and cleaners would not arrive for hours. Edward liked them to have the house to themselves as much as possible. In the kitchen all was tidy. It was a huge room, painted cream, with cream units and black marble worktops lit by the most enormous chandelier that she had ever seen. She made tea, still feeling like a visitor in the luxurious surroundings. It was hard to believe that this was her home and that this was where she could stay for as long as she liked. She stood by the two deep enamel sinks and gazed out into the distance, looking at the paddocks over the railed fencing where the horses usually grazed. At the moment, though, it was too wet and they were all safely in the warmth of the sheds, the new foals too delicate to come out in the cold wet weather.

The kettle boiled and she poured the water into two mugs, added milk and swirled the tea bags around until they turned the sludge-brown colour that Edward liked. Then nudging the kitchen door open with her knee, she carried the mugs back upstairs to the bedroom. She put them down on the bedside-table, sliding the copies of the racing newspaper away to make room, and then sat down on the bed beside Edward. She loved him so much. The twenty years in their age difference made no difference to her — it only made her more proud of him. He was incredibly handsome, a fantastic and considerate lover and the most caring man that she had ever met. She would not have cared if he had been forty years older than her. He stirred slightly and she bent down to kiss his lips. A slow smile spread slowly across his lived-in face as he woke, lifting one hand up the back of her neck and holding her there as he kissed her back.

"What a lovely way to wake up," he said, wriggling to sit up. He yawned and stretched luxuriously and then reached for the tea. Sarah took her tea to her own side of the bed and got back under the covers. They sat companionably side by side, close enough to feel each other's warmth, as they drank the hot tea. "It's started to rain," she said, looking out through the open curtains to where the rain battered against the side of the house, sending rivulets of water streaming down the pane, blurring the view of the grassland and gardens beyond.

He shuddered, in mock horror, thinking about spending the day at the races m the horrible cold weather. "The going should suit Diamond Rock, my — your," he corrected himself, "runner in the Stayer's Hurdle." He sat up slightly more to peer out of the window. He sipped his tea for another while and then said reflectively, "the rain bodes well for you to have your first winner at the Cheltenham festival, my darling."

Sarah grinned broadly. The whole concept was rather beyond her grasp; a few weeks ago she had been a groom and now she was the wife of one of the wealthiest owners in England with runners at Cheltenham in her own name. It was amazing. And for once in her life she didn't give a damn that Derry Blake would be there. He had lost his terrible power over her.

"We had better get going," said Edward, draining the last dregs of his tea and putting his mug down.

"Not yet," said Sarah, placing her own mug on the bedside-table and wriggling down so that her body was stretched out beside Edward's. She curled her legs around his, then slowly slid her hand along the taut line of his belly and began to undo the buttons of his pyjamas.

"Oh dear," he murmured, sliding down so that his body was level with hers and pulling the heavy quilt over their heads, "I think we're going to be late again."

Two hours later they were scrambling out of the helicopter and ducking low under the slowly spinning blades as they dashed across the rain-lashed grass to the racecourse complex. Ahead of them towered the magnificent stands where thousands of people would later congregate to enjoy some of the best racing that the world had to offer. Tents were emblazoned with Guinness signs and the shamrock, and Irish flags billowed in the high wind.

Edward had a hospitality box in the main stand and they dashed for the safety of the building, keen to be out of the rain and wind. Downstairs a crowd of cameramen and reporters had assembled, eager to interview owners of horses that were running that day.

One of the English interviewers grabbed Edward as he pulled open the door to the main stand and held it open for Sarah to dash inside. "Now here is one of the owners of the runners in today's Stayer's Hurdle," said the interviewer, thrusting his microphone beneath Edward's nose, making him take a step back to avoid being knocked out by it. "How do you feel the horse's chances are now that the conditions have altered so dramatically?"

He looked intently at his clipboard to ascertain any information that he could about Edward.

"Actually, I am not the owner of Diamond Rock," said Edward with a broad grin. "This is the new owner — my wife."

Instantly the media seized on the words he had said, cameras whirled and flashlights burst as they all took pictures of Edward and Sarah who grinned with embarrassment and tried to disappear behind him. He shoved her into the spotlight. "This is the lady you want," he announced, heaving her forward with a smile.

"Well, Mrs Dixon," said the interviewer, "what do you think your chances are in today's race?"

For a moment Sarah forgot all about the camera with its bright light burning into her eyes and the huge microphone that was thrust at her, and thought about the horse, Edward's favourite horse. Diamond Rock, and his jockey Sean Rudd. And she began to tell the interviewer about how well the horse was working and how she hoped that he would go well on the ground, repeating everything that she had ever heard Derry saying when he gave interviews.

"Well done. You were brilliant," said Edward as the cameras slowly drifted away.

Sarah followed him into the hospitality box. She knew what it meant to him to give her the horse: he had wanted to win the Stayer's Hurdle for years and it meant everything to her that he had sacrificed the horse, so that she could have the pleasure of having a runner at the festival. Diamond Rock was well-fancied in the betting ring, especially by the Irish who knew that the horse had been bred in Ireland and had won many races there. Also, the commentators knew that the jockey was one of the best at the moment and was highly in form.

As the horses and riders made their way onto the course it was announced that the ground was soft and heavy in places.

"I think that is an understatement," Edward said to Sarah as they watched the horses going down to the start, sticky mud flying up from behind their hooves as they cantered. Diamond Rock was running against some of the best horses and riders in England and Ireland. One of the jockeys, the announcer said, was celebrating his 21st birthday and his horse was one of the favourites. Wouldn't it make a lovely birthday treat for him to win the race?

As the horses lined up before the start of the race Sarah's jockey, Sean Rudd, trotted Diamond Rock up towards the starting-line, timing his move perfectly so that the horse would be in motion as the starting-tape shot skywards. The technique worked perfectly and as the horses leapt away from the start he quickly assumed third place behind Cardinal Red, the mount of Gerry Upton, and Diamond Rock's biggest threat, the impressive Godiva who was ridden by the only lady in the race, Kelly James.

As the field cruised towards tire top of the Cheltenham hill and began the descent away from the stands, the placings remained unaltered, with the rest of the group running in a cluster close behind the leaders. By the sixth fence Godiva had retained her lead. Then Billy Boy, the mount of Owen Bradley, blundered through the fence and knocked it to the ground. Diamond Rock, unfaltering in his run, hopped over the fallen hurdle in third place. Simpson, with Tom Ripley on board, moved up beside Warren Martin's mount, Hell's Kitchen, to race alongside Diamond Rock.

As the runners began to climb the hill again Godiva, Hell's Kitchen and Diamond Rock were side by side. With six furlongs remaining and two fences left to jump, Diamond Rock was almost cantering, covering the ground easily with his jockey crouched over his withers. Godiva was outstripped as Diamond Rock cruised easily past her. Godiva and Hell's Kitchen desperately tried to make up the ground, their jockeys spurring their mounts on but Diamond Rock powered away from them, his fast pace eating up the ground. As the final fence approached Diamond Rock led with Godiva well beaten behind him. There was just one fence left. Sean, who had been motionless as the horse cruised towards victory, came suddenly to life, gathering the horse together to remind him of the importance of the final fence. The crowd in the stand roared with excitement, all barely able to watch, willing the horse over the hurdle. As the horse glided over the fence as if in slow motion, the crowd erupted. He had leapt the final hurdle like a fresh horse and raced towards the finishing line to take his place in history.

Sean punched the air in delight, grinning from ear to ear, then leant forward to rub Diamond Rock's damp ears. He turned the horse and rode him slowly up the long sand-covered ride into the winner's enclosure. At either side a sea of faces was grinning and cheering with delight and a forest of arms reached out to try to touch the horse and shake hands with the jockey. Edward shoved his way through the crowd with Sarah clinging onto his arm so that she did not lose him, then a space cleared and they watched the horse walking towards them, his jockey barely able to contain his delight.

"Go on," said Edward, giving her a little shove. "Lead your winner in." Sarah reached out, put her hand on the horse's bridle and led him proudly through the crowds to the winner's enclosure.

Later in the day the excitement had died down and they were enjoying a quiet drink m the owners' and trainers' bar. Sarah looked around the room, as she sat alone while Edward was discussing some business with a couple of men by the bar.

And then Derry walked into the room.

He saw her and came over, his face grinning broadly in delight at seeing her.

Sarah felt her stomach churn with tension; the last person she wanted to see was Derry. She was surprised to find that she felt nothing for him, no deep suppressed longing, no stirrings of regret, just a dull feeling of familiarity: he was just someone that she knew vaguely, someone from her past.

"It's good to see you," he said, folding himself into the chair beside her and looking at her with the wolf-like appraisal that he always reserved for women, undressing them with his eyes. His eyes roved over her body, taking in the beautifully cut clothes and her new streamlined figure.

Sarah glanced at the bar and caught Edward looking at her, concern written all over his handsome face. She gave him a small smile of reassurance. Satisfied, he turned back to his business.

"You look great," Derry said and then added, as if surprised, "fantastic actually."

When she didn't respond, he said, "I saw Diamond Rock win. Well done."

Sarah looked at the pictures around the room. How things had changed between them! The balance had shifted; instead of her being the one that wanted Derry so much, now it was clear the boot was on the other foot and it was he who was longing for her.

"He's your horse now," he said with a small laugh and a toss of his head, looking at her with admiration. "Well, I have to hand it to you," he added maliciously, "you've done well for yourself."

Sarah glared at him, flushing at the insinuation. "I love him," she snapped, looking longingly at Edward, suddenly wanting him to come and rescue her.

Derry shook his head slowly. "Nah," he said, lowering his voice and leaning towards her, "you love me. You know you do!"

He looked at her. She could see the deep longing in his eyes and the sight gave her a thrill of malicious pleasure.

"Come back to me," he said. "I love you and I miss you like hell. I've been such a fool to treat you like I did — come back, please!"

Sarah looked at him, a slight smile playing on the corners of her lips, and then slowly she leant forwards.

He gazed at her expectantly.

"Derry," she breathed, "fuck off"

CHAPTER FIFTY

Tara swung herself slowly up onto Carna Boy, praying as she landed in the saddle that he would not explode as he had done once before, but the horse waited patiently until she settled herself, gathered up the reins and then gently nudged his grey sides with her heels. The wet turf sucked and squelched beneath his hooves. It was terrifying to be on him; his ears seemed to be miles away from her and his walk filled with such strength that she wanted to turn him at every second and ride him back to the safety of the stable. But as she rode, with the imposing stand and the dripping marquees in front of her, she knew that she could not turn back. Gently she eased the reins and urged him into a trot, feeling his power, her confidence growing with every stride. Where was Morgan, she wondered, her mood swinging wildly between anger at him for disappearing and enormous guilt at herself for driving him away. Feeling confident, she kicked the horse into canter, holding the reins tight, not daring to give him his head, feeling him eating up the ground with every stride even as the heavy turf sucked and dragged at his hooves. He was truly magnificent - he felt like a prince as she gave him his head finally and whooped for joy at the speed with which he accelerated, galloping for the sheer pleasure of it. The fear was gone. She felt as if she could turn him and charge at the huge fences around which she was riding and he would carry her over — his heart was brave enough for the two of them.

She tugged on the reins and he slowed his pace, dropping back to a rocking-horse canter and finally back to a long striding walk as they turned and made their way back to the stables. Now she had to face reality. Now she had only hours in which to find a jockey to ride Carna Boy.

Again she began the painful process of trying to find a jockey. In the weigh room the answer was still the same: no one would touch the horse. She toiled around the stables, the restaurants, the exercise areas, even the lorry park, feeling despair and panic mounting as every minute passed. Finally, the race about to begin, she went back to find Kate — to tell her that they would have to go home.

But Kate had got the horse ready, convinced that Tara would be able to make everything right, that she would find a jockey from somewhere, and Carna Boy was already in the paddock being led around.

"You have to declare the jockey," snapped the steward. "You only have fifteen minutes to go."

Tara and Kate hung on, hoping against hope that a miracle would happen — that some jockey would have second thoughts and appear at the last minute to ride the horse.

"Look," the steward said finally, "you're going to have to scratch him — take him out of the ring, please."

Tara's heart sank.

"Hold on," said a familiar voice.

Tara spun around and gave a whoop of delight.

Morgan was standing there, dressed in his racing silks.

She flung her arms around him, crying, "you're here!"

"You brought the horse - I can't believe that you did that!" said Morgan. "I came to watch the race, knowing we should have been here. I wanted to punish myself for driving you away." He stroked her hair and held her face as if he could not believe that she was real. "Then I saw you riding Carna Boy this morning. I couldn't believe what I was seeing! I was so proud of you!"

"I was going to try to get a jockey for him," said Tara. "Race him to show you how much I loved you." She paused. "Why didn't you come to me this morning?"

"I wanted to — I knew I'd ride him after you'd brought him here, but my silks..." he grinned, "I left them in Ireland. I had to get a new set made up quickly; I've been dashing around Cheltenham trying to get some made all day!"

Tara bit her lip. He was impossible, but it didn't matter. He was here now and they could sort all of their problems out later. After the race.

"For heaven's sake, will you go and weigh in!" snarled the ring steward.

Morgan disentangled himself and dashed away. Tara stared after him, unable to believe that he had come back. He was back and he was going to ride the horse.

Kate walked around the ring as if she was on air, a huge beam of delight splitting her face.

The bell rang and the jockeys trooped out to a great cheer from the crowd. Kate pulled Carna Boy in towards the centre of the ring where Tara stood watching the jockeys. Derry's face was like thunder as he emerged from the weigh room.

Morgan walked towards them, a huge grin on his handsome face.

"I love you," he said, stooping to drop a kiss on Tara's mouth.

"Go on," she said. "Prove to them all what you can do!" Taking his leg as he turned to the horse, she flung him straight up into the saddle.

Magnetic Attraction came jogging up with Derry on board and Floozie clinging to his bridle. "I don't fucking know why you're wasting your time," snarled Derry, shoving his feet into the irons.

"We'll see!" Morgan returned, giving Derry a long challenging stare.

The horses paraded around the ring: Derry on Magnetic Attraction, Morgan on the huge Carna Boy, and with them a host of other horses. Then at last the bell rang and Gary Brown, riding the powerful Farrier's Fortune, led them out onto the course with Crossword Puzzle ridden by the English rider Paul Duggan bringing up the rear.

Tara felt a surge of excitement rush through her, mixed with fear and desperate happiness: she wanted the race to be over so that she could have Morgan back safely. She watched as he galloped away down the course, Carna Boy's powerful quarters churning up the sticky mud.

"Come on!" Kate tugged at her elbow, pulling her towards the stand. They shoved through the crowd, hearing the moans and complaints of the other owners and trainers that the ground was too heavy and it was madness to run the race in these conditions; one complained that he had never seen ground as bad as this.

Tara felt her heart lurch. How could the horses race and jump in these conditions? Three and a half miles of the worst fences, all out of deep sticky mud that would cling to their hooves making every jump and each stride a double effort. And then, after all of that, the long strength-sapping climb from the final fence to the finishing line.

The horses surged down to the start line, plunging and as eager as their jockeys to be off. Tara gazed at the television screen over her head, watching Morgan in his familiar colours, riding with a relaxed ease. Derry, she could see from the line of his back, rode with a relaxed arrogance, trying to psyche Morgan out with his confidence.

Then the starter began the dramatic climb up the podium steps and the crowd became hushed in anticipation. The horses danced and plunged, rearing on their hind legs, wanting to be running. The starter raised his flag. For long seconds they waited, the horses' legs moving up and down as they paced in anticipation, the jockeys clinging to their reins to stop them from going. Then dramatically the starter dropped his flag and the race was on.

Like a cavalry charge they surged forward, the horses fighting for their heads, and then the first fence loomed thick and enormous in front of them. They took it as one, leaping high into the air and skimming the fence before landing. Shane Mulligan's horse Summer Fun skidded along the soft ground, his rider still sitting on him as the horse's nose ploughed a furrow in the wet turf until finally with dreadful slowness the horse's bottom overtook his nose and Shane was catapulted to the ground falling flat on his back, sprawled out like a gingerbread man. He lay stunned for a while, then got up, lashing at the ground with his whip in fury at having his chance at the race cut short. Summer Fun though was gone, charging after the other runners.

Tara gazed at the television screen, watching the horses bound over the second fence, hardly seeming to break their pace as they glided over, the leading four horses jumping it together. They charged past the stand and everyone jumped up and down bellowing the name of their horse, willing it to run faster. The heavy ground was telling on the horses; mud flew up in every direction as they charged past, their legs pulling against the sticky, heavy turf as they surged forward rounding the corner and going off into the country again.

Summer Fun ran with the other horses, giving the riders yet one more thing to worry about. The stewards ran across the course trying to stop it but it ducked out at the last minute and charged along with the race. At the next fence Mouse's Friend fell, turning a heart-stopping cartwheel in mid-air over the fence. The horse behind was caught in his flailing legs, crashing heavily to the ground — then, like dominos tumbling, more horses were brought down. The horses in the rear veered away from the fence and stopped, not wanting to risk falling as well.

Ahead, the other horses raced on. The race seemed to have slowed to a snail's pace as the horses galloped and jumped mechanically, every stride an enormous effort to pull tired legs out of the clinging relentless mud.

The leading horse, Hot Trooper, tired after the effort of being in the front for so long and began to drop back. Then Farrier's Fortune fell. Seeming not to see the fence, he charged straight through it, sending Gary Brown over the fence first before the momentum of the horse sent it sprawling sideways. The horse behind turned in mid-air to avoid landing on Farrier's Fortune and Gary instinctively rolled into a ball as the horses ran straight over him rolling and punching him with their hooves.

"Gary Brown's fallen on Farrier's Fortune! Only four horses remain in this race — one of the most exciting Gold Cups that I have ever seen!" roared the commentator, so excited that he could hardly get the words out.

The three horses in the lead, Carna Boy, Hot Trooper and Crossword Puzzle galloped side by side with the loose horse, Summer Fun, with Derry breathing down their necks. Magnetic Attraction seeming hardly to touch the ground with his feet as he charged over the thick mud.

Then, as the fourth fence from home came up, Summer Fun pulled ahead and suddenly veered along the front of the fence towards the other horses, careering into Hot Trooper, sending him sprawling sideways. Hot Trooper lurched to a halt, knocking Crossword Puzzle off course. Crossword Puzzle then refused, digging his toes in at the last moment, his momentum spinning him forward into the vast ditch in front of the fence and catapulting Paul Duggan out of the saddle onto the top of it. As the prickly fence stuck through the thin fabric of his breeches, he yowled in pain.

Summer Fun had knocked straight into Carna Boy, sending him sprawling. For a second it looked as if he would have to stop — it was impossible for him to jump — but the brave horse put in an almighty leap, clearing the sprawling Crossword Puzzle in the ditch and just getting his front legs over the fence - dragging his back legs after him, he pitched Morgan forwards so that it looked as if he must fall off.

Then by some miracle he was over the fence and Morgan was still in the saddle, clinging valiantly on.

Magnetic Attraction had time to pull away from the carnage and took the jump like a fresh horse to tremendous whoops and cheers of delight from the spectators.

"I have never seen a race like this!" the commentator was yelling. "Only two horses remain!"

The television cameras closed in on the two runners.

Magnetic Attraction was closing relentlessly on the tired Carna Boy. On the screen Tara could see Derry's demonic grin as Morgan glanced over his shoulder to see where his rival was.

Carna Boy was exhausted. Morgan gathered him for the third last fence. They could see Carna Boy put every ounce of effort into getting over the fence. Magnetic Attraction was bounding for home. Putting in a huge leap, he overtook Carna Boy as they landed. As they came to the penultimate fence the heavy ground began to tell even on the relentless Magnetic Attraction and the pace dropped, both horses moving mechanically with the effort of dragging their tired legs out of the heavy turf over and over again. At the final fence the horses were neck and neck and took it together, sprawling over it, their last reserves of strength being used. Then neck and neck they headed for the long hill, the final test of stamina before the finishing line.

Derry brought his whip down hard twice on Magnetic Attraction's sweat-drenched quarters making the horse redouble his valiant efforts and overtake Carna Boy, whose legs were moving like pistons, his ears lolling, his head down with the effort of keeping going. The crowd began to roar for the brave horses, shouting for Carna Boy, for Magnetic Attraction, not caring which won - both of the horses had run a valiant race. Neck and neck they battled towards the winning post, every stride an enormous effort. As they passed the post Carna Boy had just inched his nose in front of Magnetic Attraction.

Tara began to jump up and down, screaming with delight.

Morgan had won!

As the tired horses walked back to the gate that led them into the enclosure Morgan grinned with triumph at Derry and put out his hand. Derry glared at him and then slowly extended his hand and shook Morgan's, dropping his hand afterwards as if it had been burnt.

Tara rushed forwards, shoving the crowds out of the way as she leapt to take the horse's bridle and grin with delight up at Morgan. He bent to kiss her, leaning down from his saddle as the crowd cheered with delight at their obvious happiness.

"I can't bear to be without you," he whispered hoarsely, clinging to her shoulder, the only part of her he could reach, as if he would never let her go. At either side of them a corridor of faces grinned and roared in a sea of noise and colour. Tara clutched the reins of Carna Boy as he marched jauntily beside her, his ears proudly pricked as he walked into the winner's enclosure.

The cameramen circled around, jostling to take photographs of the horse and owners. Morgan swung down off the horse and launched himself at Tara. She felt herself being lifted and spun around in the air as Morgan gave a loud bellow of delight and she covered his face in kisses.

"This way, please!" yelled a cameraman, crouching to take the photographs. Morgan held out his arms for Sarah and Edward to join in the picture and as the camera flashes exploded Edward threw up his hat to the delight of the cameraman.

"My new partners," said Morgan hoarsely as if he could not believe his good fortune. Sarah broke away and crossed to where Derry was sullenly unsaddling the exhausted Magnetic Attraction. As she tenderly kissed the horse on his mud-splattered nose, Edward said in conspiratorial tones so that Derry could hear: "Do you think he's ready to meet Magnetic Attraction's new owner — Mrs Dixon?" Then he laughed at the expression of horror on Derry's face as he realised who had bought the horse. Then shaking his head in mock astonishment at Sarah as she embraced the horse, Edward added, "I think that horse is going to be serious competition for me!"

Sarah grinned back cheekily over her shoulder at Morgan. "He's going to be serious competition for you! We'll beat you next time!"

A reporter, purple with excitement, thrust his microphone beneath Morgan's nose, asking him about the race. And then, as they were discussing the long run up to the finishing line, a short, very plump, red-faced man shoved his way through the crowd, his shiny round face glistening with sweat, and grabbed Morgan's arm. "Have you got the room for three horses? I want to win the Galway Plate!"

Tara laughed aloud in delight, as Morgan gave her hand a triumphant squeeze and turned his attention to the Galway Plate man. Clinging to Morgan's hand, she gazed at him as if she couldn't believe he was real. Then she dropped a kiss on Carna Boy's nose. "Bloody horse!" she said fondly "You nearly tore us apart — but now you've brought us together again!"

About Louise Broderick

Louise Broderick was born in Derbyshire, England, but now lives on the west coast of Ireland. She has been involved with horses all of her life as an owner and competitor. While working as the editor of an equestrian magazine Louise published her first book. She has published books in a number of genres, using different pen names, but all feature horses and the people who love them. If you would like to join Louise's VIP Reader Club and be the first to hear about new releases and special VIP book prices please visit www.louisebroderick.com

More books by Louise Broderick
Winners
Millionaires are a girl's best friend

A plea from Louise

Thank you for taking the time to read this book. I hope you enjoyed it, I certainly enjoyed writing it. Each time I sit down to write – and that is every day – I realise just how lucky I am this is my job. I can only keep this job because people like you enjoy my books and buy them. No words can express how grateful I am for that.

If you would like to find out more about my other books please visit my web site.

www.louisebroderick.com

I love to hear from readers so please feel free to contact me on via my Facebook page or email. The details of these are all on my web site.

I hope you enjoyed this book and would like to help me carry on living the dream, writing for a living. If you would like to help please take the time to leave a book review on Amazon. Positive reviews really do help to sell a book, so if you would do that for me you are helping me to continue creating my books and continuing as a full time writer.

Can I just say a huge thank you in advance to anyone who takes the time to do this for me. I know very well how precious time is and am hugely grateful for anyone who cares enough to spend some of their valuable time helping me. Thank you!

Printed in Great Britain
by Amazon